HOT PRAISE FOR THE AUTHORS OF
Hot Ticket

New York Times Bestselling Author
Deirdre Martin

"Fun, fast-paced, and sexy."
—*USA Today* bestselling author Millie Criswell

"Deirdre Martin is the reason I read romance novels."
—*The Best Reviews*

New York Times Bestselling Author
Julia London

"Few authors can pull you into a story like Julia London."
—*The Oakland Press*

"London's characters come alive on every page."
—*The Atlanta Journal-Constitution*

National Bestselling Author
Annette Blair

"Sexy, fun, top-notch entertainment."
—*Romance Reader at Heart*

"A funny, seductive story with unique, colorful characters."
—*The Best Reviews*

Geri Buckley

"Offbeat and eccentrically charming." —*Romantic Times*

"[An] amusing contemporary romance . . . deftly handled."
—*Midwest Book Review*

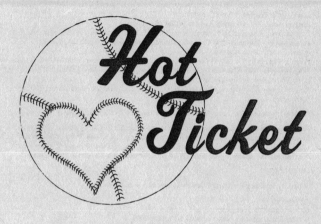

Hot Ticket

Deirdre Martin ★ Julia London
Annette Blair ★ Geri Buckley

BERKLEY SENSATION, NEW YORK

THE BERKLEY PUBLISHING GROUP
Published by the Penguin Group
Penguin Group (USA) Inc.
375 Hudson Street, New York, New York 10014, USA
Penguin Group (Canada), 90 Eglinton Avenue East, Suite 700, Toronto, Ontario M4P 2Y3, Canada
(a division of Pearson Penguin Canada Inc.)
Penguin Books Ltd., 80 Strand, London WC2R 0RL, England
Penguin Group Ireland, 25 St. Stephen's Green, Dublin 2, Ireland (a division of Penguin Books Ltd.)
Penguin Group (Australia), 250 Camberwell Road, Camberwell, Victoria 3124, Australia
(a division of Pearson Australia Group Pty. Ltd.)
Penguin Books India Pvt. Ltd., 11 Community Centre, Panchsheel Park, New Delhi—110 017, India
Penguin Group (NZ), 67 Apollo Drive, Rosedale, North Shore 0632, New Zealand
(a division of Pearson New Zealand Ltd.)
Penguin Books (South Africa) (Pty.) Ltd., 24 Sturdee Avenue, Rosebank, Johannesburg 2196,
South Africa

Penguin Books Ltd., Registered Offices: 80 Strand, London WC2R 0RL, England

HOT TICKET

A Berkley Sensation Book / published by arrangement with the authors

PRINTING HISTORY
Berkley Sensation trade paperback edition / May 2006
Berkley Sensation mass-market edition / September 2009

BERKLEY® SENSATION
Berkley Sensation Books are published by The Berkley Publishing Group,
a division of Penguin Group (USA) Inc.,
375 Hudson Street, New York, New York 10014.
BERKLEY® SENSATION and the "B" design are trademarks of Penguin Group (USA) Inc.

PRINTED IN THE UNITED STATES OF AMERICA

10 9 8 7 6 5 4 3 2 1

the Lineup

★

★

Lucky Charm

Julia London ★

CHAPTER 01

Parker Price hadn't had a hit in two weeks.

It wouldn't be a big deal if he was playing in a church league in Hoboken, but he was playing for the New York Mets, who had inked a deal to pay him one hundred ten million over seven years, plus bonuses, because they thought he *could* hit, among other things. And furthermore, it probably wouldn't have been *that* big of a deal if the Mets had at least won a game in the last two weeks.

They hadn't.

Even worse, with the humiliating end to last night's game—in which they had been swept by the team nemesis, the New York Yankees—they were on a downhill slide, picking up steam for a spectacular crash at rock bottom. And for some reason, all of New York seemed to think it was Parker Price's fault.

Okay, so he'd had a couple bad weeks, but he wasn't the only one swinging at air out there. Their big hitter, bought from the Angels for almost as much as Parker, hadn't been able to hit a damn thing, either. But did they boo him? No. Yell at him to get back on his mule and ride for Texas? Hell no. Just Parker.

Maybe these people just hated Texans in general—there had been some press to that effect when the Mets had lured him away from the Houston Astros. And maybe he really just sucked. God knew he was wondering of late—no one was more surprised than him by the base-running error he'd made last night. No, wait, that didn't do it justice—what he'd done last night had to be the most incredibly boneheaded base-running error in the history of the sport.

It was bad enough that he couldn't get out of the parking lot without hot dogs and beer bottles being thrown at his car. It was bad enough that his neighbor, Mrs. Frankel, who had to be ninety if she was a day, was waiting for him at the bottom of the drive when he arrived home. The old bat was standing in his drive, wearing her Mets jacket and Mets hat perched atop of her cotton-ball head, carrying a bat that had the words *New York Mets Swing for the Fences!* emblazoned down the side.

He knew right then it was trouble.

Parker eased himself out of his Hummer and tried to smile. "Evening, Mrs. Frankel."

"Don't *evening* me!" she shrieked, and came at him with the bat raised, blubbering something about how no one was paying *her* one hundred million dollars to hit a baseball, but she could damn sure hit a head as swollen as his.

Parker gently but firmly took the bat from her, at which point Mrs. Frankel dissolved into huge crocodile tears and sobbed how much she loved the Mets and just couldn't stand to see what was happening to them.

"Neither can I, Mrs. Frankel," he sighed and pointed her in the direction of her house. As she teetered down the drive, he called out, "You're sure you'll be all right, Mrs. Frankel?"

"Don't talk to me!" she screeched then paused and turned partially around to look at him. "May I have my bat? I got that in 1972."

Parker winced and eased the bat around behind his back. "I don't think so, Mrs. Frankel. Think I better hold on to it until you're feeling better."

That prompted her to make a derogatory remark that he heard quite clearly, but she continued her waddle down the drive, muttering to herself.

And still, that wasn't the worst of it.

This morning, he was awakened by his radio alarm just like he was every morning, and surprise, surprise; it was Kelly O'Shay of *Sports Day with Kelly O'Shay* startling him from a fitful sleep. Just like she did every freakin' morning.

"Wait, wait, wait, Guido," she was saying to her sidekick, who was, ironically, actually named Guido, "Are you trying to say the coach *didn't* signal him?"

"No, no, he *signaled* him. The Priceman either didn't see it or didn't read it right—but in either case, it's inexcusable for a top-flight professional ballplayer."

Parker bolted upright, furious. Like some punk named *Guido* could possibly understand the split-second decision-making skills baseball required.

"You're right, it's inexcusable," Kelly cheerfully agreed in that drop-dead sexy voice of hers, and someone played a tape of people booing loudly. "You expect base-running errors like that in Little League, but not the majors. The Mets can't afford to pay some bozo from Texas that kind of scratch and then let him get away with those sorts of errors, right? I'll tell you straight up, Guido—losing that game on the error last night was compounded by the fact that Price obviously can't hit, has no glove, and is just wasting an otherwise perfectly good uniform."

"I agree," Guido said, and the sound of a loud cheering section filled the room for a moment.

"I have a suggestion for the Mets, however," Kelly chirped, like she was about to impart a decorating tip, which frankly, to Parker's way of thinking, she ought to be doing.

"Oh yeah?" Guido asked, already laughing. "What's that?"

"Get some giant cue cards that say something like 'Hey, Parker, run this way and run now!'"

Guido howled.

Parker groaned, sank back into the pillows, and threw an arm over his eyes.

She did this every morning, using that sexy voice that she once used to lull him to sleep with the sports scores every night. But then they moved her to mornings with her own radio talk show, and dammit, he was convinced that if she'd just *stop,* he'd probably play like he used to. That woman had *jinxed* him. He was firmly convinced that his slump was *her* fault. Her constant ridicule was killing him, because every day she rubbed it in, the worse his slump got.

"Hey, let's go to the phones and see what New York has to say about the worst Mets ballplayer in the last one hundred years!" she cried like a cheerleader with pom-poms. "Okay, we've got Paul from Jersey. Hello, Paul! You're on the air at *Sports Day with Kelly O'Shay*. What's up?"

"Yo, Kelly, I first want to say that I love your show," a guy with a thick Jersey accent said.

"Thanks!"

"And second, I saw that base-running error in the seventh last night, and I gotta say, that was the sorriest excuse for baseball I have ever seen in my fifty-two years of following the Mets," Paul shouted over the cheering section the show was playing behind him.

"Oh yeah, it was bad," Kelly readily agreed.

"I mean, he looked like a damn freak. He can't even *run*, you know what I'm saying? Dude, *I* could run faster than that, and I'm pushing three bills!"

"Paul, I hear *exactly* what you're saying," Kelly said.

"That piece of *bleep* ain't worth no ten million!"

"No, he's not worth ten million, so it's like a *double* insult that the Mets paid him *one hundred and ten million*," Kelly gleefully corrected him.

"Yeah, yeah, that's what I meant. One hundred ten million. It's *bleep* obscene."

"But, Paul . . . I know Parker Price is slow as Christmas, but frankly, I thought that was the most artistic steal I've ever seen."

Parker uncovered his eyes and looked at the radio.

"Kelly, whaddaya saying?" Guido cried.

"I'm saying that attempted steal was poetry in motion. Beautifully executed," she continued over Guido's groans. "Really, if you think about it, the only thing missing?"

"Yeah?"

"A tutu and the final pirouette when he hit the bag."

Guido and Paul with the Jersey accent howled with laughter along with the stadium of cheers as Parker shouted at the ceiling and sank deeper into the pillows. He had to *stop* it. He *had* to stop it.

"Hey, Guido, did we get our game count of how many balls disappeared in his magic glove last night?" Kelly asked, dragging up a little stunt they did sometimes, which was to count how many errors he'd made—and count them with a giant gong, which they seemed to think was hilarious. They never cut him any slack, never counted how many spectacular, leaping grabs he had. Oooh no. That was because Kelly O'Shay had it in for him.

"Let's see, Guido, there was the line drive up the middle that nearly took his hat off, right?"

Parker didn't hear the rest because he had grabbed the radio, yanked it from the wall, and hurled it across the room. It hit the wall and fell, cracking in the center. He sat up, swung his legs over the side of the bed, grabbed his phone, punched a number, stood up, and stalked across the room to pick up the pieces of the radio.

"Sportsdaywithkellyoshay," a young man answered rapidly.

"This is Parker Price, and I want to talk to Kelly," he said gruffly as he dumped the radio into a trash can.

"Right, and I'm Tinker Bell," the guy snorted.

Parker stilled. "Look, you little ass, I *am* Parker Price, and I want a word with Kelly O'Shay right this *minute!*"

"Hey, pal, you know how many goofs call every single day claiming to be someone? And like Parker Price would have the 'nads to call this show!" He snorted again. "Save it for your girlfriend, pal," he said, and hung up before Parker could get another word out.

Parker yanked the receiver from his ear and stared at it. The kid had just hung up on him! With a roar, he hurled the phone onto his bed, but in the next instant, he pounced on it, punching in another number.

"Frank," he said when the call was answered. "Did you hear the show this morning?"

"Still hearing it," Frank, his agent, said jovially.

"It's gotta stop. I can't take that constant needling. She is single-handedly ruining my career."

"Park, Park! Calm down, now! Why don't you just listen to another station?" Frank asked as Parker padded into a massive walk-in closet.

"I can't! You *know* I can't! Frank, I have to *talk* to her. I have to explain baseball to her so she will stop jinxing me. You have to get me on that show."

He could almost hear Frank gulp. "No, Park. That is not a good idea—"

"Did you hear anything I said?" Parker shouted as he reached for a box containing a new radio alarm from a stack of boxes that contained radios identical to the one he'd broken moments ago. And yesterday. And four days ago after the San Francisco game. "I'm telling you, Frankie, if she'd just back off, I'd start hitting again!"

"Listen to me, Parker," Frank said, sounding a little frantic. "You are putting too much stock into what this chick says. She's nobody! She's just a morning trash jockey trying to keep her measly little share of the market! Look, look, look, take a walk, go out with a girl, maybe take in a movie, something like that. But don't let her get under your skin. She's not worth it."

"Frank," Parker said, stuffing the box with the new radio under his arm. "I want on that show. If you don't get me on that show, I will fire your ass and find an agent who will. Do you understand what I am saying?"

"You don't mean that."

"Like hell I don't!" Parker roared into the phone so hard that he dropped the box with the radio. *"You get me on that damn show, or I will get an agent who will!"*

"Fine, fine, fine," Frank said. "I'll call you later," he said and clicked off.

Parker tossed his phone onto the bed, then stooped to pick up the box with the new radio alarm. Frank would get him on that show. He better. The whole season was riding on it.

**CHAPTER
02**

The guy Kelly O'Shay had hired to do her makeup stood back and looked at his handiwork and nodded. "Mm-*mmm*, girl, you *definitely* got it going on."

"You did a great job," Kelly said and grinned at her reflection. Her shoulder-length hair was actually a new, luminous shade of blond, thanks to the great salon she found on the corner of Broadway and 93rd. The makeup took five years off her face, and the simple black turtleneck she was wearing made her green eyes pop.

She looked good.

She looked like an ESPN talk show host.

Yes! With any luck, after they had taped this fifteen-minute audition tape, she'd *be* an ESPN talk show host. The word was out that they were looking for a young new talent to do a new, humorous sports talk show. Kelly had practiced and practiced, called in a favor from a friend with access to a studio, and shelled out a good chunk of her savings for hair and makeup. But it was worth it. She was so excited she could hardly sit still. "Let's go," she said, popping up from the chair. "I'm ready."

She smoothed the skin-tight black pencil skirt she wore,

and with a bright smile, she strode to the set she'd created, her high-heeled, knee-high black boots clicking authoritatively across the tiled floor.

She took her place behind the desk she and Chuck, the guy helping her make the tape, had set up, and spread her hands across the wood veneer as Chuck fit her with a microphone and then switched gears to being the light guy, adjusting those on her.

On the desk in front of Kelly was the script she'd written. The director—okay, Chuck again—had gone over it with her and told her where to look. And now he stepped in the shadows behind the camera, prepared to fill the role of cameraman. "Whenever you're ready, Kelly," he said.

Oh, she was ready. She'd been working toward this for ten years and truly believed this was her shot at TV. Her radio show had been climbing steadily through the ratings. Especially since they'd let her off the graveyard shift and gave her the morning slot. The all-important twentysomething demographic loved her, but it was her scorching commentary on Parker Price, the Biggest Choker Ever, that had sent her ratings through the roof.

And thanks to the most boneheaded error in the history of baseball, she had been handed the best material of her life. Oh yeah, she was ready for this. With a grin at Chuck, she nodded. He cued her, and she began.

"Welcome to *Sports Day with Kelly O'Shay, the* source of sports news. Hey, if you're a big fan of baseball like I am, you're probably wondering—like I am—what is *up* with Parker Price of the New York Mets? Is he ill? Is he tanking? Has a body snatcher invaded his body? Here are the facts: The Mets paid one hundred and ten million for this guy to improve their record and maybe loosen the chokehold teams like the Yankees have held them in for *years*. The dude hasn't delivered. Don't talk to me about his golden glove—the guy couldn't catch a beach ball if you *rolled* it to him. And don't wave his great batting average around, either—that baby is flying below the radar. Here's another fact: Parker Price has made some of the costliest errors the Mets have ever witnessed on the field."

She smiled. "So here is my question: If a franchise pays

that sort of scratch to a guy who is essentially pegged to deliver a pennant, then who is responsible when the guy can't come through? Is it the fans? One might think so, given the price of tickets, a couple dogs, and a beer at Shea Stadium," she scoffed. "Is it the owner? The team manager? Maybe. They are the geniuses who struck the outrageous deal. But if you ask me, the one person who is responsible and must shoulder the blame is Parker Price. He was paid an obscene amount of money to deliver, and if he can't, then he is the one we should hold accountable."

She smiled into the camera and picked up a pencil. "Let's go to the local papers and see what *they* are saying about Parker Price . . ."

And on Kelly went, making a case that Parker Price should be canned for costing too much money and delivering the absolute wrong results.

Nothing personal against the guy. No, really—Kelly didn't care what they paid him, but she figured if he was fool enough to take that kind of dough to leave a team he'd played with for ten years and then blow it as bad as he had this season, it was his problem. His outrageous salary alone made him public fodder, and she wasn't saying anything the rest of the sports world hadn't said about him. But now Kelly had a front row seat at the feeding trough.

She made several jokes about Price that had Chuck laughing, while hopefully she was managing to be charming and feminine and not too girly. Men did not like getting their sports news from girly-girls. She'd learned that the hard way, early on.

Yeah, baby, this was *her* job.

When she'd finished her audition tape, Chuck complimented her. "Great job," he said. "We'll get this edited and sent around for you to look at in the next couple of days."

"Great. Thanks so much," Kelly said.

She gathered up her things, left the studio, and caught the subway—one day, maybe she'd have a car to drive her, like the big network stars—and went home, to her apartment, where she lived alone . . . and hung out alone, without the company of even a cat. After the graveyard radio slot she'd worked, she'd sort of lost touch with a lot of her friends. The morning slot wasn't much better for her social life—every night, she worked on her show for the next day, watched a little ESPN, and was in bed by nine. She was essentially undateable.

Sometimes it got to her. She was lonely. She missed companionship—especially of the male variety—but she figured it was a small sacrifice that was worth what she was working toward. She had dreams of something greater than a local radio talk show, and now, having taped her audition, all she had to do was wait.

★ The next morning, a bright-eyed Kelly O'Shay strode into the radio station offices at five-thirty and was met by her producer, Rick—a thin, young guy who smoked so much Kelly thought he was responsible for the haze over the city—who greeted her with a cup of coffee.

"How'd it go?" he asked through a massive yawn, referring to her taping yesterday.

"Great," she said. "I think I have a shot, Rick. I think I might really make it this time."

He smiled wryly. "That's great. Just be sure to remember the grunts when you hit it big. You know, the guys who made you."

She laughed. "I'll remember," she said and picked up her interoffice mail.

"Oh, hey, here's one for the record books," Rick said, sliding onto a chair, facing backward. "Frank Campanelli called yesterday—you know who he is, right? Big-time sports agent?"

"Sure, I know who he is," Kelly said with a laugh. "He reps Parker Price, among others. Let me guess—he wants me to stop unloading on Price, right?"

"He definitely wants that," Rick said with a snort. "But he also wants Parker Price to make an appearance on your show."

Kelly gasped and turned so quickly that she knocked a binder off the desk. "*What* did you say?"

Rick chuckled, watching the smile that slowly shaped her lips. She casually picked up the binder, then leaned across the desk and pinned Rick with a look. "Seriously—he wants to come on *my* show?" she repeated, certain she'd misunderstood him.

"He wants to come on your show," Rick said, smiling now. "He thinks maybe you don't get baseball," he added with a wink.

"*Ohmigod*. Ohmigod!" she cried and whirled away from Rick as a flurry of possibilities suddenly filled her head. *Parker Price on her show.* The horse's mouth and ass, neatly tied up in one appearance. "This is *fantastic*! Thank you, thank you, *thank* you! ESPN, here I come!" she sang, did a little dance move, and picked up the day's lineup. "How soon can we get him on?"

"How long do you need to prepare?" Rick asked, sipping his coffee.

"Are you kidding? I am *so* prepared I am about to *bust*. Can you get him here this morning?"

Rick laughed and shook his head. "Next Thursday. We're booked up until then."

"Next Thursday is *perfect*," she said and practically skipped out of the office and to the studio, as happy as a kid at Christmas.

CHAPTER 03

Parker and Frank arrived at the radio station promptly at six A.M. the Thursday morning Parker was scheduled to be a guest on Kelly O'Shay's show. Frank, whose doughy face appeared a little redder than usual in the fluorescent office light, was wearing his usual—dark suit, red tie, and his reddish-blond hair slicked back with a healthy dollop of something greasy.

Parker's dark hair was combed back and already falling around his eyes. He wore faded jeans, a white collared shirt, and his favorite black cowboy boots. He figured this was radio. No need to dress to impress.

Frank frowned and knocked again on the glass door of the studio. The front office staff didn't come in at this ungodly hour, so there was no one to buzz them in, and Frank did not like to be kept waiting. He was kind of a diva that way.

They stood there, Frank pressing the button over and over again until Parker figured he had awakened all of lower Manhattan by now with the incessant buzzing. And just when he thought the top of Frank's head would blow off, a woman appeared in the darkened reception area to buzz them in.

Frank opened the door and barreled inside. "Parker Price for Kelly O'Shay. We're doing the show this morning."

"Welcome!" she said and flipped on a couple lights.

Whoa. She didn't need the light because she was smiling a million-watt smile if Parker had ever seen one. And he smiled back, taking in blond hair pulled back in a sleek tail and long legs encased in nice tight jeans that rose up to just below her belly button. He knew that because she was also wearing a cropped sweater that showed off said belly button . . . and a very nice rack. Pretty eyes, pretty mouth . . . wow. "Hey," he said, and wondered, like he always did when he met a good-looking woman, if she recognized him, if he at least had that leg up.

"Hey," she responded with a funny little laugh.

Frank snorted. "We're running a little late, so if you could just round up your boss," he said impatiently.

The woman blinked. "Sure. Come with me."

She and her near-perfect derriere led them down a darkened corridor and into a dingy office. It was tiny, but they had somehow managed to shoehorn a gun-metal desk, four faux leather chairs, and a coat rack inside. The walls and desk were littered with paper and pictures Parker didn't really notice—he was too intent on the woman. She was beautiful. Absolutely beautiful. The sort of beautiful that made opera singers sing and painters paint.

"What's this?" Frank asked, clearly not as taken with the woman as Parker.

"This is where we talk with our guests before they go on the air," she said, and something about her voice made Parker start. "Please have a seat. Can I get you something to drink? Coffee? Water?"

"Coffee, black," Frank said instantly and fell into a seat with a grunt. "So when does the great Kelly O'Shay grace us with her presence?"

"I guess now," she said and folded her arms across the flat plane of her belly, challenging Frank with those green eyes to argue.

Holy shit. Of all the things Parker had thought of Kelly Shay, gorgeous was never one of them. He'd imagined . . . hell, he didn't even know what he'd imagined, but it damn sure wasn't *this.* He and Frank exchanged a look of surprise.

She laughed at their expressions. "Who were you expecting? Someone with a pointy hat, hooked nose, and a big wart?"

"Something like that," Parker muttered.

She extended her hand. "Kelly O'Shay. Pleasure to meet you, Parker Price."

He eyed her hand, half-expecting a trick zapper, and reluctantly took it. She squeezed his hand firmly and shook it vigorously.

"It's a . . . ah, nice to meet you, too," he said, still dumbfounded.

"Don't lie," she said with a wink and extended her hand to Frank. "You must be Frank Campanelli, agent extraordinaire."

Frank, the dolt, was still staring at her with his mouth gaping open. "Yeah," he said, pushing himself out of his seat. "Frank Campanelli."

"I've heard a lot about you," Kelly said, shaking his hand just as ferociously as she'd shaken Parker's. "You have quite a reputation."

"Right," Frank said, then frowned. "What's that supposed to mean?"

"Nothing!" she exclaimed with a laugh. "It's a *good* reputation—all good." She turned a surprisingly warm smile to Parker. "So how about that coffee?"

"Ah . . . water," Parker said.

"Coffee. Black," Frank repeated, apparently having regained his composure after the initial shock of learning Kelly O'Shay wasn't a hag after all.

"You got it," she said. "I'll be back in a moment." She walked out of the office.

Parker instantly turned and slapped Frank on the arm. "*Shit. Shitshitshit—that's* Kelly O'Shay?"

"This couldn't be better," Frank said, grinning. "All you have to do is turn on the charm, loverboy, and you'll have her eating out of your hand."

Parker snorted and fit his six-foot-four-inch frame into one of the chairs. "I don't get the impression that Miss O'Shay is the type to fall for a line."

"Trust me on this," Frank said, drumming his fingers impatiently on the desk. "I bet we can clear it all up right here. Just do that Texas drawl thing and smile."

Sometimes, Parker thought he had the dumbest agent in the business. "I don't have a Texas drawl, and really, this isn't about—" he started, but Kelly O'Shay walked in carrying a foam cup of coffee and a bottle of water.

"Here you go," she said, handing them their drinks. She perched one hip on the corner of the desk in front of them and smiled at Parker again. "So, Parker, thanks for coming to the show. The listeners are going to love it."

"I'm sure they will." Frank chuckled.

"My producer is running late this morning, so I am going to do your preshow interview, if that's all right?"

"Great," Parker said. "And about the show, Kelly . . . may I call you Kelly? Ah . . ." He pushed the water aside and leaned forward, looking at her earnestly. "Frankly, I wanted to come on your show because I've been in a slump like I haven't seen in my entire career."

"Yeah. I know," she said, wincing sympathetically. "I'm really sorry."

"It's been very difficult," he said, affecting his best puppy dog look. "I don't know why or how it started, but I'm having a little trouble putting on the skids."

"It must be really tough for you," she said, her eyes wide with concern.

That was just where he wanted her. "You don't know the half of it. Anyway, I was hoping that maybe you and I could come to an understanding."

"An understanding?" she asked, and slid her hands in between her knees, leaning forward, piercing him with her green eyes, and filling his nostrils with a very arousing scent. "What sort of understanding?"

"Well . . ." He cleared his throat and glanced at Frank. "The thing is, Kelly, I think that maybe . . . I don't know, but maybe . . . ah . . ."

Frank nudged him with his shoe. Parker rubbed his chin a moment. He never thought he'd be whining to a woman about his superstitions, but here he went. He looked up and smiled a little sheepishly. "I suspect that your show may be having an effect on my playing."

"Oh *no*," she said, frowning with concern. "*My* show? What do you mean?"

"Most people don't understand. It's hard to explain, but ballplayers are notoriously superstitious, and I confess, I'm one of them," he said, raising his hand with a lopsided smile.

"Ooh," Kelly said.

"And it seems that some of the things said on your show—and I'm not saying *you*, you know. You're *great*"—he quickly clarified—"but some of your callers, the negative things they say stick in my head, and then I go to the game, and I've got that negative noise going around in my head," he said, fluttering his fingers at his head. "You know, like people saying I suck, and I'm the worst ballplayer they've ever seen, that sort of thing—and then I can't seem to play. It's a psychological thing."

"Oh!" She blinked wide green eyes at him. "A *psychological* thing. I'm really sorry to hear that, Parker. I had no idea you were having psychological problems."

"No, no," he said with a laugh just as Frank blustered a hearty, *"No, no!"*

"Not *psychological* problems," Parker corrected her gently as he put a hand out to stop Frank from talking. "I just mean that negative feedback affects my head in the game. Do you see what I am saying?"

"Yes," she said, and leaned over, put a slender hand on his shoulder, and smiled so warmly he felt a little warm himself. "I understand. And I'm really sorry you are struggling."

"Thanks. Of course, there was no way you could have known. It's just a baseball player's thing. We're a pretty superstitious lot."

"Ah," she said, removed her hand, and stuffed it back between her knees.

"So I was thinking maybe we could talk about some of the great games the Mets have played this year," he suggested. "We made some great plays against the Philadelphia Phillies. And we smoked the Florida Marlins early in the season."

"Right, and the Atlanta Braves," she said, nodding.

Well, no, *not* the Atlanta Braves. That was the series that had started his slump. "Yeah, well . . . I was thinking of some of our better series."

"Right," she said. "I understand. You would rather I focus on the positive."

But there was something in the glimmer of her eyes that gave Parker pause. "If you don't mind," he said, feeling suddenly less confident.

"May I ask a few questions?" she asked, and picked up a pad of paper and pencil from the desk and made a note. "Is there anything about you personally our listeners would find interesting?"

"Ah . . . I don't know of anything."

"He's an avid fisherman," Frank interjected, which was a huge lie.

"No, I'm—"

"And he does a lot of charity work with underprivileged kids."

That much was true, but he hated that Frank made it sound like a gimmick. Not that Kelly O'Shay seemed to notice. She was jotting down something. "Anything else?"

"He loves to read," Frank blathered. "What's the last book you read, Park?"

Kelly glanced up to hear his answer.

"Jesus, Frank, I am not a big reader. I read the *History of Sports in America*, and that took me a year," he said with a laugh.

Kelly laughed, too, a melodious, sweet laugh. She glanced at the clock above their heads and said, "Oh no, look at the time. I'm on the air in ten." She flashed another winsome smile. "Come on, I'll show you where you can wait for your segment and hear the show. Rick, my producer, will come and get you when it's time." She popped up off the desk. "You can bring your drinks," she said and walked out of the room.

They quickly picked up their drinks and followed her.

CHAPTER
04

The first hour of *Sports Day with Kelly O'Shay*, which Parker listened to in a room nearby, had lots of sound effects and raucous laughter from Guido. Kelly covered tennis (the latest female teen phenom had been seen in England making out with her high-dollar trainer), women's soccer (amazing what flashing a sports bra could do for a women's sport), and bowling. No kidding. *Bowling*. Accompanied, of course, by the sound of pins falling.

At the top of the second hour, Kelly announced she had a very special guest. As she said it, a small, young man opened the door of the room and beckoned Parker to follow him.

"Remember to show her what you're working with," Frank said with a wink. Parker rolled his eyes and walked out.

He stepped into the tiny studio booth. Kelly was standing behind a stool, her arms folded. Guido, her sidekick, was seated, lounging back in his chair, feet up, tossing a Nerf ball in the air over and over.

"I wouldn't kid you, Guido," Kelly said and winked at Parker as he tried to fit headphones on his head. "This is the best guest we've ever had on this show." She gestured for Parker to sit on a stool in front of a mike. "This one is going to blow everyone's socks off."

"So who is it?" Guido asked. "Shaquille O'Neal?"

Kelly snorted. "Not *that* good."

"You're killing me here!" Guido exclaimed. "Who is it?"

"I'll tell you . . . right after these messages," she said and punched a button and leaned back in her chair. "Parker, this is Guido D'Angelo."

Parker nodded across the control panel.

"Man, you got some *cojones*," Guido said with a grin as Kelly walked around the control panel to adjust his head-phones, standing so close that her breasts were staring him in the eye.

"Oh now, Guido, don't tease him," she said, leaning back to look at him. "You don't want to scare him out of here."

Parker snorted. "He can't scare me out of here."

"Oh, that's good. I thought maybe you were . . . you know . . . a little sensitive."

Somewhere, deep down in the center of him, Common-sense Parker kicked Ego Parker and woke him up. Kelly smiled—she really did have a gorgeous smile—and Ego Parker squashed Commonsense Parker like a bug under his boot. "Nah," he said, smiling back. "I'm not sensitive at all. It's the nature of the game. I understand that."

"Great!" Kelly said, her eyes glittering. "I'll remind you of that later," she added with a laugh.

"Okay, kids, back in five," the producer said somewhere in radio space.

A moment later, Kelly said, "Welcome back to *Sports Day with Kelly O'Shay*. I'm Kelly, and this"—she waited for the foghorn sound—"is Guido D'Angelo. How you doing, Guido?"

"I couldn't be better, Kelly. The sun is shining, the birds are singing, and it's a great day here at the studio," Guido said and grinned wolfishly.

"Guido, I was telling you we had a very special guest this morning, and I am *very* pleased to introduce Parker Price of the New York Mets. Hello and welcome to our show, Parker!"

"Thanks, Kelly. It's great to be here."

"So, Parker, you have had an *amazing* career in baseball over the last several years. You played ball at the University of Texas, were named MVP two years in a row, and then you went on to play for the Houston Astros as a short stop."

"Yep. I played there for ten years."

"Right. And you were named to the All-Stars four years in a row—"

"Well," he said with a chuckle, "it was actually five."

"Oh, I'm sorry. *Five*." She smiled at him. "Very impressive. And then last year, the New York Mets brought you to town for an unprecedented one hundred and ten million dollars." She looked up. The glitter in her eyes was almost blinding. "Plus bonuses."

"Right," he said, feeling a little uncomfortable. He didn't like to talk about what the Mets were paying him, yet he'd never met anyone in the sports business who could go a minute without mentioning it.

"The Mets were lucky to get you," Kelly added.

"Thank you."

"I saw you play during the Florida Marlin series early in the season, and dude, your bat was *hot*. So was your glove for that matter. Remember that great double play you made at the top of the sixth inning?"

Like he could forget it—even he'd been impressed. "Yeah, that was definitely a great play for us. I really enjoy playing for the Mets. They are a great ball club, and I'm lucky to be a part of it."

"Yeah," Kelly said.

Was that a bit of a tone he detected?

"I was reading the back page of the *Daily News* yesterday," she said sweetly, pulling out a paper from beneath the table and spreading it before her. "Essentially, the article says you've been having a *real* good time in New York."

Damn. Frank had told him about the article, but he hadn't read it. Something to do with his social life ruining him on the field. Shit. He *really* should have read that article.

"Apparently, the city has a *lot* to offer you," Kelly said with a bit of a smirk, and Guido laughed. "I mean, a ballplayer. The ladies love a ballplayer."

He shrugged, smiled a little. "I haven't read the article, but you can't believe much of anything you read these days."

"So you're not involved with anyone?"

He blinked, trying to figure out her angle. Guido laughed. "He thinks you want to date him, Kelly."

"I guess he would, since according to the *Daily News*, every single woman who can still draw breath wants to date him."

"I, ah . . . that sort of rumor goes around all the time. In Houston, in New York—it doesn't seem to matter. They always say the same thing."

"Really? I thought maybe your nighttime habits are a contributing factor."

"A contributing factor?"

"You know, to why your batting average has sunk from a high of .349 just two seasons ago to a low of .277 this year."

Guido howled, punched a button, and the sound of a big sucking *whoosh* filled the booth.

"I don't think my social life has anything to do with it," Parker said evenly.

"Then to what would you attribute your slide? Because you were a much better batter in Houston than you are here." And Kelly smiled a warm, sweet little smile.

Guido laughed.

Parker's blood was beginning to boil. "That's an interesting theory," he said, forcing himself to sound as pleasant as possible. "But my trainer seems to think it's more to do with the shoulder injury I suffered when I caught the game-winning drive up the middle against the Phillies. I landed on the second base bag and tore my rotator cuff."

"Right, I saw it," she said, nodding eagerly. "But *before* that, you had eight errors coming into a midseason series, compared with a total of twelve errors across your entire last season with the Astros. And we haven't even hit the All-Star Break yet. At this rate, you'll hit a record of . . . what did we figure out, Guido?"

"Twenty-two errors," Guido responded helpfully.

"I had twenty-four errors one season in Houston, and I was MVP. You can't really compare the number of errors from year to year, because it depends on what team you are playing, who is pitching, what the conditions are, that sort of thing. And, you know, you have to factor in shoulder injuries that are slow to recover."

"So, Parker, what do you like to do in your spare time?" she asked, all sweetness and light as she changed the subject.

"I have a charity for underprivileged kids," he said, and

gave some of the particulars about that, for which Guido actually sounded a standing O.

"Anything else?"

"I lay pretty low," he said, not wanting to give her anything.

"Do you like to read?"

Okay, now she was *really* beginning to piss him off. His eyes narrowed. So did hers. "Yeah, I like to read. I just read the *History of Sports in America.*"

"Oh really? How long did that take you?"

Suddenly, in the hallway behind Kelly, which Parker could see because the wall was made of glass, Frank appeared and started making frantic slashing motions across his throat.

"I don't know—I savored it."

"Do you ever think about hitting a batting cage?" she asked, cheerfully changing the subject again.

"I practice batting thirty minutes every day."

"Oh, *that* long, huh? And how long do you practice fielding?"

Parker didn't answer.

"I'm only asking because a couple of your more spectacular errors were on your glove. That huge overthrow to first in the second game with the Phillies, then that line drive you just completely muffed in the series against the Angels that allowed two runs to score—"

"I remember," he said, his jaw tight and his gaze narrowed on her smiling assassin face. "I've had a slump, there's no doubt about it. I am working with the coaches and a trainer to get back to the shape I was in when I came to New York, and I have every confidence that I will. But a shoulder injury like I suffered can really take a toll. I haven't been able to resume full upper body workouts since the Atlanta game."

"Uh-huh. Well, let me ask another question, Parker." She looked up from her notes, planted her arms on the table, and leaned toward him, her eyes narrowed into little slits of green. "Don't you think that if a team pays a professional ballplayer—and not just any professional ballplayer, but an MVP and a multiyear All-Star short stop—oh, who are we kidding? Let's just say we're talking about *you*—if a team pays *you* one hundred and ten million dollars plus bonuses, don't you think *you* ought to be accountable for your level of play?"

"Of course I do." Behind Kelly's head, Frank started jumping up and down—quite a feat, given the man's girth—gesturing angrily for him to come out of the booth.

"So then don't you think *you* ought to be accountable for your declining level of play? Wouldn't it stand to reason that there is some sort of financial penalty levied if this big-time, expensive player does not deliver the results the ball club was looking for when they made that ginormous investment in you?"

"I do," he said, clearly surprising her. "But I don't think you can levy a penalty based on just a few games. I think you have to look at the season as a whole."

"So are you saying that at the end of the season, if you haven't helped the club achieve the sort of results the Mets were hoping for in their gazillion-trillion-dollar investment in you—which, incidentally, forced them to trade one of the best pitchers in the National League just to free up enough cash to *get* you—that you will give back some of that scratch?"

"I damn sure will," Parker said, and noticed, out of the corner of his eye, Frank falling up against the wall like he'd been shot and sliding down until he disappeared from sight.

Kelly reared back, blinking in surprise, and suddenly laughed. "Guido, look at the phone lines! They're on fire. Let's go to the phones!"

It went downhill from there, and by the time his hour was up, Parker had the distinct impression that Guido was feeling a little sorry for him. "I had no idea New York was that *mad*," an awestruck Guido said as they wrapped the show.

"Our thanks to Parker Price, who has been an exceptional sport by showing up here today to talk about his abysmal record. I know we'd all love to keep talking to Parker, but unfortunately, we're out of time. That's it for us at *Sports Day with Kelly O'Shay*. Tune in tomorrow when we chat about another abysmal record—the New York Knicks."

The show rolled over to commercials, and both Kelly and Guido got up, gathering their stuff to make room for the next guy. Parker followed them out into the hall—no sign of Frank, he noticed—and stepped in front of Kelly as Guido congratulated her on a great show.

She tilted her blond head back and smiled up at Parker. "I can't thank you enough for coming on this show," she said, practically bubbling with excitement. "That was just spectacular. Okay! So thanks *so* much," she said, and jostling her papers and binders, she stuck out a hand.

He expected an apology, something that indicated she knew she'd just put him through complete hell. But all he got was impatient, wiggling fingers on that extended hand. "You didn't listen to a word I said, did you?" he asked.

"I heard every word."

"But you were determined to make a putz of me, regardless of the facts."

She laughed and withdrew her hand in favor of holding all her crap. "No, I think you've done that all on your own. Listen, I'd love to chat, but I've got loads to do. So thanks again and good luck." And with that, she turned and marched off in the opposite direction.

CHAPTER
05

Kelly marched right into her office, shut the door, put down her things, and threw her arms in the air and did a Snoopy happy dance in the tiny bit of space around her desk. That had been a killer show. They had more callers than they had the day Jose Canseco's tell-all book about doping in baseball was released.

She worked on the next day's show until her stomach began to growl. She looked at a clock. High noon. No wonder she was starving—she hadn't eaten anything since a protein bar at five this morning. She could pick something up on her way home.

She packed up her stuff, said good-bye to the station staff, and walked outside into a bright New York day, headed for one of her favorite restaurants, when someone stepped in her path . . . someone about six foot four with coal black hair, steel gray eyes, and a body right out of *Sports Illustrated*. Someone who had a square jaw on which stubble had already begun to appear, a small diamond stud in one ear, and incredibly muscled arms folded across a broad chest.

Someone who was really much more handsome than she'd anticipated, which had made this meeting on the street a little rough. She didn't want to just ogle him, as she'd been tempted to do all morning. She'd always thought he was one of those overt muscle guys with spindly legs and feet and you-know-what-else. Only Parker Price didn't have a spindly bone in his body.

Too bad, she thought as she smiled up at him, that he was such a high-dollar choker. Otherwise, she might be seriously attracted to him. "Excuse me, but you are blocking my path and creating a traffic jam on the sidewalk," she said politely.

"I don't care," he said, staring down at her. "What you did in there was not cool, Kelly."

She gasped, truly affronted. The worst short stop in Mets' history was going to critique *her*? "What wasn't cool, Parker? The fact that you suck, or the fact that everyone knows you suck?"

"I don't"—he paused to lean down so that his nose was just inches from hers—"*suck*. And you ought to be ashamed for being such a mean shock jock."

"Mean?" she cried as two men walked by and suggested they move. "I'm not *mean*. I'm accurate. I have a show about *sports*, and sometimes, accurate and sports stars don't mix very well. And anyway, Tex, what'd you think it was going to be? A love fest?"

"Well now, Yank, I didn't think there was going to be any love, but I *did* think you might at least listen to what I had to say. I thought you would at least take my plea seriously."

She laughed. "How could I take you seriously?" she asked, flinging her arms wide. "You were trying to influence the way I do my show, and that is *so* not cool. As they say, if you can't stand the heat—"

Someone slammed into her from behind and knocked her right into his hard, immovable, one hundred percent male body. *Wow.* He put his hands on her arms and set her back.

"Hey, watch it!" Kelly shouted at the woman who'd bumped her.

"Get out of the way!" the woman screeched as she sailed by, followed by several more people staring darkly at them as they strode by.

"Like I was saying," Kelly continued, completely unde-terred, "the Mets paid you one hundred and ten million dollars to solve their problems, and not only have you not solved their problems, you have *added* to them. So don't you think you owe the Mets, and me, and *all* the fans out there a viable explanation as to why you stink? Something a notch above *I am superstitious*?"

"Who died and made you the supreme judge of viable explanations?" he demanded. "I just asked you to cool it, that it was getting in my head, and I figure, if you *really* want the Mets to win, maybe you could lay off a couple days."

"You've got to be kidding," she said incredulously.

"I am *so* not kidding," he said sternly. "Do you have any idea how much work I put in for this team?"

"Do you have any idea how much work I put into my show?"

"GET OFF THE SIDEWALK!" a man bellowed at them. "You're blocking foot traffic here!"

Both Parker and Kelly looked at the outraged rotund man who was shouting at them. "Just move on, pal," Kelly snapped.

"He's right. Let's go to lunch. How about Italian?" Parker responded.

Kelly gave a bark of laughter. "Now I know you're out of your mind."

"Why? We obviously have something to discuss, and this isn't the place to do it. Unless you know I'm right—"

"That's ridiculous!" she said, her eyes narrowing. "You really *have* lost your mind. Of course I'm not afraid *you* are right, because I know *I'm* right. And I don't like Italian in the middle of the day, so let's have sushi."

"I don't like sushi ever. Let's have Asian."

"No," she said, shaking her head. "Too spicy. Chicken."

He thought a moment, then nodded. "I can agree to chicken. I know a great restaurant right around the corner—"

"No," she said instantly. "I know a great place—"

"Jesus, will you just lead the way?" he demanded.

Kelly led the way, all right, wondering why it was that men who typically thought they knew *everything* and women were just minions in their world to do their bidding, had to be so damn good-looking. It wasn't fair. It threw everything off kilter and distorted the proper alignment of things.

She was marching a few steps ahead of one prime example of a man who was too good-looking for his own good, who thought he could just waltz into her show and change it to whatever he wanted.

When he put his hand protectively on the small of her back as they were jostled in a crowded cross walk, she was painfully aware of how close he was, and how good he smelled, and how dangerous that was.

In the diner, which was loud and crowded and serving standard diner fare, they got the last booth. Well, *Kelly* got the last booth. Mr. Big Shot had to stop and sign a couple autographs. By the time he sauntered to his seat, she had read the entire menu, from the salad starters all the way down to liver and onions and back up again.

Parker sat down, glanced at the menu, and then shut it and pushed it aside. "Salad. It's the only thing a person can eat in a joint like this."

Weird. Kelly was thinking *the exact same thing* at the exact same moment. She glanced at him over the top of her stained menu, which she refused to put down. "What *kind* of salad?" she asked accusingly.

He seemed to think that was a strange question but said, "Chicken Caesar."

"Augh!" she exclaimed and slapped the menu shut. "That's what *I* was going to have!"

"So have it," he said with a shrug.

That would defeat her determination to have nothing in common with him. "No thanks," she muttered and glanced at his hands. Those were some *enormous* hands. Enormous hands that were making her feel slightly flushed. Hello . . . *flushed*? The last time she'd felt slightly flushed, she'd had mononucleosis.

The waitress appeared, her ticket book out. "You know what you want, hon?" she asked Kelly.

"Chicken Caesar and water with lemon, please." Across from her, Parker lifted a brow.

"Got it," the waitress said. "And for you, sugar?"

"Same," he said.

The waitress looked up as she reached for the menus and looked at Parker fully for the first time. Her eyes went wide, and she suddenly broke into a wreath of smiles. Oh great, time for more idol worship.

"Hey, you're that baseball player!" the waitress said.

Parker smiled charmingly and shrugged a little. "I am."

"*Wow*," the waitress said, beaming. "Can I have your autograph?"

Across from him, Kelly rolled her eyes. But Parker calmly took the ticket book the waitress handed him and asked, "Who should I make it out to?"

"Lucy. Like in *I Love Lucy*," as if he couldn't get Lucy the first time. Parker started to write, but Lucy suddenly put out her hand. "No, wait! Will you make it out to my husband, Paul? He's a *huge* Mets fan."

"How about I do two? One for you and one for Paul?"

"Would you *really*?" she squealed, and squatted down at the booth, watching him write something on one ticket then on another ticket as Kelly restrained herself from barfing. Parker tore out both tickets and handed them to her. "Thank you so much," she gushed. "This will make my husband's day."

"My pleasure, Lucy," he said with a wink and watched her rush away, clutching her autographs. Then he looked at Kelly. "Would you like an autograph?"

Kelly snorted. "I just hope she didn't have the salads written on the other side of those autographed tickets, because I am starving."

"So am I," he said, pushing a hand through thick black hair. "You must have to be at work very early every morning."

"Five-thirty, Monday through Friday."

"Wow," he said, with a lopsided smile. "That's rough."

"Not if you're not a party animal," she said with a lopsided smile, too.

His smile widened to a full grin. "Now, Kelly O'Shay, you don't look like the kind of woman who believes everything she reads in the *Daily News*."

"You're right. I never believe my horoscope. But everything else, I believe. I mean, why would the *Daily News* lie to me about you? And can you honestly expect me to believe you are a good boy, early to bed, early to rise?"

He chuckled low, leaned forward so all she could see was

his gray eyes, and said, "I never claimed to be a good boy. And I won't deny that I get out every now and then. A guy can't live on frozen dinners alone, you know."

She just bet he got out every now and then. Probably in the company of little girl groupies, dressed in tiny micromini skirts and halter tops. Probably the sort that wore microminis and halter tops *and* hung on his every word. Hell, she couldn't blame the poor dumb things. Parker was *hot*.

"The last time I went out, I went to the Museum of Modern Art," he said, completely surprising her. "Have you seen it since they completed the renovations?"

"Ah . . . no." The Museum of Modern Art? A *museum*? He really didn't seem the type, did he? She couldn't picture him, a big guy, knocking around a museum. "That must be your attempt to get me to believe you are cultured and refined and not just a jock who can't bat."

"I'm not trying to get you to believe anything. I was just remarking that the last time I went out, I went to see the Museum of Modern Art. I happen to be a big fan of architecture and modern paintings."

Well, knock her over with a feather. "Right," she said, and smiled, waiting for the punch line.

"Come on, Kelly," he said genially. "Don't tell me you're suffering from the totally inappropriate, completely ignorant, and disgustingly uninformed conception that just because I am a professional athlete, I have no appreciation for the fine arts. I hope you aren't *that* narrow-minded."

In a word? *Yes*. She didn't buy for a minute that Parker appreciated the fine arts. She had him pegged as the sort of guy who came off the field, sat back, popped a couple beers, and watched *SpongeBob SquarePants* reruns. "I'm just having a hard time picturing you walking around an art gallery."

"Huh," he said, his eyes narrowing slightly. "Just how do you picture me?"

The image of him naked suddenly danced merrily across her mind's eye, and totally taken aback by it, Kelly blinked.

"What?" he demanded.

"Nothing," she said, feeling a bit of heat beneath her collar. "I don't picture you at *all*."

"Well, I wish you would try picturing me playing baseball and see if you can't turn that shock jock bit down a notch."

There was that image again, only this time it was a naked Parker in the batter's box, and Kelly could not keep the smile or the heat from her face. "I don't *picture* you," she insisted emphatically and instantly dropped her gaze to the table, working to wipe the grin off her face.

"Look at me," Parker demanded.

Kelly refused to look up but rubbed the back of her neck and wished the naked Parker would take a hike. Her face was flooding with heat.

"*Oh*. Okay. I get it," he said with a sigh.

"What?" she asked, looking up, and saw the knowing smirk. "No, no, there is no *oh*," she protested, perhaps a tad too emphatically.

"Right." He was grinning at her. A naked Parker Price was grinning at her.

She snorted and looked around for the waitress. "So how hard can it be to unwrap some premade chicken Caesars and bring them over?"

"Hey, don't freak out, Kelly. I will admit that I pictured you the same way."

That certainly got her attention—she jerked a wide-eyed gaze at him. "*Excuse* me?"

He threw up a hand. "Just keeping it real, here."

"Well . . . keep it real someplace else," she suggested, gesturing vaguely toward someplace else.

He laughed. "Didn't have you pegged for a prude." His gaze flicked the length of her. "Quite the opposite."

"I am *not* a prude," she insisted. "Just because I don't appreciate a man I've just met picturing me like *that* does not make me a prude."

"You're right. It doesn't make you a prude; it makes you uptight."

"Thanks a lot."

He grinned. "You're welcome."

He was teasing her. Okay. She sat back, crossed one leg over the other, and started swinging her foot. "So now that you have enlightened me that you are a whole person, and not just a jock who pictures women he's just met naked, maybe you will tell me the real reason you are playing so poorly."

That made Parker groan and roll his eyes to the ceiling. "May *I* ask a question for once?"

"Ask away."

"Why did you choose me to hate?"

She didn't *hate* Parker. She actually kind of liked him in a weird, distant kind of way. "I don't hate you," she scoffed, flicking her wrist at him as if that was a completely ludicrous suggestion.

"Yes, you do. You trash-talk me every day. You don't seem to have a program if you're not Parker-bashing. And I would like to know how it ever got to that point."

"Well, first of all, I trash lots of sports stars on my show— Wait. That didn't come out right. What I mean is that I have sports talk show. I have to talk about the good and the bad to be legitimate, and you just happen to be spectacularly bad at the moment. But hey, if you started hitting and fielding and living up to that truckload of dough they paid you, I'd talk about how great you are."

He suddenly leaned forward, put his arms on the table, and looked at her with an intensity that made her suck in her breath a little. "So if I play well, you'll ease up on me?"

"Absolutely!"

His eyes narrowed. "Let's put a little wager on it. We're playing the Astros at home tomorrow. If I get a base hit, you ease up a little. If I get an RBI, you not only *ease* up, you *talk* me up. And if I get a home run, you go out with me."

Kelly almost spewed her water all over the table and then laughed out loud. "Are you nuts? I'm not going out with you!"

"What's the matter? Afraid I'll get a home run?"

"You are *so* not going to hit a home run."

"Says who?'

"Says *me*. You haven't had a decent turn at bat in a month!"

"Then what's the problem? Take the bet." His gaze challenged her, daring her to do it.

Kelly drummed the table with her fingers while considering it. First of all, he'd never get a homer, at least not now, not batting like he was. And second of all, it wouldn't be the end of the world if he did, because he really was cute—and likable in a sort of full-of-himself jockish way. And third . . . She suddenly leaned forward. "Okay, how about this? Deal on the base hit. Deal on the RBI. But if you don't get a hit or an RBI or, let's be real, a *home run*, then you agree to come back on my show and let me ask you why."

His eyes narrowed. So did hers. And Lucy the waitress chose that moment to drop two chicken Caesar salads on the table. "There you go, sugar. The cook put extra chicken on your salads."

"Thank you, Lucy," he said, and gave her a smile that probably melted the woman's underpants right off her.

"Oh for Pete's sake," Kelly muttered and picked up her fork. "That's the deal, Tex."

Parker grinned. "I'm game if you are."

Kelly put down her fork and stuck out her hand. Parker took it in his big bear paw, and they shook on it. Only Parker didn't let go of her hand right away. He sort of held on to it, that charming little smile of his curling the corners of his mouth, his eyes roaming her face.

"May I have my hand, please?" she asked politely. He let go. She wished Lucy would come back and fill her water glass, because she was feeling a little parched. His smile went even deeper, and she had the distinct impression that he knew exactly how parched she was.

Kelly cleared her throat and forked a piece of chicken. "This will be the easiest bet I ever took," she said.

"I was thinking the same thing."

"I can't wait for the game tomorrow night. I'm going to listen to every play," she said, and laughed, imagining him at bat, swinging for the fences and hitting nothing but air.

"Why listen when you can see it in person? I'll leave two tickets for you and Guido."

Actually, that sounded like a perfect plan. "Seriously?" she asked.

"Absolutely. It would be my pleasure."

Not nearly as much as it would be her pleasure to watch him lose the bet. And as the conversation turned to pitching, Kelly happily thought of all the one-liners she would use when he came back on her show.

CHAPTER
06

In the bottom of the seventh, the Houston Astros were leading the Mets two to one, but the Mets had two guys on base and Parker was up to bat. He'd gotten a base hit in an earlier inning, and that had boosted his confidence. But he was mildly disappointed to look up to the seats he'd left for Kelly—choice seats, right behind the dugout—and see them empty.

Who knew why she hadn't come? Frankly, it wasn't a big deal—whatever he did tonight would be repeated over and over again on ESPN and local news. But he was playing so well, and he had an excellent feeling about this at bat, because the Astros had Orsen Harbacker warming up in the bull pen.

Orsen was a relief pitcher Parker knew almost better than anyone else in the Major Leagues. They'd played against each other in high school, together in college, and together in the minors and big league. Parker knew Orsen so well, he knew Orsen liked to throw a sinking fast ball, which most guys in the league couldn't hit.

But there wasn't another ballplayer who'd spent hours letting Orsen practice throwing sinking fast balls to them, either. Years ago, when Parker and Orsen had played college ball, the two of them had practiced many afternoons in an empty ball field.

So when Parker stepped into the batter's box with two men on, he casually knocked the dirt from his cleats and lined up. He could see Orsen size him up, could see him shake off the catcher's first two signals. Then he threw a curve ball.

"Strike!" the ump called, and Parker smiled at Orsen, stepped out of the batter's box, adjusted his helmet and his glove, and knocked the dirt off his cleats once more. Just as he was about to step into the box, he happened to glance up to the seats behind the dugout.

Damn it if his pulse didn't leap a little, because there she was, with Guido beside her. He didn't know how he might have missed her before. She was sitting with her legs crossed, leaning forward, her arms propped on her knee, watching him intently. She was wearing a Mets baseball hat, a kick-ass top with spaghetti straps, and what he guessed was some sort of short skirt—all he knew was that she had some of the shapeliest legs he'd ever seen.

Shit. Now he had a freakin' audience, like there wasn't pressure enough just from his own bench. He had to ignore those legs, that was all. He had a job to do, and that job was to get his bat on Orsen's pitch, no matter what. All he needed was a base hit to bring in one run and tie the game. Anything more was gravy.

He stepped back into the box, adjusted his grip on the bat, and glared at his old pal Orsen.

Orsen threw him a ball, much to the delight of the Mets crowd but much to Parker's dismay. For once, just once, he needed the baseball gods to be with him and make Orsen throw his sinker. *Just this once.*

Parker stepped out of the box, went through his ritual of adjusting his helmet and glove and knocking the dirt from his cleats before stepping back into the box again. And even then, he took all the time he needed to get into position, hoping to shake up Orsen a little.

It didn't shake up Orsen in the least. The next pitch he threw was a slider, and Parker was stupid enough to swing at it. The ump signaled a strike, a groan went up from the crowd, and from the corner of his eye, Parker saw the club manager shake his head and say something to the batting coach.

No, goddammit, he was not going down this time. He survived another ball, and another one after that as Orsen tried to throw another curve ball to make Parker swing. He had a full count now. He stepped out of the box and angrily knocked the dirt from his cleats. If Orsen thought he was going to walk him, he had another think coming, especially with Kelly sitting up there lapping this up like a dog. It felt like everything was riding on this full count. *Everything.*

He adjusted his helmet and glove, gripped his bat, and stepped into the box, getting in position very quickly this time. "Come on, buddy," he muttered through his teeth. "Come on . . . give me what I want."

Orsen wound up and uncorked a sinker. And by some divine miracle, Parker got under it. The ball went sailing high to right field. He dropped the bat, raced toward first, and rounded it like an old pro as a lusty cry went up from the crowd. The right fielder had missed it; the ball bounced off the back wall and away from him, and the go-ahead run was rounding third and headed for home.

As Parker hit second base, the third base coach signaled him on, and Parker felt a burst of energy like he hadn't felt since he was twelve years old. He was flying—his legs were moving under him, eating up great lengths of ground, his arms pumping like pistons. He did not break stride when he rounded third, flying over the base without knowing where the ball was. But as he came down the home stretch, he got the signal to slide and literally hurled himself through the air, sailing headfirst into home, his hand outstretched, his fingers reaching the plate just ahead of the catcher's tag.

The crowd went absolutely wild as he jumped up and brushed himself off. The dugout emptied as the entire team rushed out to high-five him. Parker clapped hands with every teammate who could reach him, and as he trotted back to the dugout, he looked up.

Miracle of all miracles, Kelly O'Shay was smiling. The girl was actually *smiling* and gave him a thumbs-up that made him feel lighter than air.

He grinned through the rest of the game and made a couple really spectacular catches, if he did say so himself. The Mets won that night, breaking a two-week losing streak. Afterward, Parker had a few beers with some of the guys to celebrate but then headed home when they all continued on into the city to do more celebrating. Not him—he wanted to be up bright and early to hear *Sports Day with Kelly O'Shay*.

The next morning, Parker awoke to the glorious sound of his radio alarm . . . but then frowned in disappointment when he was awake enough to realize it was Guido who was doing the talking.

"Full count, the go-ahead run on second, and *bam* right to the warning track! That was *off* the *hook*!"

"It was off the hook all right," Kelly agreed in her sexy— and surprisingly genial—voice. "You wouldn't think a guy that big could run that fast, but he ran like greased lightning. Guido and I were there to see it with our own two eyes."

"We saw it all right," Guido agreed, and someone sang "Take Me Out to the Ballgame."

"I'm telling you, Guido, Parker Price hit what might have been the most spectacular inside-the-park home run I've ever seen. There is no question that it saved the game."

"It may have saved the game, but, Kelly, I have to give you props," Guido said. "If it wasn't for your show, I don't believe Price would have stepped up to the plate, pardon the pun."

Wait just a damn minute . . . Parker stared disbelievingly at the radio. Guido was going to give *Kelly* credit for his game-winning home run?

"Oh, Guido, that's sweet, but *I* didn't hit that home run," Kelly said.

"Damn straight you didn't," Parker muttered.

"No, no," Guido responded, determined. "If you hadn't called this guy on the carpet for his sucky performance this season, I don't think he would have done what he did last night. That's just one man's opinion, but I defy someone to prove me wrong. Before your show, Price was sleepwalking through the season."

"Well," Kelly said airily, "sometimes, all it takes is a real-ity check. You know how these high-flying baseball players are—they've got so many managers and handlers that some-times they don't really know how they are playing in Peoria, right? But take a guy like Price, clue him in, and maybe it sinks in, maybe it doesn't, but the Mets won last night!" she sang out.

Parker kicked off the covers and stood up, his fists clenched, and stared down at the radio.

"Too bad you can't get the Knicks team in here and do some talking," Guido laughed. "They could use a turnaround, too!"

"You have *got* to be kidding!" Parker roared at the radio. "Come *on,* Kelly! You had nothing to do with that hit!"

Kelly laughed and said, "Let's go to the phones. Hello, you're on the air with Kelly O'Shay. Who are we speaking with?"

"Hi, Kelly, this is Bill in Queens. Hey, thanks for bringing Parker Price on the show. I think that really shook him up, you know?"

"That's what I'm talking about!" Guido said and played some ridiculous cheering section.

"He ought to call up and thank you," Bill added. "Honestly, you saved that guy's ass!"

Parker roared again and swiped at the radio, sent it sailing to the floor, and the power cord whipped from the wall. He glared at the radio, marched to his closet, got a replacement, and threw it on the bed before heading to the shower. *Saved his ass*! Clearly, he was going to have to go into the city and correct a couple of major misconceptions.

Rick shot Kelly a note on her laptop an hour after her show was over that Parker Price was waiting for her in the lobby.

She surprised herself by being quite pleased by that news. Well really, he'd come all the way into the city—he must have really liked the show this morning. It *had* been a good show. Kelly usually wasn't a fan of having to eat crow on the air, but then again, Parker had played so spectacularly last night that it was a glorious day for Mets fans everywhere, so she'd been happy to do it.

It helped that he'd been so damned *sexy* on the ball field. The uniform fit him like a glove in all the right places, and she noticed, as she watched him play short stop, that she was even more curious about the ol' cup than ever before.

And now look, the guy had a heart. He'd come here just to tell her how much he appreciated the show. With an uncharacteristic giggle, Kelly pulled out a small mirror from her purse, checked her hair, and dabbed on some lipstick.

But as she sailed down the hall to the lobby, she spotted Parker pacing in front of the glass doors, looking just a little bit agitated.

"Parker!" she called out as she walked into the lobby. He

instantly swung around, his face like stone. "Hey, *great* game last night," she said happily and exuberantly threw her arms wide. "On my honor, you deserve my groveling. That was as good a game as I've ever seen, and definitely worth the price of admission."

"You got in free."

"You know what I mean. It was *great*."

Instead of smiling or otherwise acknowledging the compliment, his gaze narrowed and he slowly folded his arms across his chest. "So . . . you liked what you saw, is that what you're saying?"

Hello, was he deaf? "I *loved* what I saw! Of course I did! Who wouldn't? It was a fantastic game, and you were really awesome."

"So," he said, his eyes still narrowed suspiciously, "you get that I am a professional ballplayer, with ebbs and flows in my abilities like any other human being on the planet?"

Ebbs and *flows*? What was all this oceanic crap? "I always got that."

"Then please explain *why* you would go on the air today and claim credit for that inside-the-park home run?"

Kelly burst out laughing. "Claim credit!" she cried. "How could I claim credit? I wasn't the one holding the bat!"

"*Exactly*," he said low and dropped his arms, moving toward her. "It's just a little hard to wake up to *Guido* thanking *you* for the home run last night."

Oh please. Was the man so dense that he couldn't figure out she and Guido were hyping their own show? With a roll of her eyes, she put her hands on her hips. "And here I was thinking you were a smart man, Parker."

"And here I was thinking you were a straight shooter."

"Okay, Mr. Baseball, let me see if I can explain the concept of talk radio," she said. "I have a talk radio show. And if I want people to listen to my talk radio show, which is essentially how I keep my job, then I talk about controversial things, like, say, a ballplayer getting paid loads of cash who doesn't deliver. And then, sometimes, when the ratings go through the roof because of some angle I have taken on said controversial subject—you know, like challenging you to do better—then I toot my own horn so the listeners will tune in tomorrow to see what else I can do—you know, like affect world peace or something."

He said nothing, just glared at her. But then he stepped so close that their bodies were almost touching. Up close like that, he looked huge and very, very masculine.

Kelly opened her arms wide and gave him a look right back. "I *have* to keep them coming back, don't I?"

He thought about it for a moment and nodded, his gaze falling to her lips. "Okay," he said low. "I accept your apology."

"But I didn't apologize," she said, just as low.

"You should."

"So should you," she said, fighting to keep a smile from her lips.

His dropped his gaze, skimming her body, down her pink sweater, her knee-length black skirt, her knee-high black boots. "It's hard to argue with a woman when she looks so hot."

"Thanks," she said, feeling strangely giddy. "You don't look so bad yourself." He looked fabulous, actually—black slacks, a light blue shirt that went perfectly with his eyes. Clean shaven, his hair combed . . . she wondered if he had cleaned up just for her or if he was on his way to jury duty or something.

"Are you done here, or do you have a show?" he asked.

"Ah, no . . . no. I'm really done for the day. I was just doing some paperwork and making a couple of calls."

"Well then," he said, moving a little closer so she could smell his spicy cologne, "I don't want to sound like a complete asshole here, but girl, you owe me a big fat date."

Kelly couldn't help smiling. "I know. I made a bet fair and square, and I lost."

"Don't sound so excited," he said, smiling a little.

She tilted her head back and looked him square in the eye. "Should I be excited?"

Parker arched a brow, amused. "Do you really need me to answer that for you?"

Kelly nodded.

"Then clearly, I have my work cut out for me," he said, his gaze slipping to her lips.

His gaze was so smoldering that Kelly unthinkingly put a

hand to her throat. "Ah . . . when do you want to go on this big fat date?"

"Now," he said firmly.

"Now?"

"Why not now? I came all the way down here. You said you are through for the day. We could make a day of it."

"Doing what?"

He chuckled so low that a shiver ran up her spine. "Any number of things come to mind. But I think I will start with taking you to the Museum of Modern Art to try and infuse a little culture into you. And then, over dinner, you can impress me with a recap of my most excellent home run."

"Wow," Kelly whispered. "That sounds so romantic. I think I might be excited."

"That's because I'm a very romantic guy," he said, grinning now, too, dimples and all. "But I haven't even gotten to the exciting part yet."

"Ooh, and a little titillation to boot," she muttered, staring at his mouth.

His fingers brushed hers, and the little shiver shot down her spine and into her groin. "I haven't even begun to titillate," he whispered.

Damn it if he hadn't. Her knees were getting wobbly. But she managed a smile. "Okay. You're on. Just give me a half hour to finish up here."

"Great," he drawled. "I'll wait for you on the street." He smiled again, and she noticed for the first time how his sexy smile crinkled the corners of his eyes. *Man.*

"I'll be down in a few," she responded, and stepped back, out of the sphere of his magnetism, which was just one moment shy of sucking her into its vortex.

He gave her a smile that suggested he knew how he stirred her up inside and then casually walked out of the office like a man who left women to melt in his wake all the time. Kelly watched him go, admiring him until Guido scared the crap out of her. "Kelly, are you hot for the *Priceman*?" he cried and laughed loudly as he waltzed into the reception area.

"Shut up, Guido," she shot back and marched in the opposite direction of Parker, ignoring Guido's guffaws.

"That would make a great show!" he shouted after her, but

Kelly had already dived into her office and shut the door, still smiling ridiculously.

That was when she noticed the red light indicating a message on her phone. She instantly picked up the receiver, punching in her voicemail code.

"Ah, hi," a strange voice said. "This is Dan Brown at ESPN calling for Kelly O'Shay. Kelly, we got your audition tape and thought it was absolutely great."

Shocked, Kelly fell onto her chair.

"You look great on camera, you're articulate and funny, and well, we'd love to talk to you about it. You or your agent can give me a call at the following number."

With a shriek, Kelly grabbed a pen and jotted down the number as best she could with a hand trembling with excitement. Then, to be sure she'd clearly heard what he said, she played it again, and what the hell, two more times. When she was at last convinced ESPN had really called *her* (and hadn't called to say anything about her being too fat or too hideous to be on TV, which, of course, she had secretly feared), she twirled around in her chair until her heart stopped pounding and before she made herself totally sick, and eagerly dialed the number Dan Brown had left.

"Hello?" she said when a woman answered the phone "ESPN." "This is Kelly O'Shay calling for Dan Brown."

"Hold please," the woman said, and Kelly pinched herself to keep from freaking out.

"Kelly," Dan said a moment later, just like they were old friends and had worked together for years. "How's it going?"

"It's going *great*," she said. "I am so glad you called! I am so glad you liked the tape!"

"*Loved* the tape! That was fantastic commentary. So listen, what we'd like to do is get together and talk through some things with you and your agent and see if we're all thinking alike and if there is a place for you at ESPN."

"Sure! Yes, okay," she said, and squeezed her eyes shut, waved her hand hard to keep from bursting into tears of pure delirium. "What sort of place are you thinking?"

"Well, we're thinking a humorous talk show to air Friday nights. How does that sound?"

Was he *kidding*? How did that sound? How did that *sound*?

Like all her dreams and hard work had paid off! Like she had found the pot of gold at the end of the rainbow and was now going to wallow in it, completely naked! "It sounds fantastic, Dan. I can't wait."

"Don't get too excited yet. There are a lot of details to be ironed out," he said, and began to talk through them. When she finally hung up, she couldn't wait to tell someone. *Anyone.* She dialed her mom but got the answering machine. She tried to catch her old college friend Amy at work but got her voicemail. Guido was gone for the day, and that left . . .

Oh *shit*, she'd forgotten Parker. She glanced at her watch. It had been forty-five minutes. Kelly grabbed up her stuff and sailed out the door.

He was leaning against a mailbox, one arm propped on top, one ankle crossed over the other, casually perusing the hundreds of people who went streaming by. "Parker!" she cried as she came through the revolving doors, darting in between pedestrians.

He turned toward her with a very warm, spine-tingling smile on his face. "I'm sorry," she said, juggling her things as she ran up to him. "But I got the most *amazing* phone call before I left work."

"Oh yeah?" he asked, instantly taking her laptop from her. "Let me guess—you booked the Knicks."

The world was suddenly so bright and so wonderful that Kelly laughed heartily at that. So heartily that Parker looked at her a little strangely. "No, but something just as good. *ESPN* called," she said. "They are thinking of testing me for a talk show!"

"Seriously?" Parker asked, looking quite impressed.

"*Seriously!*" she squealed. "They want to test *me* for a talk show! I am so excited, I honestly think I could fly!"

He laughed, put his hand on the small of her back, and ushered her into the stream of people on the sidewalk. "Don't fly away just yet," he said, seeming genuinely pleased for her. "But that's fantastic, Kelly. Really wonderful. I can only wonder what took them so long."

"Me, too!" She laughed again.

She talked excitedly about it as they walked down the street to a restaurant. Kelly hardly noticed—she just walked through the door, still talking as Parker opened it, then fell into a seat the maître d' showed her to, exhausted and thrilled and suddenly very happy to be with the one guy in all of New York she never thought she'd like.

It didn't hurt that he was sharing in her excitement, oohing and aahing at all the right moments, hanging on her every word—and looking so incredibly handsome while he did it.

They ordered lunch, and Kelly told him how long she had wanted this, how it was so great because ESPN was in Connecticut, still close to New York, which she loved, and how this was a dream come true.

"I know how you must feel," he said. "It's sort of like getting the call that they are bringing you up from the minors." And he went on to tell her about the day he got The Call. Even now, ten years later, he still sounded excited and grateful and proud.

"It will probably be a big adjustment for you," he said. "You'll have to work all the time to get a show like that up and running."

Kelly laughed. "I work all the time as it is, so that's nothing new."

"Oh come on—surely you don't work *all* the time. No one works *all* the time. What do you like to do when you're not working?"

"I don't know," she said, thinking about that. "I work out. I read a lot."

"Anything else?"

"Like what?"

"Like, I don't know, *guys*? Do you date? Do you have friends? Do you eat the young in your family for breakfast?"

She couldn't help laughing. "Only occasionally and always fried. Yes, of course I have friends, Parker. Hard to believe, I know, but some people actually *like* me."

"Guys?"

"Guys?"

"Do *guys* like you," he reiterated.

"Hey," she said with a laugh and forked a huge bite of cheesecake they were sharing in celebration of the ESPN call. "*Guys* like me. At least I think they do. Okay, honestly, it's been a while since I had time to date, so I'm not really sure

anymore. It's my hours," she said, by way of explanation.
"What about you? Friends? Dates who aren't groupies?
Kids?"

"No kids. Tons of friends. Lots of dates, too, but no one
steady in about five years."

"Aha," she said and pointed a fork with a hunk of cheesecake at him. "You're the old wham-bam-thank-you-ma'am
kind of guy."

"I most certainly am not," he said, taking the fork from her
hand and eating the hunk of cheesecake. "I will have you
know that I enjoy the company of a beautiful woman because
I am a man. Men like women. But that does not make me a
slut."

"Sure, Romeo," she said, and snatched her fork back, took
another piece of the cheesecake, and popped it in her mouth.

"I'm serious. I don't date a lot because most women I meet
want to go out with me because I am quasi-famous or rich,
which seems to be my best assets as far as they are concerned."

"Wow," she said, realizing, for the first time, that there
might possibly be a downside to being Parker Price on any
given day. "So what do you do with all those freeloaders when
you date them? Take them to the museum?"

He laughed. "I have reserved that for my dates who are cul-
turally challenged," he said, putting down his fork. "I don't
know. Dinner, I guess. Or maybe catch a show. And if we hit
it off, maybe a nightcap."

"Uh-huh. At your place."

"No. At a nice, quiet club."

"Huh," she said. "That actually sounds like a nice date. But
not one I'd go on."

"Why not?"

"Too boring."

"Oh yeah? What would your ideal date be?"

"Well, if I were going out with someone like you, for example, I'd probably take him to the batting cage and give him
a few pointers," she said with a wink.

Parker laughed. "God help me the day I get batting tips
from you."

"Then, if a guy like you actually started to improve his batting, I'd probably take him to a Yankees game so he could see the big boys play."

"Oh, now that's a low blow," he said, slapping a hand over his heart.

"Better than Broadway," she said.

"Depends on one's perspective."

"Museums aren't that great, either—"

"Uh-uh," he said instantly, shaking his head and signaling for the check. "You agreed and you owe me. We're going to a museum."

"Great," Kelly said with a playful sigh and polished off the cheesecake.

But actually, today, even a museum sounded good.

CHAPTER

08

Parker couldn't believe the amount of crap a two-hour morning radio show apparently generated, based on the stuff Kelly was carrying. She had a bag hanging off both shoulders, plus she had an armload of binders. When she suggested they drop off the stuff at her apartment, he couldn't agree fast enough.

Of course she lived in a walk-up. Parker was impressed that, even though she was carrying what he thought had to be thirty pounds, she jogged up the stairs to the third floor of a pre-war brownstone that had been parsed into six apartments. Hers was on the top floor, where she fit her key into the door and flung it open. He liked fit women.

Kelly's apartment was small, but it had twelve-foot ceilings, floor-to-ceiling bay windows that overlooked the community garden between buildings, and hardwood floors. She had an overstuffed brocade couch and giant chair in the middle of her living room—the only room in the place, save the bedroom—and a fireplace that had been bricked off but still had a very cool brass mantel. The kitchen was small but larger than what was typical in New York, and she had new appliances.

"Make yourself at home, and I'll be right with you!" she called, disappearing into the bedroom.

Parker put her laptop on a small table near the kitchen and walked into the big living area. There was a small TV in one corner, but at the angle it sat, he had the impression it was seldom used. She was an avid reader, too, judging by the many ways books had been stuffed into her built-in bookcases. A row of pictures along the mantel caught his eye, and he wandered over to have a look. There were pictures of Kelly with a dog and with a woman who looked a lot like her. Another was of a family gathering of some sort, a picture of her at a bar with a bunch of people.

But no guy. Excellent. No former lover. No guy pal.

"What are you doing?"

He turned around—Kelly had changed her black sweater and donned a wispy, long-sleeved flowery pirate-looking shirt through which he could see a very lacy bra, and she'd let down her hair from the ponytail; it fell in soft blond waves around her shoulders. Damn. Just when he thought she was about as hot as a woman could possibly be, she turned up the flame.

"Hello?" she said, laughing a little.

"Just looking at your pictures," he said, gesturing blindly to the mantel behind him.

"I should really put up some new ones. Those are ancient." She walked into the kitchen, opened the fridge, and pulled out a bottle of water. "Want some?"

Parker nodded and followed her into the kitchen. She ducked behind the refrigerator door and then stood up, smiling brightly, and handed him a water. When he took it from her, he couldn't help himself—he let his fingers linger on hers. And then he drank, watching her.

Kelly—beautiful, self-assured Kelly—flushed a little and put her bottle back in the fridge, closed the door, stood there looking at it, opened it again, and took the bottle out. "Water," she said, as if reminding herself what she was doing.

"Shall we get going?" Parker asked, enjoying the soft pink of her skin.

"Yeah. Can't wait to get to the museum," she said with a roll of her eyes, and opened the fridge door, put the bottle of water back in, and shut it. She glanced up at Parker, smiled, and then tried to step around him. But her kitchen was too small, and she accidentally brushed up against him.

With the woman's near-perfect body, clad in a flimsy pirate shirt and lacy bra holding round, perky breasts against him, his one hundred percent male body went into full alert at the feel of a woman's body against it. Without thinking, Parker put up an arm to stop her from going any further.

Pressed up against him, the counter behind her, and stopped by his arm, Kelly laughed softly and lifted a blistering green gaze to his face. "What are you doing?" she asked his lips.

"Don't know," he answered truthfully and lowered his mouth to hers.

He couldn't help it—she was so pretty, so spunky, so sexy. He touched her lips, lightly and carefully, just enough to taste her. But then the pure male in him sprang to rapt attention, and he put down the bottle of water he was holding and slipped his arm around her waist, drawing her in even closer, nipping lightly at her lower lip.

He expected Kelly to push him away, to slap him. But once again, she surprised him. She didn't do any of that, just opened her mouth beneath his and breathed sweet breath into his mouth. That was it, all the invitation he needed, because he was suddenly kissing her with every ounce of himself, his tongue in her mouth, his hands on her body, sliding up and down, over her breasts, down her hips.

When Kelly came up for air, she said breathlessly, "This isn't me. I don't just make out with guys I hardly know."

"Me, either," he said, and kissed her again, swallowing her laugh.

But Kelly pushed away. "No, seriously, I don't do this."

"We're not doing anything," he said, leaning down to kiss her cheek, the bridge of her nose. "We're just saying hi."

"If this is your 'hi,' I wonder what your 'so long' is like."

"Hopefully, you won't have to find out."

"Parker . . ." She reared back, looked at his eyes and then his lips, her green gaze soft.

"Hey, for what it's worth, I'm not exactly the guy who starts off like this, either."

"Then why are you?"

"Because, Kelly O'Shay, from the moment we met, I have been thinking about you," he answered honestly. "I've been thinking about how funny you are, and how you aren't wowed by celebrity and you don't think I'm the guy who can get you or keep you out of trouble. But most of all," he said, pausing to nip at her lip, "you're just so damned good-looking."

She laughed with surprise. "Really?" she asked.

"Really."

"And you're attracted to me, even after everything I said?"

"*Especially* after everything you said," he said sternly.

Kelly grabbed the collar of his shirt and yanked him close so that her luscious lips were just a moment from his. "Even when I said you couldn't hit the side of the Goodyear blimp?" she whispered.

"Don't push it," he whispered in response. "But yeah, even then."

"That's so *sweet*," she purred, and planted her mouth firmly on his, flicking her tongue against the seam of his lips.

Somewhere, in the back of his tiny little man pea brain, Parker didn't think he'd ever wanted a woman so bad in all his life as he did right then and there, and grabbed her by the waist, crushing her to him, angling his head so he could kiss her long and deep.

Kelly purred in the back of her throat, and that was about all she wrote. He suddenly twirled her around, pushed her up against the fridge, and started moving down her very curvy, very feminine, and very sweet-smelling body. Kelly laughed low and huskily as refrigerator magnets went flying and scudding across the kitchen floor.

He pressed his mouth against her belly, through the gauzy fabric of her pirate shirt, while he filled his hands with her breasts, then slid down, to the curve of her waist, and down again, digging his fingers into the meat of her hips.

"Jesus, Parker," Kelly said breathlessly. He rose back up, claimed her mouth again, his tongue tangling with hers, sliding against her teeth, the plump flesh of her mouth. Christ, she smelled so damn good—he could get high off a scent like that.

He pressed against her, and Kelly pressed back, moving seductively against his fly, which was straining to the point of bursting now. He'd had plenty of women in his arms, but he was convinced in that moment that he'd never held or felt a more beautiful or sexy woman than Kelly. He was one step

away from yanking the pirate shirt from her body when she
suddenly put her hands against his shoulders and pushed.

He raised his head, his mind swimming out of the fog of
wanting her so bad, and looked at her. Kelly was still up
against the fridge. Her hair was all mussed up. Her lips were
swollen from their passionate kisses, and her neck was still
wet where he'd kissed her. One long, booted leg was hiked up
against the fridge, too, and her skirt was pushed so far up he
could almost see Nirvana. Her eyelids hung heavy over warm
green eyes, and she was smiling. One long, satisfied little
smile stretched across her lips.

That smile did him in. He reached for her again, but Kelly
laughingly held him at arm's length. "I reserve the right to
skewer you on the air if you play bad."

"What?" he asked anxiously, her words not registering
clearly.

"I have a job to do. So if you play bad, you are fair game."

Parker laughed low in his throat and slipped his hand between her legs and one finger beneath the tiny strip of fabric
of her panties. Kelly gasped softly and closed her eyes. "I
mean it."

"Why don't we talk about that later," he suggested with a
bit of a growl, and pushed her arm aside and planted his lips
on hers again.

This time, there were no interruptions. He quickly helped
Kelly out of her shirt and lacy bra, so that her breasts were exposed and in his hands. He grabbed her up as if she weighed
nothing and twirled her around, seating her on the countertop,
then braced his arms against it as he took one breast in his
mouth and then the other.

Kelly caught her breath, arched her back, and thrust her
breast into his mouth at the same moment her hands dug into
his hair, while making sounds that suggested she was enjoying his attention to her breasts. Parker's hands were skimming
wildly over her body and her bare breasts, up her thighs and
between them. She dropped her hands to his shoulder, her
breathing raspy, and then to his shirtfront. When Parker lifted
his head from her breasts, she caught his mouth with a kiss as
she began to undo the front of his shirt.

She slipped her hands inside his shirt and sighed into his

mouth as her fingers slid over his pecs, his hardened nipples, and then down his sides. "You're gorgeous. I can't believe this," she said breathlessly as she scraped across his back and middle with her fingernails. "I wasn't going to like you."

"I wasn't going to like you, either," he said, just as breathlessly, and caught her bottom lip between his teeth, then pressed his forehead to hers. "But I'm definitely liking you now, girl."

"That's great. Do you have a condom?" she asked, sliding her hand down and over a world-class, ought-to-win-an-award erection.

"Not on me," he admitted with a wince.

Kelly suddenly pushed him away, slipped down from the counter, and hurried into the living room to an end table near the sofa. She yanked open the drawer, threw several papers and things onto the floor, then whirled around, holding up a condom in her hand. She was naked from the waist up, her chest rising and falling with her gulps for air, wearing a short skirt and boots, and damn, Parker could come just looking at her.

"It's a little old, but it oughta do the trick."

He was next to her in three strides, and in a few moments, he had removed everything from Kelly but her boots. "Let's keep the boots," he suggested with a wink as he yanked his shirt from his body, then his shoes and pants.

Kelly's eyes lit up at the sight of him—and frankly, he was a little impressed himself. Massively engorged and desperate to be in her, he stood before her, fully erect, until he reached for her, digging his fingers into the soft folds of her flesh, burying his face in her neck, and, with one arm wrapped around her waist, picking her up and then falling onto her couch with her on top.

Kelly quickly lifted one leg, planted her heel beside him, and slid back to his thighs. She dragged her fingers down his chest, to his groin, and wrapped her hand around him.

"Shit," he muttered as she took him fully in her hand and started sliding up and down. He slipped two fingers into her cleft and matched the rhythm of her hand, sliding up and down and around and around to the point that Kelly closed her eyes and dropped her head forward. The ends of her hair whispered against his belly, and Parker was thinking of taking matters to the next level when Kelly released a tiny cry and suddenly let go of him and pushed his hand away from her body. She grabbed him by the shoulder and lifted up, moving her damp body against the tip of his cock. With a very seductive smile, she started to slide her body onto his cock.

He groaned like an animal as she slid down on him; he gripped her hips and began to move with her, watching her face, watching her find pleasure in his body.

Her eyes looked like the blue-green flame of a fire, hot and intense and filled with ecstasy, and Parker experienced a strange feeling in his chest, a weird simpatico as if he had connected to someone totally and completely. Unlikely as it was, he was feeling a very deep and profound connection with Kelly at that moment.

Kelly sank her teeth into her bottom lip and began to move faster, but Parker wasn't going to let her ride away with this. He caught her by the waist and rolled off the couch, stopping their fall to the floor with one arm. Now she was on her back and he was on top of her—still connected—and her black boots around his waist.

Kelly laughed, put her arms around him, and kissed him tenderly. This was heaven, purely heaven. Parker reached between them and stroked her as he began to push deep into her. She sighed blissfully—her head rolled to one side, half covered with blond hair. She moved her hips to meet him, moving faster as she neared her release, and when she came, she let out a groan of rapture.

That groan sent Parker over the edge—he held her steady with his arm around her waist, reaching as far inside her as he could. His release was bubbling up in him, along with several deep-seated emotions that surprised him. There was something here that went beyond a primal coupling, something she had touched in him, some barrier she had broken through. Those emotions and his pleasure spiraled around one another until the bubble burst and he came, hard and long and completely.

Reduced to a mass of flesh—there was nothing left inside of him—he closed his eyes and pressed his forehead against her shoulder. Kelly wrapped her arms around his head and sighed contentedly. They remained like that for a few moments until the heel of Kelly's boot stabbed him in the butt and he yelped. "Sorry," she said, and dissolved into a fit of giggles.

So did Parker. And they lay there, giggling, until Kelly suggested that the guy across the garden could see Parker's bare ass.

Parker and Kelly did not leave that cozy apartment that afternoon, but ended up in her four-poster bed, giggling like teenagers and speaking about their lives, their dreams, and their desires. Around six that evening, when Kelly's stomach started to growl, they reluctantly got dressed and went out for what turned out to be a long, leisurely dinner. And still Parker did not leave. They returned to her apartment and made love like they'd been lovers for months instead of moments, bringing each other fulfillment in ways neither of them had experienced in a very long time.

The next morning, Parker woke to an empty apartment. He stretched, got up, found a radio, and switched it on, finding Kelly's show as they were discussing the Mets' series against the Chicago Cubs. He was leaving today.

"I'm just saying," Kelly said, "that if he could get his batting average up to around .285, .300, the guy would be unstoppable."

"You mean if he's got any glove," Guido said.

"It definitely goes without saying that if he ain't got glove, he ain't got game," Kelly quipped, and Guido provided the sound of laughter.

"But I think we might have seen a turnaround, Guido. I think maybe the Mets are back."

That was met with a stadium cheer, which Guido really seemed to like.

"Let's go to the phones—this is *Sports Day with Kelly O'Shay*. Who are we speaking with?" Kelly asked, and Parker turned it off. He didn't need to listen to her show anymore and walked into her bathroom and turned on the shower. Actually, he didn't think he needed much of anything anymore. He had a very fluid feeling that he'd found what he was looking for.

Parker called her every day from Chicago, and every day, he played spectacularly.

Every morning, Kelly sang his praises on the radio, giving him credit for single-handedly turning the Mets around. When Guido questioned that on the air, she retorted, "Hey, if he could single-handedly bring the team down, then doesn't it stand to reason that he could single-handedly build them up? You can't argue the facts, Guido. Two home runs, four RBIs, and three double plays in the last two weeks."

And for a couple of weeks after that, the Mets were suddenly so hot—thanks in large part to Parker's bat—that Kelly had to turn her on-air attention to the Yankees, who had an uncharacteristically bad slump after losing a series to the Red Sox.

In the meantime, Kelly was on cloud nine. Between her negotiations with ESPN and spending every moment she could with Parker, she felt like she was living in a dream. *Everything* was going her way. Her ratings were at an all-time high. New York, which she'd once likened to a stinking cesspool in the dead of summer, suddenly seemed beautiful, filled with flowers and bright sunshine, friendly people, and lots of shiny cabs.

Guido was beside himself over Kelly's new, positively

giddy demeanor and started teasing her mercilessly, calling her Priceman's Payment Plan, or making cooing noises when Parker would call. Once, when she said something glowing about his performance on air, Guido hit the thousand-smooches button, making the entire booth sound like it was filled with kissers.

There was a time when Kelly would have chafed beneath such teasing and thought it was undignified for a female sports radio talk show host. But now she didn't care in the least and just laughed at Guido. How could she care? She was very happy. She loved being with Parker. She loved the way he laughed, how he seemed to take everything in stride, and how he was so very attentive to her. It was true—they were hounded wherever they went by eager fans wanting an autograph or to talk baseball, and while she admired the way he spoke to each person as if they were a personal friend, he still managed to be sure she had his undivided attention.

Parker was also determined to infuse some culture into her, and marched her from one museum to another—which, Kelly was privately surprised to discover, she actually enjoyed. She would have thought she'd be deadly bored in them, but instead, she was intrigued by the art and artifacts.

They also attended some Broadway shows, which she tried very hard to like, but finally used as an excuse to insist they do some of the things *she* liked. Parker thought that was great and dove right into spending an entire Monday afternoon and evening in a movie marathon of Kelly's creation, watching the classics and sharing several big bowls of popcorn, which Parker insisted on slathering in butter.

When the Mets played in town, Kelly had great seats behind home plate. Parker made it a habit to look up and find her when he walked out to bat. She would smile and give him a thumbs-up. It worked like magic—Parker was hitting so well that the airwaves were full of Parker Price, calling him the best ballplayer of the decade. Once, when Kelly went to the game with her sister, someone tipped off the network booth as to who she was. Her picture was broadcast up on the Jumbotron in the stadium and to Mets fans across the world, along with the commentator's remark that she was Parker Price's new love interest.

Needless to say, Guido was merciless after that and had the entire radio station staff teasing her.

A few days after another fantastic afternoon game against Milwaukee in New York, Parker brought Kelly home with him to his house on Long Island. When they arrived, a blue-haired woman was waiting at the bottom of his drive, holding a box.

"Uh-oh," Parker muttered as the gate to his house swung open.

"Uh-oh? Why uh-oh?" Kelly asked, fearing a deranged stalker.

"My neighbor," he sighed as he put the car in park and got out. "Hello, Mrs. Frankel."

"Parker, you hit pretty well today," she said, nodding approvingly. "I won't lie to you—I keep waiting for the other shoe to drop, but so far, you've managed to hang on."

"Thanks, Mrs. Frankel," he said.

The woman turned to Kelly and suddenly smiled brightly. "This must be the gal they showed on the TV," she said, her old brown eyes glistening with excitement. "Honey, you're even prettier in person. I made Parker a pie I was so pleased with him today, but I want you to have it," she said, thrusting the box forward.

Kelly took the box and looked down. It was a pie, all right. Homemade and smelling like apple.

"The Mets oughta thank you," Mrs. Frankel continued as Kelly juggled the huge box of pie.

"Thank *me*?"

"Well, sure! It wasn't until Parker settled down with you that he started hitting and fielding worth a darn. You're his lucky charm. Isn't she, Parker?"

"She sure is, Mrs. Frankel," Parker said, rolling his eyes over her cotton-candy head.

"Oh, I think that's overstating it a bit—"

"It's the truth, and everyone knows it—even Parker," Mrs. Frankel interrupted, and looked at Parker for confirmation. "Just think about it, now. He doesn't play as well on the away games as he does at home. That's because *you* are here."

Parker cocked his head to one side with an expression that suggested he hadn't really thought of it before.

"Am I right?" Mrs. Frankel demanded.

"You're right," he said, nodding thoughtfully, but then grinned at Kelly. "She's definitely my lucky charm."

"Well God knows you needed one," Mrs. Frankel said, wagging a finger at him. "Don't let her go, at least not until the season is over, and you better not let the season end before October, mister. Now. Can I have my bat?"

Parker winced, shook his head. "I think I better hang on to that until the end of the season."

Mrs. Frankel huffed about that but was all smiles when she shook Kelly's hand once more. "Oh, you're so young and pretty," she said admiringly and then walked on down the street.

Kelly looked at Parker. "Her *bat*?"

"Long story," he said. "Come on, let's eat some pie—Mrs. Frankel is ornery, but she makes a great pie."

During the week, when Parker was in town, they stayed at Kelly's apartment in the city. But on weekends, they spent lazy days at Parker's palatial home, usually around the pool, talking about life and the future. Kelly was still uncertain what would happen with ESPN—having negotiated a deal, she was waiting for the muckety-mucks there to decide if they wanted to send her for a pilot test. Parker liked to make Kelly practice for her ESPN on-air audition poolside.

Wearing a bathrobe over her bikini, Kelly would laughingly swipe up a banana and begin her spiel: "Parker Price has one hundred and ten million reasons he might want to leave town if he doesn't get a hit tomorrow night," she'd start, and with Parker good-naturedly hissing and booing, she'd go on to trash the overpaid but very sexy short stop for the New York Mets.

Parker would laugh. "And don't forget," he'd remind her, "that Parker Price lost his big toes in a tragic tree-climbing accident, which makes him molasses-slow when running the bases."

Kelly laughed. "You're such a good sport, Parker."

"Nah." He grinned. "If anyone else was doing that kind of number on me, I would come out of my tree—*with* my toes. But with you? Never. This is so much better than where we started, baby. I'm just not worried about any of that anymore."

"Worried?" she said, crawling on top of him as he lay stretched out on a chaise longue. "Were you really worried?"

He smiled self-consciously. "I guess a little," he said, lifting his hands to her breasts and caressing them lightly. "I've never had a slump like that, and I've never had any trouble with my glove." He glanced up. "But I found my lucky charm."

"Stop, Parker. You know there is no such thing as a lucky charm. I had nothing to do with your slump *or* your comeback. Remember what you said one time? That you had ebbs and flows like anyone else?"

That caused him to burst out laughing. "Did I really say that?" he asked, pulling Kelly down to kiss him. "What an asshole!"

"I thought it was poetic."

"You did?"

"Yes! It was poetic in a jock sort of way."

He laughed and nibbled her lower lip. "I hope we're together for a long time," he said, kissing her cheek and the side of her mouth.

"You do?"

"Yeah." He put a hand to her face and pushed her hair out of the way. "You know that I'm falling in love with you, Kelly."

She knew. Just as well as she knew that she was falling in love with him, too. She traced a line with her finger across his bottom lip. "Are you sure?"

"Damn sure. I've never felt this way about a woman in my life. You make me happy . . . and I play so well with you in my life," he added with a grin.

"There was a time that you weren't such a big fan of mine."

"That was before I knew you . . . but you weren't exactly a fan, either," he said, stroking her cheek.

"That was before I knew what a fabulous ballplayer you are."

"Wow," he said, his brows rising up. "That is *very* high praise coming from you."

Kelly laughed and traced another line across his lip. "You know I'm falling in love with you, too, Priceman."

"I know," he whispered, and slipped a hand inside her robe.

"Hey," she said, curling her arms around his neck and glancing uneasily at his house.

"Marie is off today and no one else is around," he said, pausing to kiss her throat. "Except maybe"—he kissed the top of one breast—"a couple of squirrels." He moved to the other breast. "But pay no attention to them—I pay them well to keep their mouths shut."

Well. If he was *paying* them. She sighed as he untied her bathing top with his teeth and lowered her onto the chaise. His hand drifted down, sliding in between her legs. "Tell me again what you're going to say about me when you do your pilot test."

"That Parker Price is the sexiest guy in all of baseball."

"That's a great start," he said, and kissed her.

They made wild love on that chaise, crying out with abandon, completely in sync with one another and their blossoming relationship. They spent the entire weekend sequestered in his mansion, taking no phone calls, letting no one in—except the delivery guy, of course, who kept them in food and booze and made a tidy little sum in tips for his discretion.

They romped about Parker's huge house, talking about how many kids could live comfortably in that house, at how improbable it was that they were actually together, talking about anything and everything.

But when Sunday night came, their little retreat from the world ended when Kelly headed back to the city. "I'm gonna miss you," Parker said, wrapping her in a bear hug before they walked out to the car. "We're leaving for San Francisco tomorrow morning."

"I'll miss you, too," Kelly sighed, and pushed his hair from his forehead. "But it's just a few days."

"As long as I know you'll be here when I get back Friday. What if I swing by your place when we get in?"

"That would be great," Kelly said, rising up on her toes to kiss him once more. "I'll make you something very special."

They left it that way, both reluctant to part, both eager to be together again.

But in the middle of that week, while Parker was hitting balls out of the park and performing a double play that one sportscaster said was an impossible feat, Kelly got a call from Dan Brown at ESPN, who told her they wanted to fly her out to L.A. to get a makeover fit for television and do some tests on a few segments.

Kelly's heart started to pound like a drum as he spoke. "Seriously?"

"Seriously," he said. "We'll do a pilot segment, and if everything goes well and it gets picked up, we'd put you on the air right around October, in time for the World Series. So are you interested?"

Was he insane? Was she *interested*? "Yes!" Kelly cried, pumping her fist. "Yes, yes, *yes*!"

Kelly was waiting for Parker when he got in from San Francisco. Her apartment was swathed in candles, the tiny table had been set for two, and a bottle of wine was open and airing.

Nice ambiance, but he didn't need it, because Kelly was wearing a little red halter-top dress that hugged all her curves, and that was all the mood-setting he needed. He gathered her up in his arms, kissed her hard as he swung her around, then put her down on her feet again. "Do you know how much I missed you?" he asked, pushing her hair from her face.

"Well . . . I think the four bazillion phone calls were a pretty good indication," she said, and lifted her face to kiss him. "Come on, I made spinach lasagna, and I found this great wine—"

He caught her before she could slip away and kissed her again as his hands slid down her back to her hips.

"Parker, come on." Kelly laughed and playfully pushed him away. "The meal is ready, and I want to tell you something."

"So tell me," he murmured against her skin.

"No. I have to have your full, undivided attention."

"You've got my attention. Every fiber, every cell is focused on you, baby."

"Parker."

He sighed, dropped his hands from her body. "Okay. I'm here," he said, his gaze still skimming her body.

"Would you like a glass of wine?"

"I'd love one," he said, and walked into the living room to give her a little space. He glanced around as she poured the wine. "The place looks great," he said, nodding at all the candles. "Very romantic."

"I hoped you would think so," she said, handing him a glass of wine. "I want this to be a very romantic evening," she added as she sat on the couch. He followed her, touched his glass to hers, and sipped.

"Sorry about that last game," she said softly.

Parker shrugged. "You win some, you lose some. It'll all even out by the end of the season. If we keep up the pace, we ought to be in the running for the pennant. If not, someone ought to line us up and shoot us."

"I hope it doesn't come to *that*," Kelly laughed.

He loved the sound of her laugh and smiled, admiring her. How did he get so lucky? How did he end up with such a beautiful woman who wasn't into him for fame or money or any reason other than she wanted to be with him?

"You've got Arizona next and St. Louis right after that," she commented.

"Yep. Three days in town and then we're on the road for about ten days." He didn't want to even think of it. Summer months were tough, constantly on a ball field somewhere, constantly away from the people he loved, and now, away from Kelly. He couldn't stand it some days. "Are you okay with that?" he asked her. "The long absences?"

"Sure!" she said brightly. "I know it's part of the deal. And as a matter of fact . . ." She suddenly put her wineglass aside and faced him. "I have some great news, Parker. It looks like I'm going to be gone for a while, too."

In spite of his chuckle, Parker felt the first pinprick of trepidation. "How is it great news that you are going to be gone? Where are you going?"

She was smiling so broadly and gripping her hands so tightly that he had the impression she was fighting to keep from floating away. "Actually . . . I am going to L.A."

She waited a moment to see his reaction. But it took Parker a moment to connect the dots, and even then, he could only blink.

"Parker! I am going to L.A. to be tested for an ESPN talk show!" With a shriek of pure joy, she fell backward, her arms high above her head.

"Oh, God," he said, genuinely surprised and proud of her. "Kelly, that is fantastic!" He set aside his wine, grabbed her arm, and pulled her up to kiss her. "That's awesome! I am so damn proud of you, baby."

"*Thank* you," she said, beaming. "Parker, I am so excited I can hardly stand it. I can't *wait*! I'm going to be on ESPN with my own talk show! I mean, assuming everything goes all right and it tests out okay and they like the segments I tape and I don't come across as a big dork. Can you believe it? I have dreamed of this for years!"

"Of course I can believe it. You're smart as hell and witty and gorgeous to boot. You're the best," he said, meaning it. "So how long will you be gone?"

"Two or three weeks. Maybe longer. I'm not sure."

Maybe longer . . . that pinprick of panic was beginning to spread into a real fissure. Parker was happy for Kelly, of course he was, terribly happy . . . but . . . *but she was his lucky charm.*

"I guess I should ask them exactly how long. Guido and the producers of *Sports Day* decided I should just tell my listeners I'm going on vacation and have a couple of rotating guest hosts sit in. That way, if ESPN doesn't like the show, or doesn't pick it up for very long, I have a place to land. Isn't that *nice* of them?" she chirped, and patted Parker on the chest before popping up off the couch.

She went into the kitchen and started bustling around, gathering lasagna and salad. "I know you must be hungry. I don't know what to wear."

"What?" he asked, confused.

Kelly's laugh was bright and vibrant and reverberated in the apartment. "The two statements are not related," she said, giggling. "I mean, I don't know what to wear for the tests. Should I go casual? Or formal? Maybe a hip look?"

"Yeah, that sounds good," he said, having no clue how a hip

or casual look would differ. He got up and walked into the kitchen to help her. "So . . . after you do this testing, you're definitely coming back, right?"

"Of course!" she cried, and paused to put her hand to his face and kiss him. "If I get the show, I will be taping in Connecticut. If I don't, I will be back in New York. Don't worry, Parker. I'm definitely coming back," she said sweetly. "Come on. This lasagna has been sitting around too long."

Parker made himself eat, but he'd lost his appetite. He wasn't sure why he had such a bad sense of foreboding, but he did—a feeling that was based on absolutely nothing and bordered on highly selfish. Nevertheless, he couldn't seem to shake it.

And as the evening progressed, nothing could make it go away. Not fabulous love-making, not Kelly's show the next day, not batting practice where he was knocking them out of the park. He just couldn't shake that quiet, persistent unease that he couldn't be the same without her.

And when he left a few days later, bound for St. Louis and then Houston, he held a bubbly Kelly tightly to him, reluctant to let go, because if he did, he feared everything he'd only just found would be lost. But Kelly laughingly assured him, "It's okay, Parker. Everything is going to be just fine."

He honestly wanted to believe her. He honestly tried to believe her.

CHAPTER
11

The first couple weeks she was in L.A., Kelly woke up every morning and pinched herself. And though she left a trail of bruises, she kept doing it because she couldn't imagine what in the hell she'd ever done to deserve this fabulous new life.

First came her makeover: new haircut by Frankie Petronova, *the* hairdresser to the stars; thread lift on her brows to make her green eyes really pop; and microdermabrasion to rid her face of a couple freckles, which were not, apparently, what America wanted to see in their talk show hosts. *Plus* she was presented a hip new wardrobe from all the best designers, put together just for her by Melania Chenowith, the woman who dressed anyone who was anyone in Hollywood.

And last but not least, she got shoes. *Shoes!* Boxes and boxes of really cool high-heeled shoes to go with each outfit, even though there was no plan for the viewing audience to see her feet. But *she'd* see them, because every day she would look down at those puppies and sigh with happiness.

Kelly O'Shay had died and gone to heaven. This was heaven, the stuff of dreams. The pilot tests went great—of course they did—with the makeover and the clothes, she was practically singing her way through it, dishing the upcoming football season so well she had the crew laughing. Better yet, she had a couple of past greats to interview: Troy Aikman and Joe Montana, two very charming men who made some fun predictions and laughed at her jokes.

It just didn't get any better than that: sitting in a studio behind a desk, wearing *haute couture* with a fab new 'do, and having Troy Aikman and Joe Montana laugh at your jokes.

Frankly, the only thing missing from the fairy tale was Parker. She wished he could be here, could see her fabulous new look and watch her work.

As it was, she hardly ever spoke to him. With the time difference and the Mets' grueling season, it was difficult to catch each other on the phone. When they did connect, she told him everything—how great everyone was, how fabulous the show was going to be, how fun it was to talk to two football greats, how they were hoping to move her to Connecticut in a few days to tape some segments they would have ready to go if ESPN picked up her show.

"That's great," Parker would say, listening attentively as he always did and seeming excited right along with her. "But when are you coming home?"

It was a good question and one Kelly had no answer for. They had sent the pilot segment to Connecticut, and her agent and ESPN management told her to sit tight—they'd tell her something in the next few days.

When the call finally came—ESPN wanted six segments for the fall—Kelly was ecstatic. Unfortunately, she had no one to celebrate the news with. Her mom and sister were on the East Coast, and while they were supportive and wanted this for her, neither could take time from their jobs to come out. Parker was on the road again. So she had a split of champagne by herself, packed her bags, and flew to Bristol, Connecticut, where they put her up in a tiny corporate apartment, and got to work on her show.

Kelly was so busy writing and working with the producers that she didn't know they'd begun to air teasers for her show. Nor did she know that Parker was hitting another slump. She'd come home at night completely exhausted and go straight to bed. In the mornings, she got up with the dawn, tried at least to get a run in, and then returned to the studio.

She was disconnected from everything in the here and now, connected only with her future.

In those rare moments she actually had time to phone Parker, she could never seem to reach him. She figured he was traveling and resting between games and thought little of it, but she missed talking to him very much. She assumed he would call her in a few days to tell her how much he missed her and needed to see her, too. Of that, she was confident.

Parker was on the road a lot, but he wasn't resting. He was pacing every floor he could find, trying to stay away from TV and trying to figure out what was really in his head. Both things were difficult to achieve, because with twenty-eight guys on the active roster, someone was sure to be tuned into ESPN, and he'd be forced to endure the agony of hearing it all over again.

He just couldn't seem to think. He just couldn't seem to *breathe*.

The teasers ESPN ran for Kelly's upcoming talk show were all about him. He still couldn't wrap his heart and mind around the idea that Kelly had done this, couldn't believe she would use him so blatantly just to get a gig. He began to question if he'd ever meant anything to her, or if he was nothing but a stepping-stone on her way up the ladder.

God help him, but he was humiliated—they had flashed her picture across the big Jumbotrons in the stadium while broadcasters everywhere announced she was his girlfriend. The whole world now knew what a colossal fool he was.

It didn't help that his teammates found phrases like *"Couldn't steal a base with a gun and a mask,"* and *"Hasn't had a hit in so long that they've gone ahead and dug the grave,"* and *"The man couldn't catch a beach ball if they* rolled *it to him"* hilarious and made them locker-room jokes.

Even worse, it seemed to him like ESPN aired the clip every couple minutes, which meant that every couple minutes, he would hear that sexy voice he had so longed to hear from somewhere in the locker room, singing out, *"Parker Price couldn't catch a beach ball if they* rolled *it to him!"*

Was it any wonder, then, in a series against the Dodgers, that he missed a double play? Or the game after that, when he tried to steal a base and was tagged out several feet short of his mark? Or that his batting average began to slip? Who the hell could blame him?

He didn't answer her calls. He couldn't bear to hear her bubbly, laughing voice just now, not even to ask her what the hell she had done.

Frank, his agent, thought he had lost his mind. Sports commentators around the country were beginning to talk about his slide, and Frank was fending off questions from the press. "She's just a girl!" he bellowed at Parker after one particularly horrendous game. "When are ya gonna snap out of it?"

Parker just shrugged and drank his beer.

His lackluster play in Los Angeles prompted a call from his older brother, Jack, who had brought his partners to see the game. "What the hell?" Jack demanded. "You were playing so great! What the *hell*?"

"Dunno," Parker muttered into the phone.

"Hey," Jack said, "you're not sick or something, are you?"

"No. Yes. Sick at heart, Jack. Sick at heart."

"Oh *God*," Jack moaned. "It's not *her* again, is it? When are ya gonna snap out of it?"

Even Parker's manager pulled him in one day to ask him what the hell he was doing—or not doing—out there. "I'm having a slump, Willie. I don't know what else to say," Parker said with a sigh.

His manager glared at him through tiny little slits of eyes. "It's not that damn ESPN talk show, is it? We're not blaming this slump on a *girl* again, are we, Price?"

"Hell no," Parker said, insulted he would even ask.

But it *was* her. He felt so betrayed, so used, so foolish, so stupid. But as the week passed, and he got over the numbing shock of it, he began to get angry. Very angry. So angry, in fact, that he couldn't wait for Kelly to come home so he could explain just how angry he was.

★ Kelly finally got through to Parker one morning after catching the news and learning that the Mets had not done so well in the game against Milwaukee the night before. "Ouch," she muttered to herself when they flashed the final score up on the screen. When they flashed Parker's handsome mug up on the screen and remarked on his batting average, she winced—she hadn't realized he was slipping again. Well hell, if the guy would just answer the phone once in a while.

As soon as the sports segment ended and the morning program went back to the talking heads with giant coffee mugs, Kelly picked up her cell and dialed. Miracle of miracles, Parker actually answered. "Hey!" she cried happily, tossing aside the bagel she'd been munching. "I was beginning to wonder if I was ever going to get to speak to you again!"

"Hi, Kelly," he said. "How's it going?"

Wow. That was the most lackluster greeting she'd ever gotten. But okay, he wasn't playing well, and he was probably down in the dumps. "It's going great," she said. "But I've really missed you."

"Have you?"

"I have! And the good news is, I'm coming home Thursday!"

"Great," he said. But he didn't sound like he thought that was great at all. Frankly, he sounded like he couldn't be less interested.

Kelly frowned at the phone. "Parker? Is there something the matter?"

"Nope. Just eager to see you, that's all."

"You could have fooled me."

"No, no, I really want to see you, Kelly. I *really* do. What time are you getting in? What time will you be here?"

He sounded so odd, her internal red flags popped up. "Around five," she said uncertainly.

"That's perfect. I've got an afternoon game that day. Why don't I come by your place afterward?"

"Okay," she said. "Is everything okay, Tex?"

"I'm just tired. So great, I'll see you then," he said and promptly hung up.

She gaped at her cell phone. What was the *matter* with him? Was he miffed she hadn't been able to contact him in the last several days? That was hardly her fault—his schedule wasn't exactly conducive to phone chats, either. She couldn't imagine what else would prompt him to serve up a dish of cold shoulder like he'd just done. She glanced at the clock—she had to be at the studio in an hour. She'd think about Grump later.

But Kelly didn't think about that phone call again until Thursday at the station, waiting for her train to New York. She was sitting with a cup of coffee at a bakery, reading the paper, when some guy tapped her on the shoulder. "Hey," he said, his face lighting up. "You're her!" And he pointed at a television screen above the cash register.

Kelly gasped. That was her all right—ESPN was playing a snippet from her audition tape, promoting her new show. She had no idea they were already promoting it and smiled brightly at the guy. "That *is* me! I'm Kelly O'Shay, and I have a new show starting on ESPN next month."

"Yeah, they've been playing that over and over," the guy's companion said. "So you're the same one who does the radio show, right?"

"Right," Kelly said, turning her attention to the TV. "Really? They've been playing that clip? They didn't tell me," she said, staring curiously at it now. *"The sad truth is, folks, that Parker Price couldn't steal a base if he had a gun and a mask,"* she said, holding up a toy gun and a frilly pink sleeping mask.

"Oh *shit*," she muttered. Suddenly, everything was crystal clear to her. Parker had seen this. Parker had probably seen this a *lot*. Parker probably thought she'd been in L.A. taping *that*.

"You're right you know," one of the guys snorted to the Kelly on TV. "He went for a stolen base the other night and was tagged two feet out. What's a guy like him doing stealing bases? They got base runners for that!"

Oh*shitohshitohshit!* In all her ecstasy about the talk show, she had completely forgotten some of the things she'd said on her audition tape. "So . . . you say they've played this clip a few times, huh?" she asked, trying to sound nonchalant.

"Oh man, they probably run it twice every hour," the guy said, and then looked at her curiously. "They don't tell you stuff like that?" he asked, suddenly interested.

"Apparently not," she said with a smile painted on her face.

"Hey, you guys have a great day. I'm going to miss my train," she said, and picked up her coffee and paper and hurried out of that little bakery, walking blindly, walking deafly, seeing only Parker's face, hearing only Parker's voice on the phone the other morning.

Of course her train was late. She hit New York at the tail end of rush-hour traffic, and it seemed hours before she could get a cab. It was seven o'clock before she reached her apartment.

The place had been shut up so long that it smelled musty and dank and felt insufferably hot. She immediately set about opening windows and lighting some scented candles, trying to air out the place before Parker arrived.

Of course Parker arrived early.

She'd wanted to at least have a bath and change into something really decadent, but he buzzed her apartment while she was still running around in nothing more than a skirt, a camisole, and her bare feet. *Okay, okay,* she told herself. At least she had her fabulous new hairdo, and she rushed to a mirror in the entry to fluff it with her fingers after buzzing him in.

When he knocked at the door, she threw it open and gave him a big smile. "Hey, stranger!" she said, throwing her arms around his neck.

"Hey," Parker said, and put his hand on her waist. That was it—just the one hand, and definitely not the big bear hug she was accustomed to. Like she wanted.

"Wow," she said, stepping back. "*Wow*, Parker. That might possibly be the coldest greeting in the history of man."

He said nothing, just gazed down at her, the muscle in his jaw leaping with the clench of his teeth. He was angry—she had a sense he was doing all he could to contain himself. She stepped back again, and myriad emotions skated through his gray eyes—dismay, anger, and a couple more she couldn't quite figure out.

"You look great," he said at last, and glanced up to her hair. "Like what you've done with your hair."

"Thanks," she said, nervously touching it. "I can see you are thrilled with the new me."

He looked directly in her eyes with a cold, gray stare. "Not exactly," he said. "*Destroyed* is perhaps a better word."

"*Destroyed?*" she echoed incredulously. "Okay, that's it." She twirled away from him, marched into her living room, her hands on her hips. "What the hell, Parker? Ever since I got you on the phone this week—when I *finally* got you on the phone—you've been a total dick to me."

"Yeah, well, sometimes, when I'm getting trashed in two dozen fifteen-second spots across America each day, I'm not a particularly nice guy."

"I *knew* it," Kelly snapped, and shoved her hands through her hair.

"Did you think I wouldn't see it? I'm in a sports profession, Kelly. People in sports tend to tune in ESPN."

"I know that!" she snapped, and squeezed the bridge of her nose between her thumb and finger.

"Isn't this just fabulous," Parker said irritably. "Like an idiot, I was hoping this was the point you'd at least offer some viable explanation."

"Of course there is a viable explanation, Parker! Did you think I was using you to come up with sound bites?"

He said nothing, but the muscle in his jaw jumped again.

"Oh my *God*," she said to the ceiling.

"Well what am I missing? You used me to get the ESPN job, right? What part am I leaving out?"

"I *did* use you," Kelly admitted. "But a very long time ago."

Only Parker didn't exactly hear that, because he roared to the ceiling, "How could you *use* me like that?"

"I didn't *use* you. I didn't even know you then! I made that tape before you ever came on my show!" she responded angrily.

"That doesn't exactly make me feel better! That means four months later—*after* I've been on your show and *after* I have fallen in love with you—you used that *trash* to promote your show!"

"I didn't know they were going to play it!" she cried. "If I'd known they were going to use that, I would have asked them to use something else!"

"How could you not know it, Kelly? They run it all day long, all week. There isn't a person in America who hasn't seen that clip!"

"Well *I* didn't see it!" she insisted angrily. "I haven't watched TV in weeks! I've been working my ass off to tape segments for my show!"

"Do you have any idea what it's done to me?" he breathed angrily. "It's humiliating to know that the woman the networks have broadcast to the *world* as being my girlfriend is all over the same networks talking about what a loser I am! And I guess I am a loser, Kelly, because I'm not hitting, I'm missing balls—"

"No way, pal," she angrily interjected, pointing at him. "No way are you going to blame me for your stupid slump! I have *nothing* to do with your ability to play! It's all in your head!" she cried, waving madly at her head. "You use that superstition or whatever you call it like a crutch!"

"It's not my imagination that you used me to get a job at ESPN. And maybe you did it a long time ago, but you could have told me. At some point in the endless hours we have spent talking about *your* career, you could have *told* me instead of letting me find out in a locker room along with thirty of my closest friends!"

"I'm *sorry*! I'm sorry it happened, I'm sorry I didn't think to tell you, and I'm sorry I didn't know they were going to use that segment!"

"They just used it without your permission?" he exclaimed, disbelieving.

Kelly winced. "I gave them permission to use my materials to promote the show. I just didn't know how they planned on doing it."

"Great! So now I can sit around wondering what else is going to pop up on TV while you enjoy very high ratings at my expense! And in the meantime, I guess your beloved Mets can just go down the tubes, right?"

"Will you stop saying that? I am starting to wonder if the only reason you claim to love me is because you believe that somehow, *I* am making you play well!"

The look on Parker's face confirmed it. Kelly shrieked with impatience and whirled away from him. "Isn't *this* just fabulous! You fell in love with me for some voodooey reason, and not because you loved *me*. That's rich, Parker! And look at you, giving me such a load of shit over something you yourself admit to doing!"

He didn't say anything, and when Kelly whirled around to face him, he sighed. "I don't know anymore why I fell in love with you," he said solemnly. "I am second-guessing everything."

She gasped, but Parker clenched his jaw tightly shut, defiant and angry.

"So . . . you only loved me because you thought I was your lucky charm," she said flatly.

He didn't move, didn't confirm or deny.

"You used me, too, then."

"Maybe," he said with a shrug.

"Well at least you're honest," she muttered. "So . . . I guess there's nothing left to say, huh? I guess we're through."

He arched one brow above the other but did not argue, and God, how Kelly wanted him to argue. She wanted him to say they couldn't be through, they were too good together, it was all a big misunderstanding and they'd never make the same mistake again. She wanted him to say he loved her, he'd always loved her, and he didn't care about baseball or ESPN or anything but her and could not be without her . . .

But Parker just nodded. "I guess we're through," he agreed, and turned around and walked out of her apartment, leaving her utterly speechless and suddenly rudderless.

It wasn't that easy.

A few days had passed, but Parker still couldn't get the expression on Kelly's face out of his mind. He couldn't sleep, thinking of it. He couldn't eat, thinking of it. He couldn't seem to concentrate on the game very well because of it.

In the week leading to their breakup, he'd imagined he would catch her red-handed, so to speak, and force her to confess she had used him. He had not counted on it being an old tape, or her not knowing what ESPN was doing with her tape. And he had not imagined hurting her. But that was definitely hurt on her face—he knew it was, because he felt it, too.

He had fallen into a tailspin of emotion. He couldn't really think straight, and he couldn't really say why he had fallen in love with her, if he really even loved her, or if he loved the idea of a lucky charm. There was a time when he thought he loved her because she was beautiful and witty and didn't seek him out for fame or fortune, but genuinely seemed to like who he was. Now he wondered if he hadn't just worried all along that without her, he couldn't play. He was, like most baseball players he knew, ridiculously superstitious. This one had to top the list.

Maybe it was ridiculous, but when she was trashing him, he couldn't play. When she was praising him, he played the best baseball of his life.

Maybe he did latch on to her like she was a talisman from the baseball gods.

Maybe he did use her like she used him.

Whatever. It didn't matter now, because they were through.

A week after their breakup—and a week in which Kelly didn't call him even once—the Mets started a series with the Yankees. On the opening night, Parker arrived at Yankee Stadium early so he could work with the trainer. While the trainer worked on a tight muscle in his back, Parker watched TV, and of course, the sound bite for Kelly's new talk show popped up.

It was odd—he'd seen the clip so many times now that it didn't do anything to him . . . except make him chuckle. It was true—for some reason, lying there on the massage table, actually *listening* to what she said, he couldn't help but laugh. *Couldn't catch a beach ball if they* rolled *it to him.* He pictured himself trying to catch a rolling beach ball and laughed.

The sound bite was over, and Parker smiled, put his head down, and focused on the game he was about to play.

That night, he was first up to bat, and as he walked to home plate, some of the Yankees fans were shouting, *"Roll him a beach ball!"* And again, he chuckled to himself. Ah, how stupid people could be. They had no idea how much skill went into your average game of baseball, how hard it was to hit or catch a major league ball.

And there, without thought of lucky charms or slumps or anything else, he caught a piece of the first pitch and sent it sailing out of the ballpark. Imagine that—Parker Price hit a very rare, first pitch home run—and he laughed as he ran the bases.

The Mets ended up losing that night in spite of his spectacular opening bat, but Parker wasn't too shaken by it. He'd had a pretty good game, all in all, and had a pretty good feeling about the Mets in general.

The next morning, when his alarm went off, he opened his eyes to the sound of a stadium full of cheers. "I'm serious," Kelly was saying. "They ought to have him bat cleanup. When he gets his bat on a pitch, forget about it."

He wondered who she was talking about.

"Yeah, it's really amazing that this is the same guy who couldn't hit a beach ball at the start of the season." Guido laughed. "With the exception of that little slump a couple of weeks ago, he can't seem to miss now."

Parker bolted upright. They were talking about *him*.

"That's what I've said Guido, and you argued with me. But when Price turned it around, he turned it all the way around. Granted, he's had a couple of bad games over the last few weeks like you said, but when you compare his performance to the team as a whole, the man is responsible for most of their offensive and defensive success."

This time, Guido cued applause and whistles.

"So then how do you explain the Mets loss last night?" Guido asked. "Your boy came out firing with both barrels."

"He did, but the problem last night was in pitching. The Mets just don't have enough depth," Kelly opined.

Damn straight—Parker had said that more than once—they had too many rookie pitchers. At least Kelly was fair, but it didn't change a damn thing. He turned off the alarm and got out of bed, heading for the shower.

What needed to change was his morning station of choice. He'd try to remember to do that.

That night, the Mets loaded the bases with one out in the ninth. The go-ahead run was on second base. It looked as if the Mets would win, but the Yankees changed pitchers and brought in a closer who induced a double play and escaped the inning with a save and a game victory.

In the locker room, the Mets were pissed. They didn't want to go back to Shea without at least *one* win over the Yankees.

The next day, the mood was tense in the locker room. No one was talking. Over their heads, ESPN ran a teaser for Kelly's show. In this clip, she lifted a glove and said, "Hey, Parker! Got game?" and then smiled so prettily that Parker's heart ached with it.

"Oh, that's just great," Pablo Rena, the first baseman said next to Parker. "Guess that means you'll be too freaked out to do us any good tonight."

"What the hell is that supposed to mean?" Parker snapped.

Pablo rolled his eyes. "You know how you are—the least bit of criticism, and you fall apart."

"Hey, dude, I don't *fall apart*," he shot back. "Keep your mind on your own play, all right? You weren't exactly hitting off the hook with your bat last night."

"Hey," Pablo said, throwing up his hands, "I'm just saying. You're really sensitive when your girl talks a little smack."

"She's not my girl," Parker muttered, and slammed his locker door shut, walked out of the locker room, and onto the field.

But something Pablo said kept pricking at him as he warmed up. He *was* sensitive. He'd built it up in his own mind that everything that happened on the ball field was fate, but it was really more along the lines of what his mom used to tell him—he could be a Big Baby sometimes.

Maybe that was it after all and Kelly had nothing to do with it. Look at it—he'd played pretty well this series, in spite of the way he was feeling about her. And to prove it to himself that night, he went out on the field, had two double plays, two based hits, and one RBI, driving in the run that won the Mets the game.

That night, as he drove home, he thought it was strange that a man could play baseball all his life, and at the ripe age of thirty-two, realize that it wasn't the forces of nature or the heavens that influenced his play. It was just him. He was in full control of his actions. It was an honest-to-God epiphany.

The next morning when the alarm went off, no one was home to turn it off, and Kelly's show blared throughout the house for two hours until Marie, Parker's housekeeper, showed up and turned it off, shaking her head at the volume.

That was because Parker was in the city, standing out in the hall where Kelly's show was being aired, pacing back and forth because the receptionist wasn't there yet to let him in. But it was so early and quiet that he could hear the show over the speakers piped into the reception area. There was some talk of the game and a little of Parker's performance, but mostly they talked about the relief pitcher who had come in and saved the Mets' collective ass by getting them out of an inning in which the Yankees had put on two base runners.

When Kelly said, "Let's go to the phones," Parker hit the speed dial on his cell.

After about three tries, he got the producer. "Hey," he said, "this is Parker Price."

"Right. And I'm Arnold Schwarzenegger," the producer said, and clicked off.

"That's right, I forgot you are an ass, you little pinheaded geek," Parker muttered and dialed again. It took him several more tries to get through, but when the pinheaded geek answered, Parker said, "Yo, lemme talk to Kelly."

"What's your name, and what are you calling about?" the producer asked.

"Jeff Renteria. And I'm calling about the Mets. She's talking about the Mets, and they're, like, my favorite team ever."

"Hold, please," the producer said and clicked off. Parker grinned.

A moment later, he heard, "You're on *Sports Day with Kelly O'Shay*. What's your name?"

"P-Pete," he said.

"Hi, Pete. What do you want to say?" she asked cheerfully.

"I want to say that I think some baseball players are stupid, superstitious idiots," he said.

Kelly didn't say anything, and there was a moment of dead air until Guido jumped in. "Ah . . . we hear you, pal. They're like, *ridiculous*, man! Won't wear their socks a certain way, won't bat with the same bat twice, have to do a little dance in the batter's box before they hit. That stuff just messes with their heads."

"Yeah, I know. You pay these guys millions of dollars to just get out there and play ball, and what do you get? A bunch of sissies afraid of their own shadow."

Guido hit the laughter button.

"You know what I think?" Parker pressed on, just as the receptionist walked up and looked at him curiously. "I think a couple of them are real *jerks*."

"Why?" Kelly asked, her voice not quite as bubbly as usual.

"Well," Parker started as the receptionist opened the door and let him in, "Sometimes, they get some idea in their head that makes absolutely no sense, like maybe, you talking about them on your show affects the way they play."

"Who said *that*?" Guido scoffed.

"Parker Price. He's the biggest idiot of them all."

"He is?" Kelly asked, her voice soft. Parker started striding for the booth.

"Sir!" the receptionist yelled. "You can't go back there! Stop! If you don't stop I am calling the police!"

Apparently, the receptionist came in loud and clear, because Guido asked, "Hey, where *are* you?" as he hit the sirens button.

"Like I was saying, take Parker Price. He got it in his pea brain that some of the things you were saying about him were affecting his play. But then he figured out that was just dumb—he was the only one on that field, and if he wasn't hitting, it was because his swing was off or he wasn't concentrating. Not because of you, Kelly."

"Uh-huh. Well . . . I guess I've been a little too harsh," Kelly said as Parker rounded the corner. He saw her then, sitting on her stool, the enormous earphones on her head, staring at the windowed wall while Guido manned the phone lines. The moment she saw him, she sprang off the stool.

"No you haven't. You've been funny and dead on. If a player doesn't play well, that doesn't give him license to blame everyone else," Parker said outside the window.

"Do you mean to say that Parker Price should hold himself responsible for his performance, both good and bad?" she asked.

"I'm saying," he said, putting an arm up on the glass wall that separated him from Kelly and leaning against it, "that I made a huge mistake, Kelly. I was a jerk. I tried to blame you for my own shortcomings. I forgot that I fell in love with you, and it had nothing to do with baseball. I mean, there wasn't anything there that day but me and you—no baseball, no ESPN, nothing but us," he said, as the producer and receptionist suddenly flanked him, their hands on his arms.

Parker ignored them like a couple of gnats. "I fell in love with you because you're beautiful and funny and smart and you make a mean spinach lasagna. I fell in love with you because you don't like Broadway but you like old movies, and you think my charity is cool, but you don't think I'm so cool that I am better than the dreams you have for yourself, and a whole bunch of other reasons I swear I'll never forget again. I love you, Kelly."

Guido, he noticed, had almost fallen off of his chair.

"Ooh, that is so *hot*," the receptionist whispered. And Kelly . . . well, Kelly was gaping at him with eyes as big as home plates. And then she was trying to pull the headphones off at the same time she was climbing over Guido.

"Hey," Guido said, as Kelly threw open the door, then went out and slammed it behind her. "That's pretty sweet stuff from a guy who's scared of his own shadow. But everyone likes a good love story, right, gang?"

Whatever else he might have said, Parker didn't hear, because when Kelly launched herself at him, she knocked his cell phone from his hand.

She threw her arms around his neck and buried her face in his neck as the receptionist and producer threw themselves at the glass, gesturing wildly to Guido. "I didn't think you'd ever come back," she breathed, then lifted her head, kissed his face a thousand times. "I'll quit ESPN. I don't care—I love you, too, Parker, and that night you walked out of my apartment, I thought I would just die. Nothing mattered but you—not ESPN, not radio, nothing but you. I'll quit, I'll quit—"

"Are you kidding? You're fabulous, baby. You deserve to be on ESPN. You deserve to anchor the nightly news or whatever you want to do. Just promise me you won't go without me. I can't stand to be away from you, and it's not because of my game. It's just because I need you."

She promised with a kiss so hot that Guido felt compelled to turn on the smooch button that sounded like a giant bottom feeder having lunch. And then they cut to commercial, and the producer sagged against the wall, Guido fell back in his chair, and the receptionist ran to get the phones, which were ringing off the hook.

★ Two weeks later, when they flashed Kelly's image up on the Jumbotron before a record crowd during the pregame, the fans got to watch Parker climb up in the stands and go down on his knee, asking her to marry him in front of millions.

The next morning, the airwaves were full of commentary

about his form. Some of the sportscasters thought he really didn't bring enough emotion to it and should have done a little more genuflecting. Others—mostly Mets fans like Mrs. Frankel—argued that it was a home run, that they'd never seen anything more beautiful than that proposal in the annals of baseball history.

No one knew what Parker and Kelly thought. After they game, they locked themselves away behind his gates and weren't coming out for a few days, no matter how hot Kelly's show was or how hot the Mets suddenly got. The world could go on without them for a time.

Same Rink, Next Year

Deirdre Martin ★

CHAPTER

01

Friday, 3:10 P.M.

For most Chicagoans, January meant three things: biting cold, bitter winds, and howling snow. But for Tierney O'Connor, concierge at the Barchester, a four-star hotel on Chicago's Miracle Mile, January meant just one thing: earth-shaking, catapulting-out-of-your-body sex with David Hewson, goaltender for the Buffalo Herd.

The Herd came to town once a year, and they always stayed at the Barchester. For three years running, Tierney and David had enjoyed a one-night, no-strings-attached tryst. The arrangements were always the same: David would slip her his key before the team headed to the United Center to play. When Tierney got off work at eleven, she would go to his room and wait for him. David would show up shortly afterward, and that's when the fireworks would begin, lasting until the wee hours. The next day, David and the team would fly out for their next game, and Tierney would go home. The only person at the hotel who knew about this annual carnal rendezvous was Aggie Mullen, the hotel's head chef and Tierney's friend.

Standing behind the concierge's desk in her crisp black suit, her long brown hair pulled back in a tight, sleek ponytail and her expression inviting and open, Tierney knew she was a model of friendly efficiency. That is, until the Herd began sauntering through the door, their boisterous voices turning heads. The minute Tierney's eyes found David's, she could feel her professionalism beginning to wane as sheer animal lust took over. She wanted to push David down on the lobby's Persian carpet and have her way with him behind the potted palms. She could tell by the way he was looking at her that he was thinking the same thing. David's smile, heart stopping even when it was merely friendly, was slow and sexy. His smoky gray eyes, ever watchful from years behind the goalie's mask, grew hooded and mysterious. Desperate for a diversion, Tierney was glad when a fur-clad, middle-aged couple planted themselves in front of her, wanting to know if the Art Institute was within walking distance.

"It is," Tierney said brightly, handing them a small, complimentary map, which she used to point out to them the best route to get there.

"You want to walk?" the husband groused to his wife. "It's snowing. Not to mention the fact it's ten degrees out there."

"A little exercise wouldn't kill you," the wife shot back.

Tierney glanced away. She couldn't count all the times couples bickered in front of her. But the wife was right: the man was so big he looked like a grizzly bear in his fur coat.

"We're taking a cab," the husband declared. His eyes flicked back to Tierney. "Can you call us a cab?"

Tierney smiled again. She loved her job, but sometimes, at the end of the day, her face ached. "There should be some cabs waiting right outside the hotel, sir. If there aren't, the doorman will hail one for you."

"Thank you." Without waiting for his wife, he began barreling toward the door.

The woman shot Tierney a long-suffering look as she pulled on her gloves. "Thank you."

"My pleasure."

Tierney turned to watch them walk away, proud to have been of assistance. She loved being able to direct the hotel's guests toward the best her adopted city had to offer. Chicago had energy, culture, soul—which is why she'd fled Nebraska for the Windy City the first chance she got. As a child, she'd dreamed of living in a place where there were always new things to do and explore, a place where she'd be able to reinvent herself. That she'd been able to make her dreams come true was a constant source of pleasure as well as pride.

"They looked happy—*not*."

Tierney jolted at the sound of David's voice, amazed at his ability to sneak up on her. "Hey, you," she said quietly. "How was your flight from Buffalo?"

"Scary. A lot of turbulence. Some of the guys actually looked green around the gills."

"They're saying we might get a foot of snow overnight." It had been a year since Tierney had seen him, but it felt like just yesterday. She didn't want to think about how many times over the past twelve months her thoughts had strayed to him as she wondered what he was doing at that precise moment. But they'd agreed at the outset to keep things simple: the less they knew about each other's personal lives, the better.

"A foot of snow, huh?" David's eyes caressed hers. "Good cuddling weather if you ask me." Tierney, afraid that every unholy thought she was having could be read on her face, looked at her watch.

"Room 334," David said under his breath. "I'll bring down the key when I leave for the game."

"Gotcha."

He reached out, discreetly squeezing her hand. "You look gorgeous, by the way."

Tierney raised her eyes back to his, unable to hide her pleasure. "You say that every year."

"That's because it's true every year." David glanced over his shoulder at his waiting teammates, standing in a clump in front of the bank of elevators. "I should get going. I need to rest up before the game."

"Think you'll win?"

David flashed a confident smile. "We always do."

"Hey, watch it," Tierney warned, pointing a finger at him. "That's my team you're dissing."

"Spoken like a true Chicago girl."

Tierney swallowed, nervous of telling him the truth. She liked that he thought she was from the city.

"Yo, Hewson!" a voice called out from in front of the elevators. "C'mon!"

"Hold up!" David called back. He winked at Tierney. "See you later. Can't wait."

Tierney blushed. "Me, neither."

Friday, 7:40 P.M.

Never fond of pregame warm-ups, David especially hated them when the Herd was the visiting team. Not only was he acutely aware of bad vibes being beamed his way by the home team's fans, but he couldn't perform his powerful home ice rituals. Back in Buffalo, he knew the only thing coming between him and certain failure was the order in which he laced up his skates (left then right) and the number of times he circled the net (four times clockwise, four times counterclockwise) before standing in goal. His teammates never ribbed him about his eccentricities. All hockey players were superstitious, goalies most of all. You'd have to be a bit crazy to stand there night after night and let people shoot pucks at your head.

Fighting to focus, David performed his less-powerful away-game rituals—four splits followed by swinging his stick back and forth on the ice eleven times, the number of letters in his name—before standing in net for a drill, demonstrating to his teammates they had nothing to worry about. Kick save? No problemo. Blocker save? Puh-lease. High to the glove side? In his sleep, baby. As the drill dragged on, cockiness gave way to boredom, and he found himself daydreaming about Tierney—and all the things he planned to do to her when he got back to the hotel. Usually he was able to keep thoughts of her at bay until after the game. But tonight, he couldn't. Desire built from a whisper to a scream as he pictured himself slowly peeling off Tierney's blazer to get at the pristine white blouse below, the tiny pearl buttons like—

"Hey, Hewson! Wake up!"

David blinked at the sound of his coach's voice, mortified to see that he'd been so deep inside his own head he'd let one in through the five hole. His teammates peered at him questioningly; it wasn't like him to let a puck through his pads. Skating out of net, David approached Coach Kernan, whose scowl could reduce grown men to babbling idiots.

"What the hell just happened there?" Kernan demanded.

"Sorry," David apologized. "I lost focus for a moment."

"You lost focus? What kind of shit is that?"

David pushed his mask up onto his head so the coach could see his face. "It won't happen again."

Kernan poked him in the chest—a wasted gesture, since David couldn't feel a thing through his padding. "You're god-damn right it won't happen again. Because if it does . . ."

Kernan let the threat hang there. David nodded curtly, pulling his goalie mask down over his face. "I hear you."

"Do you?"

"Yeah."

"Then get your ass back in goal and keep your eye on the little birdy, okay? This is one team we can't afford to lose to."

Throwing another scowl over his shoulder for good measure, Kernan shuffled back to the bench, and David returned to goal, annoyed at himself for thinking about Tierney and screwing up his concentration. Usually, he thought about her when he was alone. A few times he even caught himself talking to her in his mind and was tempted to look up her home number and call her. But he held back, knowing it was a violation of the ground rules they'd so carefully laid down from the beginning.

He needed a ritual for banishing Tierney from his thoughts. Closing his eyes, he imagined the Herd decimating the Chicago team as he shifted side to side three times—one for each year of their arrangement. When he opened his eyes, he was ready to play.

Friday, 11:06 P.M.

Her shift over, Tierney decided to stop by the kitchen to see Aggie before heading upstairs to David's room. Unlike most chefs, who tended to be temperamental or dramatic, Aggie was unusually centered and calm—unless, of course, there was some major screwup in the kitchen, in which case she'd threaten to quit. She never did; like Tierney, she loved her job, pressure and all.

"I thought you might stop by," said Aggie as Tierney pulled

up a stool to sit at one of the long, stainless-steel tables at the center of the kitchen. Though room service was available to guests twenty-four hours a day, orders were few the later the night wore on. Aggie, whose primary responsibilities were dinner at the hotel's plush restaurant and handling all the hotel's catered affairs, had already handed over the culinary reins to the night staff.

She pushed a piece of chocolate ganache toward Tierney. "I saved this for you."

"Chocolate and sex in the same night," Tierney joked, her stomach growling as she dug in. "I'm going to get spoiled."

"Speaking of your boy toy and his teammates, they all ordered steak earlier," Aggie revealed. "I bet if I threw a piece of raw meat in the middle of the room, they'd fight for it like wolves."

"Not a scene I'd like witness." Tierney gazed sympathetically at Aggie as her friend yawned loudly, rubbing her eyes. "Tired?"

"Exhausted. Besides the Herd, we've got some pain in the ass British rock star and his entourage staying here. About two hours ago, they called down to order—get this—deep fried Mars Bars. When I had room service tell him Mars Bars were hard to find but we could do Snickers bars, he freaked out and threatened to jump out the window."

Tierney lowered her fork. "What did you do?"

"What do you think I did? I told room service to tell him 'Have a nice fall.' They didn't, of course. But I wish they had."

"You're bad."

"Hey. You know me: I aim to please. But I've got no patience for that kind of prima donna bullshit, you know?" Removing her chef's hat, Aggie smoothed back her short blond hair. "As if that wasn't bad enough, we've got fifteen guys in from Bangalore for some trade show down at McCormick Place. All vegetarians. *And* I've got the Mykofsky wedding on Sunday." Aggie's shoulder's sagged. "Just shoot me now, okay?"

"Oh, c'mon. You love it."

Aggie smiled sheepishly. "I do." She stifled another yawn. "I'm going to crash at the hotel tonight so I can start getting organized for the wedding bright and early tomorrow." Like

Tierney, Aggie was unattached and had no one to go home to. "The Herd lost, you know. I heard it on the radio."

"They *did*?" Tierney couldn't believe it. They'd routed Chicago the past three years.

Aggie relieved Tierney of her fork, stealing a bite of ganache. "Ever think of getting a real boyfriend? You know, the kind you can spend quality time with the other 364 days of the year?"

"I've tried," Tierney insisted. "I haven't met anyone I really like."

Which was true. Thanks to her job, Tierney had met and dated lots of men. Many were good-looking and most were rich: high-powered businessmen used to having women fall at their feet when they'd casually slip their income into the conversation. But Tierney was unimpressed. She preferred substance over income and humor over materialism. Maybe it was her rural origins; all she knew was that she'd yet to meet a man who cared more about having a real relationship than showing off his Rolex.

Aggie changed the subject. "You staying all night with hockey boy?"

"I usually do."

"Don't let Nugent catch you when you creep out of his room in the early morning hours."

"He won't."

"He might. The guy lives in the hotel, you know."

Nugent was Willy Nugent, the hotel's new manager, brought in from New York when the last manager left for a more lucrative gig in Los Angeles. Aggie hated him. A neurotic micromanager, Nugent had a tendency to stick his nose "where it didn't belong," which to Aggie meant her kitchen. But Tierney got along with him just fine.

"If I bump into him, I'll just say I stayed overnight because of the snow."

Aggie sighed. "You ain't kidding. They're saying—"

"—that we could get up to a foot of snow overnight," Tierney finished for her. One of the things she'd learned was that, like farmers, all Chicagoans were weather forecasters. In Nebraska, everyone worried about summer corn. In Chicago, it was winter snow.

Aggie shook her head. "It's enough to make me pack up and move to Key West." She patted Tierney's shoulder affectionately as she moved past her to take leave of the kitchen. "Have fun."

"I'll try," Tierney promised, finishing the last bite of chocolate cake. She smiled to herself. When it came to David Hewson, fun was a given.

Saturday, 12:12 A.M.

Stretched out on the bed in David's hotel room, Tierney wondered why he never seemed interested in returning to find her decked out in some sexy negligee, or waiting for him in a tub full of bubbles, champagne glass in hand. She'd offered, but he seemed more excited by the idea of peeling off her work clothing. Not that she minded: she loved the idea of him being turned on by her urban sophistication.

She thought back to what brought them together. She was just ending her shift when he and his teammates burst into the lobby, exuberant after beating Chicago. David told anyone who would listen how he'd just been traded to Buffalo, how he'd just played his first game for them, and how, thanks to him, they'd just achieved a shutout. Eventually, exuberance gave way to exhaustion, and one by one, his teammates drifted upstairs to their rooms. But not David. He approached the concierge desk.

"Hi," he said. "I need a wake-up call for 7:13 A.M. tomorrow morning."

Tierney pointed to the main reservation desk. "They can take care of that, sir."

"No, you don't understand. They'll wake me at 7:15. Or 7:14. Or even 7:16. I need to be awake at *exactly* 7:13 on game days."

Tierney blinked, all the while thinking, *This guy is hot, but boy, is he nuts.*

David must have read her look. "Let me explain," he said patiently. "I woke up at exactly 7:13 this morning, and we won the game. If we want to win tomorrow, I have to wake up again at exactly 7:13. Understand?"

Tierney gave a small nod, fascinated. "Yes. You're superstitious."

"All goalies are superstitious," he informed her. Since he was the first goalie she'd met, she believed him.

"I'll make sure you're awakened at *exactly* 7:13," she promised him.

David looked grateful. "One more thing. I'm on the fifth floor, and I need my room changed to the third floor."

"Let me guess: last night your room was on the third floor."

David smiled, and it was heart stopping. "You're catching on."

Tierney pointed again to the reservation desk. "A room change can be arranged."

He disappeared, only to return to the lobby ten minutes later, claiming he couldn't figure out how to program his clock radio. She was getting off work, so she offered to go back to his room with him and show him herself. When she got there, she realized his helplessness was a ruse: two Diet Cokes sat at the small table by the window, open and waiting. "I know it's not champagne, but I was hoping you could help me celebrate my victory tonight," David explained shyly.

Tierney accepted. It was way out of character for her, but that only made it more exciting. Where she came from, the only thrills to be had came from tipping cows or knocking over mailboxes. She was flattered he chose her to celebrate with.

She took her conversational cues from David, talking only about work. She had no doubt that if he knew she'd learned to drive a tractor before she could drive a car, he might not be so enamored of her. Tierney could tell he was impressed with her uniform, with her knowledge of the city, with her whole professional demeanor. She was playing a part for him, and she enjoyed it. When he eventually asked her to stay the night, she agreed, grateful for the arrangements they made the next morning to meet again the following year, and to keep personal info to a minimum.

Her reminiscence came to an end as David entered. Usually he wore faded jeans and a blue crew neck sweater. Tonight, she noticed, the sweater was rust colored.

"Hey," he said glumly.

"Hey." She sat up, folding her long legs beneath her. "Where's your blue sweater?"

"I only wear that when we *win* against Chicago. Tonight we lost. It was my fault," David lamented. "Actually, it was your fault."

"What?!"

"I was thinking about you before the game, and it totally distracted me." He shook his head. "Not good. Not good at all."

Tierney wasn't sure what to do. Usually he came in the room, bounded happily onto the bed as he crowed about the Herd's victory, and made mad, passionate love to her. Tonight he was cradling his head in his hands. "Um . . . do you want me to go?" she offered.

David slowly looked up at her, surprised. "Do you want to go?"

"No. You just seem upset."

"I *am* upset. We lost. But I'm sure you can help me get over it." He reached for her, planting a soft kiss on her mouth.

There was hunger there, blistering and real. "I've thought about this all year," he whispered, pressing his forehead to hers.

Tierney sighed. "Me, too."

"I'm sorry I blamed our loss tonight on you. I didn't mean it." There was no mistaking the hungry look in his eye. "Forgive me?"

"Done."

One minute they were kissing. The next David had lifted her off the bed as if she were light as a feather, putting her down before him so she stood between his open legs. His big, strong hands reached up to grasp her shoulders, fingers hooking under the lapels of her blazer. Then, almost as if he were a sculptor lovingly unveiling a work of art, he slowly slid her jacket off her shoulders.

Tierney shivered, closing her eyes. "How come you like me in my business suit?" she whispered.

"I love a woman in a uniform," David replied, his hands sliding down her body to cup her buttocks and draw her more closely to him. "Besides," he added as his hands slid back up her ribs to gently caress the side of her breasts, "It's a turn-on seeing you in this conservative attire, knowing what an adorable little sex kitten you are underneath."

Tierney laughed.

"What's so funny?" David asked, his hands making their way up to her neck.

"No one's ever called me a sex kitten before," Tierney admitted. "I kind of like it."

"So do I." David let his hands linger, the rough pads of his fingertips a tantalizing contrast to the soft skin of Tierney's throat. The longer he caressed her, the more Tierney longed for him to unbutton her blouse. She wanted his hands on her breasts. Wanted his mouth there, too, and everywhere else.

By the time David's hands began unbuttoning her blouse, Tierney was throbbing with desire. David was deliberately tormenting her: he'd undo one button, then kiss her mouth, undo another, then kiss her neck—on and on, until Tierney's blouse fell away and she was standing before him in the gray lace bra she'd handpicked for the occasion. She shuddered involuntarily as his hands stroked her ribs, warming to the sensation of heat as his burning fingertips began playing with her nipples through the lace.

"You like—?" he whispered.

Tierney nodded.

"Anything else I can do for you?" David continued, pressing his mouth to her right breast. The thin material between his mouth and her flesh felt like an insurmountable barrier. Tierney reached behind her, and with one snap of her left wrist, unhooked her bra. Lifting his mouth, David slid the bra off her shoulders and threw it behind him, where it landed atop one of the bedside lampshades. Tierney experienced a brief moment of panic—would it catch fire if it was too close to the bulb?—but then relaxed. She was being ridiculous.

She brought herself back to the moment, to the mounting pleasure building in her body. David's hands were cupping her breasts now, desire clouding his eyes as he nuzzled his face there.

"You taste wonderful," he murmured, taking her left nipple into his mouth. Tierney arched into him, sparks shooting through her body as her legs nearly buckled beneath her. Her hands found David's hair, and she buried her fingers deep in his curls, moaning as he suckled. She couldn't believe she'd gone a year without this delight, this heaven. She began trembling, slowly at first, and then more violently the closer she came to the edge. And just when she was almost there, David lifted his head and laughed wickedly.

"I'm kind of tired," he yawned.

"Over my dead body," Tierney growled, pushing him back onto the bed and climbing atop him. She didn't care if he hadn't finished undressing her. She wanted skin-to-skin contact. Frantic, she began rolling his sweater up his body, kissing the sculptured flesh beneath. David gasped as his mouth curled into a smile of pleasure. Lifting his torso up off the bed, he pulled his sweater off over his head and threw it to the floor.

"Better?" he asked.

"Better."

Tierney kissed his neck, then his jaw, before planting her mouth solidly on his chest. She tickled his nipples with her tongue. She traced a path with her mouth from the top of his collarbone down to the waistband of his jeans. The more aroused David became, the hotter she found herself getting, too. David was hard now. Hard and ready. Tierney reached down to unfasten his jeans.

"Oh, no, you don't," David breathed. Again, with a grace that astounded her, he turned her onto her back and resumed command.

"This skirt's gotta go," he declared. Tierney lifted her hips so he could undo the zipper at the back. She watched him pull down her skirt, taking extra care as he gently tugged it over her hips. It made no sound as it hit the carpeted floor.

She lay back, beside herself in anticipation of what might come next. David lowered his mouth to kiss each of her hipbones before peeling off her stockings and sending them sailing to the floor, too. The heat in the room kicked on, sending a warm breeze across Tierney's already-heated body. David was now stretched out beside her and was gazing at her with such unabashed tenderness Tierney's breath caught. *Hey, mister, I thought this was all about lust*, she wanted to say. Then she realized: David Hewson could look at her any way he damn well pleased, and she'd love it.

"Now what?" Tierney murmured, letting her eyes drowse shut.

"Now I torture my little sex kitten until she begs for more."

Tierney swallowed, breath frozen in her throat as he began rubbing her slowly through the silk of her panties. The sweet friction his hand caused was like an arrow aimed straight at her core. She felt greedy: the more he touched her, the more she wanted to be touched. David's hand began moving faster as wave upon wave of pleasure assailed her. Finally, Tierney's body could take it no more. Crying out, Tierney let herself go, freefalling over the precipice into her body's first white hot finale. Nothing was better than this. Nothing. Except . . .

Tierney opened her eyes to catch David watching her hungrily. Grinning mischievously, she reached down to grasp him.

"I guess I should say thank you," she sighed.

David laughed huskily. "What a polite girl you are."

"My mama taught me right," Tierney purred in a Southern accent. She turned onto her side so she was facing him and began eagerly tugging on the zipper of his jeans.

"Patience," David chided. Helping her, he slipped off his jeans and kicked them away, but not before extracting a condom from the back pocket. Finally free of his pants, he took Tierney in his arms, holding her tightly. She could feel him straining against her even as her own hips rocked involuntarily against his. The movement seemed to inflame him.

"I want you," he growled in her ear.

The mere words possessed the power to make Tierney melt.

"Say it again," she commanded dreamily.

David parted her lips with his tongue, kissing her just long enough for her to get a taste of him, cinnamon sweet. "I" . . . he kissed her neck . . . "want" . . . he flicked a hot tongue against her lobe . . . "you."

"So take me," she dared.

David smiled, rolling away from her for just a moment to take care of protection. When he was done, he pulled her on to him so Tierney was straddling his hips. His hands reached up to caress her breasts, pleasure again cascading through her as desire reignited. *Time once again to tumble over the precipice,* Tierney thought to herself feverishly. But this time would be even better. This time she'd take David with her.

She lifted up and put him inside her, squeezing tightly. David gave a long, slow moan of appreciation as his hands reached up to gently hold her by her hips. Tierney leaned forward to brush her lips against his, her hands braced on his shoulders as she began moving slowly up and down atop him. If another year was going to crawl by until she had David Hewson in bed again, she wanted to savor it. She moved slowly, deliberately, increasing the tempo in small, almost infinitesimal increments. David didn't seem to mind: his face was relaxed and happy. And the faster she moved, the happier he looked.

Tierney was close to coming now. Her eyes met David's, and for a split second she felt herself immobilized by the intensity of his gaze. It struck her how they never turned out the lights when they made love, nor did they close their eyes. They would fall into each other's reflection, speaking their own silent language that said, *This is ours, and no one can touch it. This is ours, and I cherish it.* Not once in their years of trysting had one of them ever looked away.

Breathing hard, Tierney sat up, and locking her hands in his, began moving atop him with abandon. She loved the amazement that flashed in his eyes as he blinked, stunned.

"Jesus . . ." he panted. "Tierney . . ."

The way he said her name, so desperate yet so fierce, sent a surge of power through her body. She wanted to ride him so hard he'd forgot his own damn name or where he even was. Wild now with abandon, she began pumping her hips. David's hands broke contact with hers as he reached up to pull her face down to his, kissing her roughly on the mouth. Tierney groaned, her body spasming with delight as his tongue swirled around hers. Time contracted; there was room for only this, their secret pleasure. She let go again, body soaring just as David reared up and with one final, joyous gasp, shuddered to a climax right after her. Only then, when both were sated, did they finally close their eyes.

CHAPTER

02

Saturday, 6 A.M.

"See you next year," Tierney whispered, planting a kiss on David's cheek as he slept. Six was her usual time for slipping out of his room and back into her real life. She'd already showered and dressed. Now she just needed to creep down to the employees' lounge to put on her street clothes and head back home to sleep a bit more. Not a bad way to start her weekend.

David mumbled something—"Good-bye, sex kitten"?—and turned over on his side. His breathing was slow and relaxed. Watching the steady rise and fall of his shoulders, Tierney found herself unexpectedly moved. She reached out to run her palm over the smooth, bare skin of his back, vowing to remember the feel of it so she could conjure it at will anytime she wanted over the ensuing twelve months. David seemed oblivious.

Though the heavy curtains in the room remained drawn, cracks of light still managed to filter through. Tierney could tell by the bright silver shafts scoring the carpet that it was still snowing. Light had a whole different intensity when it snowed; it seemed denser, more concentrated. She wondered how much snow had fallen.

Reluctant, Tierney finally took her leave and stole out of David's room. Up and down the hallway, half-eaten trays of food sat on the floor outside closed doors, waiting to be removed. She passed countless DO NOT DISTURB signs as she headed for the elevator. She wondered if the rock star up on thirty-seven eventually accepted the deep-fried Snickers bar as a viable alternative to suicide. She made a mental note to ask Aggie when she returned to work on Monday.

As soon as the elevator opened and she entered the lobby, she knew something was wrong. Though largely empty of guests at this hour, the place was usually abuzz with employee activity as shifts changed. Instead, the night shift remained at their various posts, grim and unsmiling.

Tierney approached Marius, the dapper, overnight concierge who worked the shift after hers.

"Is something going on?"

Marius snorted, jerking his thumb at the bank of floor-to-ceiling windows behind him. "Put on your glasses, girl. We're in the middle of a major blizzard."

Tierney approached the windows. A tempest was taking place outside, as heavy snow mixed with high winds to create a whiteout. Her heart sank. Getting home was going to be a major challenge.

"I feel sorry for anyone who needs to get to work today," she said to Marius, buttoning up her coat.

Marius thrust his head forward. "What are you talking about? The airports are closed. Union Station is closed. The *roads* are closed. The subway isn't working. We've gotten fourteen inches of snow on top of the eight that was already there, and they're saying we might get fourteen more by the time the weekend is over. You ain't goin' nowhere, honey." He narrowed his eyes. "What are you doing here, anyway?"

"I wasn't feeling too well after my shift, so I went to lie down for a minute before I headed home. I wound up falling asleep."

"Uh huh." Tierney could tell from the purse of Marius's lips that he wasn't buying a word of it. "Well, Nugent is calling a staff meeting at seven-thirty. I guess we'll find out what's going on then."

Saturday, 7:30 A.M.

By the time the staff meeting commenced, many of the hotel's guests, as well as its snowbound employees, were having a minor meltdown. Guests milled aimlessly around the lobby like refugees, hounding the poor souls behind the reception desk as if they could somehow wave a magic wand and make the blinding snow disappear. Night shift workers knew their replacements weren't going to make it in and they were stuck. The staff was trying to remain calm and put a positive face on things, but it was only a matter of time before nerves began fraying on both sides.

"I can't friggin' believe this," Aggie whispered to Tierney as the two took their seats in the smallest of the hotel's three banquet rooms. "I wake up and it's the Ice Age. I'm expecting some major deliveries today for the Mykofsky wedding tomorrow. What if they can't get through?"

"Don't think about that now," Tierney advised. Three seats down, one of the overnight housekeeping crew, Graciela, was weeping copiously. Tierney leaned over to her. "Are you okay?"

Graciela looked at her with watery eyes. "It's my cat, Jingles. Who's going to feed Jingles if I'm trapped here?"

"Don't you have a neighbor or someone you can call?" Aggie suggested.

Graciela shook her head. "I don't know any of my neighbors." She covered her face with her hands, sobbing. "Jingles, *mi corazón*, Jingles . . ."

Aggie poked Tierney in the ribs. "You never know what'll happen if people can't get to the supermarket," she whispered knowingly. "Let's just hope no one *eats* Jingles."

"You're awful."

"I can't help it. My culinary career is flashing before my eyes. Jokes are the only thing that's keeping *me* from breaking down."

"Tell me about it."

"What do you have to be upset about?" Aggie snorted. "Correct me if I'm wrong, but aren't you fresh from a night between the sheets with L'Athlete Extraordinaire?"

"Lower your voice, please," Tierney hissed, glancing

quickly around the rapidly filling banquet room. No one seemed to have heard.

"Well?" Aggie pressed quietly. "How was it?"

Tierney sighed. "Great. Fantastic. Mind-blowing."

"Yeah, thanks, rub it in. The last time I got any action Elizabeth Taylor was on husband number four."

"What about that new sous chef you just hired? He's kind of hot."

"Who, Isidore?"

Tierney nodded.

"Forget it. Can you imagine calling out 'Isidore, Isidore' in a moment of passion? I can't."

"It's not his fault he's got an unromantic name."

"I don't mix business and pleasure."

"I do."

"And therein lies the difference between us."

"Right, ladies and gents, listen up." Tierney directed her attention to the front of the room as the hotel's weed-thin manager, Willy Nugent, clapped his bony hands loudly to get everyone's attention. Aggie's response was predictable: she rolled her eyes and slumped lower in her seat.

"As you know, we are in the midst of a major blizzard, with up to a foot and a half more snow predicted." Assorted groans filled the room. "We've got quite a challenge on our hands: guests whom we thought would be checking out today are snowbound, and last night, we experienced an influx of new guests as commuters from surrounding buildings, unable to make it home, checked in. In short, the hotel is full.

"We need to concentrate on pulling together to ensure things run as smoothly as possible. To that end, I need everyone here to come forward and sign this sheet of paper indicating your usual position and shift. I'll come up with a makeshift schedule that I hope won't be too arduous for anyone. I'll be sending out periodic memos as the situation unfolds, and I expect all of you to keep *me* abreast of any developing situations with guests requiring special attention. In the meantime, please—all of you—do whatever you can to allay any anxieties our guests might be experiencing. I appreciate your cooperation. Thank you."

A collective sigh of resignation rose as the Barchester's

staff began shuffling toward the front of the room to sign Nugent's paper as instructed.

"Well, at least *you'll* be having fun," Aggie griped to Tierney.

"What are you talking about?"

"No planes in or out. Your boy's here for at least another night."

Tierney paused. She hadn't thought of that, and now that Aggie brought it up, a small frisson of delight sizzled through her. Time for more fun with David . . . maybe this blizzard wasn't so awful after all.

Saturday, 9 A.M.

As Tierney suspected, she wound up relieving Marius so he could sleep and take over *her* usual shift from 3 P.M. to 11 P.M. For now, Nugent had decided that an overnight concierge might not be necessary, since there was nowhere for people to go and no way for them to get there even if there was.

Tierney envied Marius his escape from the morning chaos. As more of the hotel's guests awoke to the news that their plans were now on hold, the lobby took on a hysterical tone. Countless guests asked Tierney to double-check that all planes were indeed grounded, and she had no choice but to comply, even though anyone with an ounce of common sense need only look out the window to understand how serious the situation was. There were rumors floating around that some roofs had collapsed beneath the weight of the snow and that the President was about to declare Chicago a disaster area. If the President wanted to see a disaster, Tierney mused, he should come to the Barchester Hotel.

"Miss?"

Tierney looked up from a crossword puzzle she'd been doing intermittently to see a group of ten women of all shapes and sizes, ranging in age from twenty-five to sixty, ringing the concierge's desk. The desperation in their eyes was all too familiar.

"Yes?" Tierney replied. If they asked her to call O'Hare she just might scream.

"We have tickets to see *Oprah* on Monday," said one slight woman with frizzy gray hair who was wringing her hands frantically like some denim-clad Lady Macbeth. "Do you think everything will be up and running by then?"

"It's really too soon to tell," Tierney said gently.

The woman's face fell. "But we have to see Oprah. We came all the way from Idaho."

"A little snow won't stop Oprah!" another woman in the group declared. Her companions nodded knowingly.

Tierney managed a sympathetic smile. "Keep checking back with me, and keep an eye on the local weather report," she urged. Placated but grumbling, the women turned and moved in a pack toward the hotel's in-house restaurant, The Mayberry. Tierney could picture them drowning their sorrows in blueberry pancakes, speculating that if *Oprah* controlled the weather, this never would have happened.

Sighing, Tierney turned to look out the window. The scene was the same: heavy snow battered the glass, accompanied by a howling wind. It was an awesome display of nature's might, though anyone daring to venture outside might view it differently. She returned to her crossword puzzle, waiting for the next guest to sidle up to the desk to ask if it was true that there was no way into the city, as well as no way out.

Saturday, 11:02 A.M.

Two hours later, Tierney spotted David emerging from the elevators across the lobby with his teammates. He looked rested and refreshed—not surprising since he'd been able to sleep in. She watched him motion for his friends to go into The Mayberry without him. Then he sauntered toward her, a Cheshire cat grin lighting up his rugged face. Tierney's toes curled with excitement.

"Hello," he said.

"Hello," Tierney replied.

He leaned over the concierge desk. For a brief, panic-filled moment, Tierney thought he was going to kiss her here, now, in public. "Last night was *amazing*," he murmured.

Tierney cleared her throat nervously. "It always is," she answered, trying to look as if she were speaking to him in a professional capacity.

"Looks like we're here for at least another night."

"Yes, I know." Tierney's eyes took a slow, appreciative tour of his body. "I get off at three, you know," she said boldly.

David looked uneasy. "Oh."

Oh?

"Look, if you don't want to," Tierney said under her breath, wounded by his lukewarm response, "it's okay. I'm a big girl. I can handle it."

"No, no, it's not that at all." David looked sheepish. "It's just . . . you know."

"No, I don't know."

"I'm kinda worried about jinxing the next game, you know?" he whispered. "I mean—you and I usually spend one night together, right? If we break with tradition, who knows what could happen?"

"Yeah, an asteroid might hit the earth." She stared at him incredulously. "You really believe all this stuff, don't you? That waking up at exactly the same time every morning you have a game means you'll win."

"Of course I believe it. Because it's true."

"Well, then, I guess I'll see you next year."

She stared hard at the computer screen in front of her, wishing he would just go away. A few seconds later, his hand touched hers. "You say you get off at three?" he murmured.

"Yes."

"Why don't you come to my room then."

"Are you sure?" Tierney asked, still staring at the screen. "I don't want to risk throwing the planets out of alignment."

"No. Come. *Please*," he added suggestively. Then he leaned closer to her. "Who knows, two nights in a row might bring me twice the luck."

Tierney finally looked at him and smiled. "Okay. Now I really should get back to work."

As if on cue, a slim, blond, perfectly made-up young woman with fire in her eyes came barreling toward Tierney, trailing a pudgy but handsome man in her wake. Tierney gripped the lip of the concierge desk. She could already tell this wasn't going to be pleasant.

"Do you know who I am?!" the woman shrieked. Before Tierney could answer, the woman continued, "I'm Mindy Mykofsky, and *I'm supposed to be getting married tomorrow!*" She was howling so loudly people in the lobby were turning to look at her. "I want you to call the mayor and tell him he has to do something *right now* to transport all our relatives and friends who are stranded at the airport here! Do you understand me?"

The man with her, who Tierney assumed was the groom-to-be, put a tentative hand on the woman's shoulder. "Now, Pookins—"

"Don't 'Pookins' me!" Mindy snarled, knocking her beloved's hand away. "Whose bright idea was it to get married in Chicago in January, huh?" She glared at Tierney. "Call the mayor. Now."

"May I suggest another course of action?" Tierney replied calmly. "I—"

"Do it!" Mindy screamed in Tierney's face.

"Hey!" David cut in angrily. "Don't talk to her like that."

Mindy's mouth fell open. "Who the hell are you?" she snapped.

"Let's call the manager and see if he has any ideas," Tierney trilled, glaring at David.

"That sounds like a good idea, doesn't it, Wuzzums?" cooed the beleaguered groom-to-be.

"I guess," Mindy muttered, glaring at Tierney as her fiancé put an arm around her shoulder.

"I'm calling the manager right now," said Tierney, making a show of picking up the phone. "Why don't you folks have a seat over there?" She pointed to the leather couches arranged in the lounge area. The couple obliged.

"Poor bastard," David muttered when they were out of earshot. "Mark my words: in a year, he'll go out for a quart of milk and never come back."

"Please don't ever do that again," said Tierney, hanging up the phone.

"Do what?"

"Interfere with my job."

David looked scalded. "I was just trying to help. She was treating you like garbage!"

"I can handle it." Tierney blew out a breath. "Don't get me wrong: I appreciate it. But it makes me look bad, and it could get me in trouble."

"Sorry." David watched her with admiration. "How do you deal with these lunatics? If it were me, I'd wind up butt ending them with my stick."

Tierney laughed. "They're not all like that. And she does have a right to be upset. Plus, these are extenuating circumstances."

"You're right."

"You can go now," Tierney whispered as Willy Nugent strode into the lobby, making a beeline toward the distressed couple.

"So, this afternoon?" David double-checked as he began walking away.

"I'll be there."

Saturday, 3:06 P.M.

By the time three o'clock rolled around, Tierney half regretted arranging to see David again. All she wanted to do was fall face first onto a big, fluffy bed and collapse. But the allure of more time with him outweighed her exhaustion. Filling in the newly refreshed Marius on where things stood, she took leave of the concierge desk, opting to take the stairs up to David's floor rather than the elevator. There was less chance of running into any other staff that way.

She knocked quietly at the door, cringing when he bellowed, "It's open!" in a voice loud enough for people two states over to hear. She found him stretched out on the bed in sweatpants and a long-sleeve T-shirt, channel surfing at a frenetic pace. He looked happy to see her.

"You look beat," he observed.

"I am. It's mayhem down there."

"The snow doesn't show any sign of letting up. At least that's what one of your local weathercasters said."

"How will that affect your playing schedule?" Tierney asked, kicking off her pumps. Her feet were killing her. In fact, her whole body ached. Stress, she supposed.

David shrugged. "We'll just make up the games somewhere else in the season schedule."

"Ah." Her eyes were drawn to the crumpled candy wrappers on the bed. "Raided the minibar, I see."

"That's what it's there for." David crawled across the bed to her, kneeling behind her as he began massaging her shoulders. "Someone needs to relax."

Tierney's head slowly dropped forward as she closed her eyes. "That feels great."

"Wait just a few more minutes, and I'll make you feel even better," David promised, nipping the back of her neck.

Tierney shuddered.

"I have a surprise for you," David continued, his fingers digging deep into her muscles. "A fun surprise."

"Really?" Tierney was intrigued. "Can I have it now? I love surprises."

"Okay."

He clambered off the bed and went to the closet, smiling proudly as he pulled out a maid's uniform—the kind Graciela would wear.

"I thought—since we're breaking our usual rules anyway—that we could play a sexy little game," David said seductively. "Maybe I'm the lord of the manor, and you—"

"Are you out of your mind?" Tierney blurted. "That's not sexy!"

David's face fell. "What?"

"A French maid's uniform is sexy. *That* is not a French maid's uniform. That's a 'Hello, My Name Is Rosa and the Management Pays Me Below Minimum Wage' uniform."

David looked at the maid's uniform in his hand. "We could *pretend* it's a French maid's uniform," he pouted.

"I don't think so." Tierney gestured down at her own clothing, hiking up her skirt a bit to flash him some thigh. "Look, I'm in my suit," she enticed. "We like that, right?"

"We do," David admitted.

Maybe it was the mini-massage, but Tierney's weariness had evaporated, replaced by an overwhelming friskiness she knew only David could satisfy. Pushing him backward toward the bed, she threw him down and straddled him, pinning his hands above his head. Then she sunk her teeth into his neck.

"How's this for different?" she growled.

"Uh, pretty damn good."

She transferred her lips to his, pressing hard, making her need known. A rush of dizziness overtook her, the delicious, scream-at-the-top-of-your-lungs kind associated with stomach-plummeting amusement park rides. It was David: only he had this effect on her, and in all the years they'd been trysting, she wasn't sure why. Was it his perfect body? The deep, sensual timbre of his voice? The fearlessness of what he did for a living? Perhaps it was the knowledge that their time together was finite and, therefore, all the more precious. All she knew was that no man had ever made her feel this way.

The room began spinning faster as bodies tumbled and clothing flew. Tierney freely plundered, her hands and mouth taking possession of David's body in a frenzy of desire. Whimpers turned to moans and moans to outright screams of delight as they took turns pleasuring each other. Tierney felt dazed, almost incoherent as their bodies came together again and again, their mutual thirst unquenchable. *I will never get enough of him,* Tierney thought greedily as he took her one final time. *Never.* Others might be cursing the weather, but not Tierney, not here, not now. She was grateful for the storm.

Saturday, 4:37 P.M.

"David?"

Tierney lay curled in his arms beneath the covers. They were both exhausted, drifting in and out of sleep. Between the afternoon sex and working a different shift, Tierney's sense of time was off. It felt like the middle of the night, even though it wasn't.

"Mmm?" David drew her closer, planting a sleepy kiss on her forehead.

"Is the reason you have your own room because you're so weird?"

David cracked open one eye and looked at her. "What do you mean, 'weird'?"

"It's just dawned on me that the other guys on the Herd share rooms. But you get your own."

David sighed, opening the other eye. "Well, I'm very particular about things."

Tierney's fingers, which had been lightly caressing the line of brown hair beneath his belly button, stopped moving. "Like your wake-up call?" she asked cautiously.

"That, and some other things. Certain rituals and routines are important to me."

"Like what?"

"Like I have to shower at exactly 7:18 in the morning, and I have to open and close the shower curtain seven times before stepping into the tub. Stuff like that."

"Why seven times?"

"Because it takes seven games to win a playoff series," he answered as if it were the most obvious thing in the world.

Tierney lifted her head to look at him. "Do you have OCD?"

"*No.* I told you when we first met: I'm a goalie."

"So, what you're saying is, you drive your teammates nuts and no one wants to room with you."

"All goalies are nuts," David replied defensively. "I told you that when we first met, too." He tickled her lightly. "You're full of questions today."

"Sorry. I know it's kind of breaking the rules."

David sighed. "The rules have already been broken because of the storm."

"True."

David's eyes danced with mischief. "Guess that means I can ask *you* some questions, then."

Tierney hesitated. "If you want."

"Yeah?" David sounded intrigued.

"Sure," Tierney answered, getting nervous.

"Okay, then." David paused for what felt like an interminable amount of time. "Where are you originally from?"

Tierney tensed. "What makes you think I'm not from Chicago?"

"I play with guys from all over the country and all over the world, Tierney. You are *not* from Chicago."

"But what makes you so sure?"

"I can hear it in your voice. You don't have a Chicago accent."

"Can't you think of a better question than 'Where are you originally from?' " Tierney shot back with a bored yawn, trying to deflect his interest.

David was beginning to look annoyed. "Cough it up, Tierney. Where are you from?"

"Nebraska," she mumbled into the pillow.

David's head shot up. *"Nebraska?"*

"Yes, Nebraska," Tierney repeated, fearful his disbelief would inevitably give way to disinterest, and their annual playdate would be cancelled. "You got a problem with cornhuskers?"

"No." David lay back down, contemplating the ceiling. "I never would have guessed you were from Nebraska."

"Why? Because I'm not wearing overalls and baling hay?"

"A little defensive, are we?"

"Maybe," Tierney sniffed. "Where are *you* from?"

"Saskatchewan. And no, I've never seen a moose."

"I wasn't going to ask that!"

"Good, because I'm the one asking the questions here, remember?" His gaze turned curious. "How did you wind up in Chicago?"

"I followed my boyfriend here. He was studying at Northwestern." She squirmed a little. "I saw it as my ticket out of Nebraska, so I took it."

"What happened to your boyfriend?"

"He hated it here and went back to Nebraska after one semester. I stayed."

David nodded. "Interesting."

"Is it?"

"Yeah."

Relaxing a bit, Tierney began stroking his cheek. Maybe the fact she was from Nebraska didn't collide with the worldly urban persona she'd created for herself. Actually, it was kind of nice talking to him like this. David's eyes lazed shut, his body sinking further into relaxation.

"Final question, Mr. Hewson. Better make it a good one."

"Do you have a boyfriend now?"

Tierney blinked. This was the last thing she imagined him asking. She was expecting something more along the lines of "Do you have brothers and sisters?" or "Do you like your job?"—something innocuous and not so deeply personal.

"That question *is* breaking the rules in a major way, don't you think?"

David gave a small shrug as he opened his eyes. "Maybe. But it's my final question, and you have to answer it."

"No, I don't have a boyfriend," Tierney revealed. "Do you have a girlfriend?"

David laced his fingers behind his head, looking at her with interest. "Are we sure we want to go down this road?"

"What road is that?"

"The road where we completely kill the mystery."

"Maybe it will enhance the mystery."

"Doubtful. But the answer is no, I don't have a girlfriend right now."

"So you're as lonely as I am," Tierney blurted.

David's gaze softened. "You're lonely?"

"No," Tierney said quickly, trying to backpedal. "I mean— maybe a little. Sometimes."

"C'mere." David took her in his arms. "Enough talking," he whispered as he softly kissed her mouth. "As long as I'm in town, you won't be lonely. I promise."

CHAPTER

03

Nebraska, David mused as he rode the elevator up three floors to see what his teammates were up to. You could have knocked him over with a feather. He'd constructed an elaborate fantasy history for Tierney, one in keeping with the well-heeled, worldly professional whose sparkling smile brought his heart to a halt every January when he stepped into the lobby of the hotel.

According to David's fantasy, Tierney was the only child of socialite parents. She grew up lonely and isolated in Newport, craving human companionship and interaction. Her father wanted her to take over his shipping business. She refused and was disowned. Forced to fall back on her own resources, she got a job at the Barchester. She rose up through the ranks to head concierge, a job she loved because it put her in touch with people. Her attraction to him was the direct result of all the effete rich boys her parents had once tried to jam down her throat, boys with three names like Justin St. Millionaire or Twee von Bogus. Tierney had rebelled by finding herself drawn to a rugged blue-collar boy from the wilds of Canada instead. Not that she had any way of *knowing* that's what he was, but never mind.

That was the Tierney he dreamed of all year long. This other Tierney—the one who probably grew up feeding the cows—unnerved him a little, because it meant they had things in common, and like it or not, it appealed to him. She was from the country, like he was. Knew all about wide open spaces and the yawning boredom that could come with it, like he did. Escaped to the city, like he did. The thought was disconcerting. The last thing he needed was for them to be a good match *outside* the bedroom. Then his unwavering dedication to the game would *really* be screwed.

Stepping out onto the sixth floor, he was greeted by the sight of two of his teammates, "Hawk" Cusack and "Thatch" Munker, hitting a stale bagel between them with their sticks. Their nicknames were self-evident: Hawk could spot a puck anywhere on the ice, while Thatch had wiry red hair that no hair-care product known to man could tame.

"If it's not David Hewson, International Man of Mystery," called Thatch, wristing the bagel directly at David's head.

David ducked, annoyed. "I get enough of that on the ice. You think maybe you could can it during my free time?"

"Touchy, touchy," said Hawk. "Seriously: where ya been?"

"Here and there."

Thatch gave a sly grin. "You nailing some chick? Giving her the big, bad 'I'm a lonely hockey player alone in a strange city' spiel?"

"Something like that."

David hadn't told any of his teammates about his annual date with Tierney, nor did he intend to. It would cheapen it somehow. Plus, he didn't want any of the guys giving Tierney a hard time when the Herd blew into town every year.

"Where's your dream girl now?" Hawk asked.

"Sleeping."

"She stranded in the hotel like everyone else?"

"Maybe. Maybe not."

Hawk looked at Thatch. "The mystery deepens."

"It's not a mystery. I just don't feel the need to take out an ad every time I sleep with someone." He kicked the bagel toward Hawk. "Where is everyone?"

"Split up between Slats in 615 and Gravy in 621. Slats has

a poker game going. Gravy's got the soap channel on. They're running the *All My Children* episode we missed yesterday."

"Think I'll hit Slats."

"Hey." Hawk's voice was casual, but David still caught the concern in those sharp blue eyes that never missed a trick on or off the ice. "You okay?"

"Yeah," David answered guardedly. "Why?"

"You seem kind of preoccupied."

"It's nothing." David started to walk away but then turned back. "You ever think something is one way, but you find out it's another way, and the change makes you kind of nervous?"

Thatch got excited. "You mean, like, you think peanuts are a vegetable, but then you find out they're really a legume, and you're, like, not sure you can ever eat peanut butter again?!"

David and Hawk exchanged looks of incredulity.

"What's eatin' you, bro?" Hawk asked.

David frowned as he started toward room 615. "Peanuts," he grumbled.

Saturday, 8 P.M.

"Do you know anything about Saskatchewan?"

Aggie's dead-eyed stare in response to Tierney's question told Tierney all she needed to know. Following her latest tryst with David, Tierney had showered and taken a small nap before checking in with Willy Nugent to find out if her help was needed anywhere else in the hotel. Commended for "doing an exemplary job so far"—a compliment that had Tierney puffing up with pride—Willy directed her toward the kitchen. He claimed the "culinary sector" of the hotel needed all the help it could get. Tierney hoped he hadn't expressed that view directly to Aggie, or he was likely to find himself sipping cyanide-laced soup.

She couldn't stop thinking about David's admission that he was from Saskatchewan. She knew he was Canadian, but in her imagination, he was a Toronto boy, born and bred. She found herself wanting to know more, which wasn't good, because what was the point? She lived in

Chicago, he lived in Buffalo, and that was that. Saskatchewan . . . an image appeared in her mind of David
wrapped in bear pelts snowshoeing across a vast, snowy
plain, followed by another of him standing knee deep in an
icy river, catching salmon with his bare hands. She giggled.

"What's so funny?" Aggie growled.

"Nothing. Look, I'm here to help," Tierney told Aggie,
who looked crazed. Her chef hat was askew, and there was a
desperation in her eyes Tierney had never seen before. In
fact, the whole kitchen was a cave of despair. "Is there anything I can do?"

"Yeah. Make the snow melt so my deliveries can get
through; put a stake through the heart of Mr. Rock Star; stuff
Nugent into a utility closet; gag the hysterical bride-to-be, and
tell the Herd that short of going down to the stockyard and
killing a steer myself, they ain't gonna get filet mignon for
dinner."

"That good, huh?"

"Oh, please." Aggie wiped her hands on her food-splattered
apron. "You don't want to know. Long story short? I'm starting to run low on food. Nugent said he might—*might*—be
able to get some staples in, but as for anything fresh, forget it.
Meantime, our fearless leader won't let me touch a lot of the
stuff I *do* have, just in case the weather lets up and that stupid
wedding goes ahead as planned tomorrow." Aggie's voice was
aggrieved. "Has Nugent even bothered to *look* outside?! Or
listen to a weather report?! The snow's not supposed to stop
until late tomorrow! A team of sled dogs couldn't get
through!" Exhausted, she slumped against the wall.

"There must be something we can do," said Tierney.

"Yeah, start cannibalizing guests."

"Seriously. What have you got in mind for dinner?"

Aggie sighed. "Potatoes. Carrots. Onions. Spices. I'm
thinking of making a stew. Why?"

"Got any beer? Guinness?"

"I don't know. I could check with Don in the bar. *Why*?"

"Spice up the stew with the beer, and give it a fake name.
Call it 'Cassoulet de Dublin.' Put it over pasta so it goes further. That's what my mom used to do when money got tight."

Aggie looked dubious. "And what if people won't eat it?"

"Of course they'll eat it. You're a fabulous cook, Aggie. I'm sure anything you whip up will be delicious."

"You're right," Aggie agreed, bypassing modesty completely, which was one of the things Tierney loved about her. "But that still doesn't take care of dessert."

"Can't you bake something? You must have stuff here for the wedding cake."

Aggie leveled her with another dead-eyed stare. "I already told you: the Führer seems to be suffering under the delusion that the Mykofsky nuptials might still take place." She drummed her fingers on a nearby countertop. "I do have Bisquick. And some industrial-size drums of fruit cocktail. Maybe if I make some biscuits and throw some fruit salad over it with some meringue, I've got . . . Frutta di Barchester!"

Tierney grinned. "There you go. See, it's not so hard."

"But what about breakfast tomorrow?" Aggie continued anxiously. "What if we're all still stuck here and there's even less to work with?"

"Don't think about that now. Just try to take it one meal at a time."

"Nugent wants to start directing people to the bar after dinner. He seems to think that if they get trashed, they might not notice they're trapped in a high-class igloo."

"Good idea—unless we run out of booze." Tierney grabbed a clean apron and put it on. "What can I do? Seriously."

"Seriously? Tell me why the hell you asked if I knew anything about Saskatchewan."

"That's where David's from."

"Hockey David?" asked Aggie in surprise as she tossed Tierney a bunch of carrots and instructed her to peel them. "You two have actually *spoken*? Full sentences beyond, 'Oooh, baby, yeah'?"

"Very funny. We've talked before. Kind of."

Aggie took hold of a gleaming blade and began mincing onions. "I take it you two hooked up again." Tierney nodded. "Let me guess: the sex was even better than last night."

"Pretty much."

"That's great," Aggie said blandly. "I'm trapped in here trying to figure out how to get creative with maraschino cherries, and you're having soul-shattering sex. There's no justice."

"Never mind the sex," Tierney chided loudly. Heads turned, including that of sous chef Isidore, who checked out Aggie before turning back to the potatoes he was chopping. "Isidore's scoping you out," Tierney whispered.

"Ain't happenin'," Aggie declared. She pushed a pile of minced onion to the left side of her cutting board, then started chopping the next one. "Why are you telling me 'Never mind the sex'? I thought it was all about the sex. All sex, all the time. Sex, sex, sex, sex, sex."

Tierney glared at her over the mounting pile of carrot peelings. "Are you done?"

"Sorry," Aggie muttered. "What's going on?"

"We had sex again," Tierney said in a low voice, "and afterward we actually talked. About ourselves."

"Most people prefer to do it the other way around, but continue."

"Do you know why he gets his own room when the team travels?"

"Snoring? Bedwetter? Hygiene issues?"

"No, because he's a goalie. He's got, like, rituals."

"Beyond having to be awakened at 7:13 exactly?" Tierney nodded, and Aggie looked disturbed. "Like what? We're not talking about sprinkling gris gris dust over a pile of bleached chicken bones, are we?"

"No, no, no. Rituals like he has to shower at exactly 7:18. And he has to open and close the shower curtain seven times before he gets into the tub. Something to do with playoff games."

"He told you this?"

Tierney nodded. "He says all goalies are nuts."

"Well, this one is. He sounds a little off kilter, Tierney."

"Actually, I think it's kind of cute," Tierney admitted reluctantly. "I think we might have more in common than we imagined. It didn't seem to faze him that I was from Nebraska."

"You *told* him you were from Nebraska? I thought that was a topic you tried to avoid."

"I tried, believe me. But he kept pushing. He wouldn't let it go."

"And what did Ronnie Ritual do with this info? Offer to dress up as a scarecrow?"

"Worse. He wanted to know how I wound up in Chicago and if I had a *boyfriend*. He seemed interested."

"Really." Aggie sounded intrigued. "Did you tell him the truth?"

"Yes."

"Another bad move. You should have said yes. Then he'd be all tied up in knots wondering if the guy was better in the sack than he was."

"He'd also wonder if I was a slut."

Aggie snorted. "This guy's got a ritual that involves a shower curtain, and you're worried about what *he* thinks?!"

"I know, I know."

"Besides, you hardly know him."

"I know he's from Saskatchewan. I know *he* doesn't have a girlfriend. And I know I want to find out more about him, even though it kind of makes me nervous."

"Why's that?"

"He lives in another city, Aggie. And I kind of liked playing the city girl role for him, you know? It was safe. And fun."

"Hey, no pain, no gain, baby."

"That's just it. I'm not sure I want gain, and I sure as hell don't want any pain."

"So what *do* you want?"

Tierney sighed. "I'm not sure. But when I figure it out, I'll let you know."

Saturday, 11:53 P.M.

"On a dark desert highvay / Cool vind in my har . . ."

Entering the hotel bar, David cringed as he listened to the boys from Bangalore butcher "Hotel California." As far as he could tell, everyone else was too soused to care. Either that, or they simply didn't have the energy to demand the drunken techies surrender control of the baby grand. He wondered where the hotel's actual piano player was. Hiding, probably. Or stranded at home.

He couldn't believe it was still snowing. He'd experienced some bad blizzards in his day, both at home in Canada and more recently in Buffalo, but this weekend's storm bordered on the catastrophic. Another day trapped inside the hotel and he just might lose his mind. Granted, he did have Tierney to help him pass the time, but now that they'd opened up to each other a little bit, he wasn't sure spending any more time with her was such a good idea. He'd already screwed up one game thinking about her. What would happen if he found out he *really* liked her and they started something? He could picture it already: the phone calls, the expectations, the visits—all anathema to his renowned single-minded focus.

No, he would just have to busy himself the way the rest of his teammates did, by watching endless TV.

He scanned the bar looking for Hawk and Thatch, who had stopped by his room earlier to invite him out for a drink. He spotted them across the room, tucked away at a small table chatting avidly to two young women who seemed to be hanging on their every word. Hawk spotted David and waved. David waved back, his heart sinking. Now that he'd been seen, there was no way he could just turn around and leave, which is what he longed to do. He couldn't think of anything more uncomfortable than watching his teammates try to score. Knowing Thatch, they'd rustle up a third woman for him, and he'd be trapped with some ditz who laughed loudly at all his jokes while running her hand up and down his thigh under the table. *Moron,* David cursed himself. He should've just stayed in his room and watched porn on pay-per-view.

He shouldered his way to the bar—thirteen and one half steps exactly from the doorway in which he was standing—and waited for the bartender, Don, to take his order. Everyone on the Herd loved Don. He was old, crusty, and full of Chicago lore. If you ever wanted to know anything about the Windy City, Don was your man.

Seeing David, Don grinned. "Well, well, well, if it's not my favorite netminder. I hear we kicked your ass."

"Don't rub it in, old man."

"There's always next year—if you're lucky," Don reminded him. "What can I do ya for?" He gestured at the table where Hawk and Thatch sat. "Your buddies are drinking pitchers of sangria. You want the same?"

David made a disparaging face. "You gotta be kidding me. I thought sangria was illegal if you're over eighteen." Don laughed appreciatively. "No, a vodka tonic will do me fine. Thanks, Don."

"You bet, big boy."

Don had no sooner loped away than David felt a tap on his shoulder. He braced, fully expecting to turn around and find Thatch grinning at him, babbling about "getting some pussy." Instead he found himself eye to eye with the soon-to-be-groom whom earlier that day he'd predicted would bolt.

"Hey," David said uncertainly.

"Bruce Goldfarb," declared the groom, sticking out a clammy hand for David to shake. "You, uh, you're the guy who was at the concierge desk earlier today, right?"

"Right." David wished Don would hurry up with his drink. He had no doubt this putz was gearing up to start a fight with him because he'd told his fiancée to stop abusing Tierney.

Bruce weaved slightly. "I just, uh, wanted to apologize to you for my fiancée's behavior—you know, when she asked you who the hell you were?" He burped. "She's a little upset right now."

"Yeah, I could see that." Don handed David his drink, and he paid up. He wasn't sure what to do: try to ditch this guy, or keep him talking until he came up with a discreet way to cut out on Hawk and Thatch.

"You married?" Bruce asked.

"Nope," said David.

"Single?"

"That's the usual alternative to being married." Bruce was so drunk his eyes were crossing. David tried to take a step back, but it was hard: the bar was packed. He wanted to be out of range should Bruce suddenly throw up.

David took a sip of his drink. The Bangalore boys had progressed to Queen's "We Will Rock You," their rousing cries of "Ve vill / ve vill / rock you!" inciting the bar's inebriated patrons to stomp their feet and clap along.

"What do you do?" Bruce asked.

"I'm a hockey player. With the Buffalo Herd."

"Wow." Bruce looked impressed, a reaction that always surprised David. He tended to take his job for granted, forgetting that to most people, earning a living as a pro athlete was somewhat exotic.

"You must have to beat off the girls with a stick," Bruce continued enviously. "A hockey stick." He snorted with laughter at his own joke.

David's smile was terse. "You bet."

David did attract his fair share of puck bunnies, but only occasionally did he take advantage of the delights they offered. Most were kind of dumb, and none came close to Tierney when it came to sheer sexiness. The truth was, it had been a long time since he met anyone who truly interested him—apart from Tierney, and it was better not to go down that road. The realization depressed him.

"Let me ask your advice," Bruce continued in a slurred voice, "since you have lots of experience with women." David recoiled as Bruce's unsteadiness had him lurching toward David. "My fiancée, Mindy?" David nodded carefully to demonstrate he knew who Bruce was referring to, but not so vigorously Bruce would think he was being encouraging. "We, uh, we've reserved the bridal suite for tomorrow night, which is our wedding night. But, um, since the wedding might not happen, I think we should use it *now*. Don't you agree?"

"Absolutely," said David. His eyes slid back to Hawk and Thatch. Hawk had his arm around one of the women, and Thatch was whispering in the ear of the other. David couldn't go over there now, even if he wanted to; he didn't want to blow it for his friends.

"Well, then, how do I convince her?" Bruce demanded. "She won't budge. You know women. How do I persuade her?"

How ironic was it that this guy was asking *him* for advice when the only "relationship" he could boast was a yearly one-night stand? Yeah, he was Mr. Romance, all right. But the guy looked so desperate David felt compelled to come up with *something*.

"Charm her."

"I've tried. It gets me nowhere. All she does is watch the Weather Channel and cry, or else call our relatives and friends trapped at O'Hare and work herself into a frenzy. I keep telling her that sex will relax her, but she says nooooo, we have to wait until we're married." He made a face.

"Tell her that because you're soulmates, you're already married in the eyes of God," David suggested.

Bruce appeared to mull this over. "Good one. But she'll never go for it." His expression turned petulant. "C'mon, man, I need your expert advice here."

"Let me ask you a question."

Bruce gulped his beer. "Shoot."

"Do you love, er—"

"Mindy."

"Do you?"

"With all my heart," Bruce declared as his eyes began to mist.

His heartfelt declaration made David feel unexpectedly envious. How was it that this maudlin, pussywhipped bastard had found someone to share his life with and *he* hadn't? Not that he would want a woman like Mindy, but still, they had something, didn't they? Love, the Weather Channel, stranded relatives, a shared dream for the future. Which was more than David could say for himself. But whose fault was that? *He* was the one who'd continually opted for minimal emotional involvement, especially with Tierney. What the hell advice could *he* offer?

Bruce tapped his wristwatch. "Time's fleeting, my friend," he said obnoxiously. "If you've got any words of wisdom, speak them now, or forever hold your—"

"You want my advice?" David cut in.

Bruce nodded eagerly.

"Wait. Do it her way. It's one more night, right?"

Bruce's face fell. "Yeah, but—"

"She obviously wants it to be special. Special's good, okay? Women like special." Special is what he and Tierney had. Sort of. Or used to have, before they took a hatchet to the mystery. He patted Bruce on the shoulder. "I've got to split, I've got some friends waiting for me. Good luck, man."

Sunday, 12:13 A.M.

"Who the hell was that?" Thatch asked as David slid into a chair at their table. The girls his teammates had been chatting up had left, much to David's surprise.

"The guy's getting married tomorrow—or was supposed to be until the blizzard hit—and he wants to use the bridal suite now."

Hawk looked completely confused. "What the hell was he talking to you for?"

David shrugged bemusedly. "I'm not sure. We met in the lobby earlier in the day. I guess he was just looking for a sympathetic ear." He stretched his legs out beneath the table. "What happened to your dream dates?"

Hawk frowned. "They said they were tired and needed sleep 'cause they had a big day tomorrow. Something about trying to find Oprah's apartment building."

David couldn't resist a little needling. "So they weren't charmed by the fact you could remove your front teeth? Maybe if you'd shown them the dents in your head . . ."

"Hey," Thatch huffed, "at least we're making an effort, which is more than I can say for you."

"Yeah, where's *your* mystery girl?" demanded Hawk, pouring himself another tall glass of sangria.

"Probably packed away in his suitcase until the next time he inflates her," Thatch chortled.

David couldn't let on, but his mystery girl had, in fact, just entered the bar with a short, tense-looking blond woman. At first, he wasn't sure it was Tierney. He was so used to seeing her in her work clothes that the sight of her in faded, form-fitting jeans and a tight sweater threw him off. She looked hot. That he thought so surprised him. Up until now, he'd been certain it was the image of Tierney as urban sophisticate that turned him on. Now he realized: he was turned on by Tierney, period. He wished they'd never opened up to each other.

"Yo, isn't that the concierge?" said Hawk, tilting his head in Tierney's direction. David played it cool as he and Thatch glanced Tierney's way.

"I think so, yeah," said David.

"Mother o' God, will you look at that ass?" Thatch marveled, practically drooling. "Who knew that under that little suit she was such a babe?"

"No shit," Hawk agreed. "I wouldn't mind getting me a piece of that."

"Hey," David said curtly. "Show a little respect, will you?"

Hawk and Thatch turned to him simultaneously. "What the hell's up with you?" Hawk asked.

"Nothing," David insisted, but inside, he was fuming. How

dare his teammates talk about Tierney like that? She was—he almost thought *his*, but stopped himself. She was only "his" once a year, and then it was just sex. Even so, it irked him that Hawk and Thatch were acting like she was some faceless piece of ass. He was about to say as much when he was struck by his own hypocrisy and laughed out loud.

Thatch looked at him in alarm. "You having one of those loony goalie moments or what?"

"Maybe." David continued watching Tierney as discreetly as he could. Her friend had disappeared. Tierney was still hovering in the doorway of the bar, looking like she couldn't make up her mind whether to go in or not.

"Let's invite her over here," Thatch suggested.

"Show her a good time," Hawk added with an elbow to David's ribs. He and Thatch touched glasses, laughing lasciviously.

David rose abruptly. If that was going to happen—if his teammates were going to lure Tierney over to the table for a drink—he didn't want to be here. There was no way he'd be able to take the strain of sitting here and pretending nothing existed between them. Yet the idea of leaving her to his friends made his guts twist. Neither of them had much respect for women. Not like him, who slept with her every year, no strings attached. Jesus, he was a mess.

"I'm getting a headache. I'll see you clowns later," he announced, draining his glass.

"Fucking goalies," he heard Thatch mutter as he started to walk away. "They're all nuts."

He began threading his way through the thick crowd. Halfway to the bar, his eye met Tierney's. Desire shot through him, undeniable and strong. He cocked his head questioningly. Tierney gave a small nod and held her hand up to indicate "five minutes." David winked to indicate his understanding and continued on.

Five minutes later, he was up in his room waiting for her.

CHAPTER 04

Sunday, 12:26 A.M.

"We need to talk."

Tierney could tell David was thinking the same thing as she sat beside him on the bed. There had been electricity in the look that passed between them in the bar, and David looked delectable right now in faded jeans and a forest green fleece. But she had to put that out of her mind. She'd come to a decision, and she needed to share it with him.

"Talk away," said David.

Tierney's hands twisted in her lap. "I don't think we should do this anymore—you know, meet for sex once a year."

David gave a long sigh—of relief or resignation, Tierney wasn't sure. "I know. Now that we've opened up to each other, there's the risk of it turning into something else, and that can't happen. I need to be able to concentrate absolutely on hockey."

"And I have no interest in having a long-distance relationship."

David nodded. "So we're on the same page. That's good." He paused. "Just one question, though."

"Yes?"

"If we're ending it, why are we here?"

"To end it."

David blinked. "We could have ended it in the bar. Or the lobby."

"True." Tierney shrugged. "I guess I wasn't thinking. I'm so used to meeting you in your room."

"I hear ya." He paused thoughtfully. "So, since this is going to be it, I guess there's no harm in finding out just a tiny bit more about each other. That way, when we think about each other years from now, we'll have more than just the sex to remember each other by, you know?"

"I agree," said Tierney. She bounced nervously on the bed. "You first."

"Ever ride a tractor?"

"Yes."

"Feed chickens?"

"Yes. I grew up on a farm."

A look of shocked pleasure crossed David's face. "So did I. Boring, wasn't it?"

"God, awful!" Tierney agreed with relief. "I couldn't wait to get out of there!"

"Me, too."

Since there was no harm in it, Tierney shared the visions of him that came to mind when she thought of Saskatchewan. David laughed. "Well, just to set the record straight, I've never gone hunting, camping, or trekking in my life."

"Ever have to live off nuts and berries?"

"Nope. I'm allergic to nuts."

"Me, too!"

"Ever go to the Nebraska State Fair? We have these fairs up in Canada, and they're a blast."

"I love the State Fair!" Tierney exclaimed. "When I was ten, my peach cobbler won first place!"

David was shaking his head in disbelief. "I had you pegged all wrong. I was so sure you were this neglected rich girl who came to the city to escape parental disapproval."

Tierney blushed a little. "I kind of like that you thought that. The real me is so boring in comparison."

"I don't think so."

They caught each other's eye and looked away quickly. David was so much easier to talk to than Tierney had imagined. And their shared background . . . she wanted to know more, but it seemed masochistic. It was better for both of them if she left the room now.

Tierney stood. "I should get going." Not sure of what else to do, she extended a hand to David. "Thanks for all the fun and, um, have a good rest of the season. I'll see you next year, I guess."

"With your clothes on," David joked nervously.

This time Tierney blushed deeply. "Yes."

David's expression was thoughtful as he continued to hold her gaze. "I've really enjoyed our, you know—"

"Incredibly hot sex?"

"Yeah." He looked relieved that she'd said it for him.

"Me, too."

"I'll miss it."

"Me, too."

"But it's for the best," David insisted.

"Absolutely."

"I've enjoyed talking to you, too," he added quietly.

Tierney swallowed. "Ditto."

He leaned over, planting a tender kiss on her cheek that lingered. "Take care of yourself, Tierney."

"You, too, David."

Starting toward the door, Tierney felt an expected wave of sadness sweep through her. She and David might not be an actual couple, but they did have a relationship in a certain sense, didn't they? And now that they'd discovered things in common, it shouldn't surprise her that she was feeling *something*.

"Tierney?"

She was just about to step over the threshhold when David called her name. She turned.

"Yes?"

David cleared his throat. "Maybe we should have one final encounter just to tie things up, you know? Farewell sex. Something to remember each other by."

"You know, I was thinking the same thing," said Tierney, closing the door. Her heart was beginning to drum as she walked back toward him. "End things the way they began."

"Exactly." David whipped his fleece off over his head and hurled it to the floor. "Symmetry. Symmetry is important."

"And closure," Tierney added, kicking off her shoes. "Let's not forget closure."

"Closure's definitely important," David agreed, hurriedly unzipping his jeans and snaking them down over his hips.

Heat swam through Tierney at the sight of him standing there in his briefs. He had a wonderful body, sculpted to perfection, she imagined, through years of arduous athletic training. She often remarked to Aggie what a pity it was he spent most of his time obscured behind a goalie's mask and heavy pads. Between his good looks and his perfectly conditioned body, Tierney could easily picture him as a model.

There was lust in David's eyes as he kicked free of his jeans and sauntered toward her, feral as a mountain lion. The look on his face—predatory, enticing—had Tierney in a frenzy as she tried to tear off her own clothing. She was burning for want of him, the need to feel his heated skin slide against hers for one final time as real as an ache.

"Here, let me help." Tierney lifted her arms high so David could pull her sweater off over her head. It landed on the floor next to his fleece.

"I hate good-byes," Tierney lamented breathily as she freed herself of her own jeans and shimmied them off.

"Me, too," agreed David, stepping into the gap between them to deftly unhook her bra and slide it off her shoulders. His lips sought hers even as his nimble fingers began toying lightly with her nipples. The effect was like a depth charge to Tierney's libido. She didn't want to play, nor did she want to toy. She wanted frenzy. Abandon. Oblivion.

David gave it to her. His mouth and hands were everywhere—her mouth, her breasts, the curve of her shoulder, her hips—as he pushed her up against the nearest wall.

"Ever do it standing?" he growled into her ear.

Tierney closed her eyes, shaking her head weakly. She felt desperate, legs trembling as he stripped her of her panties and pressed himself against her. Breathless, mind spinning faster than her body could keep up, she struggled to move her hands to his briefs, but David caught her wrists and moved her hands away.

"I say when."

Tierney swallowed, only too willing to obey. After three

years together, he knew how she liked to be kissed as well as how she liked to be touched. A low moan formed on her lips as his hand reached between her legs to tease and caress. His fingers moved slowly, expertly, then quicker as she made her increasing pleasure known. Finally, she was there, nails digging into the smooth flesh of his back, as explosion after joyous explosion ripped through her. Tierney thought her legs might give way beneath her as she began sliding down the wall, deliriously weak with satisfaction. It was David who kept her upright, gripping her hips with his hands.

Supported, Tierney struggled to catch her breath. "That was . . . that was . . ."

"I know," David murmured, pressing hard against her. Tierney could feel him: rigid, pulsing, in need of release. Slowly coming back to herself, she slyly snaked her fingers over the waist of his briefs, slipping her hand inside. "Oh, Jesus," David groaned as Tierney gripped him.

Enjoying being the one in control, she began moving her hand up and down his shaft. David's eyes lazed shut, and for a moment, his head fell back as he gave himself over to her ministrations. But just when she thought he was close to the point of no return, his eyes sprang open and he gruffly removed her hand. Tierney's smile was all tease as her fingers insisted on returning to his briefs, yanking them down while David sprang free. He grabbed a condom from the nightstand and slipped it on. There was nothing stopping them now.

Tierney felt giddy as David reached around to cup her buttocks and lift her slightly. Bracing her back against the wall, Tierney wrapped her legs around his hips. David's mouth had rediscovered her breast, his tongue wildly licking and flicking as Tierney's body shuddered in anticipation. Staring deep into his eyes, she lowered herself onto him, the moment of fit making them groan in concert. They smiled at each other as Tierney began to ride him, slow at first, and then wildly, with abandon, their guttural cries of pleasure puncturing the silence of the large, dark room.

Their last time . . . Tierney knew she should slow things down so she could savor every moment. Instead, she yearned for utter conflagration, the sort that expunges all memory and sense. She was riding him hard now, each slam of her body against his bringing her shockingly close to complete loss of consciousness. There was a split second when she thought he might halt her moving just to torment her. But one look at the wild desire in his glazed eyes told her there was no stopping. David pushed back, plunging hard and deep, sending both of them over the line into sheer euphoria. Sometimes, Tierney thought dazedly as she felt herself going under, saying good-bye wasn't so bad.

Sunday, 12:56 A.M.

"Stay?"

Tierney was snuggled in David's arms when the question took her by surprise. It had always been part of their arrangement that she stay the night. The fact that he was double-checking meant things were really over. Neither of them could take anything for granted.

"Of course," she said, burrowing deeper beneath the covers. "I do have to set the alarm for early, though. I'm on at seven."

"You know me: I always sleep through it."

True, Tierney thought to herself. For the past three years, that had indeed been one of the few things she *did* know about him: how heavily he slept. Now, thanks to the blizzard, she knew even more. Too much more. Enough to make this after-glow feel different from all the others. Bittersweet.

They settled back into companionable silence, holding each other tight. Now that they'd killed the allure of mind-blowing, almost anonymous sex, it couldn't hurt to ask a few more questions, could it?

"Do you have any siblings?" Tierney asked.

David propped himself up on his elbow, seemingly eager to talk. "I have an older brother, Les, who took over my dad's farm, and a sister, Debbie, who's a stay-at-home mom. You?"

"Only child."

"Really?" David seemed excited.

"Yes. Why?"

"Nothing, it's just that"—caution stole onto his face—"when I imagined all that stuff about you, one of the things I imagined was that you were an only child. Kinda weird that it's true."

"I guess."

"Where do you see yourself in five years?" Tierney realized she wanted to keep talking, keep *him* talking, because after she left this room, things would really be over. Suddenly she didn't want that, nor could she bear the fact that he did.

David chuckled. "Is this a job interview?"

"No, just curiosity."

David gave her a penetrating look.

"What?"

"Nothing," he murmured. "Just that curiosity can be dangerous, as I'm rapidly discovering."

"Does that mean you don't want to answer my question?"

"In five years, I'd like to have five more Stanley Cups under my belt."

"What about your personal life?" Tierney ventured.

David coughed nervously. "I guess I'd like to be married. Maybe have kids eventually. You?"

"Same."

"But you'd want to raise them here, right? I mean, you wouldn't want to go back to Nebraska or anything."

"Oh, no way."

"Well, that's good," he said with relief, then seemed to catch himself. "I mean—for you."

"Right."

She traced a line up and down his bare chest. "Do you do this with other female concierges in other cities?" It's a question she thought about every year when he came to town. Now that there was nothing to lose, she decided to ask it.

"No." David looked mildly offended. "Do you do this with other athletes who breeze through here?"

"No."

"So I'm special," he teased.

"So am I," Tierney teased back.

"Yeah, you are."

The bittersweet feeling had gone, replaced by something deeper. Tierney squeezed her eyes shut, worried she might cry. David held her tighter than ever. Both of them were done with words for now. They had to be.

Sunday, 6:45 A.M.

Tierney made a point of not looking at David as he slept before creeping out of his hotel room for the final time to make her way down to the lobby to start work. Much to her horror, it was still snowing. The airports and train station remained closed, and people were still being advised to keep off the roads, which were virtually impassable. She had no doubt Chicago would be declared a disaster area by the end of the day.

The sight of Marius behind the concierge desk gave her a start. As far as she knew, neither of them was responsible for working the overnight shift. Had something changed? Had she been so preoccupied with David that she hadn't kept abreast of Willy Nugent's latest directives? Suppose Nugent had been looking for her and hadn't been able to find her?

"Hey," she said to Marius, assuming a facade of calm. If she'd screwed up, Marius would let her know in no uncertain terms. "I'm surprised to see you here."

"Couldn't sleep," Marius sighed, "so I thought I'd come on down. Got nothin' else to do." He shook his head mournfully. "The sad truth is, I can't fall asleep unless I've got my woman wrapped around me. I've missed her bad the past two days, snoring and all."

Tierney nodded appreciatively even though a lump was forming in her throat. Normally, she liked hearing bits and pieces about Marius's life. This morning, it made her feel melancholy.

She glanced out the window. It was still dark, but the early morning sky remained illumined with snow. "I don't know if I can take another day of this."

"You and everyone else." Marius stepped out from behind the desk so he and Tierney could exchange places. "By the way, where have you been hiding?"

Tierney began fussing with the pile of paper on the desk. "What do you mean?"

Marius's dark eyes zeroed in on her. "I mean, we were all given sleeping assignments, and Julie in reservations told me she was paired with you, but she hasn't seen you in the room once." He raised his eyebrows. "You got something you want to tell Marius?"

"No." Fierce heat rushed to Tierney's cheeks. So spending time getting to know David *had* taken its toll: she knew nothing about room assignments! She made a mental note to tell Julie to mind her own business, then turned back to Marius, knowing her blush had betrayed her. "It's a long story. A long-running thing."

"It's one of those hockey boys, isn't it?"

Tierney gasped. "How did you know that?"

"You said long running. Those Herd boys are here every year, stirring up trouble." Marius looked perturbed. "Why'd you want to get mixed up with one of them for? Those boys got rocks in their head, and they don't even have their own *teeth*. If you want an athlete, old Marius can hook you up with one of the Bulls like *that*." He snapped his fingers.

"I'm not 'mixed up' with one of them, all right?" Tierney fought back tears. "And I don't have a thing for athletes. We have sex once a year, okay?"

"Well, that's one thing you and I share," Marius joked as he unbuttoned his jacket, pointing a finger at her in warning. "Just be careful, all right? If Nugent finds out you're cattin' around, you're gonna find yourself outside with the Abominable Snowman." He stifled a yawn. "I'm going to try to get some sleep. See you at three."

Sunday, 10 A.M.

"How's your headache?"

David ignored the smirk on Thatch's face as he settled into one of the chairs in his teammate's room. Word had come down that they were stuck in Chicago for another day. What had started out feeling like an adventure—ooh, snowbound, that could be fun!—now felt like a hardship. Married players were missing their families, and everyone was out of sorts. There were only so many games of poker you could play and so much TV you could watch before even that lost its appeal. It didn't help that they hadn't even been able to practice the past few days.

"I'm feeling better," David replied.

"We thought you might be," Hawk added cryptically.

David looked at his teammates. "What the hell is with you guys?"

Hawk and Thatch exchanged amused glances. "What do you think we are, retarded?" Thatch snorted. "You leave the bar with a 'headache,' and five minutes later, the concierge splits just after arriving. She's the one you've been nailing, bro."

"You're out of your mind," David scoffed, but deep down, he was surprised: he hadn't given Thatch's off-ice powers of observation much credit—until now.

"Are we?" said Hawk. "It looked pretty obvious to me."

"Yeah, well, that's what happens when you've got too much time on your hands and you view the world through sangria-colored glasses," David replied.

"C'mon, give it up," Hawk urged. "Who are we gonna tell?"

"There's nothing going on between me and the concierge," David maintained adamantly. The temptation to talk was strong. Things were over between him and Tierney; what would it matter? But there was a still a part of him that wanted to keep it private—not only for himself, but for Tierney. It was something they'd shared, something she had a say in. It wasn't right for him to talk about it without permission. So he wouldn't.

He'd woken up that morning the way he always did—alone. It felt different this time, though. Lonely. Final. A renegade thought had struck in the middle of his shower: getting to know each other had made the sex between he and Tierney even better. He'd always assumed it was the element of semi-anonymity that made things so exciting. But it wasn't. It was the two of them together, David and Tierney. What was he supposed to do with *that*?

Thatch was watching him with narrowed eyes as he devoured a Toblerone bar from the minibar in three swift bites. "So if you're not banging her, mind if I take a shot?" he asked.

"What makes you think she'd want to hook up with a loser like you?" David replied, not without affection.

"What makes you think she wouldn't?" Thatch challenged.

David shrugged. "Go for it, then." His indifference was feigned, but he didn't want to think about it right now. "Fifty bucks says she turns you down cold."

Thatch jumped off the bed and headed for the door. "We'll see about that."

CHAPTER
05

"Mass transit still isn't running. The airports remain closed. We're under a state of emergency." If Tierney had to repeat this speech one more time, she was going to start loading the desperate guests onto her back and carrying them to their destinations herself. Watching hope die every time someone walked away from her desk was getting to her. People's nerves were beyond frayed; they were about to snap. A fight had broken out in the lobby over a two-day-old newspaper. When the lights flickered from high winds, the gasps reminded Tierney of people watching a horror film—which this was, in a way. Except this was real.

"You have to do something, or I'm going to throw myself in front of a plow."

Tierney looked up to see Mindy Mykofsky rocking back and forth on the balls of her feet in front of the desk. The bride-to-be looked insane. At her side, as usual, stood the hapless groom-to-be. He looked pale and extremely hungover.

"Miss, we're doing everything we can in terms of keeping guests completely up to the moment on the latest weather reports," Tierney said gently.

Mindy sank to her knees and began to sob. "You don't understand. I'm supposed to be getting married today!" Her keening filled the lobby.

Tierney slipped out from behind the desk and crouched beside her. "I can't even imagine what you're going through," she said, putting a consoling arm around Mindy's shoulder. She glanced outside. The snow looked like it had abated somewhat, but that didn't mean trains, planes, and automobiles were up and running.

"Do you know how much money we're going to lose?!" Mindy wailed. "My grandma Ethel came all the way up from Boca! She's eighty-two, and she's sleeping on a goddamn cot at O'Hare, living on giant chocolate-chip cookies from Au Bon Pain!"

Hopeful for assistance, Tierney glanced up at Mindy's fiancé. He gestured for her to speak with him a few feet away.

"Yes?" Tierney murmured.

"I am so, so sorry about this," he apologized, his fleshy face pink with mortification. "I know you've got enough shit to deal with without Mindy going postal on you."

"It's okay. We're used to dealing with difficulties."

The groom looked somewhat relieved. "Thank your boyfriend for me when you get a chance, okay?"

Tierney was taken aback. "Excuse me?"

"The guy from the Herd. He's your boyfriend, right?"

"No." How could this guy possibly know anything about her and David?

The groom shrugged. "Oh. I thought he might be after the way he stuck up for you yesterday."

"He's just a regular guest at the hotel," Tierney said politely, finding the words unexpectedly hard to say. "Nothing more."

"Well, if you see him, thank him for the advice he gave me in the bar last night."

"What advice was that?" Tierney couldn't resist asking, even though it was completely inappropriate. Then again, Mindy's tantrum was inappropriate, too. The way Tierney figured it, Mr. Groom kind of owed her.

"Romantic advice," the groom answered. "It didn't work, but I appreciate him taking the time to talk to me. He seems like a really great guy."

"I'm sure he'd love to hear from you himself, but if I see him, I'll tell him," Tierney promised, masking her surprise. David giving romantic advice? She couldn't picture it. Maybe she didn't want to. It meant admitting that David had been in love at some point; that somewhere along the line, he *had* been able to balance hockey with a personal life. The thought irked her, and the fact she was irked bothered her even more. What did she care what he did or who he saw the other three hundred sixty-four days of the year? Besides, it was over between them.

She returned to Mindy, who had her arms raised heavenward, imploring, "Why me, God?! Why?!" It was an Oscarworthy performance, one that was beginning to pluck on Tierney's last good nerve. At least it was entertaining some of the hotel's other guests, who were looking on in horrified amusement.

Mindy finally snuffled to a full stop, pinning Tierney with pleading red-rimmed eyes. "Are you *sure* there's nothing you can do? I just have to get married today, or I'll die. *I have to.*"

Tierney swallowed. "We're doing the best we can," she repeated, knowing her words offered no comfort. She couldn't wait for her shift to be over.

Sunday, 10:40 A.M.

"Hey, pretty lady, how you holdin' up?"

Tierney immediately recognized the broadly built man with the wild red hair: he was one of David's teammates. At first she thought he was talking to Mindy. Then she realized he was addressing her. Tierney smiled cordially.

"Can I help you, sir?"

The man's smile grew more confident. "I hope so." Resting his left elbow on the desk, he cupped his chin in his hand. "My name's Thatch."

"Nice to meet you, Thatch."

"I already know *your* name," he said flirtatiously.

Tierney blinked. Her first thought was: David and his big fat mouth. It took her a few seconds before she noticed his eyes were fastened on her nametag.

"Can I help you?" Tierney repeated.

"What time do you get off work?" Thatch murmured.

"Three." Tierney was growing suspicious. "Why?"

"How would you like to come to my room for some liquid refreshment?" Thatch's voice was super-suave in an imitation of sophistication. Tierney didn't know whether to giggle or crawl under the desk until he went away.

"No, thank you."

"C'mon," Thatch cajoled. "What better way to pass the time while we're all snowbound? We could have a few drinks, get to know each other better." His eyes brushed hers seductively. "I promise you won't regret it."

Tierney wasn't sure whom she wanted to slap more: him or David. There was no mistaking what he was insinuating. David must have told his teammates that she was up for grabs, an easy lay. That son of a bitch!

"As you can see," Tierney replied as she pointed to the ring of distressed Oprah devotees now edging toward the desk, "I'm very busy here. Is there anything else I can help you with?"

"Not right now," said Thatch. "But if you change your mind, I'm up on the sixth floor. Room 662." He departed with a wink.

Tierney watched him go. David Hewson was a dead man.

Sunday, 3:30 P.M.

Thwap! The snowball hit David squarely in the left temple. Stunned, he turned, expecting to confront some crazy Chicago fan who hated the Herd. Instead, some woman in a shearling coat and earmuffs was slowly wading toward him, her movement hampered by the deep snow and heavy winds. He thought he was the only one nuts enough to venture outside. Apparently not.

"You son of a bitch!"

David squinted, moving closer. It was Tierney.

"What are you doing out here?" he called to her.

"I could ask you the same thing!" Huffing and puffing, she finally reached him. "Jerk!" She shoved him backward into the nearest snowdrift.

"Hey!" Furious, David scrambled back to his feet. "What the hell is your problem?!"

"As if you don't know!"

"I don't," David insisted, brushing snow off his coat. Damn, it was cold. Inhaling actually hurt.

"I know what you did," Tierney accused. "You told Howdy Doody that if he wanted a good time, he should come to me! How dare you?!"

She was breathing hard, her breath coming out in icy whorls. David couldn't help noticing that the tip of her nose was adorably red.

"I would never do that!"

"Then why did he come down to the concierge desk and invite me back to his room, implying sex?!"

"Hmm, let me see." David cocked his head thoughtfully, tapping his index finger against the frozen skin of his left cheek. "Maybe . . . because . . . he's a *dick*?"

"I'm sorry, but the timing is just too suspicious. You and I decide to call it quits, and all of a sudden one of your teammates comes creeping around looking for a good time? Give me a break!"

"I would never do that, Tierney!"

"How do I know that?"

"Because I'm telling you!"

"And why should I believe you? I hardly know a thing about you!" She turned and began stomping off. Without even thinking, David tackled her in the snow.

"Let me go!" Tierney spluttered.

"In a minute." He gazed down at her, pinned beneath him. "You want to know more about me? Here, I'll tell you: my way off the farm was hockey. I haven't had a girlfriend in at least three years because the last one broke my heart. When I'm not getting paid to let lunatics shoot pucks at my head, I unwind by reading mysteries and playing golf. I own a boat. I live in a really nice apartment. I hate cologne. I hate women who wear too much makeup. I love barbecue ribs. I love my brother's kids because they make me laugh. When I retire from hockey, I'll go to college. I don't know what I'll study, but whatever it is, I'll succeed at it, because I'm a stubborn, tenacious bastard who refuses to accept defeat. I believe what goes on between a man and a woman is private. I never have, and never will, tell any of my teammates what we shared." He glared at her for good measure. "That enough?"

Tierney nodded.

"Oh, and one more thing." He kissed her—hard, swift, determined.

Tierney looked stunned. "Why did you do that?"

"I don't know." David's head was spinning. His heart was still pounding from his speech. "Because it felt right." He scrambled off her, extending a hand to help her up. "So do you believe me? About not telling my teammates?"

Tierney looked humbled as she brushed the snow off her coat. "Yes. I'm sorry. And if you ever tackle me like that again, I'll—"

"You'll what?"

"I'll tell the front desk to wake you up at 7:*20*."

"You are one hard-hearted woman." David stamped his feet an effort to keep warm. "I can't believe how freakin' cold it is out here."

"This from a man who hails from Canada and lives in Buffalo?"

"Hey, I never said I *liked* the cold."

"You also never said what you were doing out here."

"Cabin fever. I had to get outside."

"Me, too," said Tierney. They both turned at the sound of a plow pushing snow to the side of the road. The snowbank it created was taller than David.

"Those guys must be getting triple overtime," David observed.

"They deserve it, too."

"By the way, where did you learn to throw a snowball like that?"

Tierney grinned. "My dad. We used to play catch together. He taught me how to throw like a guy."

"Taught you how to kill is more like it," David grumbled. "If that snowball had hit me one inch higher on the temple I'd be dead."

"It couldn't have been as fast as a puck."

"At least on the ice I have a mask on."

David looked around. Slowly but surely, a few people were

beginning to emerge from the surrounding buildings. Not many, but enough for him to feel hopeful that perhaps the worst of the storm was over. Some folks were scrambling over snowbanks to walk down the middle of the newly plowed road; others were struggling up sidewalks haphazardly shoveled, if shoveled at all. David found the quiet blanketing them intoxicating. There was something about being outdoors just after a snowfall that always made him feel at peace. He was almost able to ignore the fact he was freezing his nuts off.

"I'm going to go back inside," Tierney announced, tightening the scarf at her throat.

"Don't you want to stay out here a minute more?" said David. "Look how beautiful it is."

Tierney looked around. "Sometimes I miss living in the country," she confessed quietly.

"Me, too. When it's like this. So . . . still."

"Yeah. Are you *sure* you've never seen a moose?"

David grabbed a handful of snow and began molding it into a snowball. "Okay, okay, I take that back," said Tierney. David dropped the snowball. "I'm still going back in," she told him.

"I'll join you." David took hold of her forearm. "I think you'll find it a lot easier to walk if we do this together."

Tierney looked pleased, making David feel happy. He decided not to analyze it too much and just enjoy it. Together they started back to the Barchester.

Sunday, 4:30 P.M.

" 'And then he kissed me'—isn't that the chorus from some song from the sixties?" Aggie mused. "The Chanterelles or something?"

"Figures *you'd* think there was once a girl group named after a type of mushroom," Tierney replied. "I have no idea."

She and Aggie were sitting at the bar, stealing some time to unwind. Their boss, Nugent, had finally conceded defeat and was allowing Aggie to use some of the food for the Mykofsky wedding to feed guests later in the evening. Tierney felt badly for Aggie; she'd been in the kitchen nearly nonstop since the blizzard began. When she suggested Tierney meet her for a drink, Tierney was all for it. Especially after her outdoor adventure with David.

"Let me make sure I'm hearing you right," Aggie continued, nursing her beer. "You and David decided not to hook up anymore, then you hooked up again, then you chatted your heads off and found out you're compatible, and then he kissed you when you were both nuts enough to pretend you were strolling in a winter wonderland."

"Yes."

Aggie mimed putting an invisible microphone up to Tierney's mouth. "And how do we feel about this, Miss O'Connor?"

"Baffled. Confused. Perplexed."

"Perhaps he thinks of you as more than a fuck buddy."

Tierney grimaced. "I hate that expression!"

"Hey, if the merry widow fits . . ." Aggie shrugged and took a gulp of her beer. "Seriously, maybe he likes you."

"He barely knows me."

"Obviously he likes what he's heard. Do you like him?"

"Yes." Tierney took a tiny sip of her beer. She had to be careful; booze went straight to her head. "But what does it matter? I'm sure by late tonight, the runways at O'Hare will be cleared. He's probably leaving town tomorrow."

"So get his number."

"Why? His life is in Buffalo and mine's here. Besides, he already told me a relationship would interfere with his job. I don't want to look like I'm throwing myself at him."

"Even though you want to. What do you think, Don?" Aggie called to the crotchety, ancient bartender. "Do you think our girl here should get the phone number of one of those hockey boys?"

"Aggie!" Tierney wanted to kill her.

"Depends which one," Don answered.

"The goalie," said Aggie.

Tierney covered her face with her hands. "God help me."

"Hewson?" Don sounded interested as he scratched the wattle beneath his chin. "He's a good guy. Smart. Funny. Tough as shit out on the ice. Tips big."

"If that doesn't sound like the criteria for a dream man, I don't know what does," Tierney mocked as she uncovered her face.

"I'd still get his number," Aggie continued, undaunted. "Or

give him yours. What's the worst that happens? He never calls? You don't see him all year, anyway."

"I'd still see him next January!"

"By then you won't care whether he responded or not," was Aggie's sage reply. "Who knows? Maybe you'll even have a *real* boyfriend by then. Love works in mysterious ways—when it works at all," she finished sourly.

"Speaking of love," said Tierney, allowing herself another teeny sip of beer, "I feel badly for Mindy, even if she *is* the biggest drama queen east of L.A. All those months of planning a wedding only to have a blizzard destroy it all? That's got to suck."

"Someone was supposed to get married here today?" asked Don.

Aggie snorted. "What rock have you been hiding under?"

Don shrugged. "I don't know if it will help, but I *am* an Episcopal priest, you know."

Tierney stared at him. "You *are*?"

"Oh yeah." Don folded the dishrag in his hand into a neat square. "Haven't worn the collar or officiated anything in years, though."

Aggie looked impressed. "Don, you mystery man, you."

"Nothing mysterious about it," Don said gruffly. "I'm still listening to people's problems and offering them guidance. Only now I'm not on call twenty-four hours a day. *And* the pay's better."

Tierney took a gulp of beer, pushed the glass away, and hopped off the bar stool.

"Where do you think you're going?" Aggie called after her as Tierney started out the door.

"You'll see."

Sunday, 4:45 P.M.

"Yes?"

Mindy Mykofsky, thwarted bride-to-be, gazed suspiciously at Tierney through the open crack of her hotel-room door.

"Can I come in?" Tierney asked, trying to suppress the excited grin threatening to overtake her face.

"I guess."

Mindy seemed uncertain as she allowed Tierney to slip inside. The room was a mess; it was as if Mindy's suitcase had exploded on entry, showering the premises with clothing, shoes, toiletries, and undergarments. A large white garment bag hovered in the corner like a ghost. The groom, whose name Tierney still didn't know, was stretched out on the unmade bed watching ESPN, throwing minibar Skittles up in the air and catching them in his mouth like a seal.

"You can get married today," Tierney announced.

Mindy's eyes lit up with hope. "What? The airports are open? Oh, thank God—"

"No, not that, unfortunately. But the hotel's bartender, Don, is a minister. He could marry you."

Mindy frowned. "I don't want to be married by some martini-mixing minister! I want Rabbi Schnurn to do it!"

"Rabbi Schnurn's garage roof caved in under all the snow this morning," the groom chimed in from the bed. "He's not going anywhere." He pointed the remote at the TV, turned it off, and crawled down the bed toward where Tierney and his bride were standing.

"More, I want to hear more," he said to Tierney.

"What's your name?" Tierney finally asked.

"Bruce."

"Well, Bruce, like I just told Mindy, our bartender could marry you in a civil ceremony if you want. Then you could have a religious ceremony with family and friends at some later date."

Bruce looked at Mindy. "You hear that, Wuzzums? We could get married and use that bridal suite tonight, just like we originally planned!"

Mindy looked unsure. "I don't know."

"It was just an idea," said Tierney. "This morning you said you *had* to get married today or you would die. When I saw a way to make that possible, I thought I'd run it by you."

"I think it's a great idea," said Bruce.

"Of course you do," Mindy snapped. "Your dream is any event not attended by my mother." She looked torn. "My parents will be so upset."

"You heard what the concierge said," said Bruce. "We could always have a more formal ceremony later."

Mindy sank down on the end of the bed. "I don't know," she repeated. "A civil ceremony without any reception? How depressing is *that*?"

"You could still have a reception," Tierney pointed out. "Everyone snowed in here at the hotel could be your wedding guests. Think how much a party would cheer up everyone! Our head chef could even make your wedding cake. You could have a cake and champagne reception."

"Sounds great," Bruce enthused. He put his arm around Mindy. "What do you say, Mindywindywoodle?"

Mindy looked stressed. "Don't pressure me, Brucie. Just don't." Her face was anxious as she looked at Tierney. "When do I have to decide by?"

"Soon," Tierney said delicately, "if you want to give the chef time to make a cake."

Mindy began munching on the cuticle of her left thumb. "Even so, the 'reception' would be pretty late, wouldn't it?"

"I guess," said Tierney.

"So what?" Bruce chortled. "No one's going anywhere! I think we should do it, Min." He whispered something in her ear that made her giggle and blush.

"You're right," Mindy said, beaming. It was the first smile Tierney had seen on her face in two days.

CHAPTER

06

"I bet that dress cost more than our salaries combined."

Tierney laughed at Aggie's observation as she watched Mr. and Mrs. Bruce Goldfarb share their first dance as man and wife. As soon as Tierney had the couple's okay to go ahead with the impromptu wedding, she'd put Don on notice, got the okay from Nugent, guilted Aggie into baking a cake, and notified guests and remaining staff that they were all invited to a wedding at 10 P.M. in the hotel's main banquet room.

Apart from Don's repeatedly calling Mindy Cindy, the ceremony went off without a hitch. Tierney stood up for the bride and, ironically, David stood up for the groom. Now, more than half an hour into the reception, everyone seemed to be having a good time. There was even music because they shifted the baby grand piano from the bar to the banquet room.

"They look so happy," Tierney sighed, watching Bruce and Mindy dance.

"And it's all because of you," Aggie sighed back, draining her champagne glass. "Nugent should be kissing your ass, and I should be kicking it: you ever try baking, cooling, and frosting a wedding cake in under five hours?"

"But you did it," Tierney pointed out. "And wasn't it worth

it?" She lifted her champagne flute in the Goldfarbs' direction. "Look at them. They're ecstatic."

"Let's not get carried away here. *He* looks ecstatic. *She* looks merely relieved." Aggie's gaze lit from table to table. "Looks like Mr. Rock Star decided not to show; I don't see anyone here in spandex and a fright wig."

Tierney recoiled. "He wears spandex?"

"He did when he was hot in the eighties. Nowadays he probably wears a truss."

"May I have this dance?"

Tierney turned from Aggie to see Marius gallantly offering her his arm. Beaming with girlish pleasure, Tierney excused herself and let her coworker lead her out onto the small dance floor. One of the techies from Bangalore was tickling the ivories with a particularly smoky version of "At Last."

"I hear this bash is all your doing," Marius said.

"With a little help from Don and Aggie."

"Goddamn!" Marius marveled. "Who'd have ever believed Don was a man of faith?" He shook his head. "God moves in mysterious ways."

"Amen." Tierney's eyes strayed across the room to where the Herd and their entourage were seated. Thirty-five in all, their raucous voices and hearty bursts of laughter frequently overrode the polite murmur of voices in the room as well as the sound of the piano. Her eyes met David's for a split second before both looked away.

Marius must have noticed. "So which one of those puck-shootin' yahoos is your lover man?" he asked.

Tierney blushed. "The one at the right end of the second table."

"You mean, the one who's on his way over here?"

Tierney peered over Marius's shoulder as he turned her on the dance floor. Sure enough, David was striding in their direction. As always, the sight of him made her head swim. He looked especially handsome tonight, dressed in a jacket and tie. In fact, all the players for the Herd were in jackets and ties.

"Mind if I cut in?" David asked politely.

Marius took his time looking him up and down, sizing up David so blatantly Tierney wanted to die. "Hmmm," he said with a frown. "Depends."

David looked bemused. "On?"

"Whether Marius thinks you're good enough for this fine young lady here."

"Oh, God," Tierney squeaked.

"I think I am," David asserted boldly.

"Do you now. And what are we basing that on, Mr. I've Been Wearin' Dentures Since I Was Ten?"

"On fact."

"What do you think?" Marius asked Tierney. "Is he good enough to dance with the second-best concierge in all of Chicago?"

Tierney was so embarrassed she was having a hard time finding her voice. "I think so, yes," she choked out.

"All right, then." Marius slowly released Tierney from his embrace. "If you say so. You two kids have fun."

"God, I'm sorry," Tierney said to David as soon as Marius was out of earshot. "I had no idea he was so protective."

David stared after Marius. "You told him about us?"

"He guessed."

"I take it he doesn't approve. I kept waiting for him to pull out a can of insect repellent and spray me."

"He was worried about me losing my job if the boss found out. Plus he doesn't seem very fond of hockey players."

"Did you tell him it was over?"

"No." Maybe she was imagining it, but to Tierney, it felt like they were enveloped in sadness. She forced herself to concentrate on dancing. That's when she realized they were doing little more than swaying in place. Tierney peered up at David questioningly.

"You can't dance, can you?"

"Not really. Guess I was too busy fur trapping in my youth to learn," David teased.

"Well, you sway very well for a Canuck."

"As do you, Miss Nebraska Peach Cobbler of 1988."

"You look nice," she noted quietly, reaching up to smooth his left lapel.

David's eyes slowly raked her body. "So do you."

Tierney smiled to herself. The truth might be out about her being a country girl, but that didn't seem to stop David from still being turned on by the sight of her in a suit. Heat percolated through her as she imagined him wanting her right here, right now.

David's glance strayed to Bruce and Mindy, who were feeding each other cake. "I'm glad they were finally able to get hitched."

"Me, too."

"Though why the hell he wanted me to stand up for him is beyond me."

"Did he ever thank you?"

David looked puzzled. "For what?"

"The advice you gave him in the bar last night. He said he wanted to thank you."

"Well, he didn't, but"—David looked completely confused—"why would *you* know about him wanting to thank *me*?"

"Remember yesterday morning, when Mindy was yelling in my face and you intervened?" David nodded. "Well, Bruce assumed you were sticking up for me because you were my boyfriend."

"Ah." David's embrace seemed to grow a teeny bit stronger. "And what did you tell him?"

"That you were just a regular guest."

"Which I am. Technically. I mean, I've always *been* a guest, but until last night I was—more."

"Technically."

"Right."

"What was your advice?" Tierney asked.

"What, to Bruce?" Tierney nodded. "It was nothing."

"No, tell me. C'mon."

David rolled his eyes. "He wanted my advice on how to get Mindy into bed before they actually said 'I do.' "

Tierney stiffened. "And what did you tell him?"

"I told him that if she wanted to wait until their wedding night, then he should wait. That women like things to be special." His eyes searched hers. "Right?"

"Right."

"Speech!" someone called out. "Speech from the best man!"

The sound of the piano faded away, replaced by the clinking of metal on glass as guests tapped their silverware against their champagne flutes.

David looked horrified. "They have *got* to be kidding."

The clinking grew louder. "Speech! Speech! Speech!"

"Oh, shit," David whispered. He broke their embrace. "Excuse me a minute while I go throw myself out the nearest window."

"You can do it," Tierney encouraged.

She squeezed his arm, resuming her seat beside Aggie. David walked slowly back to the Herd table, his casual pace belying the panic building inside him. He could handle pucks being shot at his head, no problem. But public speaking? The thought made him want to throw up. All eyes in the room were on him as he picked up his champagne glass.

"What the hell should I say?" he murmured to Thatch out the side of his mouth.

"Make a bunch of jokes about the wedding night," Thatch advised. "You know, how it's a stretch that the bride is wearing white and stuff like that. The crowd'll love it, trust me."

"You're an idiot," David groaned. Bruce and Mindy, radiant with love, were looking at him expectantly. *Everyone* was looking at him expectantly. His eyes caught Tierney's. "You can do it," she mouthed.

"Yeah right," he blurted loudly. People's eyes clouded with confusion.

"Now's not the time to turn into nutty goalie man, bro," Hawk cracked under his breath.

David inhaled deeply. "Just relax," he told himself. He needed a ritual. Something to get him through, bring him luck. He blinked once, twice, three times—the number of NHL teams he'd played for so far. Coughed once into his fist to signify the number of Stanley Cups he had under his belt. Then he raised his glass.

"I'm sure everyone here joins me in wishing Bruce and Mindy the best. I don't know them very well, so I don't know if they've been together for a long time, or if they've had to battle more than the weather to say their 'I do's' tonight." The guests chuckled appreciatively. "In the end, I guess it doesn't matter how long they've been together. I know couples who have been married for years but are still strangers to one another. And then there are others who see each other rarely, but somehow, their connection is very deep." His eyes instinctively sought out Tierney's. "What matters is the quality of the time two people spend together, not the quantity." He raised his glass high. "To Bruce and Mindy. May all the time they spend together be special."

Monday, 10:30 A.M.

Tierney sighed with relief as she surveyed the crowd in the Barchester's lobby. Roads were open, trains were running, and half the runways at O'Hare were cleared and ready for business. The relief of guests was palpable as they impatiently waited their turn to check out. Tierney was busy securing everything from taxis to stretch limos for departing guests.

She'd spent a sleepless night in the room assigned her by management, haunted by David's behavior. Part of her wanted to spend one final night with him, but she was afraid he might think she just wanted sex. The truth was, she wanted more than that now. Maybe he did, too. There was that toast. And he had kissed her outside in the snow. And told her she was "special." She hated the way her mind hoarded these little tidbits, trying to make them all add up to something. Maybe they did. But maybe they didn't. What did it matter? He'd told her he didn't want to be distracted on the ice, hadn't he? *And* he was leaving town today.

"Hey."

The deep timbre of David's voice had always made her swoon a little, and now was no exception. The Herd had descended upon the lobby and had taken their place in the long, snaking checkout line. It amazed Tierney how loud they were. Their presence always seemed to dominate whatever space they inhabited.

"Hey yourself," she returned, noticing David was bleary eyed. "You look tired."

"I didn't sleep very well last night."

"Me, either."

David's eyes darted away from hers. *He doesn't want to hear that,* Tierney thought.

"Do you need me to call you guys some cabs or something?" she said, trying to keep her voice from quivering. He was disengaging. She could feel it.

"No, we're all set." David's hands dug deep into the front pockets of his jeans. "Uh, listen." He pulled out a folded piece of paper and shoved it toward her so fast she almost missed it. "That's my itinerary, and I wrote down my home number, too," he said quickly. "Just in case you ever feel lonely and want to talk. Or something." He looked away again.

"Oh." Tierney's face flashed with heat. "Okay." She took the square of paper, slipping it discreetly into the breast pocket of her jacket. "Thank you."

"No problem." David slowly raised his eyes to hers. "So I guess I'll see you next January."

"I'll be here," Tierney said, her voice ringing with false cheer.

"Have a good year."

"You, too." Tierney's throat felt tight. She was finding it hard to breathe.

David didn't move. The longer he stood there looking like he wanted to say something but couldn't find the words, the greater the odds *she* might blurt out something that would make their parting even more awkward. *Go*, she begged silently.

David turned on his heel as if he'd heard her, walking back to where his teammates were standing. He kept his back to her until the very last minute, when the Herd began shuffling out the front door of the hotel. Only then did his eyes return to hers. Tierney deliberately looked away. She didn't want him to see her cry.

Monday, 1:15 P.M.

"You were doin' that concierge chick this weekend. Admit it."

One of the things David hated about air travel was being trapped next to Thatch, who never knew when to shut up. But the two of them had sat in the same seats—12A and 12B—for every flight for the past three years. Occasionally Thatch was an okay traveling companion. But Tierney's rejection of him combined with the sight of her dancing with David at the wedding had clearly wounded Thatch's male pride. He wasn't going to let up until David conceded something, anything.

"What if I was?" David challenged.

Thatch scowled. "Then you could have told me rather than let me make a jackass of myself."

"You do that, anyway."

"Yeah, love you, too, bro." Thatch reclined his seat. "So, were you?"

"Was I what?" David replied, exasperated.

"Doing her."

"Maybe. Maybe not."

"I think you were. At least that's the way it looked to *me* when you guys were dancing together last night. There was— how shall I put it?—some real chemistry going on there."

"Whatever."

David closed his eyes, pretending to want to sleep so Thatch would leave him alone. He and Tierney had always had chemistry, right from the first moment they met. It was chemistry that led them to bed, and chemistry that led him to speak his heart during his toast to the bride and groom. He and Tierney *were* connected. What sucked was that it had taken him this long to realize it.

He'd spent the night tossing and turning, wondering what the hell to do with this realization. It seemed kind of futile to try to take things to the next level, especially since she'd specifically said she had no interest in a long-distance relationship. And now that they weren't sleeping together anymore, the connection that had drawn them together in the first place wasn't even there. Maybe he was imagining things, and their connection didn't extend beyond the sexual. Maybe he was just lonely and squirrelly with cabin fever and was making more of things than there actually was. But then why was he so bummed out to be leaving her and so miserable about not hearing her voice for a whole year?

In the end, he decided to put the ball squarely in Tierney's court by giving her his road itinerary and home number. If she called, then maybe he wasn't imagining their connection. If she didn't call, then he'd just have to deal with it.

He stifled a yawn and reclined his seat. In the past, he'd used thoughts of Tierney to help him relax. He'd picture her beautiful brown eyes, or see the two of them entwined in blissful afterglow. He let the images come. It might be the closest he would ever get to holding her again.

Monday, 2:55 P.M.

"Nugent wants to see you."

Marius's words made Tierney's heart sink. She'd been counting the minutes until her shift ended and she could head home to sleep in her own bed. She was tired of working hours she wasn't used to, tired of wearing the same clothing, tired of being cooped up in the hotel. She wanted her life back.

Turning her post over to Marius, she made her way to Willy Nugent's office. She was nervous. Suppose Nugent had somehow found out about her and David, that she'd been behaving in an unprofessional manner for three years running? Tierney's mood darkened as she braced for the possibility that after bending over backward all weekend to make sure the Barchester's snowbound guests were as comfortable as possible, she was about to be fired.

She knocked twice and entered. Nugent was seated with his feet up on his sleek, Danish modern desk, his head cocked as he balanced the phone between his ear and his shoulder. He gestured for her to sit down on the leather sofa opposite. Tierney sat, trying to quell the thoughts of doom slithering through her head.

"Tierney O'Connor." Nugent hung up the phone with an exhausted sigh. "How are you?"

"Tired, sir. And you?"

"The same. It's been quite a weekend, huh?"

"Yes."

Tierney's heart climbed into her throat as she watched Nugent swing his legs off the desk.

"I'm sure you're wondering why I wanted to see you."

"Yes, sir." *Here it comes,* thought Tierney, holding her breath.

"You've done an exemplary job this weekend, both as a concierge and behind the scenes in everything from helping out in the kitchen to getting that damn wedding off the ground."

Tierney let herself breathe.

"To show my gratitude, I'm giving you this week off, with pay. You deserve it."

Tierney was momentarily speechless. "But a lot of the staff—"

"—will be getting the week off, too," Nugent finished for her smoothly. "Don't worry; I know who rose to the occasion and who didn't."

Tierney let herself relax. "I don't know what to say."

"Thank you?"

"That goes without saying. *Thank you*." Tierney stood.

"Send Aggie in here, will you? She's also done an outstanding job."

"I will." Tierney nervously licked her lips. "Anything else, sir?"

"Go home and get some rest, Miss O'Connor. I'll see you back here next Monday. Oh, and Miss O'Connor?"

Tierney froze. "Yes?"

"Thank *you*. For all you've done."

Tierney suppressed a gasp of relief. "You're welcome."

Wednesday, 11:22 P.M.

"You were awesome tonight, my man. *Awesome*."

David grinned in response to Hawk's compliment as the Herd bounded back into their hotel after routing Los Angeles. After winning easily in Colorado, they'd flown on to California feeling cocky and confident, all of them glad to be back in the rhythm of play. Unable to get Tierney off his mind, David was fearful his lack of concentration would hurt his team and they'd fall prey to L.A.'s relentless trap. But it was just the opposite: he was responsible for another shutout. Maybe the forces of the universe had shifted, and thinking of Tierney while he was on the ice was now a good thing. He decided he'd think about her again tomorrow night, and if the Herd won in Dallas, he'd start including thoughts of Tierney in all his warm-up rituals, painful though it might be.

Hawk started toward the elevator. "You coming?"

"You go ahead," urged David. "I want to talk to someone about the water in my room. I didn't get a chance to take care of it before the game."

"See you in the morning, then," Hawk yawned, slipping into the open elevator.

"Yeah, see you."

David waited until the elevator doors had closed before approaching the hotel's front desk. "I was wondering if I had any messages?" he asked the pixie-ish blonde whose nametag indicated she was called Sara.

"What room number?" Sara asked.

"Oh, right." David shook his head, embarrassed. "Sorry about that. I'm a little tired. It's room 301. David Hewson."

"Hold on a minute."

David stared up at the ceiling while Sara checked for him. "Sorry, no messages, Mr. Hewson."

"Thanks," said David glumly. On the way back to the hotel, all he could think about was whether Tierney might have called. Now he had his answer.

Disappointed, he headed toward the elevator. He needed to face facts: she might never call. He was feeling sorry for himself. It was hard coming home from a road trip and watching how excited some of his teammates were about seeing their wives and kids, or their girlfriends. He got home from a road trip, and the only things waiting for him were milk souring in the fridge and guilt-inducing messages from his mother demanding to know why he hadn't called. He knew it was his own fault, but still, it smarted. Riding the elevator up to the third floor, he was glad as always to know he had his own room to look forward to. Being a goalie had its rewards.

He entered his room and flicked on the lights. Tierney was stretched out on his bed, wearing nothing but one of his T-shirts and the biggest smile he had ever seen in his life.

"Well?" she purred. "Aren't you even going to say hello?"

David loosened his tie. "I'm going to say a lot more than hello, Hayseed. Just give me a minute."

He threw his sports jacket over a nearby chair and sat on the end of the bed just staring at her. Tierney. In his room. In L.A. He couldn't believe it.

"Surprised?" Tierney asked.

"Surprised is an understatement."

"Good!" Tierney's eyes lit up like an excited child's. "I wanted you to be surprised." She sat up. "Is it a good surprise, or a bad surprise?"

David reached out, taking a strand of her hair and kissing it. "A good surprise. The best surprise," he murmured. He still couldn't get over it. "How did you get *in* here?"

"I know the manager. All I had to do was tell him I was your girlfriend and that I'd come to surprise you, and voilà! Here I am."

David's eyes caressed hers. "Are you?" he asked.

"Am I what?"

"My girlfriend." He reached out to touch Tierney's cheek. How soft the skin was. Soft and warm and so inviting.

"I'd like to be," Tierney said softly.

"I'd like that, too," David returned, drawing her into his arms.

"Good," said Tierney, snuggling close. She wondered if he knew the yearning that had driven her here. The minute Nugent had given her the week off, there was no doubt in her mind what she wanted to do: she wanted to be with David.

She took his palm and kissed it. "I hope my being here doesn't mess up your concentration."

David chuckled. "I think I can handle it. Can you handle us living in different cities?"

"I'm here, aren't I?"

"That you are."

His mouth touched hers, light yet insistent. She'd never tire of his kisses. Ever.

"We can't stay up too, too late, you know," she cautioned.

"Oh?" David asked, pressing his lips gently to her throat. "And why's that?"

"Because we fly out to Dallas early tomorrow morning."

David lifted an eyebrow. *"We?"*

"My boss gave me the week off because I did such a great job during the snowstorm. You're stuck with me till Monday, Hewson."

"I hope I'm going to be stuck with you a lot longer than that," David replied tenderly.

His words, so romantic and heartfelt, brought tears to Tierney's eyes. She finally understood that the loneliness that had dogged her for so long came from being incomplete. Now that she was really and truly David's, the loneliness was gone, replaced by an exquisite wholeness.

"Make love to me," she whispered.

David kissed the tip of her nose. "Saskatchewan style or Nebraska style?"

"That depends. What's the difference?"

"Here, I'll show you," said David, laying her back on the bed.

They could sleep on the plane tomorrow.

You Can't Steal First

Annette Blair ★

To Connie Bilodeau,
because she loves anthologies,
and I love her

CHAPTER 01

"Quinn Murdock, since you already have everything, except a life, we decided to jazz up your birthday memorial by getting you a man with an enormous—Ouch! Why'd you hit me? I wasn't gonna say 'dick'!"

Zapped from his comfort zone, Boston baseball megastar Juan Santiago, aka "Tiago the Stealer," heard a name that sped his hidden heart and tripped his highly publicized libido. Quinn Murdock—a hundred ten pounds of dynamite, from her nutmeg hair to the toes of her funky boots, in a short, tight black leather suit—so close to his train, he could reach out and touch her . . . and strike out again.

Tiago realized that the rapid-fire echo on the Back Bay Station platform belonged to the stiletto boot heels of the Mighty Quinn herself, and she was on the move. Accompanied by a team of gofers—a man and four women—Quinn walked so fast, her entourage had to run to keep up with her.

Inside his train, Tiago picked up his pace for the same reason.

"Tell me again," he heard Quinn say, "why you think train tickets are better for me than plane tickets."

"*Luxury* train tickets," Quinn's exotic female gofer said.

"You need a rest, a priority realignment, and the courage to face down your father and get a life. That takes time and—"

"A kick in the butt," her fashion-plate gofer said. "You get three days on the train, as opposed to three hours on a plane. Ergo, train tickets."

Intrigued, Tiago attempted to follow Quinn and her crew, but his passengers had paid big money for his attention, so he stopped long enough to accept a kiss, a bra, a G-string, and an invitation to a house party in Palm Beach.

His reputation had, as usual, preceded him, thanks to his publicist. Passenger ticket sales were split between die-hard members of Red Sox Nation and single females looking to kiss, screw, or marry, a million-dollar baseball player—not to mention adding to his bad-boy rep by letting him "steal" the panties they offered for his world-class collection.

Tiago didn't particularly care why any of them took his Hot Ticket Express to Spring Training. He liked people, and he liked to party. But he did care about the good their ticket money could accomplish.

At this moment, however, in sync with more than one hissing Amtrak engine, he found the thought of Quinn as his passenger shifting from "not this train," to "this train, this train, *thisssss trainnn*."

"What Quinn *really* needs," her fashionista gofer said, "is to open the locked closet in the boardroom basement of her psyche and release her inner vixen."

No kidding, Tiago thought. He'd known *that* since high school, though to be fair, he'd been privileged to welcome Quinn's vixen with open arms on graduation night.

But times had changed. He read enough business news to know that she was all boardroom blunt and brass balls now. And despite her kick-ass suit, she looked as if she'd locked her vixen away ages ago, possibly as far back as the morning after graduation, when she disappeared from his life.

"Speaking of the *real* you," Exotic said, placing a hand on Quinn's arm to stop her forward surge. "Did you make goal?"

Tiago stood near an open window and damned himself for caring what Quinn or her cohorts had to say.

"The *real* me?" Quinn mocked herself with a laugh. "I am so not a vixen. And yes, I did go to Daddy's office this morn-

ing, like we planned, and I said, 'Daddy, I need to cut the cord
and get a life, so I can't be your VP any longer. I quit!' "

"Go *you*!" said a brawny charm boy with the voice that belonged to the "enormous" remark.

Fashionista shook her head. "But your *father* said?"

Hah, she knew Murdock better than his daughter did. Hell,
everybody knew the old shark better.

"Daddy's decided to retire and make me president of Murdock, Inc.," Quinn said.

As stunned as her friends, Tiago noted their silence. Go
Quinn is right, if she really did want out of the paternal sink-
hole. If anybody had the guts, despite her father's presidential
offer, it was Quinn Murdock. Tiago grinned. Damn, but he'd
like to be there when she turned the old man down.

"I tried to say 'no' right off," Quinn said, "but Daddy
looked so hurt that I didn't jump at the chance, I said I'd think
about it in Florida. You brought my laptop, right?"

"Nope. Not allowed. You're lucky we let you keep your cell
phone."

"What? No e-mail?"

Quinn *cared* what they thought? If so, she'd changed. Tiago
wished he understood this life she was trying to get. What was
wrong with the one she had?

He followed her, within the confines of his train, like a two-
bit PI in a movie that tanked. Too bad he couldn't take his eyes
off her.

"Maybe you'll meet someone onboard," Charm Boy said
with a grin that earned him a glare from Exotic.

Quinn caught it, too, and missed a step. "Hey, what's going
on here?"

"Can't stop," Charm Boy said, taking Quinn's arm and hustling her along. "You'll miss your train."

"I didn't miss the look Lucie shot you."

"Oh that?" he said. "We're just foolin' around on the side."

One of the women shrieked, and they all laughed—to
Charm Boy's disgust.

"I can't wait to see my new wardrobe," Quinn told Fashionista. "Thanks for choosing and packing it for me, I think."

"Hey, the clothes are part of your gift. You should have at
least one surprise to open on your birthday."

Quinn faltered. "They're not over the top, are they?"

"Your new clothes? Nah," Fashionista said. "But I'll give you a hint. There's not a chastity belt or business suit in the lot."

"You're scaring me," Quinn said, and Tiago grinned, because he didn't think anything scared Quinn Murdock.

"Looks like we just made it," Charm Boy said. "Here's your train."

"This can't be right." Quinn stood back to examine a section of Tiago's pride and joy—nineteen pristine red, white, and blue vintage railroad cars, refurbished with love.

"This rattletrap's a throwback to the fifties, and I didn't bring my poodle skirt." She turned to Fashionista. "Did I?"

Tiago looked down at the station platform, from the parlor car in which he stood, at Quinn Murdock, all prim, and proper, and appalled, as beautiful as ever, even dissing his train.

His heart raced at the implications—Quinn, for three days, neither of them on the wrong, or right, side of the tracks, but square in the middle.

Maybe, he'd get some long-overdue answers.

Maybe . . . they'd finally kill each other.

CHAPTER
02

Quinn stepped away to read the plaque on the railroad car, and the sun came out and gilded her hair to copper. Then the wind lifted it around her face, and Tiago could swear he caught its scent. He remembered the silk of it sliding between his fingers. His body remembered as well.

"Mickey Mantle?" Quinn asked, the sudden set of her lips enhancing his hard reaction. She stepped back and read the names of the baseball greats on several cars. "You wouldn't!" She turned on her gofers, and they stepped collectively back. "I told you about Tiago in confidence!"

Tiago's heart skipped. Thirteen years and she still talked about him?

"Please!" Quinn said. "Tell me this moldering old excuse for a locomotive is *not* Tiago's Hot Ticket Express to Spring Training!"

"This is not Tiago's Hot Ticket Express to Spring Training," Charm Boy lied as ordered.

Tiago braced himself, as much against the train's first halting surge as against the razor-sharp blade of Quinn's presence slicing open his sorry past and threatening to make him bleed.

"Let's get you onboard," Charm Boy said. "Damn train's

starting to move." Despite Quinn's protest, the man shoved her, ass-up, onto the train while Tiago bit off an objection to the familiarity.

Quinn gave her attention to fighting and cursing the ham-fisted jerk behind her, so she didn't know who stepped out and caught her hand to keep her from falling on the tracks—couldn't know that touching her again revved more than the Amtrak engine up front.

"Traitors," she shouted as she turned, retrieved her hand, and caught her balance, still focused on the tricksters who got her here.

Charm Boy sprinted beside the train and tossed two suit-cases in after her. One hit the floor at her feet, split, and belched enough gauze and spandex to make a hooker proud.

The second broke the bones in Tiago's left foot.

"Effing-A," Quinn said as she fell to her knees, rescued a rippling cellophane halter top, and shoved it back in the bag's gaping belly. She rifled through the rainbow of bare-flesh wet dreams, and with rising anxiety, she checked the second bag, a street-walker's shoe store. "Where's my underwear?" she shouted. "Derek, there's no underwear!"

Her male gofer grinned, saluted, and stopped trying to keep up, and as the distance grew between them, he rubbed his hands together at a job well done. Quinn's female contingent caught up to him, and they high-fived each other.

Quinn screeched when she saw and about gave Tiago a stroke when she leaned out the door. *"Loserrrrrrs!"*

The losers grinned, nodded, and waved.

Tiago caught the death-defying tigress around the waist and hauled her back in, against her will, his heart racing over her stunt, her scent, and her lush familiar curves. "Damn, but I forgot what a pain in the ass you are."

Quinn Murdock—the only woman who ever ran away from him—in his arms again. Tiago held her against him, eye to eye, her feet about six inches off the ground.

"Son of an effing bustard," she snapped. "What the hell do you think you're doing? Put me down, you dumbass gorilla."

Tiago chuckled. "I missed you, too."

The pointed toes of her biker-type knee boots made hard contact with his shins.

He set her down. "Son of a—A few more bruises, Hot Stuff, and I'll end up shining the bench at spring training."

"Turn your back on me, and you won't make *that* cut." Despite her bluster, Quinn stepped away from him to come up against the undulating Pullman car at her back. Tiago's heart skipped when the chasm between the platform and the car opened and closed beneath her, as if trying to suck her down and swallow her whole.

"Get your sweet ass away from there." He offered his hand, but Quinn's eyes narrowed to sparks of fiery emerald, so he grabbed her by the waist, lifted her off her feet, and set her down in a safe spot between the car doors.

He brought her bags over as well. "Got any tassels in there?" he asked, catching a flying scrap of silk like a line drive to second. Then he pressed a button to shut the doors and cut the whirlwind trying to suck her wardrobe into oblivion.

Quinn snatched the silky scrap from his texture-testing fingers.

"Leave it to you to call your employees losers," he said.

She shoved the scrap in her pocket. "They're *not* my employees. They're my friends."

"You have friends?"

She placed a fast boot heel on her belching bag to nail a diaphanous strip of pink champagne and keep it from floating away.

Tiago grinned. "With all that leather you're wearing, I keep looking for your whip."

"You wouldn't know haute couture if it bit you in the butt."

"Stop it, you're turning me on."

"Bite me."

"There you go again."

Quinn tried to toss her hair over her shoulders, an assertive, attention-getter she'd used as a teen, except that her long nutmeg "wings" had been clipped, likely for the boardroom, and there was no length left. Short, stylish, and businesslike, her hair fell longest around her face, where it curled beneath her chin and met like the inside point of an inverted heart, framing her features into a sassy, sexy whole while showcasing the sweet, sublime line of her neck.

She firmed her spine and raised her chin.

Twice as hot as the designer-chic curves revealed by the calfskin outfit she'd been shoehorned into that morning, Quinn Murdock had never looked better, except for maybe the first time he saw her . . . in the sandbox.

They were five.

She gave him a black eye.

It was love at first smite.

CHAPTER

03

Dodging a corporate takeover suddenly seemed like a walk in the park to Quinn. Because this, this was like being struck by lightning, twice, in the same day. A loser double-header: her thirtieth birthday and a certain long-haired Latino ballplayer from her past appearing at the same time.

Her heart beat so fast, she feared she wouldn't survive the encounter, but maybe The Losers were right. Maybe this was a good idea, if only to rid her of an adolescent crush she refused to let go.

But damn, he looked good.

Tiago was handsome and charismatic, and his beard and shoulder-length hair, however outdated, only served to augment his allure, as did his piercing amber eyes, so compelling and penetrating that when he looked at her, she was always sure he could see clear through to her—Well, not her soul.

No wonder he collected women's underwear. He could probably see the lace and silk beneath their clothes, not to mention what lay beneath that.

Tiago was, simply put, drop-dead gorgeous. No wonder he had been her first—as she had been his—a powerful bond, after all, and probably the reason he had lingered in her mind, and heart, so long.

He cleared his throat. "Let's get you inside," he said, catching Quinn's distraction, she feared, as he indicated that she should precede him into the train.

The forties railroad car into which they stepped smelled of chocolate, radiated old-world charm, and held an invitation to leave stress behind. Art deco end tables topped by carnival glass bowls of Baby Ruth candy bars sat between chunky red easy chairs. Outside the wide picture windows, the sun was setting over an old Massachusetts mill town. A lot like Lowell, where they grew up, its granite and brick mill buildings had been transformed into trendy condos, shopping malls, and museums—improving, but not changing the face and character of New England.

While Tiago carried her broken bag under his arm, a funky runaway top tickled his chin. "Fascinating wardrobe," he said, blowing on a froth of teal and turquoise feathers.

"It's not mine," Quinn said. "I never saw those clothes before."

"Sure. Right. Okay." The twinkle in his luminous eyes skewered her to the spot.

"I resent your cocky grin," she said.

"You always did," Tiago said, following her into another car. "I resent the bruises on my shins."

"You always did." Quinn's laughter surprised them both.

"Wait!" Tiago said. "What was that sound? I barely remember it."

"Up yours, Bra Boy."

"Damn, that's another point for the visiting team." He smiled as if he were enjoying himself at her expense. "So you're going commando this trip?" he said, proving her right. "What happened to your underwear?"

"I seem doomed to having friends who steal it." Quinn found it hard to believe this was the same guy she watched play baseball with tears in her eyes because she was so proud of him.

"Surely you're not saying we were friends?" he said. "Or was that a Quinn dig at its finest?"

"If the panties fit . . ."

"They don't," he said. "Not enough room for Big Dick and the Jewels."

"Dumbass."

"Tightass."

"Nice mouth," she said.

"I remember a day you thought so."

Quinn was spared a response when a woman in a tight red designer dress sashayed—yes, that's exactly what she did, she sashayed—up to Tiago and frenched him . . . forever. "We're not having any fun without you, Sugar Pie," she drawled with a squeaky voice that lowered her IQ by twenty points.

Quinn wanted to puke, but that was nothing compared with her ghastly urge to bite the magnolia-white finger sliding down Tiago's chest.

But before she could bare her teeth, the discourteous digit drifted up and into the air, and the hussy sashayed away.

"Later, *Juguete*," Tiago said . . . playing the Latino boy toy to the hilt.

Quinn's shock morphed to disgust. "You're a regular piece of meat, you know that?"

"Want a bite?"

Quinn walked on. "You didn't try to steal a thing from The Peach Pit. I'll bet that lingerie collection of yours is as fake as you are."

Tiago shook his head with regret. "Damn, but you're right. She totally lowered my take for the day. Save my panty-stealing record, will you, and make a contribution?"

"I'd rather be strangled by a G-string. Besides, I'm wearing the only panties I have."

"Take 'em off. I can wait. I'm flexible."

"You're hopeless."

"That's what all the girls say, and that's how they like me. Want to see what I'm packing today?"

Quinn stopped and told herself she shouldn't encourage him, but unfortunately, she was curious, so she looked, and the twinkle in Tiago's eyes hit her like fireworks on the fourth, sparkling to life beneath the surface of her skin. *Déjà vu, all over again.*

Before she could recover, he'd pulled a plum-satin postage stamp from one pocket and a lemon-lace cobweb from the other.

"Spare me," Quinn said, denying jealousy, and rolling her eyes—at herself as well as at him.

"Bit late for that," Tiago said. "Years late."

"Ah, yes, I suppose this is as good a time as any to thank you for never telling the media the name of your first panty-theft victim," Quinn said, "though as it turned out, that was just the beginning."

She gave him points for the wince. "Okay," he said following her into Damon's Den. "So I stole your panties from your gym locker."

"And started down the road to glory. But *that* was almost nice," Quinn said, "or have you blocked the real embarrassment, because I wish *I* could. It was your announcement over the PA—the one telling the whole school that 'The Mighty Quinn' wore her Sunday panties on Thursday   that made me want to move to Alaska."

"I was a prepubescent male, so sue me."

"*You* were prepubescent in third grade," she said.

"It was a kiss. I stole a kiss."

"Daddy said you were showing signs of delinquency before you were twelve. He was sorry he failed you."

"I'm not a delinquent. Daddy was wrong. Think about it. Which reminds me . . . I heard you made his team."

Quinn twisted her grandmother's ring around her finger. Given the afternoon's series of humiliations, as witnessed by the nemesis of her youth, she should at least *sound* successful, so she forced a smile. "As a matter of fact, you could say I'm the president . . . elect . . . of Murdock, Inc."

Tiago hesitated just long enough to make Quinn wonder if he believed her.

She turned to hide the warmth climbing her neck.

"Well, hey," he said as she started moving again, "Congratulations. We can still make the headlines: *Tiago Steals Pants Off Murdock Pres.* Whaddya think? You make sports equipment, and I'm a jock. It could work."

Quinn tried to put some distance between them. "Grow up."

"Let it go, then," Tiago said. "We're not in junior high anymore."

She stopped and turned to face him. "And yet, you pilfer panties for publicity."

CHAPTER

04

In a parlor car with navy-striped swivel chairs, vintage pottery wall pockets of lilies, and a ceiling of gold fleur-de-lis over navy, Tiago accepted a Hot Ticket baseball cap from a waiting porter and placed it on Quinn's head.

"Take Ms. Murdock's bags to The Batter's Box, Ray," Tiago said. "I'll take her to the suite myself after the party."

"My friends said they got me the presidential suite," Quinn said.

"The Batter's Box is second only to my own suite, Home Base. I was going to upgrade you, because I was told earlier that the reservation was a no-show, but let's see your ticket. The suite's probably yours anyway."

Quinn groaned, fell into a chair, and rubbed her temple. "Damn it, Derek's still got my ticket. No wonder he put off giving it to me. The description would have given away the game."

Tiago grinned as he slouched low in the chair opposite hers, raised his size twelves to the seat of her chair, and crossed his ankles beside her.

Quinn shifted to put space between them and raised her brows. "Getting a bit familiar, are we?"

"Hey," Tiago said. "We have history."

Suddenly the rampant potential of being "with" him again brought a flutter, like the flapping of wings, to her belly, a condition Quinn dearly hoped was indigestion. "You've got balls," she said. "I'll give you that."

"Yeah, but it was always a toss-up as to which of us has the biggest set. I hear yours are made of brass."

Quinn barked a laugh. "And that doesn't bother you?"

"You're a challenge, Cupcake, that's a fact, but you never fail to make me rise to the occasion."

"A cupcake with brass balls, huh? I'm pretty sure we're tied now, but it's the top of the second, and I'm up next."

Tiago sat forward. "Okay then, here comes the pitch. *You* don't have a ticket, and *I* could throw you off the train."

"Wow, a curve ball. Well, strike me out and send me to the bench, but no deal."

"I think I lost the ball in the tall grass. Come again?"

"You're trying to score some kind of deal, right? In exchange for the suite?"

Tiago grinned like jocks do the world over. "Guess you don't read the papers. I don't need deals. If I want *any*thing, I get it." He crossed his ankles in the opposite direction, taking up a little more of her space, as if staking a claim. "No, Murdock, I'm indulging in the simple joy of baiting you. It's always been my favorite sport. Well, my third favorite, with baseball coming in a firm second."

"Thanks for sharing. But as charmed as I am, and as much as I admire your fine Italian loafers . . ." She gave her chair a swivel, and his feet hit the floor with a thud. "My space is *not* your space," she said, coming full circle.

Tiago grinned. "I wondered how long that would take."

"About as long as it'll take you to throw me off the train. Do it," she said. "Please. I'd be stupid not to get the flock out of here."

"And spoil your trip? Nah, stick around, and we can relive the good old days. You know, 'terror from the wrong side of the tracks taunts bossy debutante from the right side.' "

"I am not bossy, and keep your clown feet to yourself! The location of our respective childhood homes, in relation to the town's railroad tracks, always bothered you, not me."

"I believe you, but get your father's take on that sometime."

"Whatever that means."

"Just remember this, Murdock: *On* the tracks, we're in equal territory."

"Not in your Hot Ticket Express, we're not."

Tiago stood. "I don't care what anybody says. You're smarter than you look." He offered her a hand up.

Quinn ignored it. "High praise from a jock whose blood flows primarily south."

"Part of my enormous . . . charm. Ready to meet the gang?"

"Ignoring the reference to your best friend, where is everyone? I hate to see these gorgeous cars going to waste."

Like a child complimented by an absentee father, Tiago stopped, stunned silent, and Quinn refused to acknowledge her empathetic heart-clench. He hooked his thumbs in the back pockets of his jeans, and she half expected him to say, "Shucks." "I'll give you a tour," he said. "If you want, and if you promise to gag me when you hit detail overload. Tomorrow morning, I'll pick you up at the door to your suite like a respectable date."

" 'Tiago,' 'respectable,' and 'date,' all in the same sentence," Quinn said. "Why does that make me feel as if it's the bottom of the ninth, two outs, two strikes, bases loaded?"

"Don't worry. I won't bite . . . unless you invite me to. C'mon, the welcome party starts in the game car and continues in the club cars. We've got to pass through the blitz to get to the suites. Fair warning, it'll be loud, unruly, and you'll get hit on, but people will know you're with me, so you'll be safe."

"I'm with *you*? Well, lucky freaking me."

At Tiago's amused chuckle, Quinn changed strategy. "How's your sister, Lizzie? I heard she was pretty sick for a while, and I always wondered how she made out."

"She's good," he said. "Excellent. Thank you for asking. She's a nurse, a damned fine one. She beat the odds, Lizzie did, and she's paying it forward."

Quinn was about to ask him to explain the nature of the odds Lizzie beat when she heard a peppy rendition of "Take Me Out to the Ball Game." While he went for his shirt pocket, she pulled her cell phone from her bag and ID'd her caller.

"You got me a man with an enormous what?" she said in greeting.

"What, no hello?"

Tiago's grin told Quinn he'd heard Derek's flip response. No surprise; she had to hold the phone away from her ear so she wouldn't go deaf.

"An enormous what?" Quinn repeated, keeping the threat of castration in her tone.

"An enormous . . . train?"

"But that's not what you were going to say back at the station, was it, because you wanted to screw me."

"No, I was gonna say 'an enormous bank account,' and of course I want to screw you, but you never—"

"Derek. Focus. Why'd you call?"

"I've still got your ticket."

"No kidding, Sherlock. The Stealer's about to throw me off the train."

"We're really sorry you're pissed."

"Yeah, well, sorry doesn't buy the peace and quiet I was looking for."

"No way. You said you couldn't sit still that long. Now you won't be bored, right?"

"Bored, no. Embarrassed, yes. FedEx my damned underwear to Florida!" Quinn clapped her phone shut. "He'd better watch his sorry ass when I get home."

"Boyfriend?"

"Loser."

"It's a wonder you have any friends, bad-mouthing them like that."

"Where's my effing suite?"

"Sorry," Tiago said. "Party first . . . *bed* later."

CHAPTER

05

As they stepped into a club car named Smoky Joe's, a guy aimed a camera their way, and to Quinn's surprise, Tiago took her into his arms and kissed her.

For a second, before she gave herself up to the kiss, Quinn considered fighting the sizzle, but she felt rooted to the spot . . . or to Tiago . . . with sturdy roots—years' and years' worth.

If she tried to pull away, she'd topple, because in a place deep down, their roots were inextricably tangled.

For the first time in years, Quinn felt strong, more herself beside Tiago than away from him, a clue she should jump ship—or train—*now*. But she couldn't seem to tear herself away, literally.

"Harry, do you know the difference between The Stealer's kisses and any other man's?"

Quinn heard the disembodied voice, as if from a cloud, and tightened her hold on Tiago.

"No, what?" a second voice asked.

"The Stealer takes kisses; he don't give them. Women kiss him, but he don't kiss them back."

The voice was right. While Miss Georgia Peach had played

kissy-face, Tiago had stood like a slab of bacon . . . unlike his response at this moment. When he slanted his mouth over hers in a new and greedy way, Quinn forgot why the voices mattered.

"He's putting a whole lotta effort into kissing this one."

Yes, Quinn thought, *he is.* Tongue to tongue, he lifted her against him, aching center to pulsing rod.

"*That's* what I'm sayin'!"

"You think there's something different about this one?"

"She *is* his trip babe. She's wearing the hat."

The hat?

"That makes no never mind. I never even seen him kiss a trip babe this way. Not in public. Private property or not."

Trip babe. Quinn pulled away from Tiago with such force, she fell backward into an old man's arms, his heart at her back picking up speed for the lap dance she was giving him.

Quinn jumped to her feet so fast she got a head rush.

Tiago had not moved. He stood staring at her, stunned and disoriented.

Male fans grinned, tipped their caps, and patted him on the back—the Neanderthals—as if he "done good," while sad chic stick-women drooled like Tiago was prime rib at the health spa and they'd be going hungry.

And speaking of meat . . . Quinn swallowed a hysterical giggle, gave a low-lashed glance at Tiago's "meaty bone," and ignored her physical response to the sight.

He caught her drift and sat, looking as if she should be there with him, which made Quinn feel pretty powerful for a scary minute.

Miss Kiss-My-Cleavage, with a drink tray, bent over him and asked if she could get him *any*thing.

"Pull-eze," Quinn said. "Do you pay her to say that?"

"A brewski," Tiago said. "And bring the lady a birthday cake . . . with twenty candles. Quinn, what do you want to drink?"

She melted, more for the number of candles than the cake. "Appletini," she said.

"That'll grow hair on your chest," some bozo slurred, and a nod from Tiago got the speaker led from the club car.

A friendly type came up and asked her to dance, but when Quinn stepped into his arms, he tried to cop a feel.

Tiago cut in with a clipped, "Private property."

"Don't do me any favors," Quinn said, taking off the cap to read the embroidered slogan on the back: "Stolen by Tiago."

"I don't think so," she said, placing it on Tiago's head. "Be your own best friend."

"It doesn't mean we sleep together, if that's what you're implying."

"That's what *they* think it means. Didn't you hear them?"

"It's tradition. One girl each trip. It's a publicity stunt, not a commitment."

"Up yours, Panty Man. I won't even be your symbolic property."

"You know, Quinn, you've spelled trouble for me since we were five. I don't know why I think you should be different now."

"Me, trouble? Who stole whose panties? Who stole kisses behind the bleachers?"

"Ah senior year," he said with a grin. "So, every day after school, you hung out behind the bleachers for a different reason?"

"I needed to learn how to kiss. I used you."

"I know. Plus you were trying to outgrow your double A cups, and I really liked helping with that."

Quinn remembered his mouth on her breasts and bit her lip against a verbal response, but she wasn't the only one remembering. "Don't look now," she said, "but your calling card's making another appearance."

Tiago frowned and pulled her closer. "Nobody ever challenged me like you do."

"That's the draw," she said. "We're both fighters."

"Me? Not so much."

"The hell you're not. You got yourself a baseball scholarship to UC Berkeley, then, what, half a season on the farm team in Pawtucket, before you went to play for Boston?"

"Remind me to tell you someday how that scholarship came about."

"If we're telling secrets, I'd like to know why you ran away after we . . . after . . ."

"I didn't run," Tiago said. "You did."

Quinn went cold. She hadn't expected him to deny it. "I

thought you had more guts than that," she said. "I think I'd like to see my suite now, if you don't mind."

"Fine," he said. "Let's go."

"No, don't leave your party. Call a porter."

"I said I'll show you, and I will." Their leaving early together brought a hush over the party until the car's sliding door closed behind them.

Quinn tried to pry her fingers from Tiago's, but he wouldn't let her go. He tugged her hand up to his mouth and ran her knuckles over his parted lips, then he lowered the hand and stroked the new nails her friends had talked her into.

"Little oval ladybugs," he said. "I wouldn't have been surprised to find tiger-striped claws."

Alone in her suite, Quinn stopped pacing beside a silver ice bucket, its split of champagne calling her name. She popped the cork with a "yikes" for the froth and poured herself a flute. The sweet bubbly nectar of natural white grapes—with a touch of pear—slid down her throat like silk sunshine.

When Tiago dropped her off and said he had business to attend to, Quinn decided to skip the dining car. She didn't have suitable evening clothes, though she certainly had sluttable ones. In a way, she wished Tiago had invited her to dinner. "Don't go there," she told herself. "Tiago's train left your platform thirteen years ago."

Quinn sat on the couch and wiggled her toes, happy to be free of her knee boots. She wore only a thick white terry robe—another complimentary signature item of Tiago's—because she didn't have anything else, damn it. But she was sweltering, so she untied the belt and let the robe fall open. "Screw modesty," she said with a relieved sigh.

She sipped her champagne, ignored the clothes she'd tried to sort, and read the train's brochure for the first time. She'd get The Losers for this, she thought, wishing the train stopped in New York so she could buy some essentials, like clothes

and underwear. Instead, it stopped overnight on a spur in pic-
turesque Connecticut for their "sleeping pleasure" and only
switched tracks in New York.

Annoyed, she dialed Rouge, a clothing buyer with the fashion sense of a psychic goddess. "No underwear, Rouge?"

Her former friend chuckled. "If you're going to break out
of the boardroom, Hon, you have to free the vixen. You need
to go wild to get a life."

"Then why don't *you* have a life."

"I have issues."

"And attitude," Quinn said, "and I'm going to beat them out
of you when I get home."

"Sure you are. By the way, everything's set at the other end
of the line. Charlie's gonna meet your train in Orlando."

Quinn groaned. "How can I face Charlie looking like a
hooker?"

"Try on the clothes before you judge them."

"Underwear! I need underwear."

"Kiss, kiss," Rouge said with a laugh and hung up.

Quinn looked at the clothes . . . everywhere. Perfect drek.
Really perfect. Beautiful, haute couture designer clothes, hot
off the runway, thousands of dollars' worth, with lace and
feathers and spandex, all created with a different type of
woman in mind. A woman with a life, sex appeal, and a man.
Someone who liked daring lines that revealed cleavage, belly
button, midriff, shoulder blades, and a great deal of spine . . .
in more ways than one. They begged for a woman who wore
swatches that passed for tops, in fine, soft, clingy, second-skin
fabrics. A feminine, alluring someone with a name like
Tiffany or . . . Rouge, damn her.

"Nothing to wear beneath the clothes and nothing to sleep
in, either." Quinn sighed. "Concentrate on the positives. Room
service—fast. Filet mignon, garlic potatoes, and crème
brûlée—decadent. Suite—huge, opulent, and all mine. Second split of champagne—better than the first!" Quinn giggled
as she refilled her glass. Damn, she amused herself. Good
thing she liked her own company . . . because she'd grown up
with only the servants who raised her.

These days, however, Tiago occupied bigger, and better,
digs than she did, though she'd yet to see "Home Base." She

grinned, raised her glass, and drank to his success. "Nobody deserves it more."

These days, the boy from the row shack on the valley side of the tracks could probably *buy* the spoiled brat from the mansion on the hillside. Quinn remembered looking down at his house as a kid, wishing she'd see him at the park later in the day, but he was often delivering papers or helping his dad in her father's mill.

She didn't know back then that the shacks belonged to her father. When she joined Murdock, Inc., and found out, she was appalled. She settled their tenants in temporary housing, razed the shacks, and built townhouses. Then she sold them for a song to the families who'd lived there for generations, and she held their mortgages herself.

That had been the first, but not the last, time she and her father butted heads.

By then, she'd heard Tiago's family lived in a beautiful new house he built for them in Florida.

★ Quinn woke to the sound of doors closing.

Midnight. Tiago must be back.

Sweat-slick in her thick robe, Quinn was desperate enough to beg, even from him. She tied the belt on the robe, unlocked what she perceived to be her half of the adjoining door to his suite, and knocked.

"Who's there?" he asked.

Quinn rolled her eyes. "The big bad wolf."

"Hey," he said. "That's my line."

She smiled. "Take off your shirt."

"Are you waiting behind the bleachers?"

"Open the damned door, Bat Boy!"

When he did, he was already shirtless, barefoot, fly unsnapped . . . pecs riding high, jeans riding low. Quinn tried not to gawk and lick her lips at the same time.

"Hel-*lo*!" Tiago said. "Anybody home?"

A case of lust-induced cotton mouth stuck her tongue to her palate. "I m'need somesing do smeep in."

"Are you drunk?" Tiago slipped inside and dwarfed her suite while taking in the view: slut clothes and empty champagne bottles on the floor, knee boots, heels-up, on coat-hooks, cherry lace bra and bikinis dripping into the sink.

"Did you have an orgy? Because I'm really sorry I missed it."

Quinn downed a second glass of water. "Champagne makes my mouth dry," she said. "I tried to say that I need something to sleep in."

"Plenty of room in my bed."

She tightened the sash on her robe.

"You look like the Pillsbury Doughboy," he said.

"And I've been too long in the oven. It's hot as hell in here."

"By all means, take it off. Unless you're the sex-starved kind of hot, in which case, I'm certainly up for—"

"Okay, let's try this again. I need something to *wear* to sleep in. Got an old T-shirt you can spare?" *Pull up your jeans,* she thought. *No, lower them. No, drop them.* She backed into the wall. "T-shirt?" she squealed and rubbed her elbow.

Tiago took her hand in his—strong and tan against fish-belly white and freckled. "C'mon."

"Big and long, please," she said on the way to his bureau.

His grin grew. "You know I can accommodate that request."

"The shirt, damn it."

"Sheesh, talk about single-minded," he griped.

His suite had a gym—which would account for his six-pack abs. A sofa bed was open, bed untouched. In the corner stood a wooden circular stairway that looked as if it came from an old British library.

He tossed a "Stolen by Tiago" shirt her way. "Go change. I want to show you something."

"If I had a buck for every time I've heard that." After she changed, their adjoining door remained unlocked, so she went back to his suite. When she saw that he hadn't snapped his jeans, a tingling happy dance went on at her core.

"Well hell," he said. "You're wearing your robe instead of my shirt."

"Speaking of which, I'm surprised you don't have, 'Stolen by Tiago' tattooed on your butt."

"I'd pay big to see it tattooed on yours."

"Likewise," she said, and the air crackled with an invisible charge of electricity. "A stud till the end," she said.

"And proud of it."

"You know, Tiago, you pride yourself on stealing—kisses, panties, bases—second, third, and even home—but you do understand that you can't steal first."

"Your point?"

"You have to *earn* first base. And if you don't, the other stuff doesn't matter. It's called growing up."

"I've heard of it," he said. "Now put on my shirt. It's from my personal stash, and I like the idea of you wearing it."

"I am wearing it . . . under the robe."

"I thought you were hot."

"But not stupid."

"Right. Let's go." He led her to the stairway.

CHAPTER 07

"Are we going up?" she asked.

He sure was, Tiago thought. "Yep, I've got a surprise for you up there."

"I'll just bet you do."

"No, this is on the level. You first," he said, but he couldn't keep a straight face.

She was going commando, and they both knew it. "I have to give it to you," she said. "I'm having a good time. I forgot how entertaining you could be. But no need to be a gentleman. Do go first."

"My mama taught me better," Tiago said, admitting to himself that he hadn't had this much fun in years . . . away from the cameras.

Stepping into his upper-level glass-domed observation car at night was like riding the Milky Way. Despite its overstuffed sofas and recliners, minibar, player piano, and hot tub, the starry night sky stole the show.

With the full moon casting soft light about Quinn's hair and shoulders, she looked so radiant that their time apart seemed to slip away. They were seventeen again, and she was the center of his universe.

"I feel as if I could touch heaven," she said.

Yeah, he thought, *me, too,* amazed, still, by the sight of her, here, with him.

The first passenger, ever, to enter his sanctum sanctorum, Quinn turned in place and took it all in—the hideaway ambience, the old-world charm, the new-world luxuries.

"Do you still play the piano?" she asked.

Her dart burst his bubble and hit him where it hurt most, his pride. "You're toast if you tell the media."

Her smile grew. "I guess that would apply to your talent for tap, jazz, and ballroom dancing as well?"

"Shit, you've got a memory . . . which you will keep to yourself." He wagged a warning finger, and she caught it between her teeth. That was when Tiago knew *he* was toast, because the sizzle between them hadn't cooled in thirteen years. If anything, time and distance had heightened it.

He lowered his guard and met her gaze, and she released his finger and stepped back, something inside her speaking to the fear in him.

"Here," he said, safely back in the new millennium. "Relax and watch the sky." He pulled a sofa into a bed.

"Wait a minute," she said, her suspicion tempered by the kind of banked excitement she might be able to hide from someone else but not him.

"You watch the stars," he said. "And I'll play the piano."

She threw her robe aside and did as she was told, a rare phenomenon. "No funny business," she said, with uncertainty . . . or was it hope?

She looked lost in his shirt, which made him feel protective, and possessive, which scared the crap out of him. "I won't touch you," he promised, "believe me. Not even if you beg."

"Saint Tiago." She rose to her knees and cut him off at his. "I think they named a city after you in California."

"Well," he said, overcome by lust, "maybe if you beg."

He played and sang "their song" from senior year, "I'll Be There." He'd thought of her every time he'd heard it since.

She settled back and watched the stars while he watched her and played it again.

When he finished, he went over and found that she was still

awake. "Just call my name," he said, and she slipped her hand in his and pulled him down to the bed.

"You started sitting beside me in the first grade," she said. "Remember?"

"You had the nicest crayons."

"Man, you know all the good lines."

"Thanks, but I don't get to use that one much."

"You were my best pal," she said. "Did you know?"

"And your worst enemy."

She chuckled to cover a sob and failed, but he pretended different. "What do you think?" she asked. "Was that, like, a love/hate relationship we had, from kindergarten to twelfth grade?"

"Yeah, and I'm sorry it ended on the negative side."

She bit her lip. "Me, too, not that it matters anymore."

"Right. So why *did* you disappear the day after we had sex?" Tiago hated himself for needing to know, even now.

"Careful," she said, leaning away from him till none of their body parts touched. "The question implies you give a rat's tail."

"I do. I mean, I did."

"I woke up and you were gone," she said. "What's to explain? Twelve hours later, Daddy offered to send me to Paris until I started Harvard, and I went. Next thing I heard, you were in California. End of story."

Quinn—the kindergarten sandbox bully. Quinn—the prettiest girl in the class, the valedictorian who pushed him down on her bed and stole his virginity, more or less. Quinn—who invaded his train, and his heart, and morphed his long-held anger into a dangerous case of dissatisfaction.

His Quinn—in his bed.

Women offered themselves to him faster than he could steal bases. He was wasting his time falling again for the only woman who ever left first. "In all those years, do you know when I liked you best?" he asked.

"Please don't say the night we had sex."

"I loved the little girl who appeared in the park one day in braids and a dorky frog T-shirt. She looked me straight in the eye, that girl, and for once, she didn't come out swinging."

"I was scared wartless that you were gonna pull my braids."

"I forgot to be a terror when I looked at your pouty little mouth that day. Something happened inside me."

"You hit puberty?"

"We were eight."

"I rest my case."

Tiago smiled. "You looked like you were inviting me to kiss you."

"So you did."

"Yeah, and I asked if I could kiss you again, and you said, 'Ribbit,' like it was a yes."

"It was."

"I liked that girl. What happened to her?"

"She grew up."

"Bummer." Tiago stroked Quinn's cheek with strands of her copper hair. "Wish I'd had a frog shirt to lend you tonight."

She raised her eyes to his. "Ribbit."

And he kissed her.

CHAPTER

08

Tiago had already lost his head kissing Quinn in a railroad car full of people, so he'd have to be doubly careful now, alone with her beneath the stars . . . in a bed.

Man, he was in trouble.

He kissed her like a man drowning, he knew, but he tried to keep his hand over her shirt, along the straight of her spine, but before he knew it, he was sliding that hand up her soft, sweet leg, and she was sighing, and stretching, and rolling to her back. Oh boy.

Instead of cupping her perfect bottom as he anticipated, he found her perfect center instead, and her needy whimpers at his touch were like music that fed his heart. Quinn, slick and sleek and more than ready, was open and dew-kissed as a morning glory at dawn.

About two minutes in, she came like a firecracker.

"I think you broke the land speed record," he said, raising her up again. "When was the last time you—"

"You mean with a man?"

He was bringing her off again and having a hard time concentrating. Besides, he was throbbing so hard, his zipper was taking shark bites out of his cock.

Quinn wailed her second release, but she wasn't done, and Tiago thought maybe they'd break more than one record tonight. He tried to nudge his jeans down while giving her the kind of attention that humbled and excited him. "Yeah, with a man," he finally said.

"Max . . . somebody . . . New Year's Eve . . . two thousand . . . something."

"That's all I need to know, Baby. Have some more. That's it. Come on, you can do it. How's this, right here. Oh, that's the spot, slow and deep, I can tell." God, she was sweet—and responsive as all hell. He'd forgotten. How could he forget? "This is all for you," he said. "Let's keep it going, Sweetheart. Let's grand-slam you right out of the ballpark."

★ Quinn opened her eyes to a living dream, the one where she wakes in the morning with Tiago wrapped around her, both of them naked, the sun streaming in the windows. But for a dose of reality, this time she had the sky overhead and the incredible scent of fresh coffee wafting up the stairs. Tiago must have a standing order.

While he continued to snore softly, his morning boner patted the back of her hand, nice, big, and happy to be alive, so she gave it a "hello there" stroke. Soon enough, her hand was full and being coaxed into rhythm.

"You said you wanted it big and long," Tiago said, yawned, and stretched to his back. "Are you trying to have your wicked way with me? Say yes."

Quinn adored touching him, and not just his impressive erection, but all of him—his face, his chest, his long tapered feet, and everything in between. "Where's my shirt?" she asked.

"Don't look at me. You threw it off and said you wanted to feel your breasts against my 'nice hairy chest.' Your words."

"What a hussy."

Tiago chuckled. "You should be proud."

"I would be, but . . . I don't think you got your share, or any share."

"No foolin'."

"You didn't, did you?"

"I passed out from exhaustion, if that counts for anything."

Quinn buried her warm face in his neck. "I'm sorry."

"Sorry hell. I witnessed a miracle. You gave new meaning to the term 'multiple orgasm.' Damn, but I'd put you in the record books if I could count that high."

Quinn giggled and burrowed against him, settling in to give him his due, but someone knocked at the door downstairs.

"Much as I like what you're doing," he said, covering her hand to stop her but helping her instead, "and believe me, I do, I need to take a rain check. I have a train to run, damn it. What's say I answer the door and then we get our act together and go looking for lunch?"

"What are you going to do with this?" She knuckled his magnificent hard-on.

"I'm saving it for the Mighty Quinn. By the way, you earned that title last night. Ah, yes." He arched. "Do that again. No . . . stop. You're taking me past pecker endurance."

Quinn donned the robe, went downstairs, pilfered a cup of steaming coffee and a fresh shirt from his stash, and scooted into her suite so Tiago could answer his door.

After her shower, she found her underwear still too damp to wear.

While she waited for Tiago's shower to stop running, she grabbed the newspaper outside her door.

One glance and she choked on her coffee. *Tiago Steals Pants off Murdock President* topped the news in bold headlines, while the picture of them lip-locked and entwined like mating snakes took up half the freaking page. To add a touch of class, she could read "Stolen by Tiago" on the back of her cap.

Quinn threw open the adjoining door and stopped dead when she caught Tiago coming from the shower, towel-drying his long ebony hair.

"How could you?" she snapped, trying not to be seduced by the fact that he was hung like a stallion.

Tiago frowned. "Geez, Quinn, I'm used to being alone in here, so I walk around naked. What's the big deal?"

"Not that, you effing jock playboy traitor . . . jock . . . jerk!"

"Nice talk. Did you ever think about writing a book? You could call it *F-Word Alternatives.*"

"My father won't let me use that word around the office, so I disguise it."

"Anybody ever tell you that you suck at it?"

"Stop trying to change the subject."

"*What* subject?"

"Did you see this morning's paper?"

"Oh, oh."

"You did give them the headline. I knew it!" She smacked him with the newspaper—his arm, his head, his shoulder, his butt, wherever she could reach.

He laughed and backed away, protecting his important parts. "Ouch, stop it."

"You think this is funny?"

"I think you're kinda cute when you're mad. I always did."

"Do not point *that* at me when I'm pissed at you."

Forced to focus on his arousal, Tiago grinned. "Ah, let the big guy have some fun. He got— *No* . . . he *didn't* get screwed last night."

Quinn bit her lip. "How could you?"

"It wasn't easy. Look, the fingers on my right hand are so tired, I can hardly make a fist. I'll have to use my mouth next time."

Quinn screeched in frustration and slammed the adjoining door in his face.

CHAPTER
09

After Tiago knocked for the fourth time, he cracked the door to Quinn's suite, prepared to duck if necessary, but no need. She didn't know he was there.

Wearing one of his fresh T-shirts, her feet and long legs bare, and her head in her closet, she randomly tossed scraps of clothing over her shoulders while belting out, "To All the Girls I've Loved Before," courtesy of Julio and Willie and a little green iPod Mini.

A mass of ruffles with a metallic sheen hit him in the face. He peeled it off and held it up. "Hmm. Nice. Jewel tones."

She turned with a yelp. "You scared me!"

"This is a nice skirt." He held it up for her perusal.

She turned off the iPod. "Yeah, if you want a crotch shot."

He gave her a look. "You doubt it?"

She shook her head, returned her attention to her closet, and continued pelting him with clothes.

"I'm pretty sure this is what a bomb going off in Victoria's Secret would look like."

"Impossible. There isn't a merry widow or garter belt in the lot." She tripped on a halter top. "Damned piece of . . ." She picked it up and held it to her chest. "Whaddya think? *Too* slutty?" She tossed it.

He caught it.

"I'll never be able to show my face outside this door again," she wailed.

"Geez, it was just some heavy petting, and I didn't tell *everybody*."

"Will you stop fixating on that."

Yep. He *still* loved baiting her. "Last night might not have meant anything to you," he said, "but it was one of the highlights of *my* life. I never made a girl come a hundred thirty-three times . . . in one night."

"That's not the issue." She crawled across her sofa as if she'd made it through the desert without a camel. "It could be the reason I'm so tired, though."

"What *is* the issue, or the problem, as you perceive it?"

Quinn sighed in defeat, which worried him. Last time he heard her sigh like that, she threw down a dissecting knife and said, "Fail me."

"The problem," she said, "is threefold. One, I have two voicemails and one text message from my father. Two, I have only *wet* underwear. Three, my nipples are so big that without a bra they'll look like neon flashing, 'do me, do me, do me.' "

I will, I will, I will, Tiago thought, while his dick agreed and rose to the ready. He winked. "I . . . probably stretched the nips a bit myself last night. Sorry. And, um, I'm really turned on, here."

"Bite me," Quinn said, but her eyes widened when he looked ready to take her up on the invitation.

He stepped her way, but Quinn stopped him with a hand to his chest. "Damn," he said. "Okay, let's start again. I'm sorry about the headlines and the picture. Last night, before we came up here, I thought it would be funny, but—"

"Funny, how?"

"Funny . . . how I imagined your father looking when he saw the headlines. Did you ever see his balloon-fish face turn that deep burgundy red?"

Quinn clapped a hand to her mouth, nodded, and showed him her cell phone. The text message read, "F---! F---! F---! F---! F---!"

"Every message is the same," she said. "He won't use the word, but you have to give him points for sentiment."

"And accuracy."

"Not quite," Quinn said.

Tiago pulled her into his arms. "The point *could* be made."

"Let's not and say we did." She pushed him away. "I'm still furious with you."

"Could you find it in your heart to forgive me if I let you raid my underwear drawer?"

"A lot of good—your *collection* . . ."

He bowed and indicated his open door. "Tiago's Secret, at your service."

She threw off her anger, her sulks, and her depression over her nice big nipples and ran into his room.

"Sure go ahead, invade my privacy," he said as she opened and shut his drawers on a mad hunt for lingerie.

"You invited me." She gasped and held a hand to her heart. "All hail the mother lode."

She raised a bright yellow underwire like a flag.

Tiago grinned. "I know you graduated from double As, but I think that's a big D."

She stuck out her tongue, threw the bra at his head, and then dumped the contents of the drawer on the bed. "Okay," she said, "bras in this pile, pants in that pile. Merry widows there. Impossibles back in the drawer."

Tiago dove in up to his elbows. Yesterday this was promo. Today it was Quinn's underwear. What a turn-on.

"Yum," she said, stepping into a pair of seafoam lace bikinis. She slid them up her legs and wiggled modestly into them beneath his shirt.

"Hey, no fair. I was king of that mountain last night. Show me how they look."

She harrumphed, but she raised her shirt to her navel.

He grinned and kissed his fingers as if she were a culinary masterpiece.

"Guess these are a go," she said. "I'll make another stash for the pieces I'm borrowing."

Tiago almost told her to keep them, but maybe he'd like a memento. He stilled. How weird was that? No, how scary was that? He'd been carrying them around for days, and suddenly they were hot?

For the sake of his sanity, he'd tell her when they got to Orlando that she could keep them.

She netted only two pairs of panties that fit before she tackled the bras, discarding most before trying any on. When she got to a classy taupe underwire, she turned her back on him, took off his T-shirt—still wearing a neat little pair of red bikinis—and tried on the bra.

"Honest to Pete," he said. "You won't let me see those puppies when I fed off them for half the night?" He was getting heavy thinking about it.

"It's different in the daylight," she said, but he didn't miss the heat in her gaze when she turned to model the bra for him. "Makes me look busty, right?"

Tiago slipped his hand inside one of the cups. "*Now* it fits you."

He felt her nipple bud against his palm, as fast as his erection met her leg. He fingered the nubbin and made her moan. "In case you're interested, your nipples are the perfect size," he said, and he opened his mouth over hers.

They fell to the bed in a hungry kiss, happy to let it linger. He stroked her through her panties and let her whimper rule him until she came, and came again. Then she stopped midmoan, pushed him away, and sat up. "Damn it. Now I have only *one* pair of dry panties."

Tiago rolled to his back, laughing, moved his dick to a more comfortable spot in his slacks, and looked down at himself. "Looks like we're not getting ours again today, Big Guy. We must be losing our touch."

CHAPTER

10

When Quinn heard "Take Me Out to the Ball Game," she searched for her cell phone and laughed when Tiago answered his.

"Hello," he said, then, "I'll be there," and he hung up.

"Close friend?" Quinn slid the bikinis down her legs, brought them to her bathroom sink, and rinsed them in soapy water, pleased that Tiago followed.

"I have to make an appearance in the dining car," he said. "Some group wants to present me with an award. Guess you should get dressed if you want to be my lunch date, which I'd like. I'll give you that train tour after."

"I need a quick, quick shower," she said.

"Want company?" He wiggled his brows.

"Like you wouldn't believe, but people are waiting for you." Tiago sighed. "Right."

"Since you're already dressed, either find me an outfit that doesn't scream slut, or find me one that'll keep you hard all afternoon. Your choice."

"The sacrifices I make for my fans," he said, swatting her backside as he left her.

Tiago had a good eye and picked a rose V-neck lace-

trimmed cardigan and a terra-cotta double-flared satin skirt.
Shoes were a tough call, but he went with a pair of gold T-
strap jeweled sandals. "I could kiss Rouge," Quinn said as
they left her suite. "She was right. I feel like a new me in this."

"And Rouge is?"

"A savvy psychic fashion buyer. She's one of the people I
live with. Remind me to tell you about them later. Right now,
your fans are circling."

After the garlic and ginger salmon and before the tiramisu,
Tiago went up to receive a plaque from his fan club for the
most stolen bases last season. Quinn was inordinately proud
and thought she should probably chill, until he sat beside her
and kissed her, so she kissed him back. "Is fifty-three stolen
bases some kind of record?" she asked when they came up
for air.

"Nah. Some old Scot stole one hundred thirty-eight in one
season back in the dark ages."

But after the kiss, conversation was impossible, because his
fans kept spoon-tapping their glasses for more.

"I like kissing you," Quinn said, "but this feels so much like
a wedding reception, I'm about to have an anxiety attack."

"I've got the hives for the same reason." Tiago rubbed his
upper arm. "Think they'll forgive us if we chew and screw?"

She placed her hand in his.

"Ready?" he asked.

"Okay, but if anybody throws rice, I might need CPR."

"That base is covered."

"Good enough," Quinn said. "Let's steal home."

Not rice but a resounding cheer followed them from the
dining car.

Tiago began his tour in the Ted Williams Parlor Car, the last
car in the train. He sat beside Quinn on a stuffed circular sofa
to watch the tracks spiral to nothingness behind them through
the car's spectacular wrap-around windows.

The entire train was a masterpiece, a return to the opulence
and sophistication of another century. Tiago knew every
wood. He described the marquetry, the etched glass partitions,
the crystal chandeliers, even the baby grand piano in the Yaz
Jazz Piano Lounge.

"We're coming to my favorite car," he said.

Quinn smiled. "I'm fond of the observation car, myself."

Tiago put an arm around her waist to pull her close as they entered the Cy Young Club Car. "This used to be a smoking car," Tiago said, "and before we refurbished it, it only had facilities for 'Gents.' "

"Is that an old barber chair in the middle?"

"I love that," Tiago said. "I had the seat reupholstered and the 'barber shop' encased in glass to preserve it. I kept the two desks, or secretaries, as they were listed, in here as well. The walls are carved vermillion, and the ceiling is painted to simulate claret marble."

"I believe you had a toy train in your hand the first time you climbed into my sandbox."

"It was the park's sandbox. Not everything belonged to the Murdocks, you know."

"I just meant that I had been there first."

"Which you made abundantly clear with the black eye you gave me."

Quinn covered her mouth and giggled, and Tiago pushed her into a baggage locker and copped a butt check, a kiss, and a neck nuzzle.

Quinn loved titillation heightened by the danger of getting caught, until she realized just how turned on she'd gotten. "Damn, damn, damn."

"Has my poor pecker been thwarted again?"

"That's three for three," she said. "Damp panties wins the day. Oh, don't look so proud." She hooked a finger in his waistband and pulled him back. "Shut up and kiss me. It's too late now."

Unfortunately, she knew she wasn't the only female to kiss Tiago during the tour. He got kissed, propositioned, and proposed to, and he called every comer "Juguete."

"You call them all 'Juguete,' but what does that mean?"

"It means plaything, and I do it so I won't have to remember their names."

"Why don't you have a Latino nickname for me?"

"Wait, I'll call my mother and ask her how to say 'pain in the ass' in Spanish."

Their laughter attracted attention, and after that, he fielded invitations to host a fund-raiser, be a best man, invest in a wiener franchise, and spend Christmas in Colorado with strangers. He accepted all of it, especially the lingerie, with grace and charm, but he laughed when Quinn squeaked in delight and stuffed a fresh pair of panties into her purse. "Good thing I brought the big one," she said.

"You sure did bring the big one."

She loved that cocky grin of his.

The tour ended outside her door. "Game called on account of business," he said.

Her suite doors stood perpendicular to his, which made his look like the end of the train. "But you only showed me fourteen cars, and the brochure in the bar says the train has nineteen. What's on the other side of your suite?"

"The rest isn't open to the public," he said, "for safety and insurance reasons."

"You keep your harem in those cars, don't you? *That's* where you went last night. I saw the door on the other side of your room."

"You caught me." He chuckled but looked at his watch. "I'm on duty for a couple hours, but would you like to meet me for a private dinner upstairs in the observation car around eight?"

Quinn agreed, dipped under his arm, and shut the door to her suite. She was alerted by the difference, the . . . guilt and lack of eye contact, that accompanied his chuckle at her harem joke. What *did* he keep in those cars?

She listened for fifteen minutes of silence from his suite before she felt safe enough to enter, cross it, and open the mysterious door. It led to a corridor and a railroad car called "The Circus Train to Dreams."

Inside, Quinn found facing rows of beds disguised as circus tents, each a different color stripe, with bright circus act murals in between and strategically placed stuffed lions, giraffes, tigers, and party-hat poodles. The children hooked up to IVs broke her heart, though they certainly seemed happy, as their laughter followed a certain Latino jock, in clown garb and makeup, as he waltzed flamboyantly down the middle aisle with a stuffed floppy lady clown strapped to his feet.

"Excuse me," a nurse said, making Quinn jump, because all her senses, including her overflowing heart, were on high alert and focused on Tiago. "You're not supposed to be here."

"Lizzie?" Quinn said. "Is that you?"

The nurse stilled. "Quinn? Quinn Murdock?"

After a hug, Lizzie waved to a nurse at the other end of the car and took Quinn into a small office with charts and meds so they could sit and talk. "My brother didn't tell me you were on the train. He's such a brat. It's great to see you again. You look awesome. Do you want a cup of coffee or a soft drink?"

"No thanks," Quinn said. "You look great, too, but what is all this? I mean, I can tell what it is, and I assume the kids are headed to Orlando, but . . ."

"Tiago does this every trip. The ticket price for the main train goes a long way toward giving the kids their dream week. There's another hospital car with older kids, then a Pullman car for their families with kitchen and dining cars beyond. Tiago comes over and entertains the kids every night so their parents can dine in peace."

"Why does he keep it all such a secret?"

"He says it'll ruin his hot playboy rep, but if you ask me, he uses that rep to dodge a serious relationship."

"Makes sense," Quinn said, "So whatever made him think of something so . . . responsible?"

"It was my brush with leukemia," Lizzie said. "I was really sick when you went off to college, but I beat the odds, and

Tiago wants to help other kids do the same. He was always there for me. Well, you remember, I almost died the night you graduated from high school. Tiago had to leave your party early."

"I'll take that cold drink now," Quinn said, her mind racing. That's why he left her asleep after they'd made love? She accepted a bottle of flavored water gratefully.

Later. She'd think about all the ways her life might be different, if she'd known the truth, later. "Do you like working with children?" she asked.

"I love it," Lizzie said. "And I'm dating a wonderful doctor."

"You have a life, you lucky thing. I'm trying to get one," Quinn said. "I just got my degree in child psychology. Now all I have to do is tell my father I'm leaving the company."

"Oh, oh," Lizzie said. "He won't like that."

"Tell me about it."

"You must have been in Tiago's suite to get here," Lizzie said. "But I didn't know you two had hooked up again."

"I have the suite next to his. Taking this train was an accident. No, scratch that. It was a premeditated birthday gift from my roommates, because I mentioned your brother once or twice," or a dozen times. "I have a short-term job waiting for me in Orlando, taking my neighbor Charlie's son, Jesse, to spring training while Charlie and his new wife have a 'second' honeymoon. They're on their 'first' right now *with* Jesse. He's eleven and not happy that his father remarried."

"You have your work cut out for you."

Quinn nodded, but she couldn't let go of her shock. "So Tiago drops off the kids in Orlando and goes on to spring training. Then what, the kids and their families take the train back to Boston?"

"Yes, and the parents have the train to themselves. Tiago doesn't stop with bringing them to Orlando," Lizzie said. "He gives each family spending money. Hell, he'll even send the kids who beat the odds to college." Lizzie touched Quinn's hand. "But I don't mean to give Tiago all the credit. He got the idea from your father."

"What?" Quinn felt a bit dizzy. "What are you talking about?"

Lizzie stopped talking and started sorting charts.

"Too late, Lizzie. Now you have to tell me."

"I can't believe you didn't know your father paid my medical bills. He also paid for a family trip to Florida, and for me and Tiago to go to college."

Quinn's stupefaction was cut short by an emergency call to the bed of a five-year-old who'd spiked a fever.

"Shouldn't we call her parents?" Quinn asked when they stepped away from the bed.

"She doesn't have any," Lizzie said, "and sick kids don't get adopted, so we need to get her well."

"What's wrong with her?"

"The doctors are still trying to figure that out, but they've pretty much ruled out the worst-case scenarios."

Lizzie did everything a nurse could and lowered Colette's fever, but it took Quinn's ladybug fingernail dance, and a slice of her heart, to make the curly haired little doll stop fussing.

"You'd better get out of here," Lizzie said, checking her watch, "if you don't want to get caught. Tiago will be coming by in a minute."

"Yikes, yes, okay, thanks." She kissed Colette's cheek and then Lizzie's. "I can't believe how long we talked. Can I visit Colette again tomorrow and get your cell phone number so we can catch up more often?"

Lizzie hugged her. "I'd like that."

Back in her suite, Quinn left the door open between her room and Tiago's and speed-dialed her father.

He answered with a curt, "You want to tell me about that picture?"

"I was having a good time," Quinn said. "Couldn't you tell? I still am, and I don't wish you were here."

Her father grumbled something about smart-mouth kids.

"Tell me about the Santiago college scholarships, the medical bills, and the family trip to Orlando," she said.

"Ask Tiago."

"He's not talking, but you are. Start now."

"I paid for all of it. So what?"

"I know, but why?"

"So Tiago wouldn't ruin your life."

"No way. How could he do that?"

"The idiot asked if he could marry you the day after you graduated from high school."

Quinn's legs gave way as her heart sped. She sat, fast, shocked, thrilled, and angry that she was only now finding out. "*That's* why you sent me to Paris early. No, wait, that's not important. What did Tiago have to do in exchange for your . . . generosity?"

"You were too young to get married," her father snapped. "You needed to go to college."

"Agreed, but what did Tiago have to promise?"

"Quinn . . ."

"I'm listening."

"He promised to pick a college at the other end of the country and to stay the hell away from you for the rest of the century."

Quinn switched ears and felt light enough to float. "This is a new century, Dad."

"I knew you'd figure that out."

"Don't you want me to be happy?"

"Of course I do, but—"

"So you accept my resignation."

He blustered. No words, just the strangling sounds of a thwarted CEO.

"Dad?"

"Accepted."

"As of this minute," she said, "because I'm setting up shop as a child psychologist ASAP."

"I thought that was a phase."

"Not."

A big parental sigh. "Will that make you happy?"

"Yeah, Dad, it will."

"And Tiago?" her father asked.

"He's still gonna play baseball."

"Don't be smart. That kiss didn't look fake. What about the two of you?"

"I don't know about him, but I'm taking it one day at a time."

"Sensible." Her father cleared his throat. "Give him my best. Tell him I went hoarse during the World Series."

"I'll tell him."

Quinn heard Tiago's door open and close and then he stood in her doorway and she felt as if she were seeing him for the first time. Long hair, luminous eyes, sexy beard . . . huge heart.

"Gotta go, Dad." She clapped her phone shut.

"Hungry?" she asked, trying to put some perspective into the flaming case of hero worship speeding her heart.

"Starving," he said, raising her temperature and her heart rate and closing the distance between them.

CHAPTER
12

Tiago opened his mouth over Quinn's as if he did it every day, praying she'd welcome him. When she did, her passion fueled his. He liked her hand at his nape, the scent of her hair—like the herbs in the field where they played. "I liked finding your door open as if you were waiting for me," he said, nibbling her ear.

She stroked his beard. "I *was* waiting for you."

"Right," he said. "You must be starved. I'll call the kitchen." He picked up the house phone.

"Ask them to bring some munchies around ten," Quinn said, "and leave them in your suite."

Tiago called, still trying to figure out her game plan, both intrigued and aroused by her suggestion. "You have something else in mind for dinner?" he asked, hanging up.

"I've been thinking about jumping your bones," she said. "And I don't care to wait any longer."

"Seventeen years, and the last woman who was that direct with me was you, on graduation night. You were the stealer that night."

"I was no such—"

"You pantsed me, Murdock, and don't pretend you forgot."

Quinn raised her chin. "You were asking for it, strutting your tight butt around that party. Hell," she said, "you're asking for it now."

He took her hand and led her to the stairs. "Then you'd better give it to me good," he said.

She pulled him up short. "No strings," she said. "No commitment. Let's steal the romantic ambiance for a bit and call it a fantasy."

"And what happens when we both have to go back to reality?" he asked, leading her up the stairs, abundantly aware of her hand on his inner thigh.

"We take reality one day at a time, and . . . stay in touch." A double meaning, if ever he heard one.

He wished he knew for sure what she meant. "I go where baseball takes me; you know that," he said, to be fair and up front.

"I know," she said, "and I have plans, a new road to travel, but we have cell phones and e-mail, and we're bound to end up in the same town once in a while."

"One day at a time," Tiago said, turning Quinn in his arms. "And we stay in touch." He met her mouth with his, a feathery kiss, his lips parting hers, nibbling at their corners. "I like the idea."

"So do I," she said, getting down to business and making the big guy happy. "Pantsing you will go much easier without a party outside the door." She began to unzip his pants, taking her damned sweet torturous time.

"Are you gonna make the grab or what? Everything keeps getting tighter."

She gave him a wicked grin and knelt before him, his zipper at half mast, and she made the grab. Tiago gasped, closed his eyes, and saw stars dancing behind his lids.

"Guess I'm not the only one who goes commando around here," Quinn said, running a finger along his length.

"Call it my ready stance, to make things easier."

"Easier for who?" She tightened her fist around his happy dick and worked it like a pro. Tiago nearly jumped from his skin.

"Murdock, you're going to be the death of me." He pulled her to her feet and made short work of the buttons on the cardigan he'd helped her choose earlier, trying to get beneath the bra to the gratification inside.

By the light of the stars, they stripped each other naked, stroking and kissing every patch of bared skin along the way. Then he lifted her off her feet and carried her to the bed.

"I thought we were getting in the hot tub," she said, clinging to his neck, her eyes glazed with lust, exactly the way he wanted her.

"We will," he said. "After. Remember last night?" He grinned. "I'll take those budding nips as a yes. Last night was for you. Tonight is partner's choice, so first I'm going to make you come with my mouth and then I'm going to slip inside you and we'll both come our brains out. Then we'll get in the hot tub, and I'll let you have your wicked way with me. How's that for a deal?"

"Deal," she said. But halfway through her tenth orgasm or so, when his cock was roughly the size of a bat and twice as hard, she rolled away from him, pushed him down, and climbed on top. "Hello, Big Boy," she said impaling herself. "You like my version of a Tiago steal?" she asked, and took him home.

"Quinn?" He chuckled sometime later. "Do I make a good mattress? Are you awake?"

She raised her head from his sweat-slick chest and pushed the hair from her eyes. "I was resting."

Oh that face, that dear, sweet face. "That was some scream, Murdock."

"Yeah, well, that was some orgasm," she said. "I don't think there's a mechanical device made that can produce that."

"Tried a few, have you?" His dick came to life as he imagined it.

She rolled off him. "When you don't have a life, you take what you can get."

He led her to the hot tub, held her hand as she got in, and then he got them each an icy sparkling water from the mini-bar and joined her. "One of your gofers said something about you not having a life."

She stopped with the bottle halfway to her lips. "You heard that?"

"Tell me about the gofers."

"I told you, they're my friends—Molly, Rouge, Lucie, Goretti, and Derek. We rent a huge old townhouse on Beacon Hill."

"Friends from college?"

"No. Actually, we bonded during three hours at the 'sold out' end of a ticket line for an assertiveness training talk."

Tiago sat forward. "Assertiveness training? You?" He laughed so hard, he lost his breath. He laughed until Quinn rose like a vengeful sprite and poured ice water over his head.

Tiago sputtered and towered over her.

"Done now?" she asked, her hands on her dripping hips. "Do you want to hear the story or not?"

"Yeah, you need assertiveness training." Tiago pulled her back into the warm tingling water. "I'll try to control myself . . . more or less."

"See that you do." She snuggled against him, but he pulled her over him, took a nipple into his mouth, slipped a hand between her legs, and found her sweet spot.

CHAPTER 13

"Did the train stop moving?" she asked as she dropped her towel and crawled between the sheets.

Tiago followed suit, threw a leg over her, and pulled her close, which she found as heady and comforting as his beard against her face. "My train is about luxury and relaxation," he said. "We stable it at night, usually on a spur in some deserted field or other—prescheduled and with permission, of course—so our passengers can sleep."

"Ah, yes. I read about that. Where are we stabled now?"

"I don't precisely know—I leave that to the crew—but I can narrow it down to a spot about ten hours from Orlando. We arrive around six tomorrow night, and chartered busses will be waiting to take most of the passengers to a hotel in Fort Meyers for spring training." He kissed her brow, her nose, and her eyes. "Tell me more about your friends," he said, "the ones who needed assertiveness training. And then maybe you can tell me why you thought you did."

She tugged on a chest hair.

"Ouch!"

"That's what you get," she said, swirling the spot with slow, soothing strokes to make up for her brutality. "While the six of us waited in line for tickets, we discovered we had a lot in common. We're all in well-to-do ruts and lack any personal lives whatsoever. When tickets sold out before we got any, we went out for lunch, stayed for dinner, and talked until midnight.

"For a few weeks, we spoke on the phone daily, got together Fridays for supper, bared our souls, and found we were kindred spirits. Then we formed a club with the express purpose of helping each other get lives."

"How long have you been together?"

"Going on a year."

"Is it working, the getting lives part?"

"We've all taken steps in the right direction."

"So your friends think this trip is a step in the right direction for you. I wonder why."

"Beats me, but I *am* having a good time."

"I'm honored. Does your club have a name?"

"We can't decide between The Losers Club, because it encourages change, and The Coma Club, because it's funny."

Tiago covered her hand with his to stop her teasing swirls, as if he needed to concentrate. "Doesn't sound funny to me."

"Our goal is to help each other get lives, but failing that, we still end up old and alone, right? So we have a pact that if any of us goes into a coma, the others come in and touch up roots, pluck chin hairs, give manicures, shave legs . . . you know, keep each other from getting grungy."

Tiago's obvious amusement amused her. "Okay," she said, "so it sounds whacked, but despite our high rate of aborted attempts at social lives, we root for each other and cheer each other on. Plus, we always say something positive about any step in the right direction. I like that rule. I'd like to teach Daddy that rule."

"So this Derek guy is not your Mr. Right, I take it?"

Quinn choked on a laugh, but despite her fight for air and Tiago's back-slapping, she savored her power, because he sounded like he might be jealous.

He brought her another bottle of water, and when she could breathe again, he took her in his arms and began to kiss her, making her hot in that special way only Tiago could, until something started beeping.

Tiago got up and fished through his pants, found the culprit—
a beeper—read a message, and hit a number on his cell phone.
"Emergency?"

Quinn sat up.

"What?" he said. "The Ladybug Lady?" Then he stilled and
lifted Quinn's hand. "Hold on a sec." He held his phone to his
chest. "How long since you've been to a circus?"

Quinn cleared her throat. "Um, ah, about, oh, three, four
hours maybe."

He put the phone to his ear again. "We'll be right there."

"Get dressed," he said. "We've got a little one crying for a
ladybug dance."

"Okay," Quinn said, hustling into her clothes as fast as
Tiago did, but his silence was telling.

Quinn led the way to the hospital car.

"How'd you get away with it?" he asked before they went
inside.

"I was curious. Lizzie *said* I shouldn't be there, but we
hadn't seen each other in years, and—"

Tiago scoffed. " 'Nuff said. You and Lizzie always batted
for the same team."

Quinn smiled when he chucked his big-eyed sister under
the chin as they went by. "Brat!"

"Hey, Colette," Tiago said, sitting on her bed and taking her
on his lap. "I brought the Ladybug Lady, just like you
wanted."

Quinn drummed her nails on Colette's knee and Tiago
sang: "Gosh, little lady, don't you shrug, Tiago's gonna bring
you some ladybugs, and if those ladybugs don't dance,
Tiago's gonna bring you a box of . . . ants."

Colette giggled, and Tiago sang a few more weird verses
while Quinn kept her fingers dancing.

When the little one got drowsy, Tiago tucked her beneath
the covers and kissed her nose. Half an hour later, she fell
asleep.

Quinn kissed Colette's soft little hand and saw Tiago on the
opposite side of the bed watching her. "Sweet," she said.

He reached for her hand. "I always thought so."

* * *

★ At the train's first tentative movement, Quinn woke, her hand still in Tiago's.

On the other side of the bed, Tiago slept on, his head on Colette's pillow, her little arms around his neck.

She had never loved him more.

How stupid was that?

They'd be in Orlando in ten hours, and she didn't hold a lot of hope that they'd see each other much, if at all, after spring training.

They were free agents, both of them, going in such entirely different directions, it was laughable.

At the end of the day, his course was set . . . *Tiago Steals Pants Off . . . Anybody.*

CHAPTER 14

Quinn left the hospital car before Tiago woke. She wasn't ready to face the realization herself that she loved him, never mind facing *him* with the knowledge.

In her suite, she threw on the terry robe and skipped the farewell brunch. It had started forty-five minutes ago, anyway, so she went up to the hot tub. Tiago had evidently not yet returned to his room.

She liked sitting in the bubbling water watching the tops of trees, the bottoms of bridges, and the people in high buildings looking down at her. She waved, but nobody waved back.

She understood why Tiago loved his train. She loved it, too—its history, its healing properties, and not only in the hospital car, though that was something else. Who knew Tiago had it in him?

Ah, what was she thinking? She'd always known the kind of heart Tiago hid from the world, which probably meant she'd been in love with him, like . . . forever.

Quinn sighed, lay back, shut her eyes, and let the movement of the train and the tub's jets ease her frustration and lull her into a half sleep.

When she woke, the ancient perpetual calendar clock on the

stair wall indicated that a great deal of time had passed, and still Tiago hadn't found her. He either hadn't thought to look up here, or he hadn't cared to.

She needed to get dressed for lunch. Today was the penultimate day of the trip. Tiago said their late luncheon would be a lavish affair with speeches and such. He would play the ultimate, charismatic host, which he had not said but she knew.

Her fantasy trip was nearly over. Damn, but The Losers had been right. She missed Tiago already. "And you'd damned well better get used to it, Loser," she told herself as she stepped from the tub.

"Who's a loser?" Tiago asked as he came her way, so gorgeous in charcoal pinstripe dress pants and gray silk shirt she could eat him up with a spoon.

"Nobody who took *this* trip," she said, wrapping herself in a towel as if to protect herself from hurt. As if it wasn't already too late.

Back in her suite, after her shower, Tiago pulled Band-Aids from his pockets and put them over her nipples. "So they don't pop out," he said, "to solve what *you* think is a problem and *I* think is an asset."

After that, she let him sweet-talk her into going braless beneath a faced, black lace jacket, held together by a hook—*one* hook—between her breasts. With a muted teal corset skirt, the outfit looked great. Her ankle-wrap stiletto sandals didn't look bad, either.

Quinn liked being on Tiago's arm, except she knew this was good-bye . . . the end of the fantasy. He'd be too busy playing ball during spring training to notice her, and she'd be in the stands with Jesse, unable to get near the ballplayers.

The farewell lunch might have been delicious, but the chasm already forming between them dulled Quinn's appetite. When she lost Tiago in a crowd of well-wishers, she went back to her suite to pack her vixen clothes. She found a "Stolen by Tiago" bag in her closet where her broken bag used to be.

★ Before the train came to a full stop, she saw Charlie, waved, and called his name. He met her halfway, caught her in his arms, and gave her a big bear hug and a smacking kiss before he paid a red cap to take her bags. "Penny and I can never thank you enough for taking Jesse for the next two weeks, Quinn. But I'm warning you, he's not happy about having a new mother."

"No kid who lost his real mother is, Charlie. Give him time. He's a good kid."

"You're right. He bought you a present, though he probably won't give it to you until he finishes being a brat, after we leave you in Fort Meyers."

"I'm ready for him," Quinn said, searching the crowd as Charlie talked, but when she spotted Tiago, he was getting pulled into a white stretch limo by a tanning-salon blonde whose top-heavy silicone boobs were about to spring from her lime sundress.

Quinn put her head on Charlie's shoulder, so he placed an arm around her to lead her away. "Tired?" he asked, and she nodded.

She wished she'd known, back in the sandbox, that Tiago would grow up to break a million hearts, hers included.

★ Tiago saw genuine affection pass between Quinn and the guy with salt-and-pepper hair manhandling her on the platform. Was *he* the new direction her life was taking? A guy fifteen years older than her?

What an idiot he was, Tiago thought, to imagine for half a minute that he had a shot in hell with a Murdock. "Give it a rest, June," he told his obsessive publicist when he sat beside her in the limo. "We'll make the promo shoot with time to spare."

Why would Quinn sleep with *him*, Tiago asked himself, if a guy she cared about was meeting her in Orlando? That wasn't the Quinn he knew. "It doesn't make sense. I'm missing something," he said. "Wait a minute. I need to go and talk to—"

"Drive, Max," June said, and Max drove . . . like a maniac, but not so fast that Tiago didn't see the kid running up to Quinn and throwing his arms around her legs. "Son of a—" He'd blown his shot. So much for the fantasy.

"No, damn it! I'm *not* giving up without a fight." He speed-dialed Lizzie on his cell.

★ Three days later, when the team and the media were prepping for a promo exhibition game with a bunch of local kids looking to raise money for a field, Tiago had reason to notice Quinn.

The kid who'd welcomed her with affection in Orlando was now acting out big time. Quinn tried to keep her cool and not make a scene while the boy ran up the bleachers, spilling soda on half the crowd and then throwing the last of it Quinn's way, almost by accident.

Without thought, Tiago went over to help and gave Quinn a passing nod because she wasn't his. But after he had the kid in hand, he glanced her way again and did a double-take. She wore an aqua T-shirt with a raised mutant glitter frog on her chest.

The kid hung from his arm like a sack of potatoes, so Tiago carried him back to the dugout with a scarier sense of hope than his first day in the majors.

"Hey, you're The Stealer," the kid said when Tiago set him down. "Quinn told me she knew you, but I didn't know you stole kids."

"Cute," Tiago said. "What's your name?"

"Jesse."

"Jesse, you're benched. Don't move, and maybe Quinn won't beat you after the game."

Quinn's frog shirt made Tiago want to ask the kid a question, except he was afraid to hear the answer. Lizzie sure hadn't given him much.

Tiago hunched down before the boy. "Jesse, was that your father with you and Quinn at the train station in Orlando the other day?"

"Yeah," the boy said. "What of it?"

Despite Jesse's hostile attitude, and the odds against a second answer, Tiago decided to take the swing. "Where is your dad? Why isn't he here today?" Tiago asked, pushing it and sweating Jesse's answer.

Monster Boy returned, and Tiago ducked a flying fist before he grabbed the kid's hands and waited him out. "You wanna know where my father is?" Jesse wrenched his hands free. "He's on his honeymoon, the bastard, getting laid!"

"Don't be too hard on him," Tiago said, trying not to smile at the boy's fresh mouth or his incredible answer. "Hey, Smokey, throw me a ball and a Sharpie, will you?"

Tiago handed both to Jesse. "Keep yourself busy collecting autographs until the game starts. Smokey, keep an eye on him for a minute?"

With his teammate's nod, Tiago went to sit beside Quinn.

"Nice shirt," he said.

She raised a brow as if she doubted his sincerity. "I decorated it myself."

"No kidding. I mean . . . great job."

"Did you ever *try* to buy a frog shirt in this town? Gators they got, but frogs . . . I don't think so."

"Can't say as I knew that," Tiago said, his heart racing. She'd gone *looking* for a frog T-shirt?

"Who's the tart seducing the cameraman?" she asked.

"June. She's my publicist. Why?"

"You need a new publicist."

Tiago chuckled but stopped short, because Quinn had finally looked him in the eye, her gaze open and . . . inviting. Tiago felt a tug, and he knew his heart was coming out of hiding. He thought, hoped, prayed Quinn felt a responding tug. "Lizzie says you want to be a child psychologist."

"I suck at it. Did you see what Jesse was doing? The people he soaked are talking about giving you an award."

"He's a good kid. You would have cracked him."

"Or . . . worse."

Tiago grinned. "I thought you should know that I . . . decided to give growing up a shot. I'm going to start a foundation for sick kids and promote the hell out of it."

"That'll kill your panty-stealing rep. You ready for that?"

"I can still steal bases . . ."

"What are you gonna do with your lingerie collection? Because I'm willing to take it off your hands."

His heart beating double time, Tiago took Quinn's hand in his and rubbed her ladybugs with his thumb. "Remember how we said we'd take it one day at a time after we got off the train?"

"I remember," she said, eating him up with her expression.

"Well . . . one day away from you is one day too many. I know, because I've lived through three now, and it's killing me. You?"

Her eyes had widened and filled so that they looked like bright sparkling emeralds. "They were the longest three days of my life."

"I'm glad . . . and I mean that in a good way," Tiago said. "What d'you say we steal my plane, head for some island chapel—my family, your father, The Losers—then after the ceremony, we all go for a swim. No anxiety, no hives, just a honeymoon . . . and a life."

"Ribbit."

"I love you," Tiago said, and kissed Quinn Murdock senseless. Then he led her over to sit with the team wives.

And the crowd went ballistic.

Can't Catch This

Geri Buckley ★

CHAPTER
01

January, Northwest Florida
Arena Season Week 1

Row 1 . . . seats 12 and 13 . . . at the sideline barrier and smack center on the twenty-five-yard line.

The season-opener tickets were every arena football lover's dream, which is why Lindy Hamilton's fanny warmed the coveted seat instead of that one-minute wonder of an ex-boyfriend of hers.

Not that she was still bitter about finding him cavorting buck-naked with a bimbo who had no neck and hairy thumbs. No, she'd gotten over what's-his-name eons ago and had kept the pricey season tickets for her own use, especially since she was the one who'd eaten frost out of the freezer for a month to afford his surprise birthday gift.

He was surprised all right, right up until the moment she thwacked him upside the head with his prized stuffed trout and then peeled out of his driveway and out of his life.

Okay, she also kept the tickets so the cheapskate and his bimbo du jour would have to rot up in the civic center's nose-bleed section because all the better seats were sold out. So happy birthday to Lindy instead . . . but she wasn't bitter.

She was getting even.

From now on, no more settling, not for a mediocre love life, not for a routine relationship, and not for monotony. Instead of looking back on memories, she was going to look forward to possibilities.

It was either that or punch out the next friend or family member who spouted another platitude about being grateful she'd found out how what's-his-name really was before things got more serious between them.

"Aunt Lindy?"

Lindy strained to hear over the noisy six thousand or so people crowding into the stands, the racket intensified by music blaring from the center's gigantic speakers. New Orleans jazz echoed off the civic center's high walls with the brassy, earthy demands of the brothel juke joint. The mouthwatering aroma of hot dogs and popcorn rode the warm air that gushed out of cavernous vents in the ceiling.

She might have been attending a rock concert, except that down on the artificial turf that was the field, players littered the padded surface in pregame warm-up stretches. Multicolored ads were plastered on the sideline barriers that surrounded them, hawking everything from home security systems to running shoes. Part of the reason Lindy's seats were pricey was that the only thing separating the players from their eager—and sometimes vengeful—fans were those high-density foam rubber barriers.

The first week of the season kicked off with a new franchise called the Moccasins joining the AFL fold in the Southern Division. The Mocs were the new home team, having adopted their name and attitude from the cottonmouth snake that was native to the Florida Panhandle.

From the look of the mascot to merchandising to handing fans boxes of cotton as they entered the arena, the team name provided management with a promotional bonanza.

Lindy had no idea which team was which, but it didn't matter—between the amalgam of people in the stands and the shiny white uniforms stuck like flypaper to muscular buns, she was assured of something interesting to watch.

She settled back against her winter coat, pushed her sweater sleeves up to mid-forearm, then leaned her head to her right and smiled at her date for the evening, her eleven-year-old nephew Casey.

The apple of her eye was her brother-in-law all over again: sweet, sturdy, mature beyond his years, and elbow-deep in a pound bag of cherry Twizzlers. Like his dad, Casey was enamored of French cuisine and junk food, so much so his world revolved around food he ate and food he was going to eat. Lindy hoped exposure to some of the more physical sports might one day rub off on her husky nephew.

"Aunt Lindy?" Casey said again.

"Yes, my little Mensa sweetums," she said. "Whatcha need?"

Pudgy fingers gestured beyond her with a limp Twizzler.

"Don't look now, but isn't that what's-his-name coming toward us? Y'know, the guy you used to date?"

In a moment of wide-eyed quiet, Lindy managed to keep her game face in place. She didn't lick her lips, blink, or fiddle with Mount Vesuvius that was threatening to erupt on her chin.

Her smile twitched only once. Okay, twice.

Glancing over her shoulder, she mentally blew off her inner drama queen and braced herself for an icky run-in.

Sure enough, coming down the concrete steps like the wrath of God was none other than her ex. A show pony with a flawless hair flip stumbled in his wake on three-inch heels and wore the uncertain smile of someone who wanted to be anywhere but here.

Of all the times God could have picked to sift through the romantic wreckage of Lindy's life, why now? And why here? Didn't He like e-mail or telephones?

Her ex certainly didn't—no spectators to applaud his performance when he let his hubris run amok.

Wait a minute . . . was that still the imprint of a dorsal fin on his face? Or a trick of the fluorescent lights? Lindy couldn't decide.

She didn't care, either.

Apparently, her ex felt a tad bit touchy about it because he contemptuously shouted for her as if he were calling an ugly mutt to heel.

"*Lindy*, I'm talking to you . . . !"

"Oh, stuff it, Fish Face," she said but doubted he heard because he followed his nasty tone with a loud litany of choice words that turned heads around them, attracting the audience he craved and stiffening Lindy's spine. She was so not into witnessing more of his me-me-me indulgence.

If a man wasn't the right fit for a woman's need, the relationship wasn't working. Plain and simple.

So why go through a gnarly breakup? Why not just say it? Flat out. *I'm sorry. I truly am. I don't think this is working between us. I think we should end it now. Thanks, anyway. Bye-bye.*

It all boiled down to attitude, that's why.

And unfortunately, Lindy's attitude stunk. Nothing was sadder than an awesome beginning followed by a big ugly splat. Just ask Lindy. She'd tell you. Not only did she write the book on splatting, but she held the Guinness Book record for the most duds picked by a size-twelve bank service manager.

Honestly, were there any men who weren't just dogs?

Think happy—get happy was fine in theory, Lindy discovered, but didn't relate well at all in real life. So she was working on her attitude. Really, she was.

But bitter came easier.

Yes, taken together, all signs pointed in one direction . . . this was going to be a real sucky encounter.

Lindy started to rise from her seat to offer Fish Face a few verbal brickbats but was stopped before the fabric of her jeans even left the cushion. A drop-dead-gorgeous guy with mussed brown hair and a blunt jaw shadowed by beard stubble had leaned from behind her and kissed her on the cheek.

The devil danced in his eyes.

"Sorry I'm late, beautiful," he said, a throb of dark passion in his voice. "Did you miss me?"

A faint smile played at the corners of his mouth as one large hand kneaded her shoulder with a supersoft stroke, sending an unspoken message of help. With his other hand, he resettled a worn-in black cowboy hat on his head.

Oh, my. She'd read somewhere that hands—and what a guy did with them—could tell a woman a lot. Lindy was too busy making a rapid mental rundown of his considerable attributes to worry whether her ex was about to bust a nut.

But even if he did, so what?

Tall, dark, and hunky looked like he could take care of himself as well as make a woman's knees buckle with bliss.

In that ridiculously chivalric moment, it would have been easy for Lindy to play the passive martyr and cling to Cowboy Bob's leg like a poodle. To her credit, though, she decided to amp up the action instead.

After all, what did she have to lose?

"Well, hello there, cowboy," Lindy said with a saucy grin. "I've missed you like crazy."

Then, in one fluid motion, she surged up out of her seat, dislodging his protective hand and putting the kibosh on the notion that she lacked the strength and confidence to handle one measly ticked-off guy. On the contrary, it was Fish Face who lacked the chops to confront her in private.

She knew the cowboy had read her correctly when he said loud enough for Fish Face to hear, "Say the word, beautiful, and I'll see he doesn't bother you again."

"That's very sweet of you," Lindy returned a nanosecond before she cupped his bristly face in her hands and planted a kiss on him that would leave him grinning for a week. "Tell you what . . . keep Casey here company. I'll be right back."

The cowboy winked, gave her a rush with a lingering look, and said, "Promise?"

"Oh, yeah." Not relinquishing her hold for another moment, she heard herself practically purring. "You can count on it."

As Lindy trooped toward the aisle at the end of her row, she had one thought on her mind: *beginnings.* She was great at them. Beginnings were her thing. She excelled at beginnings. If they awarded degrees in beginnings, she'd have a dozen PhDs.

It was everything that came after *hello* that needed work.

She'd wanted possibilities . . . well, she'd gotten a possibility. The cowboy certainly offered an interesting prospect. Dare she explore the potential?

Yes. No. Maybe?

Definite maybe. Things could turn out differently, couldn't they?

And by the time Lindy bid sayonara for good to her ex and headed back to her seat, she almost believed they could.

CHAPTER

02

First Quarter

Sweet?

That wasn't the word that sprang to Josh Weldon's mind.

It was a wonder he and the luscious-smelling redhead didn't spontaneously combust right there in the middle of the stands. He could still hear her breathy voice, still feel her knowing fingers command his full attention, still taste her wicked grin.

Talk about pregame warm-up.

She was well-built and earthy and so disarming it was tough not to think sinful thoughts. His intention was to do a good turn for a pretty lady in distress, but she'd taken him by surprise.

Hoo-boy, there was definitely something to be said about a woman who used her mouth to work up a man. A couple more heated rounds like that, and Josh would go for the gusto.

To shouts and cheers, the teams ran out onto the field just as Josh stepped over the chair back and slid his keester into the redhead's seat as she'd asked. On his left perched a gassy old geezer with eyebrows like Jiffy Pop in a face that resembled the lunar landscape. On his right sat a chunky pubescent boy.

Which one was Casey?

Josh was almost afraid to find out. While the boy indulged in an Olympic-class feeding frenzy, the geezer gripped a clap stick in each meaty hand and wielded them against the blue sideline barrier as if they were light sabers ready to zap any out-of-bounds player on the helmet.

Pube-boy took the decision out of Josh's hands when he nudged his elbow and thrust a nearly empty bag of Twizzlers under his nose.

"Want one?"

"Thanks," Josh said, helping himself to one of the candy ropes.

"Better take two. You're going to need your energy."

Josh slanted the kid a curious glance but grabbed another piece of candy anyway and ventured a guess.

"I'm Josh Weldon. I take it you're Casey?"

"Casey Stuart," the kid said with a nod and a firm hand-shake. "Are you a friend of Aunt Lindy's?"

"If Aunt Lindy is the redhead . . . ?"

"That's her."

"Then I'd sure like to be." Josh ripped off a piece of the chewy candy with his teeth and leaned in closer. "So you like arena football?"

"Not really, but Aunt Lindy had an extra ticket, and I couldn't think of a good excuse fast enough."

"Yeah, I know how that goes."

"How come? You here with your aunt?"

"Might as well be," Josh grumped and then pointed toward the field. "See the quarterback over there for the Mocs?"

"Number sixteen?"

"That's him. He's my cousin. I call him Snake."

"Why? Don't you like your cousin?"

"Sure I like him. He earned the name in high school for his ability to be slippery in the pocket."

"No offense, but isn't he kind of small?"

"He may be undersized and underskilled, but he has a strong arm. It's because I like him that I'm here." Josh noted the kid's thousand-mile stare of confusion. "We're family, and family sticks together. I'm the one who talked him into play-ing ball at a two-A school in western Mississippi. Do you even know anything about this game?"

"Some. It's a quarterback-driven league, and the players are expected to protect the quarterback because it's a passing game. Sound about right?"

For a chubby kid, he did better than Josh expected.

"You're a smarty pants, aren't you?" he said. "I'm impressed."

"Don't be," Casey said, holding up the program. "I can read."

Josh muttered under his breath, then said, "Okay, tell me something else, Einstein, man to man, does Aunt Lindy have many . . . friends?"

Casey edged his face behind Josh's shoulder and glanced in his aunt's direction for a second before pulling back.

"Looks like a slot just came open if you're interested. So are you?"

The crowd erupting in a roar caught Josh's attention, and he cut his gaze to the field.

The kickoff returner for the Mocs charged down field hell bent for the goal line at the other end with most of the kickoff team hot on his heels. Josh leaped to his feet. Twenty yards . . . fifteen . . . ten . . . five . . . touchdown!—oh, please, not a flag on the play.

Amid gripes and grumbles, Josh and the rest of the crowd resumed their seats.

"Am I what?" he said to the boy.

"Interested? In my aunt?"

Just as Josh opened his mouth to answer, a syrupy voice called his name. He groaned to himself and sank lower in the seat.

"Isn't that lady calling you?" Casey said.

"Ignore her. Maybe she'll go away."

"No such luck. You are so busted."

Josh canted his head to the side to see that his date finally found her way out of the bathroom and off her cell phone. Every hair was artfully arranged, and her mouth was a glossy crimson. She looked good, he had to admit, but she'd missed the kickoff.

A woman could be anything else under the sun, but if she was more involved with herself than with him, she was out of there. The evening was young, but Josh had already decided to lose her number.

"Josh, honey," she called again from the aisle, "you're in the wrong section. We're over there."

He glanced down to row one where he sat, then up and back to where she pointed, and his gaze collided with Aunt Lindy's. The heated look in her smoky eyes made his thoughts travel along dangerous tracks, and he didn't even try to stop that train from derailing.

"To answer your question, Casey," he said as he rose to leave, "yeah, I'm interested."

CHAPTER

03

Halftime

Finding a nice guy at a football game was like finding a second husband in a small town—if he sounded too good to be true, he usually was.

For the hundredth time, Lindy shook her head in disbelief. The hunky cowboy wasn't alone; he attended the game with a date, a *d-a-t-e date*, yet he came sniffing around Lindy?

What a dog.

Where was the loyalty? Even if he was easy on the eyes, didn't she just nix it with a weenie of that stripe?

The world was full of them. Why was she surprised to unearth another one? After all, men had displayed various flavors of morality ever since they crawled out of the primordial ooze.

Lindy sincerely hoped there was a special place in hell reserved for such rounders.

For her part, sure, she was the one who'd initiated the kiss. But so what? She was a fun, fearless female and unattached, to boot.

He should've said something, done something to stop her. But did he object?

Not on his life.

Lindy sure didn't notice him putting up much of a fight at all. In fact, he seemed to enjoy their brief encounter as much as she did.

That did it. She wasn't wasting one more thought on him, even if he was mouthwatering in a leather jacket over a black turtleneck and snug jeans. And on that resolve, she washed the last of the gummy candy down with a cold draft beer.

Time expired on a fumble recovery, so at the end of the second the Moccasins led 28–17. Lindy's teeth were swimming. She needed to visit the ladies' room.

The halftime buzzer barely finished sounding before the stands resembled a busy anthill with people scurrying in all directions. Cotton balls littered the aisles.

Lindy herded Casey through the steel double doors that led toward the bathrooms and the concessions. She had a little pep in her step that had nothing to do with "Eye of the Tiger" blaring out of every speaker.

The concession venue was mega crowded with people of all ages, shapes, and sizes, and smelled of burned coffee, pizza, and sausage and peppers. Lindy made a beeline for the bathrooms and stopped short when she spotted incredibly long lines winding out of both ladies' rooms.

What else was new?

There were never any lines at the men's rooms. Why? Probably because men designed sports complexes. Just once she'd like to see guys wait in line, but that would never happen, not when they could whip out their johnsons at will and hose down the nearest wall.

When a young mother corralling two little girls exited the nearest bathroom, Lindy caught her attention to ask, "Is the wait long?"

"Unbelievable, hon. Upstairs has a plumbing problem— again—and they're detouring us down here. We were in line twenty minutes, can you believe?"

"Any idea if it's any better at the other end of the civic center—?"

"Don't bother. I tried there already. It's just as bad."

Lindy thanked her for the tip and flagged down Casey on his way out of the men's room.

"Thought you had to go," he said.

"Line's too long. I'll wait a bit until the crowd thins out."

"Can I get a snack then?"

"Sure, sweets." Lindy fished in her pocket and pulled out a few bills. "Here, get what you want. I'll go grab a table."

"You want something?"

"Surprise me."

At one end of the venue, marketers jammed the walls with arena football bric-a-brac. Bar tables were clustered on the other end for people to stand at and eat. She snagged a table before all the spots were gone and, despite herself, casually searched the crowd for the hunky cowboy.

Ball caps and cowboy hats of all colors abounded. Even so, a momentary spurt of disappointment hit her when he was nowhere to be seen.

Casey found her just as Lindy was about to go searching for him. He surprised her, all right.

He brought kraut dogs to feed a small army, an armload of chili cheese nachos . . . and her cowboy, holding a plastic cup of foamy beer in each hand.

"Look who I found," Casey said, unloading his stash of junk food along with packets of mustard and a bunch of paper napkins on the tabletop. "Aunt Lindy, this is Josh Weldon. Josh, Aunt Lindy."

Having dispensed with the superficial niceties of civilization his beleaguered mother had spent years drilling into him, Casey dove into his eats and proceeded to ignore the two of them.

Josh's roguish smile knocked Lindy's socks off.

"Hey there again, beautiful," he said.

Lindy felt her heart speed up and her ears warming at his compliment. She remained cool and tried not to grin when she said, "Hey right back at you, cowboy."

For a moment, he just blinked, apparently unsure what to make of her guarded reception. Then he seemed to shake off any doubts, relax, and set one of the beers in front of her.

"I spotted Casey loading up, and I thought you might be thirsty."

"Thanks." She pushed the cup back across the table toward him, not ready to test fate by swilling more beer. "I just finished one."

"Great," he said, unfazed by her rejection. He took a big swallow of his beer and added with a satisfied sigh, "That's more for me, then."

This time she couldn't help but chuckle.

"Weldon? The name's familiar—wait! Did I see it listed somewhere in the program—?"

"Cousins," Casey mumbled around a mouth full of nachos, then he swallowed and repeated, "Him and the quarterback for the Mocs . . . they're cousins."

"Bet that comes in handy," Lindy said, silently wondering if the quarterback cousin had the same devastating combo of long, lean body; blazing blue eyes; and rugged, healthy complexion.

She hadn't paid much attention to the individual players before. Now, she made a mental note to check out this cousin in the next quarter.

Probably heartbreakers, the both of them.

"Handy?" Josh said. "I don't get your meaning."

"Never mind. Where's your girlfriend?"

"What girlfriend?"

"How quick they forget." She rolled her gaze heavenward. "The Southern belle with you earlier . . . remember now?"

"Oh, her." He lowered his cup to the table, drumming his fingers on the plastic side . . . long, tan fingers with neatly trimmed nails. "She's in the bathroom. I don't expect she'll show her face again until halftime's over, so I've got fifteen minutes to kill . . . and she's not my girlfriend."

Lindy couldn't help but notice his hands were broad and muscular, like an athlete's. She had a weakness for a set of strong hands.

"She's not?" Lindy pinched off the end of a kraut dog, popped it into her mouth, and added, "Does she know that?"

"Oh, I'm hurt." He grabbed his chest, closer to his liver than his heart. "Is that what you really think of me?"

Either anatomy wasn't his forte, or he was hungry. She contrived to look innocent.

"I just met you. I don't really know what to think of you, but if the scum-sucking shoe fits . . ."

"We're friends, beautiful, that's it."

"You sure?"

He leaned in close to her, his voice a low, stoner drawl, effectively cutting Casey out of the convo.

"Step off my nuts already. I don't play games like your friend the total ass from earlier. No offense, but he sounded selfish, insensitive, manipulative . . . need I go on?"

"Ex-friend," Lindy corrected and wiped her greasy fingers on a napkin. "And trust me, he *knows* that."

Josh straightened, grinned in an adorably bemused way, and said, "I imagine he does at that."

"Look, I was just checking. I don't want to get in the middle of anything. Been there, done that."

He snorted.

"Quit worrying. There's nothing to come between. Bingo night at the rest home is livelier than she is. Now, can we talk about something else? Something more interesting?"

"Like what?"

"For starters, like you having dinner with me?"

"Can I come, too?" Casey said, snapping his chin up so fast he sent chili rocketing onto Josh's sleeve.

"Oh, Case!"

Josh grabbed a napkin, swiped at the bits of chili, and said, "Next time, sport."

At the same time, Lindy snatched up a napkin and said, "Blot, don't wipe!—too late, it's going to stain. Ah, Josh, look at your coat. I'm sorry."

"It's okay," he said. "Gives it character."

"No, really. Send me the cleaning bill. I insist."

"Lindy, I said it's no big deal." He wadded the messy napkins into a ball. "Now, what were we talking about? Oh, yes, dinner . . . with me. So how about it, beautiful?"

"Technically," she said, flashing her best smile at his flirty vibes, "we are having dinner."

Josh pointed to the array of junk food on the tabletop and said, "This is carnage, not dinner."

"Not what you had in mind? No? Good. Say, is your team winning?"

He laughed and said, "My team certainly is . . ."

The rest of what he said was instantly lost to Lindy. Nothing registered, not that she was bored with football talk; it was more that she had bigger troubles brewing.

Her beer had hit rock bottom, and the urge to go stepped up its demand for immediate action. She darted an anxious glance over his shoulder, toward the nearest ladies' bathroom.

The line was still long.

Josh must have pondered the meaning behind the glint in her eyes, because he turned his head, followed her gaze, and said, "Something wrong?"

Lindy drew breath to speak, but Casey didn't give her the chance.

"Aunt Lindy has to pee," he said, stuffing the last bite of hot dog in his mouth and looking up to find his aunt glaring at him. "What?" His eyes grew innocently wide, and he shrugged. "It's true, isn't it?"

"You used to be my favorite nephew," Lindy said with a pointed stare. "Now, you're out of the will."

Josh laughed and ruffled Casey's wavy brown hair.

"One day," he said, "you'll understand there are some things a man doesn't share with strangers."

"But you kissed my aunt," Casey said. "You're not a stranger."

"Good point, but actually, your aunt kissed me. There's a difference."

As the two of them dissected the fine art of tonsil hockey, Lindy experienced a worrisome moment. The urge to go became relentless. Another few minutes and she feared it would threaten her with an embarrassing leak.

The female body was built to hold off Mother Nature only so long, and now the old girl's time and patience were running out.

"I'm ducking in the men's room," Lindy said, gathering up their trash in one swipe as her feet headed in that direction. "It's never busy in there."

Both guys turned to her and blurted out in unison, "You can't do that."

Their single-mindedness brought her up short, and she angled back toward the table.

"And why not?"

"Women don't belong there," Josh said with a patronizing chuckle, "that's why. Leave us at least one place where we can go to get away from females."

Lindy's auburn eyebrows shot upward.

"You really are a cowboy, aren't you?" she said.

Any reservations or modesty or thoughts about decorum Lindy might have entertained vanished before the echo of his voice died. This wouldn't be the first time she let a superior tone goad her into unknown adventures.

"Can I help it if we live in the age of accusation and litigation?" he said.

"The old CYA shuffle?" she countered. "Except the big boys only cover their own asses. Women share their inner sanctum all the time with infants, toddlers, little kids, not to mention the beauty queens who sashay in to adjust their sugar thong around Uncle Jim and the twins. Be real. The ladies' room is like a freakin' Grand Central Station, but we're supposed to hold the men's room as sacrosanct? Oh, please."

And on that note she turned, her sights set on the forbidden chamber. Josh and Casey fell into step beside her.

"Since you feel that way," Josh said, "don't let one of the security guards see you. It'd be a shame if they nabbed you as some kind of pervert."

"I'm not ninety. I don't intend to be in there that long. I'll slip in and slip out. No problem."

"Did I mention video cameras?"

"You think I'm kidding, don't you?"

"Hey, far be it from me to stand in the way of a determined woman with a small bladder."

Lindy halted, did a bank shot with the ball of trash into a metal can by the wall, and faced them.

"Fine," she said. "Casey here will stand watch at the door for me. Won't you, Case?"

"Say what?" Casey almost choked on a slurpy inhale of his soda. "I'm too young to be sent to jail. Are you willing to risk scarring me for life?"

"What happened to being young and fearless? And don't be so dramatic. No one's going to jail. Are you taking sides with Cowboy Bob here over your own flesh and blood?"

"We guys have to stick together. Right, Josh?"

"You bet, buddy."

Lindy crossed her arms over her chest and offered a grim smile to both of them.

"It's a long walk home, nephew. If you start now, you might make it in time for breakfast. Or not."

Straw stuck in the side of his mouth, Casey sobered.

"I don't know this guy, and I don't agree with a thing he said. Which door you want to try, darling auntie? North or south?"

"Wait a minute," Josh griped. "Throw me under the bus, why don't you."

"That's my boy," Lindy said. "Now, let's try north. It's closer." She wrapped her arm around Casey's shoulder and then turned to Josh and winked. "Back in a minute."

"I've got to get going," he said, tapping his wristwatch. "Halftime's almost over."

"Oh." Her stomach fluttered, the aftermath of the kraut dog, she decided. "Okay, see you later, then."

"Yeah . . . later."

She'd plowed ahead through the milling crowd when she heard Josh behind her call, "Lindy, wait! Give me your number."

She angled her head over her shoulder but kept walking.

"Why?" she said, suspicious about what was coming next.

"I'll call you."

Bingo.

Lindy mentally cringed. The line was an innocuous one, blithely spoken, and one usually tripping off the lips of a liar.

Every woman experienced the disappointment in that phrase at least once in her life. If he was really interested, he would have been a little more original, wouldn't he? And here Lindy had a flicker of hope that she and the cowboy might actually possess the start to some serious chemistry.

"I'm in the book," she called back, figuring that was definitely the end of that.

CHAPTER 04

Fourth Quarter

What a dork.

Josh didn't catch her last name, probably because she didn't throw it. Stewart, maybe? Or did she spell it S-t-u-a-r-t?

Hell's bells.

Had to be one of them. She was Casey's aunt, after all. Surely, they'd share the same name.

Josh should've just asked her when he had the opportunity. Oh, no, that was too easy.

Much better to look for a needle in a haystack. With his luck, Lindy and Casey's mom were sisters, so her last name could be Smith for all he knew.

Twice he went by her small box section on the way back from the pretzel and soda kiosks for his date, but Lindy's seat was empty both times. Judging by Casey's empty seat, too, Josh decided they must have headed home early to beat the traffic.

He wasn't deterred. How long might it take to phone every Stewart and Stuart listed in the phone book?

Josh grinned to himself—nothing like a challenge.

Just as he was fed up with being the personal step-and-fetch-it boy of the narcissist he was with, a text message on his cell phone saved him from cracking his veneer of courtesy over her well-coifed head.

A few minutes later, in response to the message, he strolled into the new franchise owner's luxury box, located high above the arena. The posh room was an unexpected beehive of energy.

Principal team owner W. C. Corsetti stood at the plate-glass window against the backdrop of the arena's upper bleachers. He had an appreciation for the finer things in life as well as for deep-pocketed celebs who visited the Emerald Coast beaches and tipped waitresses with obnoxious abandon.

To those bicoastal star types, he extended a standing invite to watch games exclusively from his owner's box, where he preferred the conveniences of privilege, which included a full-course meal complete with accommodating wait staff. And just then, Corsetti had his thinning silver head together with a country singer cum actor Josh had seen before but couldn't put a name to.

Adjacent to them, his PR spokesman perched a hip on the corner of a massive cherry wood desk and yammered on a cell phone. Behind him, the franchise's general manager slouched on an oxblood red leather sofa that faced the picture window and chattered into a hands-free phone stuck in his ear. The team president, who was also W.C.'s oldest son, was ensconced in a deep leather chair in the corner, wearing a sweet young blonde like wet underwear and gesturing as he spoke to someone on a landline phone.

Something was definitely up.

No matter the activity they engaged in for the team, W. C. Corsetti was the maypole around which they all circled.

A hardscrabble man of the old school with a boxer's nose and bags under his eyes, he always wore a white suit and ivory string tie, no matter the season or the occasion. And in the age of permanent press, he favored pearly white silk shirts, hand-made in Hong Kong.

He dressed like a tampon, acted nuts, and the local media loved him. Even before the season had officially opened, sports reporters had dubbed him the George Steinbrenner of the South.

It was because of Corsetti that management chose Josh's

cousin Snake as potential quarterback, not only because his nickname aligned him with the mascot, but because his flamboyant and brash mannerisms endeared him early on to the predominantly Southern fans.

The new team was Corsetti's baby, comprised of a lot of free agents who were looking for good deals. But without Josh there to find an inoculation of capital, who knows if they would've survived in the league to play in the franchise's inaugural season.

Truth be told, Josh made it happen.

He was the go-to guy, a venture capitalist who owned his own firm, which, loosely translated, meant he was a workaholic and a high-priced middleman. His livelihood came from marrying money to product—in this case, a consortium out of New York entering into a limited partnership with Corsetti.

Josh acknowledged the room's occupants in a general greeting and received a variety of welcoming grunts and nods in return.

"You paged me, W.C.?" he called over the noisy voices.

Corsetti glanced up and waved Josh farther into the room.

"Junior worked the contraption for me," he said. "C'mon in. Will someone fix this boy a drink?"

At the command, a waiter in a formal white coat and dark pants stepped out from around a well-stocked bar.

"No, thanks," Josh said, waving him off. "I'm good." Then to Corsetti, he added, "What's up?"

"I'll be with you in a minute."

And Corsetti resumed his conversation with the actor.

Josh shrugged out of his jacket and hung it together with his hat on a fancy iron-scrolled hall tree near the door and then crossed the carpeted room, helping himself to a couple of peeled jumbo shrimp off a loaded hors d'oeuvre tray along the way. An envy-inducing eighty-inch plasma television dominated one wall, its hi-def picture tuned to a local channel but with the sound muted.

What with the jumble and pitch of conversations going on, no one could have heard the television anyway. Normally, Josh would have given the revolutionary electronic device an appreciative glimpse and kept moving.

But not this time.

Corsetti quit his confab and turned his attention from the

window. He stepped back toward Josh, a rocks glass filled with melting ice in his hand.

"Great view from up here," he said. "Like Zeus looking down from Mount Olympus, I see every sin that goes on down there on the field and in the stands." He canted his head in the direction of the TV on the wall. "Thought you might want to take a gander at this."

On the giant screen, a commercial touting relief for hemorrhoid sufferers faded to black.

"Appreciate the concern," Josh said with a ripple of impatience. "But I'm not bothered with hemorrhoids."

"Eighty-six the attitude, and just watch a minute. This is important."

So Josh did. And when black gave way to a lifelike color picture that filled the television screen, he made a jaw-dropping discovery.

He stopped and watched Lindy's sexy features swim into view in a plug for the late-night news, while the text scrawling across the bottom of the screen told its own tale.

Tonight at eleven. Woman charged with misdemeanor in civic center disturbance . . .

Holy Moses! Could he pick them or what?

There was no doubt his Lindy from earlier was the "woman" in question. Every feature of her was etched into his memory from her out-of-control fiery red hair to the sassy curve of her mouth.

As he watched emotions crossing her slender face—first, irritation and then calm tolerance—the unexplainable feeling hit him of riding an elevator going down too fast.

He and his macho attitude had practically double-dog-dared her to attempt a hostile takeover of the men's facilities, but he had been teasing. Apparently, she had gone through with it and her coup had been quashed.

The woman was a fireball; he'd give her that. He admired a woman willing to take the kinds of risks that led to amazing experiences.

And something told him that getting arrested tonight certainly qualified as a humdinger of an experience for her.

"Since when is using the john a misdemeanor offense?" he blurted out to the room at large.

"Misdemeanor trespassing," Corsetti corrected, then hoisted his glass in the air, gesturing to another unobtrusive waiter for a refill. "Everybody gets their fifteen minutes . . . channel seven's been airing that same picture every commercial for the past half hour."

Trespassing?

Well, who knew?

Not Josh, and certainly not Lindy, which is what it appeared she and Casey were commenting to the cop who was unnecessarily placing her in custody. No sound bites accompanied the short clip, so Josh could only guess at who might have said what.

"The coverage is a gold mine," Corsetti said. "When next you see your lady friend—"

"She's not my lady friend," Josh said absently, then pulled his attention away from the screen and back to Corsetti. "I mean, we just met. Don't even know her last name."

"That's interesting. From up here, son, it sure looked like the two of you were very . . . friendly . . . with each other."

"What we do is none of your business, W.C. Now, is that all you dragged me up here for?"

"No, I asked you up here so you could be sure to tell her thank you kindly."

"For what?" Josh said.

"For being a pain-in-the-ass female, that's what." Corsetti accepted a fresh drink from the waiter and slurped a big sip. "Her little stunt tonight was brilliant, and if you had a hand in it, kudos to you, too."

He raised his glass in salute.

"Don't thank me. I sort of goaded her into it, and now look what happened."

"Things work out for the best, son." He all but beamed. "Her set-to with the law is the fuel we needed to help rekindle our bonfire under the city fathers. I've been after those old birds to shore up this antiquated structure before we all go broke."

"She'll be thrilled to know she took a bullet for the team."

His sarcasm flew right over Corsetti's head.

"I don't mind telling you, Josh, I don't like problems. Problems take away from the gate. And I ain't happy with anything that takes away from the gate."

"So what do you plan to do about it?"

"I've called a press conference for immediately after the game. Sit, stay, and watch us win. I sympathize with your lady friend, I surely do. But got to strike while the iron's hot, y'know."

Josh narrowed his eyes at Corsetti's less-than-sympathetic tone. A press conference certainly explained a lot.

"Thanks, W.C.," he said, "but no thanks. I've got some business of my own to attend to."

"The ballsy redhead?"

"Could be."

"Suit yourself." Then Corsetti chuckled. "At least now you know where to go to find out her last name."

CHAPTER

05

Arena Season Week 2

I'll call you.

But he didn't.

In her thirty years of privileged middle-class life, Lindy had never been on the receiving end of such thoughtlessness. Okay, she was dreaming.

She knew he'd never call, predicted it, even. But deep down, she had hoped. Had hoped, too, that her hunky cowboy might feel there was something between them that needed to be explored.

That teeny flicker was enough to inspire her to glam up her everyday look and take extra care with her makeup, to wear her best moleskin pants and cashmere sweater, and to propel her out of the comfort and anonymity of her cozy house on a cold winter night and back to the scene of her crime. Besides, it wasn't in her nature to hide out at home and fester.

Well, that and the fact that her season ticket was paid for and she hated to waste the hard-earned money.

If a well-known actor could appear on a late-night talk show for all the world to see right after getting bagged for soliciting, then Lindy could certainly traipse across town to watch a public ball game. Easy-peasy. No one would even notice her.

That delusion lasted until Lindy strolled through the civic center's season ticket holder's door and she shed her coat and gloves.

Women she'd never met were suddenly calling her by name and urging, "You go, girl," or nodding in recognition as she passed them and giving her the thumbs-up. Some men, too, although not as politely.

She hadn't tuned in to every comment made about her arrest—the less said the better as far as she was concerned— nor was she masochistic enough to grant repeated interview requests from the local television reporters.

But her head wasn't stuck in the sand, either.

The bit about her the newspaper printed seemed to resurrect debate about putting a new metroplex near the underdeveloped port to further diversify the local economic base. Until Lindy's run-in with county ordinance, nary a soul got enthused about an out-of-town entertainment group hoping to make money on the backs of the taxpayers. But bring the cause closer to home, and the politicos swarmed out of the woodwork like roaches.

Now everyone, it seemed, had an opinion.

Lindy was less than thrilled to realize she'd become the poster child for downtown improvement. Gauging by her reception so far, obviously she'd been the weekly topic of conversation around more than a few water coolers.

It was going to be a long evening.

At least one thing passed the stink test for the week: Lindy walked by a slew of new portable potties lining the tunnel on her way to her seat, silent testaments to the ability of one person to shame the britches off city hall. She didn't need to visit the upper bleachers to know potties were strategically placed in the corridors up there, too.

Once she gained her coveted sideline section, doubts about coming bombarded her. She sat practically alone. A dozen or so empty seats peppered her small area.

Was everyone else running late? Even the bouncy old guy holding the ticket for the seat right next to her hadn't arrived yet.

The civic center was a repeat of what Lindy had already witnessed: catchy music blaring out of the speakers—

"YMCA" this time—and the smell of popcorn permeating the air, the noisy crowd filing into the stands with their cotton boxes at the ready, and the artificial turf field littered with muscled players warming up in skin-tight white pants.

Only Josh Weldon was missing from the scenario.

Lindy never expected to see or hear from him again, especially not after last week's fiasco was splashed all across the local news. The folks at the bank where she'd worked for ten years were taking her newfound celebrity status in stride, although her mother confessed she figured Lindy had decided to forget insanity and head straight for seriously deranged.

So no one was more surprised than Lindy when, moments before the kickoff of the second game of the season, Josh Weldon appeared at her elbow. With the loose-jointed grace of an athlete, he slid his adorable jean-clad backside into the empty seat next to her.

He'd ditched the dark Stetson and turtleneck in favor of a well-worn ball cap and gray sweatshirt with a green John Deere logo embroidered across the front, and he'd shaved. Both looks suited his relaxed manner, but this week's trim haircut and manicured nails suggested his casual outfits were the exception to his mode of dress rather than the norm.

Inwardly, she sighed. Oh, yes, she'd forgotten just how handsome he was.

"Hi there, beautiful," he said and smiled. "I owe you a phone call."

A preemptive strike? That certainly caught Lindy off guard.

As Josh turned to cheer on the kickoff run, she pondered how she was supposed to act righteously indignant about his lack of a phone call when he readily admitted up front he didn't phone. Bet he was a shrewd businessman.

This time, when he turned his attention back to her, Lindy forced herself to be impervious to the charm oozing out of that generous mouth.

"Sorry, sir, can't place the face," she said. "Do I know you?"

He shrugged out of his denim jacket and tossed it across the arms of the seat next to him.

"Not yet," he said, "but we'll fix that in short order, Miss Hamilton. See, I know your full name now. You're famous . . .

or is that *infamous*? Nice picture on the television, by the way. You do the perp walk very well."

Laughter bubbled in his voice, as refreshing as water shimmering over rocks.

"We all have our talents," she said, her smile tight. "Actually, I thought they captured my best side."

"Captured? Oh, I like that."

"Thank you. I try to keep up my end."

"I liked the handcuffs, too. Added just the right touch of bondage."

"Bet it made you goosepimply all over to see me in bracelets, didn't it?"

"Am I hearing the voice of experience?"

"Like riding a biker . . . one never forgets." She gave an exaggerated sigh and offered him her best are-you-done? smile. "Listen, this little convo's been real, doll face, but if you don't mind, the topic's getting really old. I have one last word to say to you . . . scram. Well, perhaps two. Scram. Now!"

She shot snake eyes on that one. He didn't budge, except to cross his right ankle over his left knee, set his elbows on the padded arm rests, and claim squatter's rights by sliding comfortably down a bit farther in to the cushion of his seat.

On the field, a zebra-striped official called defensive holding against a corner back, ten-yard penalty and automatic first down. Not everyone in the stands was happy with the call.

When Lindy could hear herself over the air horns and clap sticks, she said, "You're not going, are you?"

"Nope."

She sighed again, crossed her own legs, and said, "Comfy?"

"I'm good. Thanks for asking. No Casey tonight?"

"His mother is a tad peeved at me at the moment."

"Sorry to hear that. Was it a bad scene with the fam?"

"No, actually, what she had to say was short and sweet, along the lines of a snowball's chance before she lets her son out with me again. I mean the kid's almost a teenager, for crying out loud. She can't coddle him forever."

"Some mothers are touchy about jail, though."

"Tell me about it. It's not as if he was the one arrested. He got to see the inside of the sheriff's office. Big deal. I like to view it as broadening his horizons."

"I take it his mom didn't agree with that logic?"

"Not hardly."

"Too bad. I was looking forward to seeing my new buddy again."

"Maybe in your next life, if my sis is talking to me by then."

In an unexpectedly sensitive move, Josh closed his fingers around her hand and squeezed lightly, giving her a quiet jolt to the heart. Lindy fell into the kind of silence that only existed between two people in movies.

"Has it been tough this week?" Josh said.

She opened her mouth, then closed it again. The intensity of his nearness was oddly comforting.

"Awkward and mortifying," she admitted, ducking her chin, "more than tough. But I'll live." She offered a wry half smile and then asked the question upper most in her mind. "Why didn't you call? You said you would, remember?"

"I know, and I'm really sorry," he said. "Business got in the way. I was in Tokyo. Long meetings eat up the hours, you know, and the time difference . . ."

Lindy nodded, unwilling to press him further, especially when she had no right to. He didn't owe her an explanation. After all, it wasn't as if they were in a bona fide relationship.

"You look good," Josh added.

Surprised and pleased to her toes that he had noticed, she turned and stared at him.

"Thank you," she said, then covered her self-conscious hesitation with a light laugh and pointed to the seat he was warming. "You do know you're going to have to move when the old man comes?"

Josh let go of the hand he was holding, and Lindy's world resumed spinning in a rush of noise.

The arena crowd roared to life as the quarterback on the opposing team tripped and threw a short pass from his knees, only to have the ball intercepted in the end zone. The Mocs trailed by seven points.

When Josh fished a ticket out of the front pocket of his jeans and flashed it at her, he said, "This is my seat now."

She stifled the urge to grab his hand back and hang on to it. Then her eyes widened, and she stared at the ticket.

"He sold it to you?"

"Sure did."

"Why would he do that? He seemed pretty happy with it last week."

Josh shrugged.

"I made him an offer he couldn't refuse."

Lindy started to laugh at his bravado in quoting *The Godfather*, when an incredible thought occurred to her. She sobered and gestured to the nine or so empty seats beside hers that remained in her boxed section.

"And these?" She was half-kidding when she added, "Are you going to tell me all these seats are yours, too?"

He nodded.

It took a moment, but once the implication sank in, she ran some quick mental calculations. Nine seats times season ticket prices equaled an obscene amount of money.

Oh, my.

"Why did you do that?" she said.

"Call me greedy. I want it all . . . the section . . . the girl . . . is there a problem with that?"

"No, no problem—wait a minute, the girl?"

"Am I coming on too strong?"

Before Lindy could formulate a comeback, a safety shoved a receiver out of bounds and both players collided with the sideline barrier in front of her with a resounding *oomph* of air and an impact that landed them practically in her face.

Startled, she snatched her coat to her chest as if the flimsy fabric could keep her from being smushed by a two-hundred-thirty-pound tight end decked out in full pads. She recovered a second later and decided she'd had enough good time for one night.

"Say, I'm starved," she said, turning to face Josh. "Are you hungry? Want to go get something to eat?"

"Now you're playing my song, beautiful. What do you have a taste for?"

"Breakfast."

CHAPTER

06

Josh had the bizarre notion that "breakfast" meant he was going to get lucky. No quickie but an all-nighter. It was a logical conclusion for any red-blooded man to jump to.

But guess again, Tonto.

As he soon discovered, he wasn't fluent in woman-speak. She meant she really wanted to eat breakfast for dinner.

So he put his testosterone on the back burner, left her Camry in the civic center's parking lot, and drove her in his Hummer to the nearest Waffle House, where she could feast on a double order of kitchen sink hash browns.

Compared to the chilly wind outside, the inside of the diner felt warm and muggy. Josh helped Lindy out of her coat and placed it atop his on the bench seat next to him. Once he settled across from her, he pushed back his sweatshirt sleeves to his elbows.

Her hair was radiant red, her cheeks were flushed with cold, and Josh's chest swelled when she looked at him with warm approval.

When she smiled, her face lit up in an unspoken invitation, the kind that made a man want to take her in his arms and kiss her senseless. Josh imagined doing just that, long, slow, and thoroughly.

They sat across a Formica table from each other in a booth by the window, ringed by the aromas of sizzling bacon and fresh hot coffee and burned toast. Two other couples occupied similar booths closer to the counter, where a leather-clad biker type flirted with a waitress who was cleaning dishes. In the background, warbler extraordinaire Shania Twain serenaded them with her hybrid sound from a jukebox in the corner.

Lindy's appetite was a refreshing sight to behold. The platter of crispy grated spuds the waitress set before her were scattered, covered, chunked, diced, and topped to the umpteenth degree. Josh's plain BLT looked puny by comparison.

"Are you going to eat your pickles?" she said, eyeballing the small pile of dill slices decorating the edge of his plate.

Josh grinned and shook his head.

"Help yourself."

Forgoing a fork, she reached across the table as comfortable as you please and picked up the pickles with her fingers.

"What's so funny?" she said, dabbing the pickle juice off her fingertips with a paper napkin.

"Nothing. It's just rare I see a woman who can pack it away and isn't constantly dieting."

"I burn it, not store it. A couple hours at the gym tomorrow, and this'll be gone. My mom's always telling me it'll catch up to me one day if I don't watch out. When that day comes, I'll worry. Until then . . . what can I say? I take after my nephew. I love food."

"I believe it's the other way around. You came first, so he takes after you."

"Whatever." She grinned and popped a pickle chip in her mouth. "Enough about me. Tell me about Josh Weldon, besides the football-playing cousin and being instrumental in gaining the financing for the franchise's move down here."

"So you did know about that."

"Not really. We were talking last week at work about the game—I'm service manager at a bank—and your name came up."

"In a good light, I hope."

"Nothing but. One of the tellers remembered the articles in the paper when it was back and forth whether Corsetti and that bunch had the clout to bring the franchise to fruition. Obviously, they did. So tell me what I don't know about you."

Lindy picked up her fork and continued eating.

"I'm an open book," Josh said, setting his sandwich back on his plate and spreading his hands, palms up. "What do you want to know? Ask away."

"Let's see . . . drives a Hummer . . . travels for business . . . buys season tickets he doesn't need . . . Are you rich?"

"Filthy."

"Do you have a vacation home in Aspen?"

"A condo in Vail."

"Ever been to Africa?"

"North. South. Or Central?"

"All of them."

"Would it impress you if I said twice?"

Lindy tossed her head back and laughed, a musical sound that was sweet, warm, and promising. With a silly grin on his face, Josh resumed eating his sandwich.

"Your turn," he said, and wiped breadcrumbs from his hand.

"There's nothing so grand to tell about me," Lindy said. "Born and raised here. Went to school here. Work here. Will probably die here. End of story."

"Don't sell yourself short. Even I know more about you than that."

"For instance? What do you think you know?"

"Okay, try this on for size. I know you like kids."

"No fair. That one was a gimme."

"You get along well with your family."

"Most of the time, yes."

"You have lousy taste in men."

"God, yes."

Lindy leaned forward, her arms propped on the tabletop, her head nodding and her eyes shining, focused entirely on Josh, which he was eating up with a spoon.

"You're crazy and passionate and fun and good and kind," Josh continued.

"Oh, you're good," Lindy said, grinning. "Tell me more, I'm listening."

"And I want to wake up in the morning and see you lying in bed beside me."

A fat second later, Lindy's fork clattered to her half-finished plate. She protested mildly and then sat back.

"Have you been practicing that?"

Maybe he came on too strong?

Josh wiped his mouth with his napkin and said, "As a matter of fact, no. What I really wanted to say is that I want to take you home and have hot, sweaty, acrobatic, wake-up-the-neighbors sex with you. But that doesn't make my first version any less true. So how about it? Come home with me?"

A pregnant moment passed, then Lindy glanced down and tapped her bare wrist.

"Wow, will you look at that. Where did the time go?" Before he could protest, she gained her feet and reached for her coat. "You said it yourself, Josh. I have lousy taste in men. Thanks for the invite, but I think I'd better pass."

★ It was a long ride back to the civic center to pick up Lindy's car, made longer still by the hot, vivid images dancing in her mind of her and tall, dark, and hunky who was sitting beside her.

Nervous? She was about sick. His suggestion was definitely fertilizer for the creative mind.

"Look," Josh said as they pulled into the well-lit parking lot, "I'm sorry if I offended you back there in the restaurant. That wasn't my intention." He threw the gearshift into park, cut the engine, and turned in his leather seat to face her. "I'll lay it on the line. I don't have much time for dating, and when I find someone I want to be with, I go for it."

"Go for it? As in the Southern belle you were with last week? Did you say the same things to her?"

"Not at all. She was a mistake—a friend fixed us up. It'd take a bucket of Viagra and a bag over my head to get the hustle on with her. I want someone I can have fun with, not someone who takes hours to get ready." He raked his fingers through his hair. "I told you, I don't have much time for dating."

"I see. So 'go for it' in this instance means buying up a section of seats so you can be relatively alone with me? I'm someone you can have fun with?"

"Yeah, that's what it means." He flashed her a boyishly crooked grin. "I didn't say I wasn't impulsive."

"I'm not offended," Lindy said, releasing her seat belt latch. "I'm flattered. It's just that . . . well, it's a bit early in the game for me to think about the two of us playing at being the flying Wallendas."

"Do you think this is a game to me, Lindy?"

He stared at her out of guarded eyes.

"No," she said and meant it. "No, I don't. Sorry, bad choice of words. I'll be honest with you, Josh. This attention is all new to me. I'm used to carrying the yeoman's share of relationship duties. I mean, not that you and I are dating or seeing each other or anything—I'm babbling, aren't I?"

She hopped out of the car rather than wait for him to come around and open the door for her. Compared to the new car and warm leather smell of his Hummer, the cold air swirling around the civic center carried whiffs of nearby eateries and open Dumpsters. Massive halogen streetlights glowed brilliant white and flooded the lot and street like daylight.

"Will you still call me?" she said, her breath frosting.

He slammed her door closed, hit the keyless entry to lock the car, and said, "I can't promise I will."

Lindy deflated, a hollow feeling filling the pit of her stomach. What else did she expect? At least he was honest about it.

"I'm off to London tomorrow," he said, leaning against the side of the car, "then Nice after. It may be a couple of weeks before I return."

"Are you ever not working?"

"Not often." He checked his watch. "In fact, I've got to catch a conference call in an hour or so."

"Good grief, a dyed-in-the-wool company man."

Josh shrugged.

"One of the drawbacks of being the boss. If it weren't for a promise I made to my cousin to catch as many of his home games as possible, I probably wouldn't even be in town very much."

"Then I guess it was my lucky night when we met last week. I should thank your cousin."

Josh buttoned up the front of his denim jacket and straightened away from the side of the car.

"Speaking of last week . . . don't be surprised to see the Moccasin franchise milking your name in a bid to get the city and county to go in and foot the bill for new quarters."

"Good luck on that one," Lindy said. "From what I gather, the city fathers are circling the wagons. If anyone from Corsetti's office asks, I promise not to burn any bridges. Thanks for the heads-up."

With no other reason to stall, Lindy bunched her coat collar around her neck, stuffed her hands in her pockets for warmth, and started walking to her car. Josh escorted her the short distance, his running shoes quiet on the asphalt next to the clack-clacking of her low-heeled pumps.

"Your schedule doesn't leave much room for a social life, does it?" she said.

"Lindy, I—"

They reached her Camry, and she took out her keys.

"Hey, no big deal," she said. "We can still have fun. If you want, we'll get together whenever you're in town."

"Are you sure?"

She nodded and said, "Yeah, really, I'm sure."

"I'd like that."

He slipped her car keys from her hand and hit the unlock button. Later, she'd parse the finer points of the lousy deal she'd just made for herself.

For now, she offered him a crinkly smile and said, "Maybe we can even watch your cousin in a ball game or two? I mean I'd hate for all those seats to go to waste . . ."

Josh was quietly tending his own thoughts when she accepted her keys. All she had to do was climb into her car and drive off into the proverbial night.

So why was she standing there, staring at her key ring?

"I forgot to thank you for dinner," she said. "I enjoyed being with you."

"You don't have to thank me." He caressed her cheek with tender fingers and then tucked some loose hair behind her ear. "It was my pleasure."

Then, he opened the driver's side door, holding it ajar and waiting for her to scoot in behind the wheel.

"Well, good night," she said, still not budging from her spot.

"Good night, beautiful."

Neither one of them moved.

An awkward hush followed, a moment of divine insanity in which Lindy contemplated giving him a dress rehearsal of what he'd be missing. She was a dud at picking men, and only someone dead-on lucky tempted fate.

This couldn't end well.

Even as she finished the thought, she jettisoned her entire argument and reached for him.

She clutched his hand and drew him to her, relaxing into his chest, soft and pliant. He circled her arms tight around his waist, enfolding her in his embrace.

"What are you doing, beautiful?" he said.

"I think maybe you need a little something to ponder in the weeks to come while you're stuck in those boring meetings."

"Are you so sure they're boring?"

She slipped her hands free, cupped his face, and whispered, "Compared to this, I know they are."

Then she drew the tip of her tongue slowly and provocatively around her lips. His sharp intake of breath provoked a thrill that cascaded from her fingertips to her knees.

She touched her tongue to his mouth and traced the curve and texture of his smile, circling the sensitive edges of his lips and absorbing the shudder that passed through him.

"You're killing me, beautiful," he said. "You know that?"

"Ask me if I mind."

Longing uncurled deep in her stomach. Whisker stubble from his five o'clock shadow brushed against her lips, bringing a shiver of delight.

A moment later, the sound of footsteps and laughing and voices and car doors slamming around them penetrated the sensual fog.

"Game must be over," Josh said.

"Seems like it," she returned.

"Wonder if we won?"

"The season's still young."

She caressed him with her tongue until his lips parted.

"I've got to go," he said.

"Me, too."

Brushing her lips to his once, twice, she settled them with warm pressure and slid her tongue softly into his mouth, tasting his need. His throaty growl matched her pleasurable moan.

Her tongue slid deeper. His body grew harder.

And she inhaled the sweet taste of him as he slipped into her heart.

CHAPTER

07

Arena Season Week 5

Josh flipped on the flat-screen television to CNN International and then fixed himself a light scotch and water.

It was not quite nine in the morning, but he'd just returned from entertaining some European clients, first with a late dinner at Harry's Bar followed by a night with them at the casino and then drinks into the wee hours. Right about then, he was feeling bulletproof.

Outside, beyond his balcony, a heavy rain was falling and the Mediterranean was churning. His hotel room was like hundreds of others he'd stayed in, well-decorated—vivid colors, bold patterns, and rich materials—and lifeless.

Everything rested quietly in its proper place.

There was no laughter to liven the rooms. No personal touches. No homey smells. He could walk out the door, and no one could tell by the room that he'd ever existed.

He disliked the ever-constant emptiness but figured it was part of doing business and doing it successfully.

Before he hit the sack for a catnap, a stack of manila folders awaited his review, preparation for the evening's round of meetings.

He looked at the stack and then at the phone. Contrary to

what Josh had told Lindy, he had tried calling her, but he'd gotten her voicemail both times.

He hadn't left a message—other than he'd called. There was no reason to say more. He'd phoned simply to hear her voice.

Funny thing was, all Josh had to do was close his eyes, and there was Lindy.

He could easily picture her face, her brown eyes, the way she styled her fiery hair to skim her shoulders, the way she smiled when she was relaxed, the throaty way her voice sounded when she was aroused, and the way her skin felt baby smooth and silky under his touch. When he slept, in the fragile moments between dozing and full wakefulness, he could even smell the warm and enticing scent of her.

Glancing at the bedside clock, he calculated it would be a quarter to two in the morning her time. Way too early to phone. She'd be sound asleep.

He hung up his jacket, shed his tie, and loosened the top button of his dress shirt. Then he settled on the designer couch in the adjacent sitting room with his stocking feet propped on an expensive coffee table.

Two minutes later, Lindy's voice, husky with sleepy dreams and so sexy, wafted through the telephone line and was a welcome balm to the loneliness eating at him of late.

"Good morning, beautiful. How's it going?"

"Josh! You big palooka," she said, and he grinned at the warmth in her welcome. He should have known she wouldn't mind the early hour. "I'm sorry I missed your other calls. Where are you? Are you home?"

"No, Monte Carlo. I drove down yesterday morning from Nice."

"Monaco?" He knew that would bring her fully awake. "Holy smoke, talk quick. This call is costing you a fortune!"

He chuckled.

"Don't worry about it. It's worth it to hear your voice. Everything doing all right there?"

"Sure, why wouldn't it be?"

"No reason. How's your family? Is your sis talking to you yet?"

In the wistful silence, Josh heard what sounded liked pillows being ruffled and fluffed as if Lindy were adjusting them to prop herself up in bed. He wondered what she wore in bed, if anything.

Then she chuckled and said, "Oh, sis can't stay mad. She got over her tiff real quick. Is that why you called? To find out about her?"

"No, not exactly." After an awkward hesitation, Josh added, "I've missed you."

"Say what again?"

Louder, Josh repeated himself, "I said I've missed you!"

"Hey, no need to shout," she said, and he caught the smile in her voice. "I heard you the first time. I just wanted to hear you say it again."

"You're a little stinker, aren't you?"

"I miss you, too. Don't you just love mushy pillow talk?"

"I wasn't going to say any mushy stuff."

"Oh. You weren't?"

Josh laughed at the childlike disappointment he heard in her tone and relented with, "What did you have in mind?"

"Nothing much." Her voice perked up. "Maybe that you're calling so early in the morning because you can't wait to talk to me?"

He was grinning like a fool. He couldn't help himself.

"Okay," he said, swirling his scotch in the glass. "What else?"

"That you can't stop thinking about me?"

"You sound pretty sure of yourself."

"Am I on track?"

"Maybe. Keep going."

He lifted the glass to his mouth and took a big swallow.

"That I'm responsible for a good portion of your snooze-time stiffies?"

Surprised and embarrassed to admit she'd hit the nail squarely on the head, Josh burst out laughing and almost choked on his drink. As it was, he spilled more than half of the scotch down the front of his dress shirt and onto the waistband of his slacks.

Damn, it was the last clean shirt he had, too.

"Guessed right, didn't I?" Lindy said. "Okay, cowboy, breathe. It sounds like you're strangling."

"Tell you what," Josh managed to say after swallowing several times. "I'll be home in a couple days, and I deserve a break. If you're a good girl, I'll let you jump my bones. Deal?"

"Down, boy. What you deserve is open to debate."

His chuckles slid into the kind of easy tenderness that he found flowed so natural around Lindy.

"Seriously," he said, "I'm a stand-up guy. How about I pick you up, and we'll go out on the town?"

"Do I get to dress up?"

"Of course."

"I'm in."

They set a date and a few minutes later said their goodbyes. Josh reluctantly hung up the phone and then found himself whistling as he stripped out of his soggy clothes and hopped into a cold shower.

★ It was Mardi Gras day down at the bank, and by closing time, Lindy was running late.

She dragged in the front door to her townhouse, feeling as squashed as road kill. When her doorbell rang, she hadn't yet changed out of her jeans and beads into her evening dress. She threw open the door, a quick apology ready to spill off the tip of her tongue, but she stopped short.

No apology needed. Josh was wearing jeans, too.

And he also wore a look in his eye that set her pulse pounding.

"Great," he said, scoping her and her outfit up and down, and letting his gaze linger on her cleavage. "You remembered, and you're ready. I knew I could count on you."

Then he stepped over the threshold and swept her up in his arms and kissed her until her toes curled.

"Of course, I remembered," Lindy said, too giddy to have the slightest idea what he meant. "Want to come in and tell me what I remembered?"

"No time to come in," he said, checking his watch. "Kickoff's in a half hour. Grab your coat, beautiful, and let's go."

"Kickoff . . . oh, right. Tonight's football night, and you promised your cousin." She had entertained visions of a candlelit steak dinner and maybe the symphony after, but it was a given in her neck of the woods that one never let down family. "Give me a sec to change my blouse. I've been in it all day."

"Beautiful, you look great," Josh said very softly, the passion flowing very warmly. "No need to change. I love you just the way you are."

Lindy's heart melted into a dollop of pudding. She decided the symphony was overrated and grabbed her coat.

They made the kickoff with time to spare, and in the opening minutes, the Moccasins went down field in two plays and scored a touchdown. Josh's cousin was having a whale of a great season so far, and his future in the AFL was looking bright.

Because it was Mardi Gras, the civic center crowd was rowdier than usual. Members of various Krewes were scattered throughout the arena, having a good time and adding to the raucous noise. Purple, green, and gold flags were suspended from the ceiling and fluttered in the circulating air, and bunting in the same colors decorated every rail. Zydeco blared nonstop out of the speakers, and Hooters girls were stationed inside every entry door, catching pneumonia in skimpy outfits and handing out cheap beads and moon pies.

Lindy had to give props to management—they knew how to promote.

Maybe all the commotion explained why she didn't notice Casey until he trucked down the concrete steps to her section with a little friend in tow. Either that or she just couldn't keep her eyes and overactive mind off Josh Weldon.

The evening wasn't the dressy date she had imagined, but that didn't matter. Being anywhere with Josh was special.

Casey gave her a hug and a quick peck on the cheek, shook Josh's hand vigorously, and proudly introduced them both to his new friend Stevie, who was a little shy.

"I'm surprised you're here," Josh said to Casey, sliding his glance to Stevie and back, "after . . . you know."

"My television debut?" Casey said.

"Nice way to put it."

"It's cool," Casey returned. "Mom's changed the family motto to read 'the family that's bagged together stays together.' "

Josh lifted a hand to his mouth, covering a cough that Lindy suspected was really a very rude laugh.

"Is your mom here?" Lindy said before her nephew got carried away. "She didn't mention she was coming."

Casey shook his head and said, "Stevie's dad brought us. We're sitting on the other side with him. Josh? Can you do us a favor?"

"Anything, buddy. What can I help you guys with?"

"Can you ask your cousin Snake for his autograph for us?" And Casey nudged Stevie into holding up his program.

"We can do better than that," Josh said, rising from his seat. "It's almost halftime. Why don't we all ease down to the locker room and pay Snake a visit?" He wrapped an arm around each delighted boy's shoulder and winked at Lindy. "See you in a few."

Lindy stared after them and sighed in wonderment.

Dependability, stability, integrity, romance . . . he was pulling out all the stops. Or was he?

When a man was as solid as Josh was, it was hard for a woman to think straight.

Maybe, at last, Lindy was learning to spot a good guy?

Seconds before the buzzer, the Moccasins scored another touchdown, and Lindy got caught up in the wave of excitement flowing through the arena like a living thing. She jumped to her feet to cheer and stomp in time to the syncopated rhythm of the music along with the rest of the crowd. Yea, team!

For a sport that carried zero appeal for Lindy, this game was starting to grow on her.

CHAPTER

08

Lindy waltzed through her front door, exhilarated, pumped, totally wired, the sound of the arena football fans still roaring in her ears.

They'd won another game, she was taking tomorrow off, and Josh Weldon was hers tonight. Sometimes, all it took were the little things to make a girl happy in her own skin.

Lindy tossed her coat over the ladder-back chair by the door and headed for the fridge.

"Want something to eat?" she called. "Drink?"

"No, thanks," Josh said from the living room, "I'm good. You've got a nice place. It has a real homey feel."

She rounded the corner, a bottle of water in her hand, and tried to see her townhouse through his eyes. Her decoration was shabby chic—bright color to give the illusion of space, a facelift to flea market finds—and an assortment of photographs and mementoes that made the place hers.

"Glad you like it," she said, grazing her fingers near his waist. "Make yourself at home. Turn on the television to whatever you want. I'm going to run upstairs a minute."

"Take your time." He looked at her, and she saw smoldering embers in the depths of his eyes. "I'm not going anywhere."

She climbed the stairs while he did as she asked: getting comfy on the couch and slipping off his shoes, taking command of the remote and propping his feet on an ottoman that doubled as a coffee table. From midway up, she paused on a step and looked down into the living room.

There he sat, the dream life she'd been fantasizing about forever.

The thought of making something new happen was exciting and daunting at the same time.

What if this didn't work out?

Among all the "what ifs," the single image she kept coming back to was Josh. Was it so bad to feel calm, happy, and energized for as long as it lasted? And it might last. Who knew?

There was only one way to know anything for sure, and that was to dive right in.

"Hey, cowboy," she called down, leaning over the banister. "I'm taking a shower."

"Are you naked and wet?"

"Not yet. Want to help with that?"

Without waiting for an answer to her brassy offer, Lindy sauntered up to the bathroom connected to the master bedroom. Josh was waiting for her when she stepped back into the carpeted bedroom after turning on the shower faucet to let the water warm up.

"Come here," he said.

The dark throb in his voice shot heat straight to her groin. She kicked off her shoes and walked toward him like a cat on the prowl. He reached for her, yanked her to him from breastbone to pelvis, and kissed her, hard and deep and thoroughly.

"Wow," she murmured when he let her up for air.

"And that's just for starters," he said.

"My house. My rules." Lindy took a step back. "Off with the sweater first."

"Whatever you want, beautiful," he said, his eyes growing dark and hot. The crewneck sweater hit the floor in short order. "I'm here to serve."

"That's right. And what I want is to see you."

"Promise you'll be gentle?"

"I don't think so."

"Good. Take me, I'm yours."

With nimble fingers, she ripped open each button on his ox-ford shirt from the neck to the hem, dipping to sprinkle nip-ping little kisses on his exposed chest along the way. He had a scattering of soft curly dark hair that tickled her nose.

His shirt soon followed his sweater.

Lindy smiled at him, a seductive grin that drew an impa-tient growl from deep in his gut in response. With a palm to his chest, she backed him into the queen-sized bed, pushed him down atop the comforter, and knelt on the bed to straddle his hips.

"Jeans next," she ordered, then leaned over and flicked her hair behind her shoulder so she could nibble his stomach mus-cles unimpeded.

His skin was cool, smooth as a baby's butt, and smelled of clean soap and desirable man. A moment later, the jeans were unzipped and she was caressing south of his navel.

He splayed strong fingers across her back, learning the feel and landscape of her body, before he gripped her shoulders and pushed her upright.

"I need to get up to take them off," Josh said.

Lindy let him rise, but they were both too impatient.

In a heated flurry, hands swept clothes aside, until moments later they both stood naked, caressing and exploring, tasting and teasing as they sank to the cushy carpet. Josh shifted, tak-ing Lindy beneath him. Panting, gasping, mouth found mouth in an endless stream of raw sensation.

He nudged her legs apart with his thighs and settled himself against her hot sex.

"Hold up, cowboy!" Lindy said, puffing for air. "You weren't kidding when you said you don't date much. Aren't you forgetting something?"

"What? Oh . . . yeah." He looked into her flushed face and grinned. "My jacket's downstairs. Do you—?"

"The nightstand," she said, her lips twitching, and pointed toward the bed.

"Hold that thought."

"I'll wait right here for you."

When Josh returned, Lindy trapped him with her legs and took him inside her. She heard his groan and watched his eyes darken to stormy hues.

By turns slow and sensuous and then hard and wild, she gave in to the heat building between them and let him push her to the edge of the world. He followed her and gave one last thrust before plunging them both over the threshold.

Spent with his release, Josh rolled to his back, cradling Lindy in his arms so that every inch of their bare skin touched. She snuggled into his rising and falling chest, a sleepy, satisfied smile on her face.

It took a moment for the sound in the background to register.

"Water's still running," she said, laughter in her voice.

"Think it's cold yet?"

"Maybe not. It's an eighty-gallon tank."

"Quick recovery type?"

"I believe so."

Josh rolled up on his elbow, lowered his mouth to hers, and said, "Plenty of time."

★ Lindy should have been tired after a long day at work and then spending most of the night making love. Josh was certainly wiped.

But at dawn she was wide awake and starved. And she couldn't stop smiling.

After a quick shower and a spritz to the pits, she threw on a white terry robe and left him quietly snoozing, sprawled among the pillows like a sultan. She eased barefoot downstairs to fix some breakfast.

This morning she skipped her usual tired oatmeal and went for the whole megillah—bacon, eggs, toast with cinnamon butter, coffee, the daily crossword, and Josh. Josh with cinnamon butter sounded good, too. She might try it.

Unlike most days, today Lindy had enough groceries on hand for them to spend the entire day in bed eating.

Life didn't get any better than that.

Balancing the loaded breakfast tray in front of her, she nudged the bedroom door open with her hip and padded across to the bed.

"Up and at 'em, sleepyhead," she said, before she realized the bed was empty except for the stash of pillows. "Josh?"

"Here, beautiful."

Behind her, the bathroom door opened and Josh emerged, fully dressed in sweater, shirt, and jeans. Not a good sign. His hair was finger combed and damp, and his dark beard stubble gave him a rugged air.

"Well, someone certainly looks rested," she said, setting the tray on the bed. "How did you sleep?"

He answered her with a leer and a grin.

"I borrowed your extra toothbrush," he said. "Hope you don't mind."

"Not at all. Help yourself to whatever you need."

"In that case . . ."

Josh took her in his arms and kissed her head, her forehead, her nose, making a slow foray toward her mouth, all the while running his hands over her body, his fingers relearning secrets he'd uncovered during the night. Lindy kissed him back with all the energy and steamy passion he aroused in her.

"That's so nice," she said, pressing into him. "You're a good kisser."

He smiled with satisfaction and brushed stray hairs behind her ears with his fingertips.

"Good morning to you, too. You're up early. You doing okay?"

She smiled back, holding him around his waist. He smelled of her perfumed shower gel. She made a mental note to stock the bathroom with some guy soaps.

"Never better," she said. "Let's eat and jump back in bed. What do you say?"

"The food smells heavenly. Coffee! Woman, you read my mind."

Lindy released him to pour him a cup and said, "We can spend the day holed up in here, talking about the first thing that pops up." She wiggled her eyebrows suggestively. "Or playing video games, whichever you like."

"Wish I could, beautiful, but I can't. I've got to go. I'm late as it is. Have you seen my shoes?"

"Downstairs."

"Thanks."

On his way out of the bedroom door, he took two big swallows of coffee and snatched up a piece of toast. Lindy padded down the stairs after him.

"Got to go? But you just got here—well, a few hours ago— and what do you mean late? Aren't you staying? I've got breakfast in bed. It's fixed. It's ready."

She heaved a sigh worthy of a martyr.

"I know," he said, slipping his feet into his shoes. "And I'm sorry. I didn't intend for you to go to so much trouble."

"It wasn't any trouble. I wanted to do it."

Josh looked around for his jacket, spotted it on a chair, and tossed it over his arm.

"I've got a business to run, beautiful. I've got to work. I'm due to catch a plane in two hours, and I'm not packed yet." He smooched her on the nose. "You understand, don't you? I would've packed last night, except someone sidetracked me into staying over and being her sex slave."

"Since you put it that way . . ." Lindy flashed an unrepentant grin. "I guess you can go, if you must."

"I must. I'd rather stay here with you. You know that?"

She nodded and opened the front door for him, and he paused to kiss her again on his way out.

Somewhere, a neighbor's dog was barking. The buildings in her complex stood shoulder to shoulder, and the sun was peeking over the building across the way, the day already smelling crisp and cool. Lindy pulled her robe closer to keep out the chill.

"I'll try to call," Josh said. He stepped off the stoop, then angled back. "Do me a favor?"

"If I can."

"Go to the games while I'm gone. Snake's under the impression you're his good luck charm."

Lindy leaned against the doorframe and said, "Sure, Josh, I don't mind going, but where in the world did he get that idea? He doesn't even know me."

"Who knows? Caught you on television, I guess."

"Who in the Panhandle didn't," Lindy muttered. "The infamous Lindy Hamilton strikes again."

"Snake's having a great season, one of his best. You've been at the games. Somehow he's connected the two and decided he's played well because you've got the mojo working. So you've become his totem, of sorts. Will you go to the games, beautiful, for me?"

"Of course, I will, Josh." Her grin turned saucy. "For you, big boy, anything."

"That's my girl."

"Am I? Am I really?"

"You better believe it." He kissed her again, softly this time, but with purpose and longing. "I'll miss you."

Lindy sobered, and said, "I'll miss you, too."

And he was gone.

Arena Season Week 10

Less than half a season to go, and the playoff races were tightening up. A major television network bid for a live feed of the Moccasins versus the Orlando Predators rivalry, and everyone in town was making a big deal about the broadcast appearing during weekend sports primetime.

All week long, the newspaper devoted extra pages in the sports section for pregame forecasts and guest columnists. Not to be outdone, the local affairs channel on cable television hosted a special talk show call-in every night where viewers interacted with a panel of area coaches.

Unfortunately, Lindy got caught up in the hype and couldn't seem to untangle herself.

Word had leaked about her bringing luck for the Moccasins quarterback. Dredge up her toilet faux pas at the start of the season, and the lucky charm story took on a life of its own.

Suddenly, fans—dubbed the Privy Council—appeared at games sporting T-shirts airbrushed with a picture of a bad-ass viper twining around an outhouse. Privy Council visors made from twisting balloons were big hits with the animal house set.

Lindy had no proof, but having witnessed the promotion

machine the Moccasins franchise had in place, she suspected Corsetti and that bunch orchestrated the whole thing in hopes of bumping up attendance for the big night.

The day of the televised live game, she was ensconced on her couch in front of the television, wrapped in her favorite blanket and snug in her flannel strawberry jammies, the ones she favored the most when she was sick. An array of cold remedies littered the coffee table in front of her, along with a box of tissues, a half-finished can of ginger ale, a twenty-ounce bottle of apple juice, and a few dozen breakfast bar wrappers.

Feed a cold, starve a fever. Or was it starve a cold, feed a fever? She never could keep those two straight.

Around her, the house was a wreck: dirty dishes stacked in the sink, kitchen garbage needing to go out, laundry piled on the floor, dust bunnies the size of small dogs frolicking in the corners. That wasn't how she kept house, but she felt too bad to clean.

"No, I'm sorry," she was saying into the portable phone, or trying to around fits of sneezing. "As I told the last young man who called from Mr. Corsetti's office, I won't be at tonight's game. Thank you for asking. I've caught a wicked cold, and I think it's better if I stay in."

She glanced to the cases of sport drink and canned chicken soup delivered a half hour ago and sitting on the floor by her front door.

"And please tell Mr. Corsetti that I appreciate the drinks and soup. I'll be sure and stay hydrated."

Lindy hung up the phone, blew her raw nose for the zillionth time, and muttered, "Get a life, people."

Some of them were taking this good luck charm thing far too seriously.

The phone shrilled again, and Lindy picked it up. She expected to hear either another reporter or another one of Corsetti's people on the other end, so her greeting was cool at best, stuffy head nasally, at worst.

"Oh, you sound pitiful, beautiful."

"Josh!" She wiped her drippy nose again and sank back into the sofa cushion, feeling better just for hearing his voice. "You think it's bad on your end, you should be on this side of the phone. Spring colds are the worst."

"How are you feeling?"

"I'm dying."

"You're not dying."

"Yes, I am. We can put a man on the moon, but we can't cure the common cold?"

"Because there's no money in a cure. The money's in treatment."

"That is just wrong."

As they talked, the obnoxious call-waiting beep started and kept signaling.

"Is that you or me?" Josh said.

"Me. They'll go away. The phone hasn't stopped since I told a reporter this morning that I was sick and not going to the game tonight. Where are you?"

"I'm in Atlanta now. Barring any problems, I'll be home in an hour." His volume dropped a notch. "And you know how I look forward to coming home."

Did she ever.

Passion-fueled memories of previous homecomings sent a yummy thrill through Lindy. Not that she was in any shape to act on it. But that was okay. Their relationship was more than just peel-me-off-the-ceiling sex.

No matter what she and Josh were doing, whenever they looked at each other, they couldn't stop grinning.

Yet with all that, there was still one annoying fly in Lindy's ointment of happiness. Because of his business, she and Josh spent as much time apart as they spent together.

"Got to go," he said. "My plane is boarding. Crawl back in bed. I'll see you soon."

At any other time, Lindy would have jumped up to clean house with a rag in her teeth if she had to, rather than let anyone, especially Josh, see her home looking like a landfill on a busy day. But right now, her head hurt.

She didn't know how long she'd dozed on the couch before the doorbell woke her up. Lindy and Josh hadn't exchanged keys or shared closet space yet, mainly because they signaled commitment and Lindy wasn't sure enough about where this thing between the two of them was going.

The phone rang as she opened the front door, the sound impatient and demanding. She let it ring.

To her surprise, Josh stood in her doorway wearing a windbreaker over jeans and a navy blue golf shirt. Usually, when he came straight from the airport, he wore a suit or dress shirt and slacks. He'd obviously stopped and changed first.

One look at her sorry state and he put a broad palm to her forehead, his gorgeous blue eyes awash with concern. Then, with the phone rudely shrilling in the background, he said the most welcome words she'd heard all day.

"Dr. Josh is here and will take care of everything."

★ What a sap.

That's how Josh saw himself. He'd been played by Corsetti, the low-down son of a bitch, and lied to by his cousin Snake.

When Lindy had opened her front door, Josh could see she felt puny. She had puffy eyes and a feverish glow, and a wealth of tenderness had filled him.

So he ushered her back to the sofa and then headed straight for the kitchen to fix her a hot toddy. He answered the phone on the way—a reporter. And he answered it two more times while putting together the toddy—Corsetti's people.

A picture quickly gelled in Josh's mind of his cousin Snake in collusion with Corsetti's antics.

"I can't believe I let Snake sucker me in," Josh said, helping Lindy into the steamy shower, where she could let the warm water run on her stuffy sinuses. "The bastard lied to me. He sounded so real when he talked about you being lucky for him."

"Maybe it's not all his fault," Lindy said, soaping up. "Maybe you heard what you wanted to hear because you know me and like me."

With the steam billowing over the top of the shower curtain, the bathroom was muggy. Josh perched on her vanity seat, holding a bath sheet to wrap her in so she wouldn't catch a chill, and wiped the sweat off his face.

"Snake charm, my ass," he said. "It ends here. You're not playing in this charade anymore. I'll make sure Snake understands that."

After Lindy got out of the shower, Josh rubbed Vicks on her chest and on the soles of her feet and bundled her in socks, a fresh T-shirt, and sweat pants so she'd stay warm. Then he blew her hair dry and tucked her into bed with a new box of tissues and a glass of juice at the ready on the nightstand.

"Better, my little Rudolph?" he said, sitting on the bed beside her and holding her hand.

Her nose was cherry red. She had no makeup on, and she was sneezing her brains out, but he couldn't seem to get enough of touching her.

"Much. I'm very relaxed right now."

"Can you sleep?"

"I think so."

"Good. You rest while I fix you something to eat." Josh leaned over, cupped her jaw in his palm, and kissed her cheek. "I'll wake you when it's ready."

He started out the doorway, but when Lindy called, he angled back toward her.

"I'm glad you're home," she said. "I missed you."

He threw her an air smooch, her words wrapping around his heart.

Local coverage of the game was blacked out, so Josh had no idea how the Moccasins were doing. Whatever the outcome, he hoped Snake was getting sacked repeatedly. It served him right.

In short order, Josh had Lindy's townhouse shipshape, not that he thought it was terribly messy to begin with, more like well-lived-in. The dishwasher was loaded, a load of laundry was going, the clutter was picked up, and the floors were dusted. Meatloaf in the oven made the place smell homey . . . and comfortably inviting.

He heard her moving upstairs, so it didn't surprise him when she answered the phone before he did.

When he heard Lindy say, "Hi, Casey . . ." he hung up the kitchen receiver and ladled some hot soup into a coffee mug. He found the spoons, a napkin, and the crackers; arranged it all on the bed tray; and headed upstairs.

She was putting on her shoes when he walked into the bedroom. Her hair was pulled back into a simple ponytail, and she had changed into jeans with a light sweater set.

"You look better," he said, narrowing his eyes. "I brought you an appetizer. The entrée will be ready in a few minutes."

"Thanks, I feel better. At least the sneezing has stopped, and my chest doesn't feel so tight. Is that meatloaf I smell?"

"Yes. Why are you dressed?"

"They're losing."

She didn't have to say who "they" were; Josh knew she meant the Moccasins.

"Let them lose," he said, setting the tray on the bed. "Maybe it'll take Snake down a notch and improve his character."

Lindy shook her head and said, "I'm going to the civic center."

Josh picked up the mug of soup and handed it to her.

"So you're going to play Corsetti's game? Are you really okay with that?"

"No," Lindy said, spooning the soup. "I'm not going for Corsetti or for your cousin. I'm going for Casey and Stevie and all the other little kids who believe in Santa Claus, the tooth fairy, and the integrity of sports heroes. There's plenty of time for them to find out that heroes are human, that they're flawed . . . but not tonight. Tonight, anything is possible."

CHAPTER

10

Fourth Quarter

Forty-five seconds remained on the clock when Josh escorted a bundled-up Lindy to her seat. A roar arose in the stands, and it took a moment for Josh to realize the Privy Council was chanting Lindy's name.

It looked like snow, so many cotton balls flew everywhere. The fans were understandably concerned, but Josh felt the hype had gone too far.

All season Snake had shown the remarkable ability to come back in the final quarter. Gauging by Lindy's reception though, that fact seemed to have escaped everyone's notice. Now with Snake's lucky charm present, the energy and volume in the civic center became a palpable thing.

Josh leaned over to Lindy and said, "We're leaving as soon as this is over. I want you back home in bed."

"I'm okay," she said and squeezed his hand. "Really. I had some great doctoring."

With the ball on their own twenty-two following the kick-off, the Moccasins set out on their drive. Snake dropped back in the pocket and looked for an open receiver.

But the pocket collapsed, and Snake had to scramble, as he had all season, to avoid the rush. Josh watched as he rolled out of the pocket right and abruptly tried to reverse his fields but was blindsided by a three-hundred-twenty-pound defensive tackle and driven headfirst into the turf.

"Oh, Josh," Lindy said, grabbing his arm. "Think he's hurt?"

"He got his clock cleaned on that one, that's for sure."

The crowd became silent as Snake lay motionless.

Trainers and the team doctor sprinted onto the field and soon revived him. Josh and Lindy watched two minutes tick by, then three, before Snake got off the field under his own power but in an obviously groggy state.

"That doesn't look good," Lindy said.

"It isn't," Josh said. "My guess is concussion."

The fans erupted in a standing ovation. But Josh knew, for Snake, this game was over.

As the untested second-string quarterback jogged onto the field, the crowd hushed once more. Ten seconds left on the clock. To a person, they all knew the chances of winning without Snake just went down the toilet.

"This is nerve-wracking," Lindy said. "What happens now?"

"Hail Mary is all he's got left," Josh said.

"What's that?"

Josh smiled and said, "Just what it sounds like. Throw the ball and pray."

And the quarterback did exactly as Josh predicted.

When he dropped back, everyone headed to the end zone. All the defensive backs dropped back, too, to protect the zone. The seconds ticked down while the quarterback looked for someone open and finally rocketed the ball toward the crowd of players congregated at the end zone.

The ball deflected off the helmet of a defensive back, off a shoulder pad of a receiver, and, as the ball fell toward the turf, one of the Moccasins' wide receivers dove underneath and caught the ball with his fingertips.

Touchdown! Mocs won 51–45.

★ Pandemonium erupted on the field.

Lindy saw Corsetti, in his usual white suit, stroll out of the tunnel surrounded by gray-suited bodyguards. Reporters with cameramen in tow raced to his side. One such reporter stuck a microphone in Corsetti's face and asked his opinion of Snake.

"Little did we know," Corsetti boomed, all smiles, "this small college renegade would lead us to a possible playoff berth in our very first year in the league . . ."

Lindy followed close in Josh's wake as he cleared a path through the jostling crowd and out the door. When they were in the comfort of his Hummer, Josh turned in his seat to face her. The intensity of his steady regard suddenly worried her, her concern buoyed by an undercurrent of emotion, one that dominated the air but defied description.

"What's wrong?" she said. "Are you still peeved that we came?"

"No, I have something I want to say to you."

Oh, no.

With his flat prelude, dread formed up and marched smartly across Lindy's heart. She tried to put a brave face on, but it was hard to do with the sniffles.

"So say it, already," she said, wiping her nose with a tissue.

"I don't know any other way, except straight out."

"Fine. I'm listening."

"You and I—we're in for some changes ahead."

Nerves strung out, Lindy unleashed her fear. "Look, are you trying to break up with me?" She pointed at him with the soggy tissue. "Because if you are, don't try to sugarcoat it. Just once I'd like to hear a guy be honest and put his cards on the table in plain English . . . this isn't working. We should end it now. Thanks. Bye."

Josh cupped her cheek in his palm and said, "This isn't working."

Sometimes the truth really stinks. Lindy sucked in a breath so fast she brought on a coughing fit.

When she calmed down, Josh said, "I mean I won't be traveling as much. Instead, I'll be staying in town more."

"That's all?"

"No, there's more."

The seriousness in his gaze still worried her.

"Is everything okay with your business?"

"Business is fine." He sandwiched her hand in his, rubbing her skin with light, tantalizing strokes. She loved his hands. "I've spent a lot of years building up my business. But what's the point if I don't take time off to enjoy the fruits of my labor?"

"Josh?" She narrowed her eyes. "What are you saying?"

"I'm saying I miss you like crazy when I'm away, Lindy, and I think what you and I share is more than a casual thing. And I think you feel the same way, don't you?"

She melted into the seat.

"Yes, I do. I love you, Josh."

"I love you, too, Lindy." His expression softened. He squeezed her fingers and kissed her hand with promise before turning the key in the ignition. The Hummer's engine roared to life. "We've got some plans to make."

Lindy smiled—she couldn't help herself.

"That just proves what I've always suspected," she said.

Pulling out of the parking lot, he canted his head toward her and asked, "What's that, sweatheart?"

"That I might just be at my best in the fourth quarter."

Hot romance featuring the **cool** hockey
players of the New York Blades

by **Deirdre Martin**

who "always delivers heat and romance."
(Romantic Times)

Body Check

Fair Play

The Penalty Box

Chasing Stanley

---

penguin.com

M204AS1107

First in the all-new contemporary romance series featuring men who find love the most extreme sport of all

From National Bestselling Author

Julia London

Wedding Survivor

Survivor meets *Bridezilla* in this all-new series about a members-only adventure service that caters to the rich and famous. In this captivating opener, one of its founders is about to embark on the thrill ride of his life—meeting a woman he can't live without.

"Sprightly and fresh... A gifted and versatile writer."
—*Publishers Weekly*

"Writing that sparkles with sexy, sassy charm."
—*Booklist*

penguin.com

Penguin Group (USA) Online

What will you be reading tomorrow?

Tom Clancy, Patricia Cornwell, W.E.B. Griffin,
Nora Roberts, William Gibson, Robin Cook,
Brian Jacques, Catherine Coulter, Stephen King,
Dean Koontz, Ken Follett, Clive Cussler,
Eric Jerome Dickey, John Sandford,
Terry McMillan, Sue Monk Kidd, Amy Tan,
John Berendt…

You'll find them all at
penguin.com

Read excerpts and newsletters,
find tour schedules and reading group guides,
and enter contests.

Subscribe to Penguin Group (USA) newsletters
and get an exclusive inside look
at exciting new titles and the authors you love
long before everyone else does.

PENGUIN GROUP (USA)
us.penguingroup.com